Bestselling author Tess Gerritsen is also a doctor, and she brings to her novels her first-hand knowledge of emergency and autopsy rooms.

But her interests span far wider than medical topics. As an anthropology undergraduate at Stanford University, she catalogued centuries-old human remains, and she continues to travel the world, driven by her fascination with ancient cultures and bizarre natural phenomena.

Now a full-time novelist, she lives with her husband in Maine.

For more information about Tess Gerritsen and her novels, visit her website at www.tessgerritsen.co.uk

www.rbooks.co.uk

BODY DOUBLE

Dr Maura Isles has seen more than her share of corpses.
But never has the body on the autopsy table been her own...

'It's scary just how good Tess Gerritsen is. This is crime
writing at its unputdownable, nerve-tingling best'
Harlan Coben

VANISH

When medical examiner Maura Isles looks down at the body
of a beautiful woman she gets the fright of her life.
The corpse opens its eyes...

'A horrifying tangle of rape, murder and blackmail'
Guardian

THE MEPHISTO CLUB

Can you really see evil when you look into someone's eyes?
Dr Maura Isles and detective Jane Rizzoli encounter
evil in its purest form.

'Gruesome, seductive and creepily credible'
The Times

KEEPING THE DEAD

She's Pilgrim Hospital's most unusual patient –
a mummy thought to have been dead for centuries.
But when Dr Maura Isles attends the CT scan,
it reveals the image of a very modern bullet...

'A seamless blend of good writing and pulse-racing tension'
Independent

Have you read Tess Gerritsen's stand-alone thrillers?

GIRL MISSING

Her stunning first thriller

The first body is a mystery. The next body is
a warning. The final body might be hers…

'You are going to be up all night'
Stephen King

THE BONE GARDEN

Boston 1830: A notorious serial killer preys on his victims,
flitting from graveyards and into maternity wards.
But no one knows who he is…

'Fascinating…gory…a fast-paced novel that will leave
you with a real appreciation of just how far medicine
has come in the past century'
Mail on Sunday

HARVEST

How far would you go to save a life? A young surgical
resident is drawn into the deadly world of organ smuggling.

'Suspense as sharp as a scalpel's edge.
A page-turning, hold your breath read'
Tami Hoag

LIFE SUPPORT

A terrifying and deadly epidemic is about to be unleashed.

'If you like your crime medicine strong,
this will keep you gripped'
Mail on Sunday

THE SINNER

Tess Gerritsen

BANTAM BOOKS

LONDON • TORONTO • SYDNEY • AUCKLAND • JOHANNESBURG

TRANSWORLD PUBLISHERS
61-63 Uxbridge Road, London W5 5SA
A Random House Group Company
www.rbooks.co.uk

THE SINNER
A BANTAM BOOK: 9780553815023

First published in Great Britain
in 2003 by Bantam Press
an imprint of Transworld Publishers
Bantam edition published 2004

Addresses for Random House Group Ltd companies outside the UK
can be found at: www.randomhouse.co.uk
The Random House Group Ltd Reg. No. 954009

The Random House Group Limited supports The Forest Stewardship
Council® (FSC®), the leading international forest-certification organisation.
Our books carrying the FSC label are printed on FSC®-certified paper.
FSC is the only forest-certification scheme supported by the leading
environmental organisations, including Greenpeace. Our
paper procurement policy can be found at
www.randomhouse.co.uk/environment

MIX
Paper from
responsible sources
FSC® C016897

Typeset in 11/12.5pt Sabon by Falcon Oast Graphic Art Ltd.
Printed and bound in Great Britain by Clays Ltd, St Ives PLC

26 28 30 29 27 25

To my mother, Ruby J. C. Tom, with love.

Acknowledgments

My warmest thanks to:

Peter Mars and Bruce Blake, for their insights into the Boston Police Department.

Margaret Greenwald, M.D., for allowing me to look into the medical examiner's world.

Gina Centrello, for her unflagging enthusiasm.

Linda Marrow, every writer's dream editor.

Selina Walker, my miracle worker on the other side of the Pond.

Jane Berkey, Donald Cleary, and the wonderful team at the Jane Rotrosen Agency.

Meg Ruley, my literary agent, champion, and guiding light. Nobody does it better.

And to my husband Jacob, still my best friend after all these years.

THE SINNER

Prologue

The driver refused to take him any farther.

A mile back, right after they passed the abandoned Octagon chemical plant, the pavement had given way to an overgrown dirt road. Now the driver complained that his car was getting scraped by underbrush, and with the recent rains, there were muddy spots where their tires could get mired. And where would that leave them? Stranded, 150 kilometers from Hyderabad. Howard Redfield listened to the long litany of objections, and knew they were merely a pretext for the real reason the driver did not wish to proceed. No man easily admits that he is afraid.

Redfield had no choice; from here, he would have to walk.

He leaned forward to speak in the driver's ear, and caught a gamey whiff of the man's sweat. In the rearview mirror, where rattling beads dangled, he saw the driver's dark eyes staring at him. 'You'll wait here for me, won't you?' Redfield asked. 'Stay right here, on the road.'

'How long?'

'An hour, maybe. As long as it takes.'

'I tell you, there is nothing to see. No one is there anymore.'

'Just wait here, okay? Wait. I'll pay you double when we get back to the city.'

Redfield grabbed his knapsack, stepped out of the air-conditioned car, and was instantly swimming in a sea of humidity. He hadn't worn a knapsack since he was a college kid, wandering through Europe on a shoestring, and it felt a little would-be, at age fifty-one, to be slinging one over his flabby shoulders. But he was damned if he went anywhere in this steamhouse of a country without his bottle of purified drinking water and his insect repellant and his sunscreen and diarrhea medicine. And his camera; he could not leave behind the camera.

He stood sweating in the late afternoon heat, looked up at the sky, and thought: Great, the sun is going down, and all the mosquitoes come out at dusk. Here comes dinner, you little buggers.

He set off down the road. Tall grass obscured the path, and he stumbled into a rut, his walking shoes sinking ankle-deep in mud. Clearly no vehicle had come this way in months, and Mother Nature had quickly moved in to reclaim her territory. He paused, panting and swatting at insects. Glancing back, he saw that the car was no longer in sight, and that made him uneasy. Could he trust the driver to wait for him? The man had been reluctant to bring him this far, and had grown more and more nervous as they'd bounced along the increasingly rough road. Bad people were out here, the driver had said, and terrible things happened in this area. They could both disappear, and who would bother to come looking for them?

Redfield pressed onward.

The humid air seemed to close in around him. He could hear the water bottle sloshing in his knapsack, and already he was thirsty, but he did not stop to drink. With only an hour or so left of daylight, he had to keep moving. Insects hummed in the grass, and he heard what he thought must be birds calling in the canopy of trees all around him, but it was unlike any birdsong he'd ever heard before. Everything about this country felt strange and surreal, and he trudged in a dreamlike trance, sweat trickling down his chest. The rhythm of his own breathing accelerated with each step. It should be only a mile and a half, according to the map, but he seemed to walk forever, and even a fresh application of insect repellant did not discourage the mosquitoes. His ears were filled with their buzzing, and his face was an itching mask of hives.

He stumbled into another deep rut and landed on his knees in tall grass. Spat out a mouthful of vegetation as he crouched there, catching his breath, so discouraged and exhausted that he decided it was time to turn around. To get back on that plane to Cincinnati with his tail tucked between his legs. Cowardice, after all, was far safer. And more comfortable.

He heaved a sigh, planted his hand on the ground to push himself to his feet, and went very still, staring down at the grass. Something gleamed there among the green blades, something metallic. It was only a cheap tin button, but at that moment, it struck him as a sign. A talisman. He slipped it in his pocket, rose to his feet, and kept walking.

Only a few hundred feet farther, the road suddenly opened up into a large clearing, encircled by tall trees. A lone structure stood at the far edge, a squat cinder block building with a rusting tin roof. Branches clattered and grass waved in the gentle wind.

This is the place, he thought. This is where it happened.

His breathing suddenly seemed too loud. Heart pounding, he slipped off his knapsack, unzipped it, and pulled out his camera.

Document everything, he thought. Octagon will try to make you out as a liar. They will do everything they can to discredit you, so you have to be ready to defend yourself. You have to prove that you are telling the truth.

He moved into the clearing, toward a heap of blackened branches. Nudging the twigs with his shoe, he stirred up the stench of charred wood.

He backed away, a chill crawling up his spine.

It was the remains of a funeral pyre.

With sweating hands, he took off his lens cap and began to shoot photos. Eye pressed to the viewfinder, he snapped image after image. The burned remains of a hut. A child's sandal, lying in the grass. A bright fragment of cloth, torn from a sari. Everywhere he looked, he saw Death.

He swung to the right, a tapestry of green sweeping past his viewfinder, and was about to click off another photo when his finger froze on the button.

A figure skittered past the edge of the frame.

He lowered the camera from his eye and straightened, staring at the trees. He saw nothing now, only the sway of branches.

There – was that a flash of movement, at the very periphery of his vision? He'd caught only a glimpse of something dark, bobbing among the trees. A monkey?

He had to keep shooting. The daylight was going fast.

He walked past a stone well and crossed toward the tin-roofed building, his pants swishing through grass, glancing left and right as he moved. The trees seemed to have eyes, and they were watching him. As he drew near the building, he saw that the walls were scorched by fire. In front of the doorway was a mound of ashes and blackened branches. Another funeral pyre.

He stepped around it, and looked into the doorway.

17

At first, he could make out very little in that gloomy interior. Daylight was rapidly fading, and inside, it was even darker, a palette of blacks and grays. He paused for a moment as his eyes adjusted. With growing bewilderment, he registered the glint of fresh water in an earthenware jar. The scent of spices. How could this be?

Behind him, a twig snapped.

He spun around.

A lone figure was standing in the clearing. All around them, the trees had gone still, and even the birds were silent. The figure came toward him, moving with a strange and jerky gait, until it stood only a few feet away.

The camera tumbled from Redfield's hands. He backed away, staring in horror.

It was a woman. And she had no face.

One

They called her the Queen of the Dead.

Though no one ever said it to her face, Dr. Maura Isles sometimes heard the nickname murmured in her wake as she traveled the grim triangle of her job between courtroom and death scene and morgue. Sometimes she would detect a note of dark sarcasm: *Ha ha, there she goes, our Goth goddess, out to collect fresh subjects.* Sometimes the whispers held a tremolo of disquiet, like the murmurs of the pious as an unholy stranger passes among them. It was the disquiet of those who could not understand why she chose to walk in Death's footsteps. Does she enjoy it, they wonder? Does the touch of cold flesh, the stench of decay, hold such allure for her that she has turned her back on the living? They think this cannot be normal, and they cast uneasy glances her way, noting details that only reinforce their beliefs that she is an odd duck. The ivory skin, the black hair with its blunt Cleopatra cut. The red slash of lipstick. Who else wears lipstick to a death scene? Most of all, it's her calmness that disturbs them, her coolly regal gaze as she surveys the horrors that they themselves can barely stomach. Unlike them, she does not avert her gaze. Instead she bends close and stares, touches. She sniffs.

And later, under bright lights in her autopsy lab, she cuts.

She was cutting now, her scalpel slicing through chilled skin, through subcutaneous fat that gleamed a greasy yellow. A man who liked his hamburgers and fries, she thought as she used pruning shears to cut through the ribs and lifted the triangular shield of breastbone the way one opens a cupboard door, to reveal its treasured contents.

The heart lay cradled in its spongey bed of lungs. For fifty-nine years, it had pumped blood through the body of Mr. Samuel Knight. It had grown with him, aged with him, transforming, as he had, from the lean muscle of youth to this well-larded flesh. All pumps eventually fail, and so had Mr. Knight's as he'd sat in his Boston hotel room with the TV turned on and a glass of whiskey from the minibar sitting beside him on the nightstand.

She did not pause to wonder what his final thoughts might have been, or whether he had felt pain or fear. Though she explored his most intimate recesses, though she flayed open his skin and held his heart in her hands, Mr. Samuel Knight remained a stranger to her, a silent and undemanding one, willingly offering up his secrets. The dead are patient. They do not complain, nor threaten, nor cajole.

The dead do not hurt you; only the living do.

She worked with serene efficiency, resecting the thoracic viscera, laying the freed heart on the cutting board. Outside, the first snow of December swirled, white flakes whispering against windows and slithering down alleys. But here in the lab, the only sounds were of running water and the hiss of the ventilator fan.

Her assistant Yoshima moved in uncanny silence, anticipating her requests, materializing wherever she needed him. They had worked together only a year and a half, yet already they functioned like a single organism, linked by the telepathy of two logical minds. She did not need to ask him to redirect the lamp; it was already done, the light shining down on the dripping heart, a pair of scissors held out and waiting for her to take them.

The darkly mottled wall of the right ventricle, and the white apical scar, told her this heart's sad story. An old myocardial infarction, months or even years old, had already destroyed part of the left ventricular wall. Then, sometime in the last twenty-four hours, a fresh infarction had occurred. A thrombus had blocked off the right coronary artery, strangling the flow of blood to the muscle of the right ventricle.

She resected tissue for histology, already knowing what she would see under the microscope.

Coagulation and necrosis. The invasion of white cells, moving in like a defending army. Perhaps Mr. Samuel Knight thought the discomfort in his chest was just a bout of indigestion. Too much lunch, shouldn't have eaten all those onions. Maybe Pepto-Bismol would do the trick. Or perhaps there'd been more ominous signs which he chose to ignore: the weight on his chest, the shortness of breath. Surely it did not occur to him that he was having a heart attack.

That, a day later, he would be dead of an arrhythmia.

The heart now lay open and sectioned on the board. She looked at the torso, missing all its organs. So ends your business trip to Boston, she thought. No surprises here. No foul play, except for the abuse you heaped on your own body, Mr. Knight.

The intercom buzzed. 'Dr. Isles?' It was Louise, her secretary.

'Yes?'

'Detective Rizzoli's on line two for you. Can you take the call?'

'I'll pick up.'

Maura peeled off her gloves and crossed to the wall phone. Yoshima, who'd been rinsing instruments in the sink, shut off the faucet. He turned to watch her with his silent tiger eyes, already knowing what a call from Rizzoli signified.

When at last Maura hung up, she saw the question in his gaze.

'It's starting early today,' she said. Then she

stripped off her gown and left the morgue, to usher another subject into her realm.

The morning's snowfall had turned into a treacherous mix of both snow and sleet, and the city plows were nowhere in sight. She drove cautiously along Jamaica Riverway, tires swishing through deep slush, windshield wipers scraping at hoar-frosted glass. This was the first winter storm of the season, and drivers had yet to adjust to the conditions. Already, several casualties had slid off the road, and she passed a parked police cruiser, its lights flashing, the patrolman standing beside a tow truck driver as they both gazed at a car that had tipped into a ditch.

The tires of her Lexus began to slide sideways, the front bumper veering toward oncoming traffic. Panicking, she hit the brakes and felt the vehicle's automatic skid control kick into action. She pulled the car back into her lane. Screw this, she thought, her heart thudding. I'm moving back to California. She slowed to a timid crawl, not caring who honked at her or how much traffic she held up. Go ahead and pass me, idiots. I've met too many drivers like you on my slab.

The road took her into Jamaica Plain, a west Boston neighborhood of stately old mansions and broad lawns, of serene parks and river walks. In the summertime, this would be a leafy retreat from the noise and heat of urban Boston, but today, under bleak skies, with winds sweeping across barren lawns, it was a desolate neighborhood.

The address she sought seemed the most forbidding of all, the building set back behind a high stone wall over which a smothering tangle of ivy had scrambled. A barricade to keep out the world, she thought. From the street, all she could see were the gothic peaks of a slate roof and one towering gable window which peered back at her like a dark eye. A patrol car parked near the front gate confirmed that she had found the correct address. Only a few other vehicles had arrived so far – the shock troops before the larger army of crime-scene techs arrived.

She parked across the street and braced herself against the first blast of wind. When she stepped out of the car, her shoe skidded right out from under her, and she barely caught herself, hanging onto the vehicle door. Dragging herself back to her feet, she felt icy water trickle down her calves from the soaked hem of her coat, which had fallen into the slush. For a few seconds she just stood there, sleet stinging her face, shocked by how quickly it had all happened.

She glanced across the street at the patrolman sitting in his cruiser, and saw that he was watching her, and had surely seen her slip. Her pride stung, she grabbed her kit from the front seat, swung the door shut, and made her way, with as much dignity as she could muster, across the rime-slicked road.

'You okay, Doc?' the patrolman called out through his car window, a concerned inquiry she really did not welcome.

'I'm fine.'

'Watch yourself in those shoes. It's even more slippery in the courtyard.'

'Where's Detective Rizzoli?'

'They're in the chapel.'

'And where's that?'

'Can't miss it. It's the door with the big cross on it.'

She continued to the front gate, but found it locked. An iron bell hung on the wall; she tugged on the pull rope, and the medieval clang slowly faded into the softer tick, tick of falling sleet. Just beneath the bell was a bronze plaque, its inscription partially obscured by a strand of brown ivy.

Graystones Abbey
The Sisters of Our Lady of Divine Light
The harvest is indeed great, but the laborers are few.
Pray, therefore, to send laborers
Into the harvest.

On the other side of the gate, a woman swathed in black suddenly appeared, her approach so silent that Maura gave a start when she saw the face staring at her through the bars. It was an ancient face, so deeply lined it seemed to be collapsing in on itself, but the eyes were bright and sharp as a bird's. The nun did not speak, posing her question with only her gaze.

'I'm Dr. Isles from the Medical Examiner's office,' said Maura. 'The police called me here.'

The gate squealed open.

Maura stepped into the courtyard. 'I'm looking for Detective Rizzoli. I believe she's in the chapel.'

The nun pointed directly across the courtyard. Then she turned and shuffled slowly into the nearest doorway, abandoning Maura to make her own way to the chapel.

Snowflakes whirled and danced amid needles of sleet, like white butterflies circling their lead-footed cousins. The most direct route was to cross the courtyard, but the stones were glazed with ice, and Maura's shoes, with their gripless soles, had already proven no match for such a surface. She ducked instead beneath the narrow covered walkway that ran along the courtyard's perimeter. Though protected from the sleet, she found little shelter here from the wind, which sliced through her coat. She was shocked by the cold, reminded yet again of how cruel December in Boston could be. For most of her life, she had lived in San Francisco, where a glimpse of snowflakes was a rare delight, not a torment, like these stinging nettles that swirled under the overhang to nip her face. She veered closer to the building and hugged her coat tighter as she passed darkened windows. From beyond the gate came the faint swish of traffic on Jamaica Riverway. But here, within these walls, she heard only silence. Except for the elderly nun who had admitted her, the compound seemed abandoned.

So it was a shock when she saw three faces staring at her from one of the windows. The nuns stood in a silent tableau, like darkrobed ghosts behind glass, watching the intruder make her way deeper into their sanctuary. Their gazes swerved in unison, following her as she moved past.

The entrance to the chapel was draped with a strand of yellow crime scene tape, which had sagged in the doorway and hung crusted with sleet. She lifted the tape to step beneath it and pushed open the door.

A camera flash exploded in her eyes and she froze, the door slowly hissing shut behind her, blinking away the afterimage that had seared her retinas. As her vision cleared, she saw rows of wooden pews, whitewashed walls, and at the front of the chapel, an enormous crucifix hanging above the altar. It was a coldly austere room, its gloom deepened by the stained glass windows, which admitted only a murky smear of light.

'Hold it right there. Be careful where you step,' said the photographer.

Maura looked down at the stone floor and saw blood. And footprints – a confusing jumble of them, along with medical debris. Syringe caps and torn wrappings. The leavings of an ambulance crew. But no body.

Her gaze moved in a wider circle, taking in the piece of trampled white cloth lying in the aisle, the splashes of red on the pews. She could see her own breath in this frigid room, and the temperature seemed to drop even colder, her chill deepening as she read the bloodstains, saw the successive splashes moving up the rows of benches, and understood what had happened here.

27

The photographer began to click off more shots, each one a visual assault on Maura's eyes.

'Hey Doc?' At the front of the chapel, a mop of dark hair popped up as Detective Jane Rizzoli rose to her feet and waved. 'The vic's up here.'

'What about this blood here, by the door?'

'That's from the other victim, Sister Ursula. Med-Q boys took her to St. Francis. There's more blood along that center aisle, and some footprints we're trying to preserve, so you'd better circle around to your left. Stick close to the wall.'

Maura paused to pull on paper shoe-covers, then edged along the perimeter of the room, hugging the wall. Only as she cleared the front row of pews did she see the nun's body, lying faceup, the fabric of her habit a black pool blending into a larger lake of red. Both hands had already been bagged to preserve evidence. The victim's youth took Maura by surprise. The nun who had let her in the gate, and those she had seen through the window, had all been elderly. This woman was far younger. It was an ethereal face, her pale blue eyes frozen in a look of eerie serenity. Her head was bare, the blond hair shorn to barely an inch long. Every terrible blow was recorded in the torn scalp, the misshapen crown.

'Her name's Camille Maginnes. Sister Camille. Hometown, Hyannisport,' said Rizzoli, sounding Dragnet-cool and businesslike. 'She was the first novice they've had here in fifteen years. Planned to take her final vows in May.'

She paused, then added: 'She was only twenty,' and her anger cracked through the facade.

'She's so young.'

'Yeah. Looks like he beat the shit out of her.'

Maura pulled on gloves and crouched down to study the destruction. The death instrument had left raggedly linear lacerations on the scalp. Fragments of bone protruded through torn skin, and a clump of gray matter had oozed out. Though the facial skin was largely intact, it was suffused a dark purple.

'She died facedown. Who turned her onto her back?'

'The sisters who found her,' said Rizzoli. 'They were looking for a pulse.'

'What time were the victims discovered?'

'About eight this morning.' Rizzoli glanced at her watch. 'Nearly two hours ago.'

'Do you know what happened? What did the sisters tell you?'

'It's been hard getting anything useful out of them. There are only fourteen nuns left now, and they're all in a state of shock. Here they think they're safe. Protected by God. And then some lunatic breaks in.'

'There are signs of forced entry?'

'No, but it wouldn't be all that hard to get into the compound. There's ivy growing all over the walls – you could hop right over without too much trouble. And there's also a back gate, leading to a field, where they have their gardens. A perp could get in that way, too.'

'Footprints?'

'A few in here. But outside, they'd be pretty much buried under snow.'

'So we don't know that he actually broke in. He could have been admitted through that front gate.'

'It's a cloistered order, Doc. No one's allowed inside the gates except for the parish priest, when he comes in to say Mass and hear confession. And there's also a lady who works in the rectory. They let her bring her little girl when she can't get child care. But that's it. No one else comes in without the Abbess's approval. And the sisters stay inside. They leave only for doctors' appointments and family emergencies.'

'Who have you spoken to so far?'

'The Abbess, Mother Mary Clement. And the two nuns who found the victims.'

'What did they tell you?'

Rizzoli shook her head. 'Saw nothing, heard nothing. I don't think the others will be able to tell us much, either.'

'Why not?'

'Have you seen how old they are?'

'It doesn't mean they don't have their wits about them.'

'One of them's gorked out by a stroke and two of them have Alzheimer's. Most of them sleep in rooms facing away from the courtyard, so they wouldn't have seen a thing.'

At first Maura simply crouched over Camille's body, not touching it. Granting the victim a last moment of dignity. Nothing can hurt you now, she thought. She began to palpate the scalp, and felt the crunch of shifting bone fragments beneath the skin. 'Multiple blows. All of them landed on the crown or the back of the skull . . .'

'And the facial bruising? Is that just lividity?'

'Yes. And it's fixed.'

'So the blows came from behind. And above.'

'The attacker was probably taller.'

'Or she was down on her knees. And he was standing over her.'

Maura paused, hands touching cool flesh, arrested by the heartbreaking image of this young nun, kneeling before her attacker, blows raining down on her bowed head.

'What kind of bastard goes around beating up nuns?' said Rizzoli. 'What the fuck is wrong with this world?'

Maura winced at Rizzoli's choice of words. Though she couldn't remember the last time she'd set foot in a church, and had ceased believing years ago, to hear such profanity in a sanctified place disturbed her. Such was the power of childhood indoctrination. Even she, for whom saints and miracles were now merely fantasies, would never utter a curse in full view of the cross.

But Rizzoli was too angry to care what words came tumbling out of her mouth, even in this sacred place. Her hair was more disheveled than usual, a wild, black mane glistening with melted sleet. The bones of her face jutted out in sharp angles beneath pale skin. In the gloom of the chapel, her eyes were bright coals, lit with rage.

Righteous anger had always been Jane Rizzoli's fuel, the essence of what drove her to hunt monsters. Today, though, she seemed feverish with it, and her face was thinner, as though the fire was now consuming her from within.

Maura did not want to feed those flames. She kept her voice dispassionate, her questions businesslike. A scientist dealing in facts, not emotions.

She reached for Sister Camille's arm and tested the elbow joint. 'It's flaccid. No rigor mortis.'

'Less than five, six hours then?'

'It's also cold in here.'

Rizzoli gave a snort, exhaling a puff of vapor in the frigid air. 'No kidding.'

'Just above freezing, I'd guess. Rigor mortis would be delayed.'

'How long?'

'Almost indefinitely.'

'What about her face? The fixed bruising?'

'Livor mortis could have happened within half an hour. It doesn't help us all that much with time of death.'

Maura opened her kit and set out the chemical thermometer to measure ambient temperature. She eyed the victim's many layers of clothing and decided not to take a rectal temperature until after the body had been transported to the morgue. The room was poorly lit – not a place in which she could adequately rule out sexual assault prior to the insertion of the thermometer. Wrestling off clothes might also dislodge trace evidence. Instead she took out syringes to withdraw vitreous fluid for postmortem potassium levels. It would give her one estimate for time of death.

'Tell me about the other victim,' Maura said as she pierced the left eye and slowly withdrew vitreous fluid into the syringe.

Rizzoli gave a groan of disgust at the procedure and turned away. 'The vic found by the door was Sister Ursula Rowland, sixty-eight years old. Must be a tough old bird. They said she was moving her arms when they loaded her into the ambulance. Frost and I got here just as they were driving away.'

'How badly injured was she?'

'I didn't see her. Latest report we got from St. Francis Hospital is that she's in surgery. Multiple skull fractures and bleeding into the brain.'

'Like this victim.'

'Yeah. Like Camille.' The anger was back in Rizzoli's voice.

Maura rose to her feet and stood shivering. Her trousers had absorbed freezing water from the soaked hem of her coat, and her calves felt encased in ice. She had been told on the phone that the death scene was indoors, so she had not brought her scarf or wool gloves from the car. This unheated room was scarcely warmer than the sleet-swept courtyard outside. She shoved her hands into her coat pockets, and wondered how Rizzoli, who was also without warm gloves and scarf, could linger so long in this frigid chapel. Rizzoli seemed to carry her own heat source

33

within her, the fever of her outrage, and although her lips were turning blue, she did not seem in a hurry to seek a warmer room anytime soon.

'Why is it so cold in here?' asked Maura. 'I can't imagine they'd want to hold Mass in this room.'

'They don't. This part of the building's never used in winter – it's too expensive to heat. There are so few of them still living here, anyway. For Mass, they use a small chapel off the rectory.'

Maura thought of the three nuns she'd seen through the window, all of them elderly. These sisters were dying flames, flickering out one by one.

'If this chapel's not used,' she said, 'what were the victims doing in here?'

Rizzoli gave a sigh, exhaling a dragon's breath of vapor. 'No one knows. The Abbess says the last time she saw Ursula and Camille was at prayers last night, around nine. When they didn't appear at morning prayers, the sisters went looking for them. They never expected to find them in here.'

'All these blows to the head. It looks like sheer rage.'

'But look at her face,' said Rizzoli, pointing to Camille. 'He didn't hit her face. He spared her face. That makes it seem a lot less personal. As if he's not swinging at her specifically, but at what she is. What she stands for.'

'Authority?' said Maura. 'Power?'

'Funny. I would have said something along the lines of faith, hope, and charity.'

'Well, I went to a Catholic high school.'

'You?' Rizzoli gave a snort. 'Never would've guessed.'

Maura took a deep breath of chilly air and looked up at the cross, remembering her years at Holy Innocents Academy. And the special torments meted out by Sister Magdalene, who had taught history. The torment had not been physical but emotional, dispensed by a woman who was quick to identify which girls had, in her opinion, an unseemly excess of confidence. At the age of fourteen, Maura's best friends had not been people, but books. She'd easily mastered all her classwork, and had been proud of it, too. That was what had brought Sister Magdalene's wrath down upon her shoulders. For Maura's own good, that unholy pride in her own intellect needed to be beaten into humility. Sister Magdalene went about the task with vicious gusto. She had held Maura up to ridicule in class, had written cutting comments in the margins of her immaculate papers, and sighed loudly whenever Maura raised her hand to ask a question. In the end, Maura had been reduced to conquered silence.

'They used to intimidate me,' said Maura. 'The nuns.'

'I didn't think anything scared you, Doc.'

'Lots of things scare me.'

Rizzoli laughed. 'Just not dead bodies, huh?'

'There are far scarier things in this world than dead bodies.'

They left the body of Camille lying on her bed

of cold stone and moved back around the room's perimeter, toward the bloodstained floor where Ursula had been found, still alive. The photographer had completed his work and departed; only Maura and Rizzoli remained in the chapel, two lone women, their voices echoing off stark walls. Maura had always thought of chapels as universal sanctuaries, where even the spirit of the unbeliever might be comforted. But she found no comfort in this bleak place, where Death had walked, contemptuous of holy symbols.

'They found Sister Ursula right here,' said Rizzoli. 'She was lying with her head pointed toward the altar, her feet toward the door.'

As though prostrating herself before the crucifix.

'This guy's a fucking animal,' said Rizzoli, the angry words clipped off like shards of ice. 'That's what we're dealing with. Out of his mind. Or some coked-up asshole looking for something to steal.'

'We don't know it's a man.'

Rizzoli waved toward the body of Sister Camille. 'You think a woman did that?'

'A woman can swing a hammer. Crush a skull.'

'We found a footprint. There, halfway up the aisle. Looked to me like a man's size twelve.'

'One of the ambulance crew?'

'No, you can see the Med-Q team's footprints here, near the door. That one in the aisle's different. That one's *his*.'

The wind blew, rattling the windows, and the

door creaked as though invisible hands were tugging at it, desperate to get in. Rizzoli's lips had chilled to blue, and her face had taken on a corpselike pallor, but she showed no intention of seeking a warmer room. That was Rizzoli, too stubborn to be the first to capitulate. To admit she had reached her limit.

Maura looked down at the stone floor where Sister Ursula had been lying, and she could not disagree with Rizzoli's instincts, that this attack was an act of insanity. This was madness she saw here, in these bloodstains. In the blows slammed into Sister Camille's skull. Either madness, or evil.

An icy draft seemed to blow straight up her spine. She straightened, shivering, and her gaze fixed on the crucifix. 'I'm freezing,' she said. 'Can we get warm somewhere? Get a cup of coffee?'

'Are you finished here?'

'I've seen what I need to. The autopsy will tell us the rest.'

Two

They emerged from the chapel, stepping over the strand of police tape which by now had fallen from the doorway and lay encased in ice. The wind flapped their coats and whipped their faces as they headed beneath the walkway, their eyes narrowed against rebel gusts of snowflakes. As they stepped into a gloomy entranceway, Maura registered barely a whisper of warmth against her numb face. She smelled eggs and old paint and the mustiness of an ancient heating system, radiating dust.

The clatter of chinaware drew them down a dim hallway, into a room awash in fluorescent light, a disconcertingly modern detail. It glared down, stark and unflattering, on the deeply lined faces of the nuns seated around a battered rectory table. Thirteen of them – an unlucky number. Their attention was focused on squares of bright floral cloth and silk ribbons and trays of dried lavender and rose petals. Craft time, thought Maura, watching as arthritic hands scooped up herbs and wound ribbon around sachets. One of the nuns sat slumped in a wheelchair. She was tilted to the side, her left hand curled into a claw on the armrest, her face sagging like a partly melted mask. The cruel aftermath of a stroke. Yet she was the first to notice the two intruders, and she gave a moan. The other sisters looked up, turning toward Maura and Rizzoli.

Gazing into those wizened faces, Maura was startled by the frailty she saw there. These were not the stern images of authority she remembered from her girlhood, but the gazes of the bewildered, looking to her for answers to this tragedy. She was uneasy with her new status, the way a grown child is uneasy when he first realizes that he and his parents have reversed roles.

Rizzoli asked, 'Can someone tell me where Detective Frost is?'

The question was answered by a harried-looking woman who had just come out of the adjoining kitchen, carrying a tray of clean coffee cups and saucers. She was dressed in a faded blue jumper stained with grease, and a tiny diamond glinted through the bubbles of dishwater on her left hand. Not a nun, thought Maura, but the rectory employee, tending to this ever more infirm community.

'He's still talking to the Abbess,' the woman said. She cocked her head toward the doorway, and a strand of brown hair came loose, curling over her frown-etched forehead. 'Her office is down the hall.'

Rizzoli nodded. 'I know the way.'

They left the harsh light of that room and continued down the hallway. Maura felt a draft here, a whisper of chill air, as though a ghost had just slipped past her. She did not believe in the afterlife, but when walking in the footsteps of those who had recently died, she sometimes wondered if their passing did not leave behind some imprint, some faint disturbance of energy that could be sensed by those who followed.

Rizzoli knocked on the Abbess's door, and a tremulous voice said: 'Come in.'

Stepping into the room, Maura smelled the aroma of coffee, as delicious as perfume. She saw dark wood paneling and a simple crucifix mounted on the wall above an oak desk. Behind that desk sat a stooped nun whose eyes were magnified to enormous blue pools by her glasses. She appeared every bit as old as her frail sisters seated around the rectory table, and her glasses looked so heavy they might pitch her face-forward onto her desk. But the eyes gazing through those thick lenses were alert and bright with intelligence.

Rizzoli's partner, Barry Frost, at once set down his coffee cup and rose to his feet out of politeness. Frost was the equivalent of everybody's kid brother, the one cop in the homicide unit who could walk into an interrogation room and make a suspect believe Frost was his best friend. He was also the one cop in the unit who never seemed to mind working with the mercurial Rizzoli, who even now was scowling at his cup of coffee, no doubt registering the fact that while she had been shivering in the chapel, her partner was sitting comfortably in this heated room.

'Reverend Mother,' said Frost, 'This is Dr. Isles, from the Medical Examiner's office. Doc, this is Mother Mary Clement.'

Maura reached for the Abbess's hand. It was gnarled, the skin like dry paper over bones. As she shook it, Maura spotted a beige cuff peeking out from under the black sleeve. So this was how the nuns tolerated such a cold building. Beneath her woollen habit, the Abbess was wearing long underwear.

Distorted blue eyes gazed at her through thick lenses. 'The Medical Examiner's office? Does that mean you're a physician?'

'Yes. A pathologist.'

'You study causes of death?'

'That's right.'

The Abbess paused, as though gathering the courage to ask the next question. 'Have you already been inside the chapel? Have you seen . . .'

Maura nodded. She wanted to cut off the question she knew was coming, but she was incapable of rudeness to a nun. Even at the age of forty, she was still unnerved by the sight of a black habit.

'Did she . . .' Mary Clement's voice slipped to a whisper. 'Did Sister Camille suffer greatly?'

'I'm afraid I have no answers yet. Not until I complete the . . . examination.' *Autopsy* was what she meant, but the word seemed too cold, too

41

clinical, for Mary Clement's sheltered ears. Nor did she want to reveal the terrible truth: That in fact, she had a very good idea of what had happened to Camille. Someone had confronted the young woman in the chapel. Someone had pursued her as she fled in terror up the aisle, wrenching off her white novice's veil. As his blows avulsed her scalp, her blood had splashed the pews, yet she had staggered onward, until at last she stumbled to her knees, conquered at his feet. Even then her attacker did not stop. Even then, he had kept swinging, crushing her skull like an egg.

Avoiding Mary Clement's eyes, Maura briefly lifted her gaze to the wooden cross mounted on the wall behind the desk, but that imposing symbol was no more comfortable for her to confront.

Rizzoli cut in, 'We haven't seen their bedrooms yet.' As usual, she was all business, focusing only on what needed to be done next.

Mary Clement blinked back tears. 'Yes. I was about to take Detective Frost upstairs to their chambers.'

Rizzoli nodded. 'We're ready when you are.'

The Abbess led the way up a stairway illuminated only by the glow of daylight through a stained glass window. On bright days, the sun would have painted the walls with a rich palette of colors, but on this wintry morning, the walls were murky with shades of gray.

'The upstairs rooms are mostly empty now.

Over the years, we've had to move the sisters downstairs, one by one,' said Mary Clement, climbing slowly, grasping the handrail as though hauling herself up, step by step. Maura half expected her to tumble backwards, and she stayed right behind her, tensing every time the Abbess paused, wobbling. 'Sister Jacinta's knee is bothering her these days, so she'll take a room downstairs, too. And now Sister Helen has trouble catching her breath. There are so few of us left . . .'

'It's quite a large building to maintain,' said Maura.

'And old.' The Abbess paused to catch her breath. She added, with a sad laugh, 'Old like us. And so expensive to keep up. We thought we might have to sell, but God found a way for us to hold onto it.'

'How?'

'A donor came forward last year. Now we've started renovations. The slates on the roof are new, and we now have insulation in the attic. We plan to replace the furnace, next.' She glanced back at Maura. 'Believe it or not, this building feels quite cozy, compared to a year ago.'

The Abbess took a deep breath and resumed climbing the stairs, her rosary beads clattering. 'There used to be forty-five of us here. When I first came to Graystones, we filled all these rooms. Both wings. But now we're a maturing community.'

'When did you come, Reverend Mother?' asked Maura.

43

'I entered as a postulant when I was eighteen years old. I had a young gentleman who wanted to marry me. I'm afraid his pride was quite wounded when I turned him down for God.' She paused on the step and looked back. For the first time, Maura noticed the bulge of a hearing aid beneath her wimple. 'You probably can't imagine that, can you, Dr. Isles? That I was ever that young?'

No, Maura couldn't. She couldn't imagine Mary Clement as anything but the wobbly relic she was now. Certainly never a desirable woman, pursued by men.

They reached the top of the stairs, and a long hallway stretched before them. It was warmer up here, almost pleasant, the heat trapped by low dark ceilings. The exposed beams looked at least a century old. The Abbess moved to the second door and hesitated, her hand on the knob. At last she turned it, and the door swung open, gray light from within spilling onto her face. 'This is Sister Ursula's room,' she said softly.

The room was scarcely large enough to fit all of them at once. Frost and Rizzoli stepped in, but Maura remained by the door, her gaze drifting past shelves lined with books, past flowerpots containing thriving African violets. With its mullioned window and low-beamed ceiling, the room looked medieval. A scholar's tidy garret, furnished with a simple bed and dresser, a desk and chair.

'Her bed's been made,' said Rizzoli, looking down at the neatly tucked sheets.

'That's the way we found it this morning,' said Mary Clement.

'Didn't she go to sleep last night?'

'It's more likely she rose early. She usually does.'

'How early?'

'She's often up hours before Lauds.'

'Lauds?' asked Frost.

'Our morning prayers, at seven. This past summer, she was always out early, in the garden. She loves to work in the garden.'

'And in the winter?' asked Rizzoli. 'What does she do so early in the morning?'

'Whatever the season, there's always work to be done, for those of us who can still manage it. But so many of the sisters are frail now. This year, we had to hire Mrs. Otis to help us prepare meals. Even with her help, we can scarcely keep up with the chores.'

Rizzoli opened the closet door. Inside hung an austere collection of blacks and browns. Not a hint of color nor embellishment. It was the wardrobe of a woman for whom the Lord's work was all-important, for whom the design of clothing was only in His service.

'These are the only clothes she has? What I see in this closet?' asked Rizzoli.

'We take a vow of poverty when we join the order.'

'Does that mean you give up everything you own?'

Mary Clement responded with the patient smile one gives to a child who has just asked an absurd question. 'It's not such a hardship, Detective. We keep our books, a few personal mementoes. As you can see, Sister Ursula enjoys her African violets. But yes, we leave almost everything behind when we come here. This is a contemplative order, and we don't welcome the distractions of the outside world.'

'Excuse me, Reverend Mother,' said Frost. 'I'm not Catholic, so I don't understand what that word means. What's a contemplative order?'

His question had been quietly respectful, and Mary Clement favored him with a warmer smile than she had given Rizzoli. 'A contemplative leads a reflective life. A life of prayer and private devotion and meditation. That's why we retreat behind walls. Why we turn away visitors. Seclusion is a comfort to us.'

'What if someone breaks the rules?' asked Rizzoli. 'Do you kick her out?'

Maura saw Frost wince at his partner's bluntly worded question.

'Our rules are voluntary,' said Mary Clement. 'We abide by them because we wish to.'

'But every so often, there's got to be some nun who wakes up one morning and says, "I feel like going to the beach." '

'It doesn't happen.'

'It must happen. They're human beings.'

'It doesn't happen.'

'No one breaks the rules? No one jumps the wall?'

'We have no need to leave the abbey. Mrs. Otis

46

buys our groceries. Father Brophy attends to our spiritual needs.'

'What about letters? Phone calls? Even in high security prisons, you get to make a phone call every so often.'

Frost was shaking his head, his expression pained.

'We have a telephone here, for emergencies,' said Mary Clement.

'And anyone can use it?'

'Why would they wish to?'

'How about mail? Can you get letters?'

'Some of us choose not to accept any mail.'

'And if you want to send a letter?'

'To whom?'

'Does it matter?'

Mary Clement's face had frozen into a tight, lord-give-me-patience smile. 'I can only repeat myself, Detective. We are not prisoners. We choose to live this way. Those who don't agree with these rules may choose to leave.'

'And what would they do, in the outside world?'

'You seem to think we have no knowledge of that world. But some of the sisters have served in schools or in hospitals.'

'I thought being cloistered meant you couldn't leave the convent.'

'Sometimes, God calls us to tasks outside the walls. A few years ago, Sister Ursula felt His call to serve abroad, and she was granted exclaustration – permission to live outside while keeping her vows.'

'But she came back.'

'Last year.'

'She didn't like it out there, in the world?'

'Her mission in India wasn't an easy one. And there was violence – a terrorist attack on her village. That's when she returned to us. Here, she could feel safe again.'

'She didn't have family to go home to?'

'Her closest relative was a brother, who died two years ago. We're her family now, and Graystones is her home. When you're tired of the world and in need of comfort, Detective,' the Abbess asked gently, 'don't you go home?'

The answer seemed to unsettle Rizzoli. Her gaze shifted to the wall, where the crucifix hung. Just as quickly, it caromed away.

'Reverend Mother?'

The woman in the grease-stained blue jumper was standing in the hall, looking in at them with flat, incurious eyes. A few more strands of brown hair had come loose from her ponytail and hung limp about her bony face. 'Father Brophy says he's on his way over to deal with the reporters. But there are so many of them calling now that Sister Isabel's just taken the phone off the hook. She doesn't know what to tell them.'

'I'll be right there, Mrs. Otis.' The Abbess turned to Rizzoli. 'As you can see, we're overwhelmed. Please take as much time as you need here. I'll be downstairs.'

'Before you go,' said Rizzoli, 'which room is Sister Camille's?'

'It's the fourth door.'

'And it's not locked?'

'There are no locks on these doors,' said Mary Clement. 'There never have been.'

The smell of bleach and Murphy's Oil Soap was the first thing Maura registered as she stepped into Sister Camille's room. Like Sister Ursula's, this room had a mullioned window facing the courtyard and the same low, wood-beamed ceiling. But while Ursula's room felt lived-in, Camille's room had been so thoroughly scrubbed and sanitized it felt sterilized. The whitewashed walls were bare except for a wooden crucifix hanging opposite the bed. It would have been the first object Camille's gaze would fix upon when she awakened each morning, a symbol of her focused existence. This was a chamber for a penitent.

Maura gazed down at the floor and saw where areas of fierce scrubbing had worn down the finish, leaving patches of lighter wood. She pictured fragile young Camille down on her knees, clutching steel wool, trying to sand away . . . what? A century's worth of stains? All traces of the women who had lived here before her?

'Geez,' said Rizzoli. 'If cleanliness is next to Godliness, this woman was a saint.'

Maura crossed to the desk by the window, where a book lay open. *Saint Brigid of Ireland: A Biography*. She imagined Camille reading at this pristine desk, the window light playing on her delicate features. She wondered if, on warm days, Camille ever removed her novice's white veil and sat bareheaded, letting the breeze through the window blow across her cropped blond hair.

'There's blood here,' said Frost.

Maura turned and saw that he was standing by the bed, staring down at the rumpled sheets.

Rizzoli peeled back the covers, revealing bright red stains on the bottom sheet.

'Menstrual blood,' said Maura, and saw Frost flush and turn away. Even married men were squeamish when it came to intimate details of women's bodily functions.

The clang of the bell drew Maura's gaze back to the window. She watched as a nun emerged from the building to open the gate. Four visitors wearing yellow slickers entered the courtyard.

'CSU's arrived,' said Maura.

'I'll go down and meet them,' said Frost, and he left the room.

Sleet was still falling, ticking against the glass, and a layer of rime distorted her view of the courtyard below. Maura caught a watery view of Frost stepping out to greet the crime-scene techs. Fresh invaders, violating the sanctity of the abbey. And beyond the wall, others were waiting to invade as well. She saw a TV news van creep past the gate, cameras no doubt rolling. How did they find their way here so quickly? Was the scent of death so powerful?

She turned to look at Rizzoli. 'You're Catholic, Jane. Aren't you?'

Rizzoli snorted as she picked through Camille's closet. 'Me? Catechism dropout.'

'When did you stop believing?'

'About the same time I stopped believing in Santa Claus. Never did make it to my confirmation, which to this day still pisses off my dad. Jesus, what a boring closet. *Let's see, shall I wear the black or the brown habit today?* Why would any girl in her right mind want to be a nun?'

'Not all nuns wear habits. Not since Vatican II.'

'Yeah, but that chastity thing, that hasn't changed. Imagine no sex for the rest of your life.'

'I don't know,' said Maura. 'It might be a relief to stop thinking about men.'

'I'm not sure that's possible.' She shut the closet door and slowly scanned the room, looking for . . . what? Maura wondered. The key to Camille's personality? The explanation for why her life had ended so young, so brutally? But there were no clues here that Maura could see. This was a room swept clean of all traces of its occupant. That, perhaps, was the most telling clue of all to Camille's personality. A young woman scrubbing, always scrubbing away at dirt. At sin.

Rizzoli crossed to the bed and dropped down to her hands and knees to look underneath. 'Geez, it's so clean under here you can eat off the goddamn floor.'

Wind shook the window and sleet clattered against the glass. Maura turned and watched Frost and the CSTs cross toward the chapel. One of the techs suddenly slid across the stones, arms flung

51

out like a skater as he struggled to stay upright. We're all struggling to stay upright, Maura thought. Resisting the pull of temptation, just as we fight the pull of gravity. And when we finally fall, it's always such a surprise.

The team stepped into the chapel, and she imagined them standing in a silent circle, staring down at Sister Ursula's blood, their breaths marked by puffs of steam.

Behind her there was a thud.

She turned and was alarmed to see Rizzoli sitting on the floor next to the toppled chair. She had her head hanging between her knees.

'Jane.' Maura knelt beside her. 'Jane?'

Rizzoli waved her away. 'I'm okay. I'm okay . . .'

'What happened?'

'I just . . . I think I got up too fast. I'm just a little dizzy . . .'

Rizzoli tried to straighten, then quickly dropped her head again.

'You should lie down.'

'I don't need to lie down. Just give me a minute to clear my head.'

Maura remembered that Rizzoli had not looked well in the chapel, her face too pale, her lips dusky. At the time she'd assumed it was because the detective was chilled. Now they were in a warm room, and Rizzoli looked just as drained.

'Did you eat breakfast this morning?' Maura asked.

'Uh . . .'

'Don't you remember?'

'Yeah, I guess I ate. Sort of.'

'What does that mean?'

'A piece of toast, okay?' Rizzoli shook off Maura's hand, an impatient rejection of any help. It was that fierce pride that sometimes made her so difficult to work with. 'I think I'm coming down with the flu.'

'You're sure that's all it is?'

Rizzoli shoved her hair off her face and slowly sat up straight. 'Yeah. And I shouldn't have had all that coffee this morning.'

'How much?'

'Three – maybe four cups.'

'Isn't that overdoing it?'

'I needed the caffeine. But now it's eating a hole in my stomach. I feel like puking.'

'I'll walk you to the bathroom.'

'No.' Rizzoli waved her away. 'I can make it, okay?' Slowly she rose to her feet and just stood for a moment, as though not quite confident of her footing. Then she squared her shoulders, and with a hint of the old Rizzoli swagger, walked out of the room.

The clang of the gate bell drew Maura's gaze back to the window. She watched as the elderly nun once again emerged from the building and shuffled across the cobblestones to answer the call. This new visitor did not need to plead his case; the nun at once opened the gate. A man dressed in a long black coat stepped into the courtyard and laid his hand on the nun's shoulder. It was a gesture of comfort and familiarity. Together they walked toward the building, the man moving slowly to match her arthritic gait, his head bent toward her as though he did not want to miss hearing a single word she said.

Halfway across the courtyard, he suddenly stopped and looked up, as though he sensed that Maura was watching him.

For an instant, their gazes met through the window. She saw a lean and striking face, a head of black hair, ruffled by the wind. And she caught a glimpse of white, tucked beneath the raised collar of his black coat.

A priest.

When Mrs. Otis had announced that Father Brophy was on his way to the abbey, Maura had imagined him to be an elderly, gray-haired man. But the man gazing up at her now was young – no older than forty.

He and the nun continued toward the building, and Maura lost sight of them. The courtyard was once again deserted, but the trampled snow bore a record of all who had walked across it that morning. The morgue transport team would soon arrive with their stretcher and add yet more foot-prints to the snow.

She took a deep breath, dreading the return to the cold chapel, to the grim task that still lay before her. She left the room and went down to await her team.

Three

Jane Rizzoli stood at the bathroom sink, staring at herself in the mirror, and not liking what she saw. She could not help comparing herself to the elegant Dr. Isles, who always seemed regally serene and in control, every black hair in place, her lipstick a glossy slash of red on flawless skin. The image Rizzoli saw in the mirror was neither serene nor flawless. Her hair was as wild as a banshee's, the black coils overwhelming a face that was pale and strained. I'm not myself, she thought. I don't recognize this woman looking back at me. When did I turn into this stranger?

Another wave of nausea suddenly washed through her and she closed her eyes, fighting it, resisting it as fiercely as though her life depended on it. Sheer willpower couldn't hold back the inevitable. Clapping a hand to her mouth, she made a dash for the nearest toilet stall, getting there just in time. Even after her stomach had emptied itself, she lingered there with her head hung over the bowl, not yet daring to leave the security of the stall. Thinking: *It's got to be the flu. Please, let it be the flu.*

When at last her nausea had passed, she felt so drained she sat down on the toilet and slumped sideways against the wall. She thought about the work that lay before her. All the interviews still to be done, the frustrations of trying to tease out any useful information from this community of stunned and silent women. And the standing around, worst of all, the exhaustion of just standing around while CSU performed its microscopic treasure hunt. Usually she was the one eagerly sifting for evidence, always more evidence, the one who fought for control of every crime scene. Now here she was, holed up in a toilet stall, reluctant to step back into the thick of it, where she always strove to be. Wishing she could hide out here, where it was blessedly silent, and where no one could glimpse the turmoil written on her face. She wondered how much Dr. Isles had already noticed; perhaps nothing. Isles had always seemed more interested in the dead than the living, and when confronting a homicide scene, it was the corpse who commanded her attention.

At last, Rizzoli straightened and stepped out of the stall. Her head felt clear now, her stomach settled. The ghost of the old Rizzoli, creeping back into its skin. At the sink, she scooped icy water into her mouth to rinse out the sour taste, then splashed more water on her face. Buck up, girl. Don't be a wimp. Let the guys see a hole in your armor, and they'll aim straight for it. They always do. She grabbed a paper towel, blotted her face dry, and was about to drop the paper into the trash can when she paused, remembering Sister Camille's bed. The blood on the sheets.

The trash can was about half full. Among the mound of crumpled paper towels was a small bundle of toilet paper. Quelling her distaste, she unwrapped the bundle. Although she already knew what it contained, she was still jolted by the sight of another woman's menstrual blood. She dealt with blood all the time, and had just seen a lake of it beneath Camille's corpse. Yet she was far more shaken by the mere glimpse of this sanitary pad. It was soaked, heavy. This was why you left your bed, she thought. The warmth seeping between your thighs, and the dampness of the sheets. You got up and came into the bathroom to change pads, depositing this soiled one in the trash can.

And then . . . what did you do then?

She left the bathroom and returned to Camille's chamber. Dr. Isles had left, and Rizzoli was alone in the room, frowning at the bloodstained sheets, the one bright blot in this colorless room. She crossed to the window and looked down, at the courtyard.

Multiple footprints now tracked across the frosting of sleet and snow. Beyond the gate, yet another TV news van had pulled up outside the wall, and was setting up its satellite feed. The dead nun story, beamed straight into your living room. Sure to be a lead at five, she thought; we're all curious about nuns. Swear off sex, retreat behind walls, and everyone wonders what it is you're hiding underneath that habit. It's the chastity that intrigues us; we wonder about any human being who girds herself against the most powerful of all urges, who turns her back on what nature intended us to fulfill. It's their purity that makes them titillating.

Rizzoli's gaze swung back across the courtyard, to the chapel. Where I should be right now, she thought, shivering with the CSU crew. Not lingering up here in this room that smelled of Clorox. But only from this room could she picture the view that Camille must have seen, returning from her nocturnal trip to the bathroom on a dark winter's morning. She would have seen light, shining through the chapel's stained-glass windows.

A light that should not have been there.

Maura stood by as the two attendants laid out a clean sheet and gently transferred Sister Camille. She had watched transport teams remove other bodies from other sites. Sometimes they performed the task with perfunctory efficiency, other times with evident distaste. But every so often, she saw them move a victim with special tenderness. Young children received this attention, their small heads cradled with care, their still forms caressed through the body pouch. Sister Camille was treated with just such tenderness, just such sorrow.

She held open the chapel door as they wheeled out the stretcher, and followed it as it made its slow progress toward the gate. Beyond the walls, the news media swarmed, cameras ready to capture the classic image of tragedy: the body on the stretcher, the plastic shroud containing a clearly human shape. Though the public could not see the victim, they would hear that she was a young woman, and they would look at that bag and mentally dissect its contents. Their ruthless imaginations would violate Camille's privacy in ways Maura's scalpel never could.

As the stretcher rolled out the abbey gate, a ring of reporters and cameramen surged forward, ignoring the patrolman yelling at them to stand back.

It was the priest who finally managed to hold the pack at bay. An imposing figure in black, he strode out of the gate and swept into the crowd, his angry voice carrying over the sounds of chaos.

'This poor sister deserves your respect! Why don't you show her some? Let her pass!'

Even reporters can sometimes be shamed, and a few of them stepped back to allow the transport team through. But the TV cameras kept rolling as the stretcher was loaded into the vehicle. Now those hungry cameras turned to their next prey: Maura, who had just slipped out of the gate and was headed toward her car, hugging her coat tight, as though it would shield her from notice.

'Dr. Isles! Do you have a statement?'

'What was the cause of death?'

'—any evidence this was a sexual assault?'

With reporters bearing down on her, she

fumbled in her purse for the keys and pressed the remote lock release. She'd just opened her car door when she heard her name shouted out. But this time, it was in alarm.

She looked back, and saw that a man was sprawled on the sidewalk, and several people were bending over him.

'We've got a cameraman down!' someone yelled. 'We need an ambulance!'

Maura slammed her car door shut and hurried back toward the fallen man. 'What happened?' she asked. 'Did he slip?'

'No, he was running – just kind of keeled over—'

She crouched down at his side. They had already rolled him onto his back, and she saw a heavyset man in his fifties, his face turning dusky. A TV camera, emblazoned with the letters WVSU, was lying in the snow beside him.

He wasn't breathing.

She tilted his head backwards, extending the beefy neck to open the airway, and leaned forward to start resuscitation. The smell of stale coffee and cigarettes almost made her gag. She thought of hepatitis and AIDS and all the other microscopic horrors one could catch from body fluids, and forced herself to seal her mouth over his. She blew in a breath and saw the chest rise, the lungs inflating with air. Blew in two more breaths, then felt for a carotid pulse.

Nothing.

She was about to unzip the man's jacket, but

someone else was already doing it for her. She looked up and saw the priest kneeling opposite her, large hands now probing the man's chest for landmarks. He placed his palms over the sternum, then looked at her, to confirm he should begin chest compressions. She saw startling blue eyes. An expression of grim purpose.

'Start pumping,' she said. 'Do it.'

He leaned into the task, counting aloud with each compression so she could time the breaths. 'One one-thousand. Two one-thousand . . .' No panic in his voice, just the steady count of a man who knows what he's doing. She didn't need to direct him; they worked together as though they had always been a team, twice switching positions to relieve each other.

By the time the ambulance arrived, the front of her slacks was soaked from kneeling in the snow, and she was sweating despite the cold. She rose stiffly to her feet and watched, exhausted, as the EMTs inserted IVs and an endotracheal tube, as the stretcher was loaded into the ambulance.

The TV camera the man had dropped was now being wielded by another WVSU employee. The show must go on, she thought, watching the reporters mill about the ambulance, even if the story is now about your own colleague's collapse.

She turned to the priest standing beside her, the knees of his pants soaked with melted snow. 'Thank you for the help,' she said. 'I take it you've done CPR before.'

He gave a smile, a shrug. 'Only on a plastic

61

dummy. I didn't think I'd ever have to actually use it.' He reached out to shake her hand. 'I'm Daniel Brophy. You're the medical examiner?'

'Maura Isles. This is your parish, Father Brophy?'

He nodded. 'My church is three blocks from here.'

'Yes, I've seen it.'

'Do you think we saved that man?'

She shook her head. 'When CPR goes on that long, without a pulse, it's not a very good prognosis.'

'But there's a chance he'll live?'

'Not a good one.'

'Even so, I'd like to think we made a difference.' He glanced at the TV reporters, still fixated on the ambulance. 'Let me walk you to your car, so you can get out of here without having a camera shoved in your face.'

'They'll go after you next. I hope you're ready for them.'

'I've already promised to make a statement. Though I don't really know what they want to hear from me.'

'They're cannibals, Father Brophy. They want nothing less than a pound of your flesh. Ten pounds, if they can get it.'

He laughed. 'Then I should warn them, it's going to be pretty stringy meat.'

He walked with her to her car. Her wet slacks were clinging to her legs, the fabric already stiffening in the chill wind. She would have to change into a scrub suit when she returned to the morgue, and hang the slacks to dry.

'If I'm to make a statement,' he said, 'is there anything I should know? Anything you can tell me?'

'You'll have to speak to Detective Rizzoli. She's the lead investigator.'

'Do you think this was an isolated attack? Should other parishes be concerned?'

'I only examine the victims, not the attackers. I can't tell you his motives.'

'These are elderly women. They can't fight back.'

'I know.'

'So what do we tell them? All the sisters living in religious communities? That they're not safe even behind walls?'

'None of us is entirely safe.'

'That's not the answer I want to give them.'

'But it's the one they have to hear.' She opened her car door. 'I was raised Catholic, Father. I used to think nuns were untouchable. But I've just seen what was done to Sister Camille. If that can happen to a nun, then no one is untouchable.' She slid into her car. 'Good luck with the press. You have my sympathies.'

He closed her car door and stood looking at her through the window. As striking as his face was, it was that clerical collar that drew her gaze. Such a narrow band of white, yet it set him apart from all others. It made him unattainable.

He raised his hand in a wave. Then he looked

toward the pack of reporters, who were even now closing in on him. She saw him straighten and take a deep breath. Then he strode forward to meet them.

'In light of the gross anatomical findings, as well as the subject's known history of hypertension, it is my opinion that this death was from natural causes. The most likely sequence of events was an acute myocardial infarction, occurring within the twenty-four hours prior to death, followed by a ventricular arrhythmia, which was the terminal event. Presumptive cause of death: fatal arrhythmia secondary to acute myocardial infarction. Dictated by Maura Isles, M.D., Office of the Medical Examiner, Commonwealth of Massachusetts.'

Maura turned off the Dictaphone and stared down at the preprinted diagrams on which she had earlier recorded the landmarks of Mr. Samuel Knight's body. The old appendectomy scar. The blotches of lividity on his buttocks and the underside of his thighs, where blood had pooled during the hours he had sat, lifeless, on his bed. There had been no witnesses to Mr. Knight's final moments in his hotel room, but she could imagine what went through his mind. A sudden fluttering in his chest. Perhaps a few seconds' panic, when he realizes that the fluttering is his heart. And then, a gradual fadeout to black. You were one of the easy ones, she thought. A swift dictation, and Mr. Knight could be set aside. Their brief acquaintance would end with the scrawl of her name on his autopsy report.

More reports sat in her in-box, a stack of transcribed dictations needing her review and signature. In cold storage, yet another new acquaintance waited for her: Camille Maginnes, whose autopsy was scheduled for nine o'clock the next morning, when both Rizzoli and Frost could attend. Even as Maura flipped through reports, jotting corrections in the margins, her mind was still on Camille. The chill she'd felt in the chapel that morning had not left her, and she kept her sweater on as she worked at her desk, bundled against the memory of that visit.

She rose from her chair to feel whether her wool slacks, which she'd left hanging over the radiator, were now dry. Close enough, she thought, and quickly untied her waist drawstring and slipped out of the scrub pants she'd worn all afternoon.

Sinking back into her chair, she just sat for a moment, eyeing one of the floral prints on her wall. To counteract the grimness of her job, she had decorated her office with reminders of life, not death. A potted ficus thrived in the corner of the room, the happy recipient of constant fussing and attention by both Maura and Louise. On the wall were framed images of flowers: a bouquet of white peonies and blue irises. Another with a vase of centifolia roses, the blossoms so lush with petals that the stems drooped. When the stack of files grew too tall on her desk, when the weight of death seemed overwhelming, she would look up at those prints and think of her garden, and of the smell of rich soil and the bright green of spring grass. She would think of things growing, not dying. Not decaying.

But on this December day, spring had never seemed so distant. Freezing rain was tapping against the window, and she dreaded the drive home. She wondered if the city had salted the roads yet, or if it would still be an ice rink out there, cars sliding like hockey pucks.

'Dr. Isles?' said Louise over the intercom.

'Yes?'

'There's a Dr. Banks on the phone for you. He's on line one.'

Maura went very still. 'Is it . . . Dr. Victor Banks?' she asked softly.

'Yes. He said he's with the charity One Earth International.'

Maura said nothing, her gaze fixed on the phone, her hands frozen on the desk. She was scarcely aware of the sleet hitting the window. She heard only the pounding of her own heart.

'Dr. Isles?'

'Is he calling long distance?'

'No. He left a message earlier. He's staying at the Colonnade Hotel.'

Maura swallowed. 'I can't take his call right now.'

'It's the second time he's called. He said he knows you.'

Yes. He certainly does.

'When did he call before?' Maura asked.

66

'This afternoon, while you were still at the scene. I did leave his message on your desk.'

Maura found three pink *while you were out* memos, which were hidden beneath a stack of folders. There it was. *Dr. Victor Banks. Called at 12:45 P.M.* She stared at the name, her stomach churning. Why now? She wondered. After all these months, why do you suddenly call me? What makes you think you can step back into my life?

'What should I tell him?' asked Louise.

Maura took a deep breath. 'Tell him I'll call back.' *When I'm goddamn ready.*

She crumpled the slip and threw it into the rubbish can. Moments later, unable to focus on her paperwork, she rose and pulled on her coat.

Louise looked surprised to see her emerge from her office, already bundled up for the weather. Maura was usually the last to leave, and almost never out the door before five-thirty. It was barely five now, and Louise was just shutting down her computer for the night.

'I'm going to get a head start on the traffic,' said Maura.

'I think it's too late for that. Have you seen the weather? They've already closed most city offices for the day.'

'When was that?'

'At four o'clock.'

'Why are you still here? You should have gone home.'

'My husband's coming to get me. My car's in the shop, remember?'

Maura winced. Yes, Louise had told her about the car that morning, but of course she'd forgotten. As usual, her mind had been so focused on the dead, she had not paid enough attention to the voices of the living. She watched Louise wrap a scarf around her neck and pull on her coat and thought: I don't spend enough time listening. I don't take the time to acquaint myself with people while they're alive. Even after a year of working in this office, she knew little about her secretary's personal life. She'd never met Louise's husband, and knew only that his name was Vernon. She could not recall where he worked, or what he did for a living, partly because Louise seldom shared personal information about her life. Is that my fault? Maura wondered. Does she sense that I'm not a willing listener, that I'm more comfortable with my scalpels and Dictaphone than I am with the feelings of people around me?

Together, they walked down the hall, toward the exit leading to the staff parking lot. No small talk, just two parallel travelers, headed toward the same destination.

Louise's husband was waiting in his car, its windshield wipers swinging furiously against the falling sleet. Maura gave a goodbye wave as Louise and her husband drove off, and got a puzzled look from Vernon, who probably wondered who that woman was, waving as though she knew them.

As though she really knew anyone.

She crossed the parking lot, slipping on the

glazed blacktop, her head bent under stinging pellets of sleet. She had one more stop to make. One more duty to execute before her day was over.

She drove to St. Francis Hospital to check on the status of Sister Ursula.

Although she had not worked in a hospital ward since her internship years ago, the memories of her final rotation in the intensive care unit remained vividly unpleasant. She remembered moments of panic, the struggle to think through the fog of sleep deprivation. She remembered a night when three patients had died on her shift, and everything had gone wrong at once. She could not walk into an ICU now without feeling haunted by the shadow of old responsibilities and old failures.

The surgical intensive care unit at St. Francis had a central nursing station surrounded by twelve patient cubicles. Maura stopped at the ward clerk's desk to show her identification.

'I'm Dr. Isles, from the Medical Examiner's office. May I see the chart for your patient, Sister Ursula Rowland?'

The ward clerk eyed her with a puzzled look. 'But the patient hasn't expired.'

'Detective Rizzoli asked me to check on her condition.'

'Oh. The chart's in that slot over there. Number ten.'

Maura crossed to the row of cubbyholes and pulled out the aluminum cover containing Bed #10's hospital chart. She opened it to the preliminary operative report. It was a handwritten summary, scrawled by the neurosurgeon immediately after surgery:

'Large subdural hematoma identified and drained. Open right parietal comminuted skull fracture debrided, elevated. Dural tear closed. Full operative report dictated. James Yuen, M.D.'

She turned to the nurses' notes, and skimmed the patient's progress since surgery. The intracranial pressures were holding steady, with the help of intravenous Mannitol and Lasix, as well as forced hyperventilation. It appeared that everything that could be done was being done; now it was a waiting game, to see how much neurological damage would result.

Carrying the chart, she crossed the unit to Cubicle #10. The policeman sitting outside the doorway gave her a nod of recognition. 'Hey, Dr. Isles.'

'How is the patient doing?' she asked.

'About the same, I guess. I don't think she's woken up yet.'

Maura looked at the closed curtains. 'Who's in there with her?'

'The doctors.'

She knocked on the doorframe, and stepped through the curtain. Two men were standing by the bed. One was a tall Asian man with a darkly piercing gaze and a thick mane of silver hair. The neurosurgeon, she thought, seeing his name tag: *Dr. Yuen*. The man who stood beside him was younger – in his thirties, with robust shoulders filling out his white coat. His long blond hair had been pulled back into a neat ponytail. Fabio as M.D., thought Maura, regarding the man's tanned face and deep-set gray eyes.

'I'm sorry to intrude,' she said. 'I'm Dr. Isles, from the Medical Examiner's office.'

'The M.E.'s office?' said Dr. Yuen, looking baffled. 'Isn't this visit a little premature?'

'The lead detective asked me to check in on your patient. There is another victim, you know.'

'Yes, we've heard.'

'I'll be doing that postmortem tomorrow. I wanted to compare the pattern of injuries between these two victims.'

'I don't think there's much you'll be able to see here. Not now, after surgery. You'll learn more by looking at her admission X-rays and head scans.'

She gazed down at the patient, and could not disagree with him. Ursula's head was encased in bandages, her injuries by now altered, repaired by the surgeon's hand. Deeply comatose, she was breathing with the aid of a ventilator. Unlike the slender Camille, Ursula was a woman of large proportions, big-boned and solid, with the plain, round face of a farmer's wife. IV lines coiled over meaty arms. On her left wrist was a Medic Alert bracelet, engraved with 'Allergic to Penicillin.' An ugly scar tracked, thick and white, over the right elbow – the aftermath of an old injury, badly sutured. A souvenir from her work abroad? Maura wondered.

'I've done what I could in the O.R.,' said Yuen.

'Now let's hope Dr. Sutcliffe here can head off any medical complications.'

She looked at the ponytailed physician, who gave her a nod, a smile. 'I'm Matthew Sutcliffe, her internist,' he said. 'She hasn't been in to see me for several months. I didn't even know she was admitted to the hospital until a little while ago.'

'Do you have her nephew's phone number?' Yuen asked him. 'When he called me, I forgot to get it from him. He said he'd be talking to you.'

Sutcliffe nodded. 'I have it. It'll be easier if I'm the one who stays in touch with the family. I'll let them know her status.'

'What is her status?' asked Maura.

'I'd say she's medically stable,' said Sutcliffe.

'And neurologically?' She looked at Yuen.

He shook his head. 'It's too early to say. Things went well in the O.R., but as I was just telling Dr. Sutcliffe here, even if she regains consciousness – and she very well may not – it's likely she won't remember any details of the attack. Retrograde amnesia is common in head injuries.' He glanced down as his beeper went off. 'Excuse me, but I need to get this call. Dr. Sutcliffe can fill you in on her medical history.' In just two quick strides, he was out the door.

Sutcliffe held out his stethoscope to Maura. 'You can examine her, if you'd like.'

She took the stethoscope and moved to the bedside. For a moment she just watched Ursula's chest rise and fall. Seldom did she examine the living; she had to pause to call back her clinical skills, acutely aware that Dr. Sutcliffe was a witness to just how out of practice she felt when examining a body whose heart was still beating. She had worked so long with the dead that she now felt clumsy with the living. Sutcliffe stood at the head of the bed, an imposing presence with his broad shoulders and intent gaze. He watched as she shone a penlight into the patient's eyes, as she palpated the neck, her fingers sliding across the warm skin. So different from the chill of refrigerated flesh.

She paused. 'There's no carotid pulse on the right side.'

'What?'

'There's a strong pulse on the left, but not the right.' She reached for the chart and opened it to the O.R. notes. 'Oh. The anesthesiologist mentions it here. "Absent right common carotid artery noted. Most likely a normal anatomical variation." '

He frowned, his tanned face flushing. 'I'd forgotten about that.'

'So it's an old finding? The lack of a pulse on this side?'

He nodded. 'Congenital.'

Maura slipped the stethoscope onto her ears and lifted the hospital gown, exposing Ursula's large breasts. The skin was still pale and youthful despite her sixty-eight years. Decades of protection beneath a nun's habit had spared her from the sun's aging rays. Pressing the diaphragm of the stethoscope to Ursula's chest, she heard a steady, vigorous heartbeat. A survivor's heart, pumping on, undefeated.

A nurse poked her head into the cubicle. 'Dr. Sutcliffe? X-ray called to say that the portable chest film's ready, if you want to go down and see it.'

'Thanks.' He looked at Maura. 'We can look at the skull films too, if you'd like.'

They shared the elevator with six young candy stripers, freshfaced and glossy-haired, giggling among themselves as they shot admiring glances at Dr. Sutcliffe. Attractive though he was, he seemed oblivious to their attention, his solemn gaze focused instead on the changing floor numbers. The glamour of a white coat, thought Maura, remembering her own teenage years working as a volunteer in St. Luke's Hospital in San Francisco. The doctors had seemed untouchable to her. Unassailable. Now that she herself was a doctor, she knew only too well that the white coat would not protect her from making mistakes. It would not make her infallible.

She looked at the candy stripers in their crisp uniforms, and thought of herself at sixteen – not giggly, like these girls, but quiet and serious. Even then, aware of life's dark notes. Instinctively drawn to melodies in a minor key.

The elevator doors opened, and the girls spilled out, a sunny flock of pink and white, leaving Maura and Sutcliffe alone in the elevator.

'They make me tired,' he said. 'All that energy. I wish I had a tenth of it, especially after a night on call.' He glanced at her. 'Do you have many of those?'

'Nights on call? We rotate.'

'I guess your patients don't expect you to rush in.'

'It's not like your life here in the trenches.'

He laughed, and suddenly he was transformed into a blond surfer boy with smiling eyes. 'Life in the trenches. That's what it feels like sometimes. The front lines.'

The X-rays were already waiting for them on the clerk's counter. Sutcliffe carried the large envelope into the viewing room. He slid a set of films under the clips and flipped on the switch.

The light flickered on through images of a skull. Fracture lines laced across bone like lightning strikes. She could see two separate points of impact. The first blow had landed on the right temporal bone, sending a single fine crack downward, toward the ear. The second, more powerful, had fallen posterior to the first blow, and this one had compressed the plateau of cranium, crushing it inward.

'He hit her first on the side of the head,' she said.

'How can you tell that was the first blow?'

'Because the first fracture line stops the propagation of an intersecting fracture from a second blow.' She pointed to the fracture lines. 'You see how this line stops right here, where it reaches the first fracture line? The force of impact can't jump across the gap. That tells me this blow to the right temple came first. Maybe she was turning away. Or she didn't see him, coming at her from the side.'

'He surprised her,' said Sutcliffe.

'And it would have been enough to send her reeling. Then the next blow landed, farther back on the head, here.' She pointed to the second fracture line.

'A heavier blow,' he said. 'It compressed the skull table.'

He took down the skull films and put up the CT scans. Computerized axial tomography allowed one to look into the human cranium, revealing the brain slice by slice. She saw a pocket of collected blood that had leaked from torn vessels. The mounting pressure would have squeezed the brain. It was an injury as potentially devastating as that done to Camille.

But human anatomy and human endurance are variable. While the much younger nun had succumbed to her injuries, Ursula's heart kept beating, her body unwilling to surrender its soul. Not a miracle, merely one of those quirks of fate, like the child who survives a fall from a sixth-floor window, and is only scratched.

'I'm amazed she survived at all,' he murmured.

'So am I.' She looked at Sutcliffe. The glow of the light box lit half his face, glancing across the strong angles of his cheek. 'These blows were meant to kill.'

Four

Camille Maginnes had young bones, thought Maura, gazing at the X-rays hanging on the morgue light box. The years had not yet chewed away at the novice's joints, nor collapsed her vertebrae or calcified the costal cartilage of her ribs. Now the years never would. Camille would be placed into the earth, her bones forever arrested in a state of youth.

Yoshima had X-rayed the body while it was fully dressed, a standard precaution to locate loose bullets or other metal fragments that might be lodged in clothing. Except for the crucifix, and what were clearly safety pins over the chest, no other pieces of metal were visible on the X-rays.

Maura pulled down the torso views, and the stiff X-rays made a musical *boing* as they bent in her hands. She reached for the skull films, and slid them under the light box clips.

'Jesus,' Detective Frost murmured.

The damage to the cranium was appalling. One of the blows had been heavy enough to drive bone fragments deep below the level of surrounding skull. Although Maura had not yet made a single incision, she could already envision the damage inside the cranium. The ruptured vessels, the taut pockets of hemorrhage. And the brain, herniating under the mounting pressure of blood.

'Talk to us, Doc,' said Rizzoli, crisp and to the point. She was looking healthier this morning, had walked into the morgue that morning with her usual brisk stride, the warrior woman back in action. 'What are you seeing?'

'Three separate blows,' said Maura. 'The first one hit here, on the crown.' She pointed to a single fracture line, running diagonally forward. 'The other two blows followed, at the back of the head. My guess is, she was facedown by that time. Lying helpless and prone. That's when the last blow crushed through the skull.'

It was a finale so brutal that she and the two detectives fell silent for a moment, imagining the fallen woman, her face pressed to the stone floor. The attacker's arm rising, hand gripping the death weapon. The sound of shattering bone breaking the silence of that chapel.

'Like clubbing a baby seal,' said Rizzoli. 'She didn't have a chance.'

Maura turned to the autopsy table, where Camille Maginnes lay, still clothed in her blood-soaked habit. 'Let's undress her.'

A gloved and gowned Yoshima stood waiting, the ghost of the autopsy room. With silent efficiency, he had assembled the tray of instruments, angled lights and readied specimen containers. Maura scarcely needed to speak; with only a look, he could read her mind.

First they removed the black leather shoes, ugly and practical. Then they paused, eyeing the victim's many layers of clothing, preparing for a task they had never before attempted: the disrobing of a nun.

'The guimpe should come off first,' said Maura.

'What's that?' asked Frost.

'The shoulder capelet. Only I don't see any fasteners on the front. And I didn't see any zippers on X-ray. Let's turn her onto her side, so I can check the back.'

The body, now stiff in rigor mortis, was light as a child's. They logrolled her sideways, and Maura peeled apart the edges of the capelet.

'Velcro,' she said.

Frost gave a startled laugh. 'You're kidding.'

'The medieval meets the modern age.' Maura slid off the capelet, folded it, and set it onto a plastic sheet.

'Somehow, that's really disappointing. Nuns using Velcro.'

'You want to keep 'em in the Middle Ages?' said Rizzoli.

'I just kind of figured they'd be more traditional or something.'

'I hate to disillusion you, Detective Frost,' said Maura, as she removed the chain and crucifix. 'But some convents even have their own Web sites these days.'

'Oh, man. Nuns on the Internet. That blows my mind.'

'The scapular looks like it comes off next,' said Maura, indicating the sleeveless overgarment that draped from shoulders to hem. Gently she lifted the scapular over the victim's head. The fabric was soaked with blood, and stiff. She laid this on a separate plastic sheet, followed by the leather belt.

They were down to the final layer of wool – a black tunic, draped loosely over Camille's slim form. Her last barrier of modesty.

In all her years of undressing corpses, Maura had never felt such reluctance to strip a victim nude. This was a woman who had chosen to live hidden from the eyes of men; now she would be cruelly revealed, her body probed, her orifices swabbed. The prospect of such an invasion brought a bitter taste to Maura's throat and she paused to regain her composure. She saw Yoshima's questioning glance. If he was disturbed, he did not show it. His impassive face was a calming influence in that room, where the very air seemed charged with emotion.

She refocused on the task. Together, she and Yoshima lifted the tunic, sliding it up over the thighs and hips. It was loosely fitted, and they were able to remove it without breaking rigor mortis of the arms. Beneath it were yet more garments – a white cotton hood that had slid down around her neck, the front flaps safety-pinned to a bloodstained T-shirt. The same pins that had appeared on the X-ray. Heavy black tights covered her legs. They removed the tights first, revealing white cotton panties beneath. They were absurdly modest briefs, designed to cover as much skin as possible, the underwear of an old lady, not a nubile young woman. A sanitary pad bulged beneath the cotton. As Maura had suspected earlier, from the bloodstained bed sheets, the victim was menstruating.

Next Maura tackled the T-shirt. She unfastened a safety pin, peeled apart more Velcro flaps, and slid off the hood. The T-shirt, however, would not come off so easily due to rigor mortis. She reached for scissors and cut straight up the center of the shirt. The fabric parted, revealing yet another layer.

This one took her aback. She stared at the band of cloth wrapped tightly around the chest, fastened at the front with two safety pins.

'What's that for?' asked Frost.

'It looks like she bound her breasts,' said Maura.

'Why?'

'I have no idea.'

'Substitute for a bra?' Rizzoli suggested.

'I can't imagine why she'd choose to wear this instead of a bra. Look how tightly it's wrapped. It had to be uncomfortable.'

Rizzoli snorted. 'Yeah, like a bra's comfortable?'

'It's not some kind of religious thing, is it?' said Frost. 'Part of their habit?'

'No, this is just standard Ace wrap. The same

wrapping you'd buy at a drugstore to bind a sprained ankle.'

'But how do we know what nuns usually wear? I mean, for all we know, under all those robes, they could be dressed in black lace and fishnet.'

No one laughed.

Maura gazed down at Camille, and was suddenly struck by the symbolism of bound breasts. Womanly features disguised, suppressed. Squeezed into submission. What had gone through Camille's mind as she'd wound the cloth around her chest, pulling the elastic taut against her skin? Had she felt disgust about these reminders of womanhood? Had she felt cleaner, purer, as her breasts vanished beneath the strips of bandage; her curves flattened, her sexuality denied?

Maura undid the two safety pins and set them on the tray. Then, with Yoshima's assistance, she began to unwrap the binding, baring successive bands of skin. But even smothering elastic could not make healthy flesh shrivel away. The last strip came off, revealing ripe young breasts, the skin stippled with the imprint of the fabric. Other women would have been proud of those breasts; Camille Maginnes had concealed them, as though ashamed.

There was one last item of clothing to remove. The cotton briefs.

Maura slid the elastic waistband down over the hips and peeled it past the thighs. The sanitary napkin, affixed to the underwear, was stained with only a scant amount of blood.

'Fresh pad,' noted Rizzoli. 'Looks like she'd just changed it.'

But Maura was not looking at the pad; her gaze was focused on the toneless abdomen, sagging and loose between jutting hipbones. Silvery streaks marred the pale skin. For a moment she said nothing, silently absorbing the significance of those streaks. She was thinking, too, of the tightly wrapped breasts.

Maura turned to the tray, where she had left the bundle of Ace wrap, and slowly unrolled it, inspecting the fabric.

'What're you looking for?' asked Rizzoli.

'Stains,' said Maura.

'You can already see the blood.'

'Not bloodstains . . .' Maura paused, the Ace wrap spread across the tray to reveal dark rings where fluid had dried. My god, she thought. How can this be possible?

She looked at Yoshima. 'Let's set her up for a pelvic.'

He frowned at her. 'Break rigor mortis?'

'She doesn't have a lot of muscle mass.' Camille was a slender woman; it would make their task easier.

Yoshima moved to the foot of the table. While Maura held down the pelvis, he slid his hands under the left thigh and strained to flex the hip. Breaking rigor mortis was as brutal as it sounded – the forcible rupture of rigid muscle fibers. Never a pleasant procedure, it clearly horrified Frost, who stepped back from the table, his face paling.

Yoshima gave a firm shove, and Maura felt, transmitted through the pelvis, the snap of tearing muscle.

'Oh man,' said Frost, turning away.

But it was Rizzoli who moved unsteadily toward the chair near the sink, and sank into it, dropping her head in her hands. Rizzoli the stoic, who never complained of the sights or the smells of the autopsy suite, now seemed unable to stomach even these preliminaries.

Maura circled to the other side of the table, and again held down the pelvis while Yoshima worked on the right thigh. Even she had a twinge of nausea as they strained to break the rigidity. Of all the ordeals she'd known during her medical training, it was her rotation in orthopedic surgery that had most appalled her. The drilling and sawing into bone, the brute force needed to disarticulate hips. She felt that same abhorrence now as she felt the snap of muscle. The right hip suddenly flexed, and even Yoshima's normally bland expression betrayed a flash of distaste. But there was no other way to fully visualize the genitals, and she felt some urgency about confirming her suspicions as quickly as possible.

They rotated both thighs outward, and Yoshima aimed a light directly on the perineum. Blood had pooled in the vaginal canal – normal menstrual blood, Maura would have assumed earlier. Now she stared, stunned by what she was seeing. She reached for gauze and gently wiped away the blood to reveal the mucosa beneath it.

'There's a second degree vaginal tear at six o'clock,' she said.

'You want to take swabs?'

'Yes. And we'll need to do a bloc removal.'

'What's going on?' asked Frost.

Maura looked at him. 'I don't do this very often, but I'm going to remove the pelvic organs in one mass. Cut through the pubic bone and lift it all out.'

'You think she was sexually assaulted?'

Maura didn't answer him. She circled to the instrument tray and picked up a scalpel. Moved to the torso to begin her Y incision.

The intercom buzzed. 'Dr. Isles?' Louise said over the speakerphone.

'Yes?'

'There's a call for you on line one. It's Dr. Victor Banks again, from that organization, One Earth.'

Maura froze, hand gripping the scalpel. The tip just touching the skin.

'Dr. Isles?' said Louise.

'I'm unavailable.'

'Shall I tell him you'll return his call?'

'No.'

'It's the third time he's called today. He asked if he could reach you at home.'

'Do *not* give him my home phone number.' Her answer came out more harshly than she'd intended, and she saw Yoshima turn to look at her. She felt Frost and Rizzoli watching her as well. She took a breath and said, more calmly: 'Tell Dr.

Banks I'm not available. And keep telling him that until he stops calling.'

There was a pause. 'Yes, Dr. Isles,' Louise finally responded, sounding more than a little stung by the exchange. It was the first time Maura had ever spoken sharply to her, and she'd have to find some way to smooth over the rift and repair the damage. The exchange left her flustered. She looked down at the torso of Camille Maginnes, trying to refocus her attention on the task at hand. But her thoughts were scattered, and her grip was unsteady around the scalpel.

The others could see it.

'Why's One Earth bugging you?' asked Rizzoli. 'They hitting you up for donations?'

'This has nothing to do with One Earth.'

'So what is it?' pressed Rizzoli. 'Is this guy harassing you?'

'He's just someone I'm trying to avoid.'

'Sounds like he's pretty persistent.'

'You have no idea.'

'You want me to get him off your back? Tell him where to go?' This was more than just Rizzoli the cop talking; it was also Rizzoli the woman, and she had no tolerance for overbearing men.

'It's a personal matter,' said Maura.

'You need help, all you have to do is ask.'

'Thank you, but I'll handle him.' Maura pressed the scalpel to skin, wanting nothing more than to drop the subject of Victor Banks. She took a breath, and found it ironic that the scent of dead flesh was less disturbing to her than the mere utterance of his name. That the living tormented her far more than the dead ever could. In the morgue, no one hurt her, or betrayed her. In the morgue, she was the one in control.

'So who is this guy?' asked Rizzoli. The question that was still on all their minds. The question Maura would have to answer, sooner or later.

She sank the blade into flesh and watched skin part like a white curtain. 'My ex-husband,' she said.

She cut her Y-incision, then reflected back flaps of pale skin. Yoshima used common pruning shears to cut through the ribs, then lifted the triangle of ribs and breastbone to reveal a normal heart and lungs, disease-free liver and spleen and pancreas. The clean, healthy organs of a young woman who has abused neither tobacco nor alcohol, and who has not lived long enough for her arteries to narrow and clog. Maura made few comments as she removed organs and placed them in a metal basin, moving swiftly toward her next goal: the examination of the pelvic organs.

A pelvic bloc excision was a procedure she usually reserved for fatal rape cases, as it allowed a far more detailed dissection of those organs than the usual autopsy did. It was not a pleasant procedure, this coring out of pelvic contents. As she and Yoshima sawed through the bony pubic rami, she was not surprised to see Frost turn away. But Rizzoli, too, shrank from the table. No one spoke now of the calls from Maura's ex-husband; no one pressed her for personal details. The autopsy had suddenly turned too grim for conversation, and Maura was perversely relieved by this.

She lifted the entire bloc of pelvic organs, external genitalia, and pubic bone, and moved it to a cutting board. Even before she sliced into the uterus, she knew, just by its appearance, that her fears were already confirmed. The organ was larger than it should be, the fundus well above the level of the pubic bone, the walls spongey. She slit it open, to reveal the endometrium, the lining still thick and lush with blood.

She looked up at Rizzoli. Asked, sharply: 'Did this woman leave the abbey at any time during the last week?'

'The last time Camille left the abbey was back in March, to visit her family on Cape Cod. That's what Mary Clement told me.'

'Then you have to search the compound. Immediately.'

'Why? What are we looking for?'

'A newborn.'

This seemed to hit Rizzoli with stunning force. She stared, white-faced, at Maura. Then she looked at the body of Camille Maginnes, lying on the table. 'But . . . she was a nun.'

'Yes,' said Maura. 'And she's recently given birth.'

Five

It was snowing again when Maura stepped out of the building that afternoon, soft, lacy flakes that fluttered like white moths, to light gently on the parked cars. Today she was prepared for the weather, and had worn ankle boots with rugged soles. Even so, she was cautious as she walked across the parking lot, her boots slipping on the snow-dusted ice, her body braced for a fall. When she finally reached her car, she released a sigh of relief, and dug in her purse for her keys. Distracted by the search, she paid scant attention to the thud of a nearby car door slamming shut. Only when she heard the footsteps did she turn to face the man who was now approaching her. He came to within a few paces and stopped, not saying anything. Just stood looking at her, his hands tucked in the pockets of his leather jacket. Falling snowflakes settled on his blond hair, and clung to his neatly trimmed beard.

He looked at her Lexus and said, 'I figured the black one would be yours. You're always in black.

Always walking on the dark side. And who else keeps a car that neat?'

She finally found her voice. It came out hoarse. A stranger's. 'What are you doing here, Victor?'

'It seemed like the only way I could finally see you.'

'Ambushing me in the parking lot?'

'Is that what it feels like?'

'You've been sitting out here, waiting for me. I'd call that an ambush.'

'You didn't leave me much choice. You weren't returning any of my calls.'

'I haven't had the chance.'

'You never sent me your new phone number.'

'You never asked.'

He glanced up at the snow, fluttering down like confetti, and sighed. 'Well. This is like old times, isn't it?'

'Too much like old times.' She turned to her car and pressed the key remote. The lock snapped open.

'Don't you want to know why I'm here?'

'I need to get going.'

'I fly all the way to Boston, and you don't even ask why.'

'All right.' She looked at him. 'Why?'

'Three years, Maura.' He stepped closer, and she caught his scent. Leather and soap. Snow melting on warm skin. Three years, she thought, and he's hardly changed. The same boyish tilt of his head, the same laugh lines around his eyes. And even in December, his hair looked sun-bleached, not artificial highlights from a bottle, but honest blond streaks from hours spent outdoors. Victor Banks seemed to radiate his own gravitational force, and she was just as susceptible to it as everyone else. She felt the old pull drawing her toward him.

'Haven't you wondered, just once, if it was a mistake?' he asked.

'The divorce? Or the marriage?'

'Isn't it obvious which one I'm talking about? Since I'm standing here talking to you.'

'You waited a long time to tell me.' She turned back to her car.

'You haven't remarried.'

She paused. Looked back at him. 'Have you?'

'No.'

'Then I guess we're both equally hard to live with.'

'You didn't stay around long enough to find out.'

She laughed. A bitter, distasteful sound in that white silence. 'You were the one who was always heading for the airport. Always running off to save the world.'

'I'm not the one who ran from the marriage.'

'I'm not the one who had the affair.' She turned and yanked open the car door.

'Goddamn it, can you just wait? *Listen* to me.'

His hand closed around her arm, and she was startled by the anger she felt transmitted in that grasp. She stared at him, a cold look that told him he had gone too far.

He released her arm. 'I'm sorry. Jesus, this isn't the way I wanted it to go.'

'What were you expecting?'

'That there'd be something left between us.'

And there was, she thought. There was too much, and that's why she couldn't let this conversation go on any longer. She was afraid that she'd be sucked in again. She could already feel it happening.

'Look,' he said. 'I'm only in town for a few days. I have a meeting tomorrow at the Harvard School of Public Health, but after that, I have no plans. It's almost Christmas, Maura. I thought we could spend the holidays together. If you're free.'

'And then you'll just go flying off again.'

'At least we could catch up on things. Couldn't you take a few days off?'

'I have a job, Victor. I can't just leave it.'

He glanced at the building, and gave a disbelieving laugh. 'I don't know why you'd even want a job like that.'

'The dark side, remember? That's me.'

He looked at her, and his voice softened. 'You haven't changed. Not a bit.'

'Neither have you, and that's the problem.' She slid into her car and pulled the door shut.

He rapped on the window. She looked at him, gazing in at her, snowflakes glistening on his lashes, and she had no choice but to roll down the glass and continue the conversation.

'When can we talk again?' he asked.

'I have to go now.'

'Later, then. Tonight.'

'I don't know when I'll get home.'

'Come on, Maura.' He leaned close. Said softly, 'Take a chance. I'm staying at the Colonnade. Call me.'

She sighed. 'I'll think about it.'

He reached in and squeezed her arm. Again, the scent of him stirred warm recollections, of nights they had slept beneath crisp sheets, legs twined around each other. Of long, slow kisses, and the taste of fresh lemons and vodka. Two years of marriage leave indelible memories, both good and bad, and at that moment, with his hand on her arm, it was the good memories that dominated.

'I'll wait for your call,' he said. Already presuming he had won.

Does he think it's so easy? she wondered as she drove out of the parking lot and headed toward Jamaica Plain. One smile, one touch, and all is forgiven?

Her tires suddenly skittered across the ice-crusted road, and she gripped the wheel, her attention instantly focused on regaining control of the car. She had been so agitated, she hadn't realized how fast she was going. The Lexus fishtailed, tires spinning, searching for purchase. Only when she had steered it back into a straight line did she allow herself to breathe again. To be angry again.

First you break my heart. Then you almost get me killed.

An irrational thought, but there it was. Victor inspired irrational thoughts.

By the time she pulled up across the street from Graystones Abbey, she felt wrung out by the drive. She sat for a moment in the car, wrestling her emotions under control. *Control* was the word she lived by. Once she stepped out of the car, she was a public person, visible to law enforcement and to the press. They expected her to appear calm and logical, and so she would. Much of the job was simply looking the part.

She stepped out, and this time she crossed the road with confidence, her boots gripping the road. Police cars lined the street, and two TV news crews sat in their vans, waiting for some breaking development. Already, the wintry light was fading into evening.

She rang the gate bell, and a nun appeared, black habit emerging from the shadows. The nun recognized Maura and admitted her without a word of conversation passing between them.

Inside the courtyard, dozens of footprints had churned the snow. It was a different place than on the morning Maura first walked in. Today, all semblance of tranquility was disrupted by the search now under way. Lights shone in all the windows, and she could hear men's voices echoing from archways. Stepping into the entrance hall, she smelled the scent of tomato sauce and cheese, unpleasant odors that conjured up memories of the bland and leathery lasagna that had been served so often in the cafeteria of the hospital where she'd trained as a medical student.

She glanced into the dining room and saw the

sisters seated at the rectory table, silently eating their evening meal. She saw tremulous hands lift unsteady forks to toothless mouths, and saw milk dribble down wrinkled chins. For most of their lives, these women had lived behind walls, growing old in seclusion. Did any of them harbor regrets about what they had missed, what lives they might otherwise have lived, had they simply walked out the gate and never returned?

Continuing down the hall, she heard men's voices, foreign and startling in that house of women. Two cops waved at her in recognition.

'Hey, Doc.'

'Have you found anything?' she asked.

'Not yet. We're calling it quits for the night.'

'Where's Rizzoli?'

'Upstairs. The dormitory.'

Climbing the stairway, Maura saw two more members of the search party on their way down – police cadets, who looked scarcely old enough to be out of high school. A young man, his face still spotty with acne, and a woman, wearing that aloof mask that so many female cops seemed to adopt as a matter of self-preservation. They both dropped their gazes in respect when they recognized Maura. It made her feel old, watching these youngsters deferentially step aside to let her pass. Was she so intimidating that they didn't see the woman beneath, with her bundle of insecurities? She had perfected the act of invincibility, and she played the part even now. She dipped her head in polite greeting, her gaze moving swiftly past them.

Aware, even as she climbed the stairs, that they were watching her.

She found Rizzoli in Sister Camille's room, sitting on the bed with her shoulders slumped in exhaustion.

'Looks like everyone's going home but you,' said Maura.

Rizzoli turned to look at her. Her eyes were dark and deeply hollowed, and there were lines of fatigue in her face that Maura had never seen before.

'We haven't found a thing. We've been searching since noon. But it takes time, combing through every closet, every drawer. Then there's the field and the gardens out back – who knows what's underneath the snow? She could have wrapped it up and just thrown it in the trash a few days ago. Could have handed it to someone outside the gate. We could spend days looking for something that may or may not be here.'

'What does the Abbess say about it?'

'I haven't told her what we're looking for.'

'Why not?'

'I don't want her to know.'

'She might be able to help.'

'Or she might take steps to make sure we *don't* find it. You think this archdiocese needs any more scandals? You think she wants the world to know that someone in this order killed her own baby?'

'We don't know that the child's dead. We just know it's missing.'

'And you're absolutely sure of your autopsy findings?'

'Yes. Camille was in the advanced stages of pregnancy. And no, I don't believe in immaculate conception.' She sat down on the bed beside Rizzoli. 'The father may be key to the attack. We have to identify him.'

'Yeah, I was just thinking about that word. Father. As in priest.'

'Father Brophy?'

'Good-looking man. Have you seen him?'

Maura remembered the brilliant blue eyes that had gazed at her across the fallen cameraman. Remembered how he had strode through the abbey gate like a black-robed warrior, to challenge that wolf pack of reporters.

'He had repeated access,' said Rizzoli. 'He said Mass. He heard confession. Is there anything more intimate than sharing your secrets in a confession booth?'

'You're implying the sex was consensual.'

'I'm just saying, he's a good-looking guy.'

'We don't know that the baby was conceived in this abbey. Didn't Camille visit her family, back in March?'

'Yeah. When her grandmother died.'

'It's the right time frame. If she conceived in March, she'd be in her ninth month of pregnancy now. It could have happened during that visit home.'

'And it could have happened right here. Inside these walls.' Rizzoli gave a cynical snort. 'So much for that vow of chastity.'

They sat without talking for a moment, both of them gazing at the crucifix on the wall. How flawed we humans are, thought Maura. If there is a god, why does he hold us to such unattainable standards? Why does he demand goals we can never reach?

Maura said, 'I wanted to be a nun, once.'

'I thought you didn't believe.'

'I was only nine years old. I'd just found out I was adopted. My cousin let the cat out of the bag, one of those nasty revelations that suddenly explained everything. Why I didn't look like my parents. Why I didn't have any baby pictures. I spent the whole weekend crying in my room.' She shook her head. 'My poor parents. They didn't know what to do, so they took me to the movies to cheer me up. We saw the *Sound of Music*, only seventy-five cents, because it was an old movie.' She paused. 'I thought Julie Andrews was beautiful. I wanted to be just like Maria. In the convent.'

'Hey, Doc. You want to hear a secret?'

'What?'

'So did I.'

Maura looked at her. 'You're kidding.'

'I may have been a catechism dropout. But who can resist the pull of Julie Andrews?'

At that, they both laughed, but it was uneasy laughter that quickly stuttered into silence.

'So what made you change your mind?' Rizzoli asked. 'About being a nun?'

Maura rose to her feet and wandered over to the window. Looking down at the dark courtyard, she said: 'I just grew out of it. I stopped believing in things I couldn't see or smell or touch. Things that couldn't be scientifically proved.' She paused. 'And I discovered boys.'

'Oh, yeah. Boys.' Rizzoli laughed. 'There's always that.'

'It's the real purpose of life, you know. From a biological point of view.'

'Sex?'

'Procreation. It's what our genes demand. That we go forth and multiply. We think we're the ones in control of our lives, and all the time, we're just slaves of our DNA, telling us to have babies.'

Maura turned and was startled to see tears shimmering on Rizzoli's lashes; just as quickly they were gone, dashed away by a quick swipe of her hand.

'Jane?'

'I'm just tired. I haven't been sleeping very well.'

'There's nothing else going on?'

'What else would there be?' The answer was too quick, too defensive. Even Rizzoli realized it, and she flushed. 'I need to use the bathroom,' she said and stood up, as though eager to escape. At the door she stopped and looked back. 'By the way, you know that book on the desk over there? The one Camille was reading. I looked up the name.'

'Who?'

'Saint Brigid of Ireland. It's a biography. Funny, how there's a patron saint for everything, every occasion. There's a saint for hat makers. A saint for drug addicts. Hell, there's even a saint for lost keys.'

'So whose saint is Brigid?'

'Newborns,' Rizzoli said softly. 'Brigid is the saint of newborns.' She walked out of the room.

Maura looked down at the desk, where the book was lying. Only a day ago, she had imagined Camille sitting at this desk, quietly turning pages, drawing inspiration from the life of a young Irish woman destined for sainthood. Now a different picture emerged – not Camille the serene, but Camille the tormented, praying to St. Brigid for her dead child's salvation. *I beg you, take him into your forgiving arms. Bring him into the light, though he be unbaptized. He is an innocent. He is without sin.*

She looked around the stark room with new comprehension. The spotless floors, the smell of bleach and wax – it all took on new meaning. Cleanliness as a metaphor for innocence. Camille the fallen had desperately scrubbed away her sins, her guilt. For months she must have realized she was carrying a child, hidden beneath the voluminous folds of her habit. Or did she refuse to accept reality? Did she deny it to herself, the way pregnant teenagers sometimes deny the evidence of their own swollen bellies?

And what did you do, when your child came into the world? Did you panic? Or did you coldly and calmly dispose of the evidence of your sin?

She heard men's voices outside. Through the window, she saw the shadowy forms of two cops

100

emerging from the building. They both paused to pull their coats tighter, to glance up at the snow, tumbling like glitter from the night sky. Then they walked out of the courtyard, and the hinges squealed as the gate shut behind them. She listened for other sounds, other voices, but heard nothing. Only the stillness of a snowy night. So quiet, she thought. As though I am the only one left in this building. Forgotten, and alone.

She heard a creak, and felt the whisper of movement, of another presence in the room. The hairs on the back of her neck suddenly stood up and she gave a laugh. 'God, Jane, don't sneak up on me like . . .' Turning, her voice died in mid-sentence.

No one was there.

For a moment she didn't move, didn't breathe, just stared at empty space. Vacant air, polished floor. *The room is haunted* was her first irrational thought, before logic reasserted control. Old floors often creaked, and heating pipes groaned. It was not a footstep but the floorboards, contracting in the cold. There were perfectly reasonable explanations for why she had thought someone else was in the room.

But she still felt its presence, still sensed it watching her.

Now the hairs on her arms were standing up as well, every nerve singing with alarm. Something skittered overhead, like claws against wood. Her gaze shot to the ceiling. *An animal? It's moving away from me.*

She stepped out of the room, and the panicked drumming of her own heartbeat almost drowned out any sounds from overhead. There it was – moving farther down the hallway!

Thump-thump-thump.

She followed the noise, her gaze on the ceiling, moving so fast she almost collided with Rizzoli, who'd just emerged from the bathroom.

'Hey,' said Rizzoli. 'What's the rush?'

'Shhh!' Maura pointed to the dark-beamed ceiling.

'What?'

'Listen.'

They waited, straining to hear any new sound. Except for the pounding of her own heart, Maura heard only silence.

'Maybe you just heard water running in the pipes,' said Rizzoli. 'I did flush the toilet.'

'It wasn't the pipes.'

'Well, what did you hear?'

Maura's gaze snapped back to the antique beams running the length of the ceiling. '*There.*'

The scrabbling sound again, at the far end of the hall.

Rizzoli stared upward. 'What the hell is that? Rats?'

'No,' whispered Maura. 'Whatever it is, it's bigger than a rat.' She moved quietly down the corridor, Rizzoli right behind her, approaching the spot where they had heard it last.

Without warning, a chorus of thumps drummed

across the ceiling, moving back the way they had come.

'It's headed into the other wing!' said Rizzoli.

With Rizzoli in the lead, they pushed through a door at the end of the hallway, and Rizzoli flipped on the light switch. They gazed down a deserted corridor. It was chilly in here, the air closed-in and damp. Through open doorways, they saw abandoned rooms and the ghostly shapes of sheet-draped furniture.

Whatever had fled into this wing was now silent, revealing no hint of its whereabouts.

'Your team searched this end of the building?' Maura asked.

'We made a sweep of all these rooms.'

'What's upstairs? Above this ceiling?'

'It's just attic space.'

'Well, something's moving up there,' Maura said softly. 'And it's intelligent enough to know we were chasing it.'

Maura and Rizzoli crouched in the chapel's upper gallery, studying the mahogany panel that Mary Clement had told them would lead to the building's crawl space. Rizzoli gave the panel a gentle push; noiselessly it swung open, and they stared into the darkness beyond, listening for sounds of movement. A whisper of warmth touched their faces. The crawl space was a trap for the building's rising heat, and they could feel it spilling out through the panel opening.

Rizzoli shone her flashlight into the space. They

103

glimpsed massive timbers and the pink matting of newly installed insulation. Electrical wires snaked across the floor.

Rizzoli was first to step through the opening. Maura turned on her own flashlight and followed. The space was not tall enough for her to stand up straight; she had to keep her head bent to avoid the oak beams arching across the ceiling. Their lights swept in wide arcs, carving a circle in the darkness. Beyond that circle was unseen frontier; Maura could feel her breaths coming too fast. The low ceiling, the stale air, made her feel entombed.

She almost jumped when she felt a hand touch her arm. Wordlessly, Rizzoli pointed to the right.

Timbers creaked under their weight as they moved through shadows, Rizzoli in the lead.

'Wait,' whispered Maura. 'Shouldn't you call for backup?'

'Why?'

'For whatever's up here.'

'I'm not calling for backup, if all we're hunting down is just some stupid raccoon . . .' She paused, her flashlight arcing left, then right. 'I think we're over the west wing now. It's getting nice and warm up here. Turn off your flashlight.'

'What?'

'Turn it off. I want to check out something.'

Reluctantly, Maura switched off her light. So did Rizzoli.

In the sudden blackness, Maura felt her pulse throbbing. *We can't see what's around us. What might be moving toward us.* She blinked, trying to force her eyes to accommodate to the darkness. Then she noticed the light – slivers of it, shining through cracks in the floor. Here and there, a wider shaft, where the boards had pulled apart, or where knotholes had contracted in the dry winter air.

Rizzoli's footsteps creaked away. Her shadowy form suddenly dropped to a crouch, her head bent toward the floor. For a moment she held that pose, then she gave a soft laugh. 'Hey. It's just like peeking into the boys' locker room at Revere High.'

'What are you looking at?'

'Camille's room. We're right above it. There's a knothole here.'

Maura eased her way through the darkness, to where Rizzoli was crouched. Dropping to her knees, Maura peered through the opening.

She was staring down directly at Camille's desk.

She straightened, a chill suddenly running its cold fingers up her spine. *Whatever was up here could see me, in that room. It was watching me.*

Thump-thump-thump.

Rizzoli spun around so fast, her elbow slammed into Maura.

Maura fumbled to turn on her flashlight, her beam jerking in all directions as she hunted for whoever – whatever – was in this crawlspace with them. She caught glimpses of feathery cobwebs, of massive crossbeams, hanging low overhead. It was so warm up here, the air close and stifling, and the sense of suffocation fed her panic.

105

She and Rizzoli had instinctively moved into defensive positions, back to back, and Maura could feel Rizzoli's tense muscles, could hear her rapid breathing as they both scanned the darkness. Searching for the gleam of eyes, a feral face.

So swiftly did Maura scan her surroundings, she missed it in the first sweep of her flashlight. It was only as she brought it back that the farthest reach of her beam rippled across an irregularity on the rough-planked floor. She stared, but did not believe what she was looking at.

She took a step toward it, her horror mounting as she moved closer, as her beam began to pick up other, similar forms lying nearby. So many of them . . .

Dear god, it's a graveyard. A graveyard of dead infants.

The flashlight beam wavered. She, whose scalpel hand had always been rock-steady at the autopsy table, could not stop shaking. She came to a stop, her beam shining directly down on a face. Blue eyes glittered back at her, shiny as marbles. She stared, slowly grasping the reality of what she was seeing.

And she laughed. A startled bark of a laugh.

By now, Rizzoli was right beside her, flashlight playing over the pink skin, the kewpie mouth, the lifeless gaze. 'What the hell,' she said. 'It's just a friggin' doll.'

Maura waved her beam at the other objects lying nearby. She saw smooth plastic skin, plump limbs. The sparkle of glass eyes stared back at her.

'They're all dolls,' she said. 'A whole collection of them.'

'See how they're lined up, in a row? Like some kind of weird nursery.'

'Or a ritual,' said Maura softly. An unholy ritual in God's sanctuary.

'Oh, man. Now you've got *me* spooked.'

Thump-thump-thump.

They both whirled, flashlights slicing the darkness, finding nothing. The sound had been fainter. Whatever had been inside the crawlspace with them was now moving away, retreating far beyond the reach of their lights. Maura was startled to see that Rizzoli had drawn her weapon; it had happened so quickly, she had not even noticed it.

'I don't think that's an animal,' Maura said.

After a pause, Rizzoli said: 'I don't think so either.'

'Let's get out of here. Please.'

'Yeah.' Rizzoli took in a deep breath, and Maura heard the first tremolo of fear. 'Yeah, okay. Controlled exit. We take it one step at a time.'

They stayed close together as they moved back the way they'd come. The air grew cooler, damper; or maybe it was fear that chilled Maura's skin. By the time they neared the panel doorway, she was ready to bolt straight out of the crawl space.

They stepped through the panel opening, into the chapel gallery, and with the first deep breaths of cold air, her fear began to dissipate. Here in the light, she felt back in control. Able, once again, to think logically. What had she seen, really, in that dark place? A row of dolls, nothing more. Plastic skin and glass eyes and nylon hair.

'It wasn't an animal,' Rizzoli said. She was crouched down, staring at the gallery floor.

'What?'

'There's a footprint here.' Rizzoli pointed to smudges of powdery dust. The tread mark of an athletic shoe.

Maura glanced down behind her own shoes, and saw that she too had tracked dust onto the gallery. Whoever left that footprint had fled the crawl space just ahead of them.

'Well, there's our creature,' said Rizzoli, and she shook her head. 'Jesus. I'm glad I never took a shot at it. I'd hate to think . . .'

Maura stared at the footprint and shuddered. It was a child's.

Six

Grace Otis sat at the convent dining table, shaking her head. 'She's only seven years old. You can't trust anything she says. She lies to me all the time.'

'We'd like to talk to her anyway,' said Rizzoli. 'With your permission, of course.'

'Talk to her about what?'

'What she was doing up in the crawl space.'

'Did she damage something, is that it?' Grace glanced nervously at Mother Mary Clement, who had been the one to summon Grace from the kitchen. 'She'll be punished, Reverend Mother. I've tried to keep track of her, but she's always so quiet about her mischief. I never know where she's gone off to . . .'

Mary Clement placed a gnarled hand on Grace's shoulder. 'Please. Just let the police speak to her.'

Grace sat for a moment, looking unsure. Evening cleanup in the kitchen had left her apron stained with grease and tomato sauce, and strands of dull brown hair had worked free from her ponytail and hung limp about her sweating face. It was a raw, worn face that had probably never been beautiful, and it was further marred by lines of bitterness. Now, while others awaited her decision, she was the one in control, the one who held power, and she seemed to relish it. To be drawing out the decision as long as possible while Rizzoli and Maura waited.

'What are you afraid of, Mrs. Otis?' Maura asked quietly.

The question seemed to antagonize Grace. 'I'm not afraid of anything.'

'Then why don't you want us to speak to your daughter?'

'Because she's not reliable.'

'Yes, we understand that she's only seven—'

'She lies.' The words shot out like the snap of a whip. Grace's face, already unattractive, took on an even uglier cast. 'She lies about everything. Even silly things. You can't believe what she says – any of it.'

Maura glanced at the Abbess, who gave a bewildered shake of her head.

'The girl has usually been quiet and unobtrusive,' said Mary Clement. 'That's why we've allowed Grace to bring her into the abbey while she works.'

'I can't afford a baby sitter,' cut in Grace. 'I can't afford anything, really. It's the only way I can manage to work at all, if I keep her here after school.'

'And she just waits here for you?' asked Maura. 'Until you're done for the day?'

'What am I supposed to do with her? I have to work, you know. It's not as if they let my husband stay there for free. These days, you can't even die unless you have money.'

'Excuse me?'

'My husband. He's a patient in St. Catherine's Hospice. Lord knows how long he'll have to be there.' Grace shot a glance at the Abbess, sharp as a poison dart. 'I work here, as part of the arrangement.' Clearly not a happy arrangement, Maura thought. Grace could not be much older than her mid-thirties, but it must seem to her that her life was already over. She was trapped by obligations, to a daughter for whom she clearly had little affection; to a husband who took too long to die. For Grace Otis, Graystones Abbey was no sanctuary; it was her prison.

'Why is your husband in St. Catherine's?' Maura asked gently.

'I told you. He's dying.'

'Of what?'

'Lou Gehrig's disease.. ALS.' Grace said it without emotion, but Maura knew the terrible reality behind that name. As a medical student, she had examined a patient with amyotrophic lateralizing sclerosis. Though completely awake and aware and able to feel pain, he could not move because his muscles had wasted away, reducing him to little more than a brain trapped in a useless body. As she had examined his heart and lungs and palpated his abdomen, she had felt his gaze on her, and had not wanted to meet it, because she knew the despair she would see in his eyes. When she'd finally walked out of his hospital room, she had felt both relief as well as a twinge of guilt – but only a twinge. His tragedy was not hers. She was just a student, passing briefly through his life, under no obligation to share the burden of his misfortune. She was free to walk away, and she had.

Grace Otis could not. The result was etched in resentful lines in her face, and in the prematurely gray streaks in her hair. She said, 'At least I've warned you. She's not reliable. She tells stories. Sometimes they're ridiculous stories.'

'We understand,' said Maura. 'Children do that.'

'If you want to talk to her, I need to be in the room. Just to make sure she behaves.'

'Of course. It's your right, as a parent.'

At last, Grace rose to her feet. 'Noni's hiding out in the kitchen. I'll get her.'

It was several minutes before Grace reappeared, tugging a darkhaired girl by the hand. It was clear that Noni did not want to come out, and she resisted it all the way, every fiber of her little body straining against Grace's relentless pull. Finally, Grace just picked up the girl under the arms and plopped her into a chair – not gently, either, but with the tired disgust of a woman who has reached the end of her rope. The girl sat still for a moment, looking stunned to find herself so swiftly conquered. She was a curly-haired sprite with a square jaw and lively dark eyes that quickly took in everyone in the room. She spared only a glance at Mary Clement, then her gaze lingered a little longer on Maura before it finally settled on Rizzoli. There it stayed, as though Rizzoli was the only one worth focusing on. Like a dog who chooses to annoy the only asthmatic in the room, Noni had settled her attentions on the one person who was least fond of children.

Grace gave her daughter a nudge. 'You have to talk to them.'

Noni's face scrunched up in protest. Out came two words, hoarse as a frog's croak. 'Don't wanna.'

'I don't care if you don't want to. These are the police.'

Noni's gaze remained on Rizzoli. 'They don't look like the police.'

'Well, they are,' Grace said. 'And if you don't tell the truth, they'll put you in jail.'

This was exactly what cops hated to hear a parent say. It made children afraid of the very people they were supposed to trust.

Rizzoli quickly motioned to Grace to stop talking. She dropped to a crouch in front of Noni's chair, so that she and the girl were eye to eye. They were so strikingly alike, both with curly dark hair and intense gazes, that Rizzoli could have been facing a young clone of herself. If Noni was equally stubborn, then there were fireworks ahead.

'Let's get something clear right off, okay?' Rizzoli said to the girl, her voice brusque and matter-of-fact, as though she was speaking not to

113

a child but to a miniature adult. 'I won't put you in jail. I don't ever put kids in jail.'

The girl eyed her dubiously. 'Even bad kids?' she challenged.

'Not even bad kids.'

'Even really, really bad kids?'

Rizzoli hesitated, a spark of irritation in her eyes. Noni was not about to let her off the hook. 'Okay,' she conceded. 'The really, *really* bad ones I send to juvenile hall.'

'That's jail for kids.'

'Right.'

'So you do send kids to jail.'

Rizzoli shot Maura a *can you believe this?* look. 'Okay,' she sighed. 'You got me there. But I'm not gonna put you in jail. I just want to talk to you.'

'How come you don't have a uniform?'

'Because I'm a detective. We don't have to wear uniforms. But I really am a policeman.'

'But you're a woman.'

'Yeah. Okay. Policewoman. So you wanna tell me what you were doing up there, in the attic?'

Noni hunched down in the chair and just stared like a gargoyle at her questioner. For a solid minute, they eyed each other, waiting for the other one to break the silence first.

Grace finally lost her patience and gave the girl a whack on the shoulder. 'Go on! Tell her!'

'Please, Mrs. Otis,' said Rizzoli. 'That's not necessary.'

'But you see how she is? Nothing's ever easy with her. Everything's a struggle.'

'Let's just relax, okay? I can wait.' *I can wait as long as you can, kid*, Rizzoli's gaze told the girl. 'So c'mon, Noni. Tell us where you got those dolls. The ones you were playing with up there.'

'I didn't steal them.'

'I never said you did.'

'I found them. A whole box of them.'

'Where?'

'In the attic. There are other boxes up there, too.'

Grace said, 'You weren't supposed to be up there. You're supposed to stay near the kitchen and not bother anyone.'

'I wasn't bothering anyone. Even if I wanted to, there's no one in this whole *place* to bother.'

'So you found the dolls in the attic,' Rizzoli said, directing the conversation back to the subject at hand.

'A whole box of them.'

Rizzoli turned a questioning look at Mary Clement, who answered: 'They were part of a charity project some years ago. We sewed doll clothes, for donation to an orphanage in Mexico.'

'So you found the dolls,' Rizzoli said to Noni. 'And you played with them up there?'

'No one else was using them.'

'And how did you know how to get into the attic?'

'I saw the man go in there.'

The man? Rizzoli shot a glance at Maura. She leaned closer to Noni. 'What man?'

'He had things on his belt.'

'Things?'

'A hammer and stuff.' She pointed to the Abbess. 'She saw him too. She was talking to him.'

Mother Mary Clement gave a startled laugh. 'Oh! I know who she means. We've had a number of renovations in the last few months. There've been men working in the attic, installing new insulation.'

'When was this?' asked Rizzoli.

'In October.'

'Do you have the names of all these men?'

'I can check the ledgers. We keep a record of all payments we've made to the contractors.'

So it was not such a startling revelation after all. The girl had spied workmen climbing into a hidden space she hadn't known about. A mysterious space, reachable only through a secret door. To take a peek inside would be irresistible for any child – especially one this inquisitive.

'You didn't mind the dark up there?' asked Rizzoli.

'I have a flashlight, you know.' *What a stupid question*, Noni's tone of voice implied.

'You weren't afraid? All by yourself?'

'Why?'

Why indeed? thought Maura. This little girl was fearless, intimidated by neither the dark nor the police. She sat with her gaze perfectly steady on her questioner, as though she, not Rizzoli, was directing this conversation. But self-possessed as she appeared, she was very much a child, and a ragged one at that. Her hair was a tangle of curls,

116

powdery with attic dust. Her pink sweatshirt looked like a well-worn hand-me-down. It was a few sizes too large, and the rolled-back cuffs were soiled. Only her shoes looked new – brand new Keds with Velcro flaps. Her feet did not quite touch the floor, and she kept swinging them back and forth in a monotonous rhythm. A metronome of excess energy.

Grace said, 'Believe me, I didn't know she was up there. I can't go chasing after her all the time. I have to get the meals on the table, and then I have to clean up afterwards. We don't get out of here until nine o'clock, and I can't get her into bed until ten.' Grace looked at Noni. 'That's part of the problem, you know. She's tired and cranky all the time, so everything turns into an argument. Last year, she gave me an ulcer. Made me so stressed out my stomach started digesting itself. I could be doubled over in pain, and she wouldn't care. She still puts up a fuss about going to bed, or taking a bath. No concern for anyone else. But that's the way children are, completely selfish. The whole world revolves around *her*.'

While Grace vented her frustration, Maura was watching Noni's reaction. The girl had gone perfectly still, her legs no longer swinging, her jaw clamped tight in an obstinate square. But the dark eyes briefly glistened with tears. Just as quickly, the tears were gone, erased by the furtive swipe of a dirty cuff. She's not deaf and dumb, thought Maura. She hears the anger in her mother's voice. Every day, in a dozen different ways, Grace surely

117

conveys her disgust for this child. And the child understands. No wonder Noni is difficult; no wonder she makes Grace angry. It's the only emotion she can wrest from her mother, the only proof that any feeling at all exists between them. Just seven years old, and already she knows she's lost her futile bid for love. She knows more than adults realize, and what she sees and hears is surely painful.

Rizzoli had been crouched too long at the child's level. Now she rose and stretched her legs. It was already eight o'clock, they had skipped supper, and Rizzoli's energy appeared to be wearing thin. She stood eyeing the girl, both of them with equally disheveled hair, equally determined faces.

Rizzoli said, with weary patience, 'So, Noni, have you been going up to the attic a lot?'

The dusty mop of curls bounced in a nod.

'What do you do up there?'

'Nothing.'

'You just said you play with your dolls.'

'I already told you *that*.'

'What else do you do?'

The girl shrugged.

Rizzoli pressed harder.'Come on, it's gotta be boring up there. I can't imagine why you'd want to hang around in that attic unless there's something interesting to see.'

Noni's gaze dropped to her lap.

'You ever peek at the sisters? You know, just sort of watch what they're doing?'

'I see them all the time.'

'How about when they're in their rooms?'

'I'm not allowed to go up there.'

'But do you ever watch them when they're not looking? When they don't know it?'

Noni's head was still bent. She said, into her sweatshirt, 'That's *peeping*.'

'And you know better than to do that,' said Grace. 'It's an invasion of privacy. I've told you that.'

Noni crossed her arms and declared in a stentorian voice: ''vasion of *privacy*.' It sounded like a mocking of her mother. Grace reddened and moved toward her daughter, as though to strike her.

Rizzoli halted Grace with a swift gesture. 'Would you and Mother Mary Clement mind stepping out of the room for a minute, Mrs. Otis?'

'You said I could stay,' said Grace.

'I think Noni might need a little extra police persuasion. It will work better if you're not in the room.'

'Oh.' Grace nodded, an unpleasant gleam in her eye. 'Of course.' Rizzoli had read this woman correctly; Grace was not interested in protecting her daughter; rather, she wanted to see Noni disciplined. Cowed. Grace shot Noni a *now you're in for it* look, and walked out of the room, followed by the Abbess.

For a moment, no one spoke. Noni sat with head ducked, hands in her lap. The picture of childish obedience. What an act.

Rizzoli pulled up a chair and sat down, facing the girl. There she waited, not speaking. Letting the silence play out between them.

At last, from beneath a wayward curl of hair, Noni cast a sly glance at Rizzoli. 'What're you waiting for?' she said.

'For you to tell me what you saw in Camille's room. Because I know you were peeking at her. I used to do the same thing when I was a kid. Spy on the grownups. See what kind of weird things they do.'

'It's a 'vasion of privacy.'

'Yeah, but it's fun, isn't it?'

Noni's head came up, her eyes focusing with dark intensity on Rizzoli. 'This is a trick.'

'I don't play tricks, okay? I need you to help me. I think you're a very smart girl. I bet you see things that grownups don't even notice. What do you think?'

Noni gave a sullen shrug. 'Maybe.'

'So tell me some of the things you see the nuns do.'

'Like the weird things?'

'Yeah.'

Noni leaned toward Rizzoli and said softly: 'Sister Abigail wears a diaper. She pees in her pants because she's really, really old.'

'How old, do you think?'

'Like, fifty.'

'Wow. That *is* old.'

'Sister Cornelia picks her nose.'

'Yuck.'

120

'And she shoots it on the floor when she thinks nobody's looking.'

'Double yuck.'

'And she tells me to wash my hands because I'm a dirty little girl. But she doesn't wash her hands, and she's got boogers on hers.'

'You're ruining my appetite, kid.'

'So I told her why didn't she wash off the boogers, and she got mad at me. She said I talk too much. Sister Ursula said so too, because I asked her why that lady didn't have any fingers, and she told me to be quiet. And my mommy makes me apologize all the time. She says I'm 'barrassing to her. That's because I'm out and about where I shouldn't be.'

'Okay, okay,' said Rizzoli, looking as if she was getting a headache. 'That's a lot of really interesting stuff. But you know what I want to hear about?'

'What?'

'What you saw in Camille's room. Through that peephole. You were looking, weren't you?'

Noni's gaze dropped to her lap. 'Maybe.'

'Weren't you?'

This time Noni gave a submissive nod. 'I wanted to see . . .'

'See what?'

'What they wear underneath their clothes.'

Maura had to catch herself from bursting out in laughter. She remembered her years at Holy Innocents, when she, too, had wondered what the sisters wore beneath their habits. Nuns had seemed like such mysterious creatures, their bodies disguised and shapeless, black robes fending off the gazes of the curious. What did a bride of Christ wear against her bare skin? She had imagined ugly white pantaloons that pulled all the way up over the navel, and cotton bras designed to disguise and diminish, and thick stockings like sausage casings over legs with bulging blue veins. She had imagined bodies imprisoned by layers and layers of bland cotton. Then one day, she had seen pinch-lipped Sister Lawrencia lift her skirt as she climbed the stairs, and had caught a startling glimpse of scarlet beneath the nun's raised hem. It was not just a red slip, but a red *satin* slip. She had never again looked at Sister Lawrencia, or at any nun, in quite the same way.

'You know,' said Rizzoli, leaning toward the girl, 'I always wondered what they wear under their habits, too. Did you see?'

Gravely, Noni shook her head. 'She never took off her clothes.'

'Not even to go to bed?'

'I have to go home before they go to bed. I never saw.'

'Well, what did you see? What did Camille do up there, all alone in her room?'

Noni rolled her eyes, as though the answer was almost too boring to mention. 'She cleaned. All the time. She was the *cleanest* lady.'

Maura remembered the scrubbed floor, the varnish rubbed down to bare wood.

'What else did she do?' asked Rizzoli.

'She read her book.'

'What else?'

Noni paused. 'She cried a lot.'

'Do you know why she was crying?'

The girl chewed on her bottom lip as she thought about it. Suddenly she brightened as the answer came to her. 'Because she was sorry about Jesus.'

'Why do you think that?'

The girl gave an exasperated sigh. 'Don't you know? He died on the cross.'

'Maybe she was crying about something else.'

'But she kept looking at him. He's hanging on her wall.'

Maura thought of the crucifix, mounted across from him Camille's bed. And she imagined the young novice, prostrated before that cross, praying for . . . what? Forgiveness for her sins? Deliverance from the consequences? But every month, the child would be growing inside her, and she would begin to feel it moving. Kicking. No amount of prayer or frantic scrubbing could wash away that guilt.

'Am I done?' asked Noni.

Rizzoli sank back in her chair with a sigh. 'Yeah, kid. We're all done. You can go join your mom.'

The girl hopped off the chair, landing with a noisy clomp that made her curls bounce. 'She was sad about the ducks, too.'

'Man, that sounds good for dinner,' said Rizzoli. 'Roast duck.'

'She used to feed them, but then they all flew away for the winter. My mommy says some of them won't come back, because they get eaten up down south.'

'Yeah, well, that's life.' Rizzoli waved her off. 'Go on, your Mom's waiting.'

The girl was almost at the kitchen door when Maura called out: 'Noni? Where were these ducks that was Camille feeding?'

'The ones in the pond.'

'Which pond?'

'You know, in the back. Even when they flew away, she kept going out to look for them, but my mommy said she was wasting her time because they're probably in Florida. That's where Disney World is,' she added, and skipped out of the room.

There was a long silence.

Slowly Rizzoli turned and looked at Maura. 'Did you just hear what I heard?'

'Yes.'

'Are you thinking . . .'

Maura nodded. 'You have to search the duck pond.'

It was nearly ten when Maura pulled into her driveway. The lights were on in her living room, giving the illusion that someone was at home, waiting for her, but she knew the house was empty. It was always an empty house that greeted her, the lights turned on not by human hands but by a trio of $5.99 automatic timers bought in the local Wal-Mart. During the short days of winter, she set them for five o'clock, ensuring that she would not come home to a dark house. She had chosen this suburb of Brookline, just west of Boston, because of the sense of security she felt in its quiet, treelined streets. Most of her neighbors were urban professionals who, like her, worked in the city and fled every evening to this suburban haven. Her neighbor on one side, Mr. Telushkin, was a robotics engineer from Israel. Her neighbors on the other side, Lily and Susan, were civil rights attorneys. In the summertime, everyone kept their gardens neat and their cars waxed – an updated version of the American dream, where lesbians and immigrant professionals happily waved to each other across clipped hedges. It was as safe a neighborhood as one could find this close to the city, but Maura knew how illusory notions of safety were. Roads into the suburbs can be traveled by both victims and predators. Her autopsy table was a democratic destination; it did not discriminate against suburban housewives.

Though the lamps in her living room offered a welcoming glow, the house felt chilly. Or perhaps she had simply brought winter inside with her, like one of those cartoon characters over whom storm clouds always hang. She turned up the thermostat and lit the flame in the gas fireplace – a convenience that once struck her as appallingly fake, but which she had since come to appreciate. Fire was fire, whether it was lit with the flick of a switch, or by fussing over wood and kindling. Tonight, she craved its warmth, its cheery light, and was glad to be so quickly gratified.

She poured a glass of sherry and settled into a chair beside the hearth. Through the window, she could see Christmas lights adorning the house across the street, like twinkling icicles drooping from the eaves – a nagging reminder of how out-of-touch she was with the holiday spirit. She had not yet bought a tree, or shopped for gifts, or even picked up a box of holiday cards. This was the second year in a row that she'd played Mrs. Grinch. Last winter, she had just moved to Boston, and in the midst of unpacking and settling into her job, she had scarcely noticed Christmas whizzing by. And what's your excuse this year? she thought. She had only a week left to buy that tree and hang the lights and make eggnog. At the very least, she should play a few carols on her piano, as she used to do when she was a child. The book of holiday songs should still be in the piano bench, where it had been stored since . . .

Since my last Christmas with Victor.

She looked at the phone on the end table. Already, she could feel the effects of the sherry, and she knew that any decision she made now would be tainted by alcohol. By recklessness.

Yet she picked up the phone. As the hotel operator rang his room, she stared at the fireplace, thinking: This is a mistake. This is only going to break my heart.

He answered: 'Maura?' Without her saying a word, he had known she was the one calling.

'I know it's late,' she said.

'It's only ten thirty.'

'Still, I shouldn't have called.'

'So why did you?' he asked softly.

She paused and closed her eyes. Even then, she could still see the glow of the flames. *Even if you don't look at them, even if you pretend they aren't there, the flames are still burning. Whether or not you see them, they burn.*

'I thought it was time to stop avoiding you,' she said. 'Or I'll never get on with my life.'

'Well, that's a flattering reason for you to call.'

She sighed. 'It's not coming out right.'

'I don't think there's any way to say it kindly, what you want to tell me. The least you can do is say it to me in person. Not over the phone.'

'Would that be kinder?'

'It'd be a hell of a lot braver.' A dare. An attack on her courage.

She sat up straighter, her gaze back on the fire. 'Why would it make a difference to you?'

'Because let's face it, we both need to move on. We're stuck in place, since neither of us really understands what went wrong. I loved you, and I think you loved me, yet look where we ended up. We can't even be friends. Tell me why that is. Why can't two people, who just happened to be married to each other, have a civilized conversation? The way we would with anyone else?'

'Because you're not anyone else.' *Because I loved you.*

'We can do that, can't we? Just talk, face to face. Bury the ghosts. I won't be in town long. It's now

127

or never. Either we go on hiding from each other, or we bring this out in the open and talk about what happened. Put the blame on me, if you want to. I admit, I deserve a lot of it. But let's stop pretending the other one doesn't exist.'

She looked down at her empty sherry glass. 'When do you want to meet?'

'I could come over now.'

Through the window, she saw the decorative lights across the street suddenly go dark, the twinkling icicles vanishing into a snowy night. A week before Christmas, and in all her life, she had never felt so lonely.

'I live in Brookline,' she said.

Seven

She saw his headlights through the falling snowflakes. He drove slowly, in search of her house, and came to a stop at the end of her drive-way. Are you having doubts too, Victor? she thought. Are you wondering if this is a mistake, if you should turn around and go back to the city?

The car pulled over to the curb and parked.

She stepped away from the window and stood in the living room, aware that her heart was pounding, her hands sweating. The sound of the doorbell made her draw in a startled breath. She was unprepared to face him, but he was here now, and she couldn't very well leave him standing outside in the cold.

The bell rang again.

She opened the door and snowflakes whirled in. They sparkled on his jacket, glittered in his hair, his beard. It was a classic Hallmark moment, the old lover standing on her doorstep, his hungry gaze searching her face, and she couldn't think of anything to say except, 'Come in.' No kiss, no hug, not even a brushing of hands.

He stepped inside and shrugged off his jacket. As she hung it up, the familiar smell of leather, of Victor, brought an ache to her throat. She shut the closet and turned to look at him. 'Would you like a drink?'

'How about some coffee?'

'The real stuff?'

'It's only been three years, Maura. You have to ask?'

No, she didn't have to ask. High-octane and black was the way he always drank it. She felt an unsettling sense of familiarity as she led him into the kitchen, as she took the bag of Mt. Sutro Roasters coffee beans from the freezer. It had been their favorite brand in San Francisco, and she still had a fresh bag of it shipped to her from the shop every two weeks. Marriages may end, but some things one simply couldn't give up. She ground the beans and started the coffeemaker, aware that he was slowly surveying her kitchen, taking in the stainless steel Sub-Zero refrigerator, the Viking stove, and the black granite countertops. She had remodeled the kitchen soon after she'd bought the house, and she felt a sense of pride that he was standing in *her* territory, that she had earned everything he was now looking at, with her own hard work. In that regard, their divorce had been relatively simple; they had asked for nothing from each other. After only two years of marriage, they'd simply reclaimed their separate assets, and gone their own ways. This home was hers alone, and each evening, when she walked in the door, she knew that everything would be where she had left it. That every stick of furniture had been her purchase, her choice.

'Looks like you finally got the kitchen of your dreams,' he said.

'I'm happy with it.'

'So tell me, do meals really taste better when they're cooked on a fancy six-burner stove?'

She didn't appreciate his undertone of sarcasm, and she shot back: 'As a matter of fact, they do. And they taste better on Richard Ginori china, too.'

'What happened to good old Crate and Barrel?'

'I've decided to indulge myself, Victor. I've stopped feeling guilty about having money and spending money. Life's too short to keep living like a hippie.'

'Oh come on, Maura. Is that what it felt like, living with me?'

'You made me feel as if splurging on a few luxuries was a betrayal of the cause.'

'What cause?'

'For you, everything was a cause. There are people starving in Angola, so it's a sin to buy nice linens. Or eat a steak. Or own a Mercedes.'

'I thought you believed it, too.'

'You know what, Victor? Idealism becomes exhausting. I'm not ashamed of having money, and I won't feel guilty about spending it.'

She poured his coffee, wondering if he was

131

conscious of the ironic little detail that he, an addict of Mt. Sutro coffee beans, was drinking a brew made from beans shipped across the country (wasted jet fuel!) Or that the cup in which she served it was emblazoned with the logo of a pharmaceutical company (corporate bribery!) But he was silent as he took the cup. Strangely subdued, for a man who'd always been so driven by his idealism.

It was that very passion that had first drawn her to him. They had met at a San Francisco conference on third world medicine. She had presented a paper on overseas autopsy rates; he had delivered the keynote address about the many human tragedies encountered by One Earth's medical teams abroad. Standing before the smartly dressed audience, Victor had looked more like a tired and unshaven backpacker than a physician. He had, in fact, just stepped off the plane from Guatemala City, and had not even had the chance to iron his shirt. He'd walked into the room carrying only a box of slides. He'd brought no written speech, no notes, just that precious collection of images, which played across the screen in tragic progression. The young Ethiopian mother, dying of tetanus. The Peruvian baby with the cleft palate, abandoned at the roadside. The Kazakh girl, dead of pneumonia, wrapped in her burial shroud. Every one of them was a preventable death, he'd emphasized. These were the innocent victims of war and poverty and ignorance that his organization, One Earth, could have saved. But there would never be enough money, or enough volunteers, to meet the needs of every humanitarian crisis.

Even halfway back in that dark room, Maura had been moved by his words, by how passionately he spoke of tent clinics and feeding stations, of the forgotten poor who died unnoticed every day.

When the lights came up, she no longer saw just a rumpled doctor standing behind the podium. She saw a man whose sense of purpose made him larger than life. She, who insisted on order and reason in her own life, found herself attracted to this man of almost frightening intensity, whose job took him to the most chaotic places on earth.

And what had he seen in her? Certainly not a sister crusader. Instead, she'd brought stability and calm to his life. She was the one who balanced their checkbook and organized the household, the one who waited at home while he traveled from crisis to crisis, continent to continent. His life was lived out of a suitcase, and was rich with adrenaline.

Has that life been so much happier without me? she wondered. He did not look particularly happy, sitting here at her kitchen table, sipping coffee. In many ways, he was still the same Victor. His hair was a little shaggy, his shirt in need of a good pressing, and the edges of the collar were frayed – all evidence of his disdain for the superficial. But in other ways he was different. An older, wearier Victor who seemed quiet, even sad, his fire dampened by maturity.

She sat down with her own cup of coffee and they looked at each other across the table.

'We should have had this talk three years ago,' he said.

'Three years ago, you wouldn't have listened to me.'

'Did you try? Did you ever once come out and tell me that you were sick of being the activist's wife?'

She looked down at her coffee. No, she had not told him. She had held it in, the way she held in emotions that disturbed her. Anger, resentment, despair – they all made her feel out of control, and that she could not abide. When she'd finally signed the divorce papers, she'd felt eerily detached.

'I never knew how hard it was for you,' he said.

'Would it have changed anything if I'd told you?'

'You could have tried.'

'And what would you have done? Resigned from One Earth? There was no way to compromise. You get too much of a thrill from playing Saint Victor. All the awards, all the praise. No one gets on the cover of *People* just for being a good husband.'

'You think that's why I do it? For the attention, the publicity? Jesus, Maura. You know how important this is! Give me some credit, at least.'

She sighed. 'You're right, that wasn't fair of me. But we both know you'd miss it.'

'Yes, I would,' he admitted. Then added, quietly: 'But I didn't know how much I'd miss *you*.'

134

She let those last words slip past without a response. Let the silence hang between them. In truth, she didn't know what to say, his admission had so taken her aback.

'You look great,' he said. 'And you seem content. Are you?'

'Yes.' Her answer was too quick, too automatic. She felt herself flush.

'The new job's working out?' he asked.

'It keeps me challenged.'

'More fun than terrorizing medical students at U.C.?'

She gave a laugh. 'I did not terrorize medical students.'

'They might beg to differ.'

'I held them to higher standards, that's all. And they almost always met them.'

'You were a good teacher, Maura. I'm sure the university would love to have you back.'

'Well, we all move on, don't we?' She could feel his gaze on her face, and she purposefully kept her expression unreadable.

'I saw you on TV yesterday,' he said. 'The evening news. About the attack on those nuns.'

'I was hoping the cameras would miss me.'

'I spotted you right away. They showed you walking out the gate.'

'It's one of the job hazards. You're always in the public eye.'

'Especially that particular case, I imagine. It was on every TV station.'

'What are they saying about it?'

'That the police have no suspects. That the motive remains unknown.' He shook his head. 'It does sound completely irrational, attacking nuns. Unless there was some kind of sexual assault.'

'That makes it rational?'

'You know what I mean.'

Yes, she did know, and she knew Victor well enough not to be offended by his comment. There was indeed a difference between the coldly calculating sexual predator and the psychotic who had no grip on reality.

'I did the autopsy this morning,' she said. 'Multiple skull fractures. Torn middle meningeal artery. He hit her again and again, probably with a hammer. I'm not sure you could classify this attack as rational.'

He shook his head. 'How do you deal with it, Maura? You went from performing autopsies on nice, neat hospital deaths to something like this.'

'Hospital deaths aren't exactly nice and neat.'

'But a postmortem on a homicide victim? And she was young, wasn't she?'

'Only twenty.' She paused, on the verge of telling him what else she'd found at autopsy. When they were married, they'd always shared medical gossip, trusting each other to keep such information confidential. But this subject was too grim, and she didn't want to invite Death any deeper into the conversation.

She rose to refill their cups. When she returned to the table with the coffeepot, she said: 'Now tell me about you. What's Saint Victor been up to?'

'Please don't call me that.'

'You used to think it was funny.'

'Now I think it's ominous. When the press starts calling you a saint, you know they're just waiting for the chance to knock you off the pedestal.'

'I've noticed you and One Earth have been popping up quite a bit in the news.'

He sighed. 'Unfortunately.'

'Why unfortunately?'

'It's been a bad year for international charities. So many new conflicts, so many refugees on the move now. That's the only reason we're in the news. Because we're the ones who have to step in. We're just lucky we got a huge grant this year.'

'A result of all that good press?'

He shrugged. 'Every so often, some big corporation develops a conscience and decides to write a check.'

'I'm sure the tax deduction doesn't hurt them, either.'

'But that money goes so fast. All it takes is some new maniac launching a war, and suddenly we're dealing with a million more refugees. A hundred thousand more kids dying of typhoid or cholera. That's what keeps me up at night, Maura. Thinking about the kids.' He took a sip of coffee, then put it down, as though he could no longer stomach its taste.

She watched him sitting so quietly, and noticed the new threads of gray in his tawny hair. He might be getting older, she thought, but he'd lost none of his idealism. It was that very idealism that

137

had first drawn her to him – and what had eventually driven them apart. She could not compete with the world's needs for Victor's attention, and she never should have tried. His affair with the French nurse had not, in the end, been surprising. It was his act of defiance, his way of asserting his independence from her.

They were silent, their gazes not meeting, two people who had once loved each other, and now could think of nothing to say. She heard him rise to his feet, and watched as he stood at the sink to rinse out his cup.

'So how is Dominique these days?' she asked.

'I wouldn't know.'

'Does she still work for One Earth?'

'No. She left. It wasn't comfortable for either one of us, after . . .' He shrugged.

'You two don't keep in touch?'

'She wasn't important to me, Maura. You know that.'

'Funny. But she became very important to me.'

He turned to face her. 'Do you think you'll ever get over being angry about her?'

'It's been three years. I suppose I should.'

'That doesn't answer the question.'

She looked down. 'You had an affair. I needed to be angry. It was the only way.'

'The only way?'

'That I could leave you. That I could get over you.'

He walked toward her. Placed his hands on her shoulders, his touch warm and intimate. 'I don't want you to get over me,' he said. 'Even if it means you hate me. At least you'd feel *something*. That's what bothered me the most, that you could just walk away. That you seemed so cold about it all.'

It's the only way I know how to cope, she thought, as his arms slipped around her. As his breath warmed her hair. She had learned long ago how to box up all those messy emotions. They were so poorly matched, the two of them. Exuberant Victor, married to the Queen of the Dead. Why did they ever think it would work?

Because I wanted his heat, his passion. I wanted what I myself can never be.

The ringing telephone made Victor's hands go still on her shoulders. He stepped away, and left her longing for his warmth. She rose and went to the kitchen phone. One glance at the caller I.D., and she knew that this call would send her back into the night, into the snow. As she spoke to the detective and jotted down directions, she saw Victor give a resigned shake of his head. Tonight, she was the one called to duty, and he was the one left behind.

She hung up. 'I'm sorry, I have to leave.'

'The Grim Reaper calls?'

'A death scene in Roxbury. They're waiting for me.'

He followed her down the hallway, toward the front door. 'Would you like me to come with you?'

'Why?'

'To keep you company.'

'Believe me, there's plenty of company at a death scene.'

He glanced out the living room window, at the thickly falling snow. 'It's not a good night to be driving.'

'For either of us.' She bent down to pull on boots. She was glad he couldn't see her face as she said, 'There's no need for you to drive back to the hotel. Why don't you just stay here?'

'Spend the night, you mean?'

'It might be more convenient for you. You can make up the bed in the guest room. I'll probably be gone for a few hours.'

His silence made her flush. Still not looking at him, she buttoned her coat. Suddenly anxious to escape, she opened the front door.

And heard him say, 'I'll wait up for you.'

Blue lights flashed through the gauze of falling snow. She pulled up right behind one of the cruisers and a patrolman approached, his face half hidden behind his raised collar, like a turtle retracted into its shell. She rolled down her window and squinted against the glare of his flashlight. Snow blew in, skittering across her dashboard.

'Dr. Isles, M.E.'s office,' she said.

'Okay, you can park right where you are, ma'am.'

'Where's the body?'

'Inside.' He waved his flashlight toward a building across the street. 'Front door's padlocked –

gotta go in the alley entrance. Electricity's off, so watch your step. You'll need your flashlight. All kinds of boxes and shit piled up in that alley.'

She stepped out of the car, into a curtain of lacy white. Tonight she was fully prepared for the weather, and grateful that her feet were warm and dry inside Thinsulate boots. At least six inches of new snow layered the road, but the flakes were soft and feathery and offered not even a whisper of resistance as her boots cut a trough through the drifts.

At the alley entrance, she turned on the flashlight, and saw a strand of sagging police tape, the yellow almost obscured by a coating of white. She stepped over it and dislodged a shower of flakes. The alley was obstructed by several amorphous piles obscured by snow. Her boot connected with something solid, and she heard the clatter of bottles. The alley had been used as a trash dump, and she wondered what distasteful items were hidden beneath this white blanket.

She knocked on the door and called out: 'Hello? Medical Examiner.'

The door swung open, and a flashlight glared in her eyes. She could not see the man holding it, but she recognized Detective Darren Crowe's voice.

'Hey, Doc. Welcome to roach city.'

'Would you mind shining that light somewhere else?'

The flashlight beam dropped from her face and she saw his silhouette, broad-shouldered and vaguely threatening. He was one of the younger

141

detectives in the Homicide Unit, and every time she worked a case with him, she felt she was walking onto the set of a TV show, and Crowe was the series star, a movie-star cop with blow-dried hair and the attitude to match, cocky and self-assured. The only thing that men like Crowe respected in a woman was icy professionalism, and that's what she showed him. While the male M.E.s might banter with Crowe, she could not; the barriers had to be maintained, the lines drawn, or he would find a way to chip at her authority.

She pulled on gloves and shoe-covers and stepped into the building. Shining her flashlight around the room, she saw metallic surfaces reflect back at her. A huge refrigerator and metal countertops. A commercial stove top and ovens.

'This used to be Mama Cortina's Italian restaurant,' said Crowe. 'Until Mama went out of business and filed for bankruptcy. Building got condemned two years ago, and the entrances were both padlocked. Alley door looks like it was broken open some time ago. All this kitchen equipment's up for auction, but I don't know who'd want it. It's filthy.' He shone his flashlight at the gas burners, where years of accumulated grease had thickened to a black crust. Roaches scurried away from the light. 'The place is crawling with 'em. All this yummy grease to feed on.'

'Who found the body?'

'One of our boys from the narcotics division. They had a drug bust going down, about a block from here. The suspect bolted, and they thought he came down this alley. They noticed the door had been pried open. Came inside looking for their perp, and got quite a surprise.' He pointed his flashlight at the floor. 'Some scrape marks across the dust here. Like the perp dragged the victim across this room.' He waved the light toward the other end of the kitchen.

'Body's that way. We gotta go through the dining room.'

'You've already videotaped in here?'

'Yeah. Had to lug in two battery packs to get enough light. Already ran 'em both down. So it's gonna be a little dim in there.'

She followed him toward the kitchen doorway, holding her arms close to her body, a reminder not to touch any surface – as if she would want to. She heard rustling all around her in the shadows, and thought of thousands of insect legs skittering across the walls and clinging to the ceiling above her head. She might be stoic about the gory and grotesque, but scavenging insects truly repelled her.

Stepping into the dining area, she smelled the tired bouquet of scents that always clings to alleys behind old restaurants: the smell of garbage and stale beer. But here, there was also something else, an ominously familiar odor that made her pulse quicken. It was the object of her visit here, and it stirred in her both curiosity and dread.

'Looks like bums have been crashing in here,' said Crowe, aiming his flashlight at the floor, where she saw an old blanket and bundles of newspapers. 'And there are some candles over there. Lucky they didn't burn the place down, with all this trash.' His flashlight moved across a mound of food wrappers and empty tin cans. Two yellow eyes stared at them from the top of the pile – a rat, unafraid, even cocky, daring them to advance on it.

Rats and roaches. With all these scavengers, what would be left of the body? she wondered.

'It's around that corner.' Crowe picked his way with athletic confidence past tables and stacked chairs. 'Stay to this side. There are some footprints we're trying to preserve. Someone tracked blood away from the body. They fade out right about there.'

He led her into a short hallway. Faint light spilled out a doorway at the end. It came from the men's restroom.

'Doc's here,' Crowe called out.

Another flashlight beam appeared in the doorway. Crowe's partner, Ed Sleeper, stepped out of the restroom and gave Maura a tired wave of his gloved hand. Sleeper was the oldest detective in the Homicide Unit, and every time she saw him, his shoulders seemed to be sagging a little deeper. She wondered how much of his dispiritedness had to do with being paired with Crowe. Neither wisdom nor experience could trump youthful aggression, and Sleeper had long since ceded control to his overbearing partner.

'It's not a pretty sight,' said Sleeper. 'Just be glad it's not July. I don't want to think about what it'd smell like if it wasn't so damn cold in here.'

Crowe laughed. 'Sounds like someone's ready for Florida.'

'Hey, I got a nice little condo all picked out. Only one block from the beach. I'm gonna wear nothing but swim trunks all day. Let it all hang out.'

Warm beaches, thought Maura. Sugary sand. Wouldn't they all love to be there right now, instead of in this grim little hallway, lit only by their trio of flashlights.

'All yours, Doc,' said Sleeper.

She moved to the doorway. Her flashlight beam fell on dirty floor tiles, laid in a black-and-white checkerboard pattern. It was tracked over with footprints and dried blood.

'Stay along the wall,' said Crowe.

She stepped into the room and instantly jerked backwards, startled by a streak of movement near her feet. 'Jesus,' she said, and gave a startled laugh.

'Yeah, those rats are big mothers,' said Crowe. 'And they've had themselves a little feast in there.'

She saw a tail slither beneath the door of a bathroom stall, and thought of the old urban legend of rats swimming through sewer systems and popping out of toilets.

Slowly, she played her beam past two sinks with missing faucets, past a urinal, its drain clogged by trash and cigarette butts. Her beam dropped, to the nude body lying on its side beneath the urinal.

The gleam of exposed facial bones peeked through tangled black hair. Scavengers had already been gorging on this bounty of fresh meat, and the torso was punctured by numerous rat bites. But it was not the damage caused by sharp teeth that horrified her most; it was the diminutive size of the corpse.

A child?

Maura dropped to a crouch beside the body. It lay with its right cheek pressed against the floor. As she bent closer, she saw fully developed breasts – not a child at all, she thought, but a mature woman of small stature, her features obliterated. Feasting scavengers had gnawed hungrily on the exposed left side of the face, devouring skin and even nasal cartilage. The skin still remaining on the torso was deeply pigmented. Hispanic? she wondered, her light beam moving across bony shoulders, and down the knobby ridge of spine. Dark, almost purplish nodules were scattered across the nude torso. She focused her light on the left hip and buttock, and saw more lesions. The angry eruption ran all the way down the thigh and calf to the . . .

Her flashlight beam froze on the ankle. 'My God,' she said.

The left foot was missing. The ankle ended in a stump, the raw edge black with putrefaction.

She shifted her beam to the other ankle, and saw another stump. The right foot was missing as well.

'Now check out the hands,' said Crowe, who'd moved close beside her. He added his beam to

146

hers, pooling their light on the arms, which had been tucked into the shadow of the torso.

Instead of hands, she saw two stumps, the edges ragged with the teeth marks of scavengers.

She rocked back, stunned.

'I take it rats didn't eat those clean off,' said Crowe.

She swallowed. 'No. No, these were amputations.'

'You think he did it while she was still alive?'

She stared down at the stained tiles, and saw only small black pools of dried blood near the stumps, no machine-gun splatter. 'There was no arterial pressure when these cuts were made. The parts were removed postmortem.' She looked at Crowe. 'Did you find them?'

'No. He took them. Who the hell knows why?'

'There's a logical reason he might have done it,' said Sleeper. 'We don't have fingerprints now. We can't I.D. her.'

Maura said, 'If he was trying to obliterate her identity . . .' She stared at the face, at the gleam of bone, and felt a fresh thrill of horror at its significance. 'I need to roll her over,' she said.

She took a disposable sheet from her kit and spread it out beside the body. Together, Sleeper and Crowe logrolled the corpse onto the sheet.

Sleeper gave a gasp and flinched away. The right side of the face, which had been pressed against the floor, now came into view. So, too, did the single bullet hole, punched into the left breast.

But it was not the bullet wound that had

repelled Sleeper. It was the victim's face, its lidless eye staring up at them. Lying against the bathroom tiles, the right side of the face should have been inaccessible to rodent teeth, yet the skin was gone. Exposed muscle had dried in leathery strands, and a pearly nubbin of cheekbone poked through.

'The rats didn't do that, either,' said Sleeper.

'No,' said Maura. 'This damage wasn't done by scavengers.'

'Christ, did he just tear it off? It's like he peeled away a . . .'

A mask. Only this mask had not been made of rubber or plastic, but of human skin.

'He cut off the face. The hands. He's left us with no way to identify her,' said Sleeper.

'But why take the feet?' said Crowe. 'That doesn't make any sense. No one gets identified by their toe prints. Besides, she doesn't look like the kind of vic who'd be missed. What is she, black? Latina?'

'What does her race have to do with whether she's missed or not?' asked Maura.

'I'm just saying, this isn't some housewife from the suburbs. Or why would she end up in this neighborhood?'

Maura stood up, her dislike for Crowe suddenly so strong she found it hard to be near him. She waved her flashlight around the room, her beam streaking across sinks and urinals.

'There's blood there, on the wall.'

'I'd say he whacked her right in here,' said

Crowe. 'Dragged her in, shoves her up against the wall, and pulls the trigger. Then he does the amputations, right where she falls.'

Maura stared down at blood on the tiles. Only a few smears, because by then the victim is already dead. Her heart has stopped beating, stopped pumping. She feels nothing as the killer crouches beside her, and his blade sinks deep into her wrist, prying apart joints. As he slices through her flesh, peeling away her face as though he is skinning a bear. And when he is done collecting his prizes, he leaves her here, like a discarded carcass, an offering to the scavengers that infest this abandoned building.

Within a few days, with no clothing to hinder sharp teeth, the rats would have been down to muscle.

Within a month, down to bone.

She looked up at Crowe. 'Where are her clothes?'

'All we found was a single shoe. Tennis shoe, size four. I think he dropped it on the way out. It was lying in the kitchen.'

'Was there blood on it?'

'Yeah. Got splattered across the top.'

She looked down at the stump where the right foot should have been. 'So he undressed her here, in this room.'

'Postmortem sexual assault?' said Sleeper.

Crowe snorted. 'Who'd want to screw a woman with this creeping crud all over her skin? What is that rash, anyway? It's not infectious, is it? Like smallpox or something?'

149

'No, these lesions look chronic, not acute. See how some of them are crusted over?'

'Well, I can't see anyone wanting to touch her, much less screw her.'

'It's always a possibility,' said Sleeper.

'Or he may have undressed her just to expose the corpse,' said Maura. 'To speed up its destruction by scavengers.'

'Why bother to take the clothes with him?'

'It could be one more way to strip her identity.'

'I think he just wanted them,' said Crowe.

Maura looked at him. 'Why?'

'For the same reason he took the hands and the feet and the face. He wanted souvenirs.' Crowe looked at Maura, and in the slanting shadows, he seemed taller. Threatening. 'I think our boy's a collector.'

Her porch light was on; she could see its yellowish glow through the lace of falling snow. Hers was the only house on the block lit up at this hour. So many other nights, she had returned to a house where the lamps were turned on not by human hands but by electric timers. Tonight, she thought, someone is actually waiting for me.

Then she saw that Victor's car was no longer parked in front of her house. He's left, she thought. I'm coming home, as usual, to an empty house. The glowing porch light, which had seemed so welcoming, now struck her as coldly anonymous.

Her chest felt hollow with disappointment as

she turned into her driveway. What disturbed her most was not that he had left; it was her reaction to it. Just one evening with him, she thought, and I'm back where I was three years ago, my resolve shaken, my independence cracking.

She pressed the garage remote. The door rumbled open and she gave a startled laugh as a blue Toyota was revealed, parked in the left stall.

Victor had simply moved his car into the garage.

She pulled in beside the rented Toyota, and as the garage door shut behind her, she sat for a moment, acutely aware of her own quickening pulse, of anticipation roaring through her bloodstream like a drug. From despair to jubilation in ten seconds flat. She had to remind herself that nothing had changed between them. That nothing *could* change between them.

She stepped out of the car, took a deep breath, and walked into the house.

'Victor?'

There was no answer.

She glanced in the living room, then went up the hall to the kitchen. The coffee cups had been washed and put away, all evidence of his visit erased. She peeked in the bedrooms and her study – still no Victor.

Only when she returned to the living room did she spot his feet, clad in sensible white socks, protruding from one end of the couch. She stood and watched him as he slept, his arm trailing limp toward the floor, his face at peace. This was not the Victor she recalled, the man whose volcanic

151

passions had first attracted her, and then driven her away. What she remembered of their marriage were the arguments, the deep wounds that only a lover can inflict. The divorce had distorted her memories of him, turning him darker, angrier. She had nursed those memories, had fed off them for so long that seeing him now, unguarded, was a moment of startling recognition.

I used to watch you sleep. I used to love you.

She went to the closet for a blanket, and spread it over him. Reached out to touch his hair, then stopped, her hand hovering above his head.

His eyes were open and watching her.

'You're awake,' she said.

'I never meant to fall asleep. What time is it?'

'Two thirty.'

He groaned. 'I was going to leave—'

'You might as well stay. It's snowing like crazy.'

'I moved the car into the garage. I hope you don't mind. The city plow was coming by—'

'They would have towed you, if you hadn't moved it. It's okay.' She smiled, and said softly, 'Go back to sleep.'

They looked at each other for a moment. Caught between longing and doubt, she said nothing, knowing only too well the consequences of a wrong choice. Surely they were both thinking the same thing: that her bedroom was right up the hall. It took only a short walk, an embrace, and there she'd be, back again. In a place she'd worked so hard to escape.

She rose, an act that took as much fortitude as

152

if she was struggling out of quicksand. 'I'll see you in the morning,' she said.

Was that disappointment she saw in his eyes? she wondered. And couldn't help feeling a small dart of happiness at that possibility.

Lying in bed, she couldn't sleep, knowing that he was under the same roof. Her roof, her territory. In San Francisco, they had lived in the house he'd owned before they married, and she had never really thought of it as hers. Tonight, the circumstances were reversed, and she was the one in control. What happened next was her choice.

The possibilities tormented her.

Only when she startled awake did she realize she had actually slept. Daylight already glowed in the window. She lay in bed for a moment, wondering what had awakened her. Wondering what she would say to him. Then she heard the garage door rumble open, and the growl of a car engine backing out her driveway.

She climbed out of bed and looked out the window, just in time to see Victor's car drive away and vanish around the corner.

Eight

Jane Rizzoli awakened in the early dawn. The street outside her apartment building was still quiet; the morning commute had not yet started in earnest. She stared up at the gloom, thinking: Come on, you gotta do it. You can't keep your goddamn head stuck in the sand.

She switched on the lamp and sat on the side of the bed, stomach cramping with nausea. Though the room was chilly, she was sweating, and her T-shirt clung to her damp underarms.

It was time to face the music.

She walked barefoot into the bathroom. The package lay on the counter, where she had left it the night before, to ensure that she wouldn't forget to use it this morning. As if she needed any reminder. She opened the box, tore open the foil packet, and removed the test stick. Last night she had read the instructions several times, had practically committed them to memory. Nevertheless, she paused now to read them again. Stalling just a little longer.

At last she sat down on the toilet. Holding the test stick between her thighs, she peed on the tip, soaking it in the stream of early morning urine.

Wait two minutes, the instructions said.

She set the test stick on the countertop, and went into the kitchen. Poured herself a glass of orange juice. The same hand that could grip a weapon and squeeze off shot after shot, hitting every target, was now shaking as she lifted the glass of juice to her lips. She stared at the kitchen clock, watching the second hand make its jerky revolution. Feeling her pulse quicken as the two minutes counted down to zero. She had never been a coward, had never shrunk from facing down the enemy, but this was a different sort of fear, private and gnawing. The fear that she would make the wrong decision, and would spend the rest of her life suffering for it.

Goddamn it, Jane. Get on with it.

Suddenly angry at herself, disgusted by her own cowardice, she set down the juice and walked back to the bathroom. Did not even pause in the doorway to steel herself, but crossed straight to the counter and picked up the test stick.

She did not need to read the instructions to know what that purple line across the test window meant.

She didn't remember returning to the bedroom. She found herself sitting on the bed, the test stick on her lap. She'd never liked the color purple; it was too girly and flamboyant. Now the very sight of it made her sick. She thought she'd been fully prepared for the result, but she was not ready at all. Her legs went numb from sitting too long in the same position, yet she couldn't seem to stir. Even her brain had shut down, every thought mired by shock and indecision. She could not think of what to do next. The first impulse that came to mind was childish and utterly irrational.

I want my Mom.

She was thirty-four years old and independent. She had kicked down doors and tracked down murderers. She had killed a man. And here she was, suddenly hungry for her mother's arms.

The phone rang.

She looked at it in bewilderment, as though not recognizing what it was. On the fourth ring, she finally picked it up.

'Hey, you still at home?' said Frost. 'The team's all here.'

She struggled to focus on his words. The team. The pond. Turning to look at her bedside clock, she was startled to see it was already eight-fifteen.

'Rizzoli? They're ready to start dragging. You want us to go ahead?'

'Yeah. I'll be right there.' She hung up. The sound of the receiver thudding in the cradle was like the snap of a hypnotist's fingers. She sat up straight, the trance broken, the job once again demanding her complete focus.

She threw the test stick into the trash can. Then she got dressed, and went to work.

* * *

156

The Rat Lady.

This is what an entire lifetime gets distilled down to, thought Maura as she gazed down at the body lying on the table, its horrors concealed beneath a sheet. Nameless, faceless, your existence summed up in three words which only emphasize the indignity with which your life ended. As fodder for rodents.

It was Darren Crowe who'd dubbed the corpse last night, while they had stood surrounded by vermin skittering just beyond the range of their flashlights. He had casually tossed off the nickname to the morgue retrieval crew, and by the next morning, when Maura walked into her office, her staff was calling the victim Rat Lady as well. She knew it was just a convenient moniker for a woman who'd otherwise be known merely as Jane Doe, but Maura could not help wincing when she heard even Detective Sleeper use it. This is how we get beyond the horror, she thought. How we keep these victims at arm's length. We refer to them by a nickname, or a diagnosis, or a case file number. They don't seem like people then, so their fates cannot break our hearts.

She looked up as Crowe and Sleeper walked into the lab. Sleeper was exhausted from last night's exertion, and the harsh light of the autopsy room cruelly emphasized his baggy eyes and his sagging jowls. Beside him, Crowe was like a young lion, tan and fit and confident. Crowe was not someone you ever wanted to humiliate; beneath the veneer of an arrogant man, cruelty usually lurked. He was looking down at the corpse with his lips curled in disgust. This would not be a pleasant autopsy, and even Crowe seemed to regard the prospect of this postmortem with a hint of trepidation.

'The X-rays are hanging,' said Maura. 'Let's go over them before we begin.'

She crossed to the far wall and flipped on a switch. The light box flickered on, illuminating ghostly images of ribs and spine and pelvis. Scattered within the thorax, like a galaxy of stars spread across the lungs and heart, were bright metallic flecks.

'That looks like shotshell,' said Sleeper.

'That's what I thought, at first,' said Maura. 'But if you look here, next to this rib, you see this opaque shadow? It's almost lost against the rib's outline.'

'Metal jacket?' said Crowe.

'That's what it looks like to me.'

'So this isn't a shotshell cartridge.'

'No. This looks like Glaser ammo. Judging by the number of projectiles I see here, it's most likely a blue-tip. Copper jacket, packed with number twelve shot.'

Designed to produce far more devastating damage than a conventional bullet, Glaser-type ammo hit its target as a single unit, and then fragmented after impact. She did not need to cut open the torso to know that the damage caused by that single bullet was devastating.

She took down the chest films and clipped up

two new ones. These were somehow more disturbing images, because of what was missing from them. They were gazing at the right and left forearms. The radius and ulna, the two long bones of the forearm, normally extended from the elbow to the wrist, where they joined with the dense pebblelike carpal bones. But these arm bones ended abruptly.

'The left hand was disarticulated here, right at the joint between the styloid process of the radius and the scaphoid bone,' she said. 'The killer removed all the carpal bones, along with the hand. You can even see some of the nick marks, on the other views, where he scraped along the edge of the styloid process. He separated the hand just where the arm bones meet the wrist bones.' She pointed to the other X-ray. 'Now look at the right hand. Here, he wasn't quite as neat. He didn't slice straight across the wrist joint, and when he removed the hand, he left the hamate bone behind. You can see how the knife made a cut here. It looks like he couldn't quite find the joint, and he ended up sawing around blindly, till he found it.'

'So these hands weren't just chopped off, say, with an axe,' said Sleeper.

'No. It was done with a knife. He cut off the hands the way you'd disjoint a chicken. You flex the limb to expose the joint space, and cut through the ligaments. That way, you don't have to saw through bone itself.'

Sleeper grimaced. 'I don't think I'll be eating chicken tonight.'

'What kind of knife did he use?' asked Crowe.

'It could be a boning knife, it could be a scalpel. The stump's been too chewed up by rats, so we can't tell by the wound margin. We'll need to boil off the soft tissues and see how the cut marks look under the microscope.'

'I don't think I'll be eating soup tonight either,' said Sleeper.

Crowe glanced at his partner's ample belly. 'Maybe you ought to hang around the morgue more often. Might lose some of that tire.'

'You mean, instead of wasting my life in the gym?' Sleeper shot back.

Maura glanced at him, surprised by the retort. Even the usually tractable Sleeper could only take so much of his partner.

Crowe merely laughed, oblivious to the irritation he stirred in others. 'Hey, when you're ready to bulk up – I mean, *above* the waist – you're welcome to join me.'

'There are other X-rays to look at,' cut in Maura, pulling down the films with businesslike efficiency. Yoshima handed her the next films, and she slid them under the mounting clips. Images of the Rat Lady's head and neck glowed from the light box. Last night, looking at the corpse's face, she'd seen only raw meat, ravaged even more by hungry scavengers. But beneath the stripped flesh, the facial bones were eerily intact, except for the missing tip of the nasal bone, which had been sheared off when the killer had peeled off his trophy of flesh.

'The front teeth are missing,' said Sleeper. 'You don't think he took those, too?'

'No. These look like atrophic changes. And that's what surprises me.'

'Why?'

'These changes are usually associated with advanced age and bad dentition. But that doesn't fit a woman who otherwise appears fairly young.'

'How can you tell, with her face gone?'

'Her spine films show no evidence of the degenerative changes you usually see with age. She has no gray hairs, either on her head or her pubis. And no arcus senilis in her eyes.'

'How old would you say she is?'

'I would have put her age at no older than forty.' Maura looked at the X-ray hanging on the light box. 'But these films are more consistent with a woman of advanced age. I've never seen such severe bony resorption in anyone, much less a young woman. She wouldn't have been able to wear dentures, even if she could afford them. Clearly, this woman didn't get even basic dental care.'

'So we're not gonna have dental X-rays for comparison.'

'I doubt this woman has seen a dentist in decades.'

Sleeper sighed. 'No fingerprints. No face. No dental X-rays. We'll never I.D. her. Which may be the whole point.'

'But it doesn't explain why he cut off the feet,' she said, her gaze still fixed on the anonymous skull glowing on the light box. 'I think he did this for other reasons. Power, maybe. Rage. When you strip off a woman's face, you've taken more than just a souvenir. You've stolen the essence of who she is. You've taken her soul.'

'Yeah, well, he scraped the bottom of the barrel for this one,' said Crowe. 'Who'd want a woman with no teeth and sores all over her skin? If he's gonna start collecting faces, you'd think he'd go after one that'd look nicer on the mantelpiece.'

'Maybe he's just starting,' Sleeper said softly. 'Maybe this is his first kill.'

Maura turned to the table. 'Let's get started.'

As Sleeper and Crowe tied on their masks, she peeled back the sheet, and caught a strong whiff of decay. She'd drawn vitreous potassium levels last night, and the results told her this victim had been dead approximately thirty-six hours prior to its discovery. Rigor mortis was still present, and the limbs were not easily manipulated. Despite the meat-locker chill at the death scene, decomposition had commenced. Bacteria had begun their work, breaking down proteins, bloating air spaces. Cold temperatures had only slowed, but not stopped, the process of decay.

Though she had already seen that ruined face, the sight of it startled her anew. So too did the many skin lesions, which, under the bright lights, stood out in dark, angry nodules punctuated by rat bites. Against that background of ravaged skin, the bullet wound seemed unimpressive – just a small entry hole at the left of the sternum. Glaser bullets were designed to minimize ricochet danger, while inflicting maximum damage once they have entered the body. A clean penetration is followed by the explosion of lead pellets contained within the Glaser's copper jacket. This small wound gave no hint of the devastation inside the thorax.

'So what's this skin crud?' asked Crowe.

Maura focused on the areas undamaged by rodent teeth. The purplish nodules were scattered across both torso and extremities, and some had crusted over.

'I don't know what this is,' she said. 'It certainly seems to be systemic. It could be a drug reaction. It could be a manifestation of cancer.' She paused. 'It could also be bacterial.'

'You mean – infectious?' said Sleeper, taking a step back from the table.

'That's why I suggested the masks.'

She ran a gloved finger across one of the crusted lesions, and a few white scales flaked off. 'Some of these remind me a little of psoriasis. But the distribution is all wrong. Psoriasis usually affects primarily the elbows and knees.'

'Hey, isn't there treatment for that?' said Crowe. 'I used to see it advertised on TV. The heartbreak of psoriasis.'

'It's an inflammatory disorder, so it responds to steroid creams. Ultraviolet light therapy helps, too. But look at her dentition. This woman didn't have the money to pay for expensive creams or doctors' bills. If it's psoriasis, she probably went untreated for years.'

What a cruel affliction such a skin condition would have been, thought Maura, especially in the summertime. Even on the hottest days, she would have wanted to wear pants and long-sleeved shirts to conceal the lesions.

'Not only does our perp choose a victim who's got no teeth,' said Crowe, 'he whacks off a face with skin like this.'

'Psoriasis does tend to spare the face.'

'You think that's significant? Maybe he only sliced off the parts where the skin was okay.'

'I don't know,' she said. 'I can't begin to understand why anyone would do something like this.'

She turned her attention to the right wrist stump. White bone gleamed through raw flesh. Hungry rodents' teeth had gnawed the open wound, destroying the cut marks left by the knife, but scanning electron microscopy of the cut surface of bone might reveal the blade's characteristics. She lifted the forearm from the table, to examine the underside of the wound, and a fleck of yellow caught her eye.

'Yoshima, can you hand me the tweezers?' she said.

'What is it?' asked Crowe.

'There's some kind of fiber adhering to the wound edge.'

Yoshima moved so silently, the tweezers seemed to magically appear in her hand. She swung the magnifying lens over the wrist stump. With the tweezers, she plucked the fragment from its crust of blood and dried flesh and laid it on a tray.

Through the magnifying lens, she saw a thick coil of thread, dyed a startling shade of canary yellow.

'From her clothes?' asked Crowe.

'It looks awfully coarse for a clothing fiber.'

'Carpet, maybe?'

'Yellow carpet? I can't imagine.' She slipped the strand into an evidence bag that Yoshima was already holding open, and asked:

'Was there anything at the death scene that would match this?'

'Nothing yellow,' said Crowe.

'Yellow rope?' said Maura. 'He may have bound her wrists.'

'And then took the cut ropes away?' Sleeper shook his head. 'Weird, how this guy's so neat.'

Maura looked down at the corpse, small as a child. 'He hardly needed to bind her wrists. She would have been easy to control.'

How simple it would have been, to take her life. Arms this thin could not have struggled long against an attacker's grip; legs this short could not have outrun him.

You have already been so violated, she thought. And now my scalpel will make its mark on your flesh as well.

She worked with quiet efficiency, her knife slicing through skin and muscle. The cause of death was as obvious as the bits of shrapnel glowing on the X-ray box, and when at last the torso gaped open, and she saw the taut pericardial sac and the pockets of hemorrhage throughout the lungs, she was not surprised.

The Glaser bullet had punctured the thorax and then exploded, sending its deadly shrapnel throughout the chest. Metal had ripped through arteries and veins, punctured heart and lungs. And blood had poured into the sac that surrounded the heart, compressing it so that it could not expand, could not pump. A pericardial tamponade.

Death had been relatively swift.

The intercom buzzed. 'Dr. Isles?'

Maura turned toward the speaker. 'Yes, Louise?'

'Detective Rizzoli is on line one. Can you answer?'

Maura stripped off her gloves and crossed to the phone. 'Rizzoli?' she said.

'Hey, Doc. It looks like we need you here.'

'What is it?'

'We're at the pond. It took us a while to scoop off all the ice.'

'You've finished dragging it?'

'Yeah. We found something.'

Nine

Wind sliced across the open field, whipping Maura's coat and wool scarf as she walked out the rear cloister gate and started toward the somber gathering of cops who waited for her at the pond's edge. A layer of ice had formed over the fallen snow, and it cracked beneath her boots like a sugar crust. She felt everyone's gaze marking her progress across the field, the nuns watching from the gate behind her, and the police awaiting her approach. She was the lone figure moving across that white world, and in the stillness of that afternoon, every sound seemed magnified, from the crunch of her boots, to the rush of her own breath.

Rizzoli emerged from the knot of personnel and came forward to greet her. 'Thanks for getting here so quick.'

'So Noni was right about the duck pond.'

'Yeah. Since Camille spent a lot of time out here, it's not too surprising she thought of using the pond. The ice was still pretty thin. Probably froze over only in the last day or two.' Rizzoli looked at the water. 'We snagged it on the third pass.'

It was a small pond, a flat black oval that in the summertime would reflect clouds and blue sky and the passage of birds. At one end, cattails protruded, like ice-encrusted stalagmites. All around the perimeter, the snow was thoroughly trampled, its whiteness churned with mud.

At the water's edge, a small form lay covered by a disposable sheet. Maura crouched down beside it, and a grim-faced Detective Frost peeled back the sheet to reveal the swaddling, caked in wet mud.

'It felt like it was weighed down with rocks,' said Frost. 'That's why it's been sitting on the bottom. We haven't unwrapped it yet. Thought we'd wait for you.'

Maura pulled off her wool gloves and pulled on latex ones. They offered no protection against the cold, and her fingers quickly chilled as she peeled back the outer layer of muslin. Two fist-sized stones dropped out. The next layer was equally soaked, but not muddy. It was a woolen blanket of powder blue. A color one would swaddle an infant in, she thought. A blanket to keep him safe and warm.

By now her fingers were numb and clumsy. She peeled back a corner of the blanket, just enough to catch a glimpse of a foot. Tiny, almost doll-like, the skin a dusky and marbled blue.

That was all she needed to see.

She covered it again, with the sheet. Rising to

her feet, she looked at Rizzoli. 'Let's move it directly to the morgue. We'll finish unwrapping it there.'

Rizzoli merely nodded, and gazed down in silence at the tiny bundle. The wet wrappings were already starting to crust over in the icy wind.

It was Frost who spoke. 'How could she do it? Just toss her baby in the water like that?'

Maura stripped off the latex gloves and thrust numb fingers into the woolen ones. She thought of the light blue blanket wrapped around the infant. Warm wool, like her gloves. Camille could have wrapped the baby in anything – newspapers, old sheets, rags – but she had chosen to wrap it in a blanket, as though to protect it, to insulate it from the frigid water of the pond.

'I mean, drowning her own kid,' said Frost. 'She'd have to be out of her mind.'

'The infant may already have been dead.'

'Okay, so she killed it first. She'd still have to be crazy.'

'We can't assume anything. Not until the autopsy.' Maura glanced toward the abbey. Three nuns stood like dark-robed wraiths beneath the archway, watching them. She said to Rizzoli: 'Have you told Mary Clement yet?'

Rizzoli didn't answer. Her gaze was still fixed on what the pond had yielded up to them. It took only one pair of hands to slip the bundle into the oversize body bag, to seal it with an efficient tug of the zipper. She winced at the sound.

Maura asked, 'Do the sisters know?'

At last Rizzoli looked at her. 'They've been told what we found.'

'They must have an idea who the father is.'

'They deny it's even possible she was pregnant.'

'But the evidence is right here.'

Rizzoli gave a snort. 'Faith is stronger than evidence.'

Faith in what? Maura wondered. A young woman's virtue? Was there any house of cards more rickety than the belief in human chastity?

They fell silent as the body bag was carried away. There was no need to bring a stretcher through the snow; the attendant had scooped the bag into his arms as tenderly as though he was lifting his own child, and now he walked with grim purpose across the windy field, toward the abbey.

Maura's cell phone rang, violating the mournful silence. She flipped it open and answered quietly: 'Dr. Isles.'

'I'm sorry I had to leave without saying goodbye this morning.'

She felt her face flush and her heartbeat go into double time. 'Victor.'

'I had to get to my meeting in Cambridge. I didn't want to wake you. I hope you didn't think I was running out on you.'

'Actually, I did.'

'Can we meet later, for dinner?'

She paused, suddenly aware that Rizzoli was watching her. Aware, too, of her own physical reaction to Victor's voice. The quickened pulse, the happy anticipation. Already he's worked his

170

way back into my life, she thought. Already, I'm thinking of the possibilities.

She turned from Rizzoli's gaze, and her voice dropped to a murmur. 'I don't know when I'll be free. There's so much going on right now.'

'You can tell me all about your day over dinner.'

'It's already turning into a doozy.'

'You have to eat sometime, Maura. Can I take you out? Your favorite restaurant?'

She answered too quickly, too eagerly. 'No, I'll meet you at my house. I'll try to be home by seven.'

'I don't expect you to cook for me.'

'Then I'll let you do the cooking.'

He laughed. 'Brave woman.'

'If I'm late, you can get in through the side door to the garage. You probably know where the key is.'

'Don't tell me you're still hiding it in that old shoe.'

'No one's found it yet. I'll see you tonight.'

She hung up, and turned to find that now both Rizzoli and Frost were watching her.

'Hot date?' asked Rizzoli.

'At my age, I'm lucky to have any date,' she said, and slipped the phone in her purse. 'I'll see you both in the morgue.'

As she tramped back across the field, following the trail of broken snow, she felt their gazes on her back. It was a relief to finally push through the rear gate and retreat behind abbey walls. But only a few steps into the courtyard, she heard her name called.

She turned to see Father Brophy emerge from a doorway. He walked toward her, a solemn figure in black. Against the gray and dreary sky, his eyes were a startling shade of blue.

'Mother Mary Clement would like to speak to you,' he said.

'Detective Rizzoli is the person she should probably talk to.'

'She'd prefer to speak to you.'

'Why?'

'Because you're not a policeman. At least you seem willing to listen to her concerns. To understand.'

'Understand what, Father?'

He paused. The wind flapped their coats and stung their faces.

'That faith isn't something to be ridiculed,' he said.

And that was why Mary Clement did not want to talk to Rizzoli, who could not hide her skepticism, her disdain toward the church. Something as deeply personal as faith should not be subjected to another person's contempt.

'This is important to her,' said Father Brophy. 'Please.'

She followed him into the building, down the dim and drafty hallway, to the Abbess's office. Mary Clement was seated behind her desk. She looked up as they walked in, and the eyes staring through those thick lenses were clearly angry.

'Sit down, Dr. Isles.'

Although Holy Innocents Academy was years

behind Maura, the sight of an irate nun could still rattle her, and she quietly complied, sinking into the chair like a guilty schoolgirl. Father Brophy stood off to the side, a silent observer of this coming ordeal.

'We were never told the reason for this search,' said Mary Clement. 'You've disrupted our lives. Violated our privacy. From the beginning, we've cooperated in every way, yet you've treated us as though we're the enemy. You owed us the courtesy of at least telling us what you were searching for.'

'I do think that Detective Rizzoli is the one you should speak to about this.'

'But you're the one who initiated the search.'

'I only told them what I found on autopsy. That Sister Camille recently gave birth. It was Detective Rizzoli's decision to search the abbey.'

'Without telling us why.'

'Police investigations are usually played close to the vest.'

'It's because you didn't trust us. Isn't that right?'

Maura looked into Mary Clement's accusing gaze and found she could not respond with anything but the truth. 'We had no choice but to proceed with caution.'

Rather than make her angrier, that honest answer seemed to defuse the Abbess's outrage. Looking suddenly drained, she leaned back in her chair, transforming into the frail and elderly woman she really was. 'What a world it is, when even we cannot be trusted.'

'Like everyone else, Reverend Mother.'

'But that's just it, Dr. Isles. We are not like everyone else.' She said this without any note of superiority. Rather, it was sadness that Maura heard in her voice, and bewilderment. 'We would have helped you. We would have cooperated, if we'd known what you were looking for.'

'You really had no idea that Camille was pregnant?'

'How could we? When Detective Rizzoli told me this morning, I didn't believe it. I still can't believe it.'

'I'm afraid the proof was in the pond.'

The Abbess seemed to shrink even smaller into her chair. Her gaze fell on her arthritis-gnarled hands. She was silent, staring at those hands as though they did not belong to her. Softly she said: 'How could we not have known?'

'Pregnancies can be concealed. Teenage girls have been known to hide their condition from their own mothers. Some women deny it even to themselves, until the moment they give birth. Camille herself may have been in denial. I have to admit, I was completely taken aback at autopsy. It wasn't at all what I expected to find in . . .'

'A nun,' Mary Clement said. She looked straight at Maura.

'That's not to say nuns aren't human.'

A faint smile. 'Thank for you acknowledging that.'

'And she was so young—'

'Do you think only the young struggle with temptation?'

174

Maura thought of her restless night. Of Victor, sleeping right down the hall.

'All our lives,' said Mary Clement, 'we're enticed by one thing or another. The temptations change, of course. When you're young, it's a handsome boy. Then it's sweets or food. Or, when you get old and tired, just the chance to sleep an extra hour in the morning. So many petty desires, and we're just as vulnerable to them as everyone else, only we're not allowed to admit it. Our vows set us apart. Wearing the veil may be a joy, Dr. Isles. But perfection is a burden that none of us can live up to.'

'Least of all, such a young woman.'

'It gets no easier with age.'

'Camille was only twenty. She must have had some doubts about taking her final vows.'

Mary Clement did not answer at first. She stared out the window, which faced only a barren wall. A view that would remind her, every time she glanced out, that her world was enclosed by stone. She said, 'I was twenty-one when I took my final vows.'

'And did you have doubts?'

'Not a single one.' She looked at Maura. 'I knew.'

'How?'

'Because God spoke to me.'

Maura said nothing.

'I know what you're thinking,' Mary Clement said. 'That only psychotics hear voices. Only psychotics hear the angels speak to them. You're a doctor, and you probably see everything with a scientist's eye. You'll tell me it was just a dream. Or a chemical imbalance. A temporary bout of schizophrenia. I know all the theories. I know what they say about Joan of Arc – that they burned a madwoman at the stake. It's what you're thinking, isn't it?'

'I'm afraid I'm not religious.'

'But you were, once?'

'I was raised Catholic. It's what my adoptive parents believed.'

'Then you're familiar with the lives of the saints. Many of them heard God's voice. How do you explain that?'

Maura hesitated, knowing that what she said next would likely offend the Abbess. 'Auditory hallucinations are often interpreted as religious experiences.'

Mary Clement did not seem to take offense, as Maura had expected. She simply gazed back, her eyes steady. 'Do I seem insane to you?'

'Not at all.'

'Yet here I am, telling you that I once heard the voice of God.' Her gaze wandered, once again, to the window. To the gray wall, its stones glistening with ice. 'You're only the second person I've told this to, because I know what people think. I would not have believed it myself, if it hadn't happened to me. When you're only eighteen years old, and He calls you, what choice do you have, but to listen?'

She leaned back in her chair. Said, softly: 'I had

a sweetheart, you know. A man who wanted to marry me.'

'Yes,' said Maura. 'You told me.'

'He didn't understand. No one understood why a young woman would want to hide from life. That's what he called it. Hiding, like a coward. Surrendering my will to God. Of course, he tried to change my mind. So did my mother. But I knew what I was doing. I knew it from the moment I was called. Standing in my backyard, listening to the crickets. I heard His voice, clear as a bell. And I knew.' She looked at Maura, who was shifting in her chair, anxious to break off this conversation. Uncomfortable with this talk of divine voices.

Maura looked at her watch. 'Reverend Mother, I'm afraid I have to leave.'

'You wonder why I'm telling you this.'

'Yes, I do.'

'I've told this to only one other person. Do you know who that was?'

'No.'

'Sister Camille.'

Maura looked into the Abbess's distorted blue eyes. 'Why Camille?'

'Because she heard the voice, too. That's why she came to us. She was raised in an extremely wealthy family. Grew up in a mansion in Hyannisport, not far from the Kennedys. But she was called to this life, just as I was. When you're called, Dr. Isles, you know you've been blessed, and you answer with joy in your heart. She had no doubts about taking her vows. She was fully committed to this order.'

'Then how do we explain the pregnancy? How did that happen?'

'Detective Rizzoli has already asked that question. But all she wanted to know was names and dates. Which repairmen came to the compound? Which month did Camille leave to visit her family? The police care only about concrete details, not about spiritual matters. Not about Camille's calling.'

'She did become pregnant. Either it was a moment of temptation, or it was rape.'

The Abbess was silent for a moment, her gaze dropping to her hands. She said, quietly: 'There is a third explanation, Dr. Isles.'

Maura frowned. 'What would that be?'

'You'll scoff at this, I know. You're a doctor. You probably rely on your laboratory tests, on what you can see under the microscope. But haven't there been times when you've seen the inexplicable? When a patient who should be dead suddenly revives? Haven't you witnessed miracles?'

'Every physician has been surprised at least a few times in his career.'

'Not just surprised. I'm talking about something that astounds you. Something that science can't explain.'

Maura thought back to her years as an intern at San Francisco General. 'There was a woman, with pancreatic cancer.'

'That's incurable, isn't it?'

'Yes. It's almost as good as a death sentence. She shouldn't have lived. When I first saw her, she was considered terminal. Already confused and jaundiced. The doctors had decided to stop feeding her, because she was so close to death. I remember the orders on the chart, to simply keep her comfortable. That's all you can do, at the end, is dull their pain. I thought her death was a matter of days.'

'But she surprised you.'

'She woke up one morning and told the nurse she was hungry. Four weeks later, she went home.'

The Abbess nodded. 'A miracle.'

'No, Reverend Mother.' Maura met her gaze. 'Spontaneous remission.'

'That's just a way of saying you don't know what happened.'

'Remissions do occur. Cancers shrink on their own. Or the diagnosis was wrong to begin with.'

'Or it was something else. Something science can't explain.'

'You want me to say it was a miracle?'

'I want you to consider other possibilities. So many people who've recovered from near death report they saw a bright light. Or they saw their loved ones, telling them it's not their time. How do you explain such universal visions?'

'The hallucinations of an oxygen-deprived brain.'

'Or evidence of the divine.'

'I would love to find such evidence. It would be

179

a comfort to know there's something beyond this physical life. But I can't accept it on faith alone. That's what you're getting at, isn't it? That Camille's pregnancy was some sort of miracle? Another example of the divine.'

'You say you don't believe in miracles, but you can't explain why your patient with pancreatic cancer lived.'

'There's not always an easy explanation.'

'Because medical science doesn't completely understand death. Isn't that true?'

'But we do understand conception. We know it requires a sperm and an egg. That's simple biology, Reverend Mother. I don't believe in immaculate conception. What I do believe is that Camille had a sexual encounter. It may have been forced, or it may have been consensual. But her child was conceived in the usual way. And the father's identity could well have a bearing on her murder.'

'What if no father is ever found?'

'We'll have the child's DNA. We only need the father's name.'

'You have such confidence in your science, Dr. Isles. It's the answer to everything!'

Maura rose from her chair. 'But at least those answers, I can believe in.'

Father Brophy escorted Maura from the office, and walked with her, back up the dim corridor, their steps creaking on well-worn floorboards.

He said, 'We might as well bring up the subject now, Dr. Isles.'

'Which subject is that?'

He stopped and looked at her. 'Whether the child is mine.' He met her gaze without flinching; she was the one who wanted to turn away, to retreat from the intensity of his gaze.

'It's what you're wondering, isn't it?' he said.

'You can understand why.'

'Yes. As you said just a moment ago, the unavoidable laws of biology require a sperm and an egg.'

'You're the one man who has regular access to this abbey. You say Mass. You hear confession.'

'Yes.'

'You know their most intimate secrets.'

'Only what they choose to tell me.'

'You're a symbol of authority.'

'Some view priests that way.'

'To a young novice, you certainly would be.'

'And that makes me automatically suspect?'

'You wouldn't be the first priest to break your vows.'

He sighed, and for the first time his gaze dropped from hers. Not in avoidance, but a sad nod of acknowledgment. 'It's not easy, these days. The looks people give us, the jokes behind our backs. When I say Mass, I look at the faces in my church, and I know what they're thinking. They wonder whether I touch little boys, or covet young girls. They're all wondering, just as you are. And you assume the worst.'

'Is the child yours, Father Brophy?'

The blue eyes were once more focused on her.

His gaze was absolutely steady. 'No, it's not. I have never broken my vows.'

'You understand, don't you, that we can't just take your word for it?'

'No, I could be lying, couldn't I?' Though he didn't raise his voice, she heard the note of anger. He drew closer, and she stood very still, resisting the urge to retreat. 'I could be compounding one sin with another, and yet another. Where do you see that spiral, that chain of sins, leading to? Lying. Abuse of a nun. Murder?'

'The police have to look at all motives. Even yours.'

'And you'll want my DNA, I suppose.'

'It would eliminate you as the baby's father.'

'Or it would point to me as a prime murder suspect.'

'It could work either way, depending on the results.'

'What do *you* think it will show?'

'I have no idea.'

'But you must have a hunch. You're standing here, looking at me. Do you see a murderer?'

'I trust only the evidence.'

'Numbers and facts. That's all you believe in.'

'Yes.'

'And if I told you that I'm perfectly willing to submit my DNA? That I'll give you a blood sample right here and now, if you're ready to take it?'

'It doesn't require a blood sample. Just a swab from the mouth.'

'A swab, then. I just want to be clear that I'm volunteering for this.'

'I'll tell Detective Rizzoli. She'll collect it.'

'Will that change your mind? About whether I'm guilty?'

'As I said, I'll know when I see the results.' She opened the door and walked out.

He followed her into the courtyard. He was not wearing a coat, yet he seemed impervious to the cold, his attention focused only on her.

'You said you were raised Catholic,' he said.

'I went to a Catholic high school. Holy Innocents, in San Francisco.'

'Yet you believe only in your blood tests. In your science.'

'What should I rely on instead?'

'Instincts? Faith?'

'In you? Just because you're a priest?'

'*Just* because?' He shook his head and gave a sad laugh, his breath white in the chill air. 'I guess that answers my question.'

'I don't make guesses. I don't assume anything about other human beings, because too often, they surprise you.'

They reached the front gate. He opened it for her, and she stepped out. The gate swung shut between them, suddenly separating his world from hers.

'You know that man who collapsed on the sidewalk?' he said. 'The one we did CPR on?'

'Yes.'

'He's alive. I went to visit him this morning. He's awake and talking.'

'I'm glad to hear that.'

'You didn't think he'd make it.'

'The odds were against him.'

'So you see? Sometimes the numbers, the statistics, are wrong.'

She turned to leave.

'Dr. Isles!' he called. 'You grew up in the church. Isn't there anything left of your faith?'

She looked back at him. 'Faith requires no proof,' she said. 'But I do.'

The autopsy of a child was a task every pathologist dreaded. As Maura pulled on gloves and readied her instruments, she avoided looking at the tiny bundle on the table, trying to distance herself, as long as possible, from the sad reality of what she was about to confront. Except for the clang of instruments, the room was silent. None of the participants standing around the table felt like saying a word.

Maura had always set a respectful tone in her lab. As a medical student, she'd observed the autopsies of patients who had died under her care, and although the pathologists performing those postmortems regarded the subjects as anonymous strangers, she had known those patients while they were alive, and could not look at them, laid out on the table, without hearing their voices or remembering how awareness had lit up their eyes. The autopsy lab was not the place to crack jokes or discuss last night's date, and she didn't tolerate such behavior. One stern look from her could subdue even the most disrespectful cop. She knew that they were not heartless, that humor was how they coped with the darkness of their jobs, but she expected them to check their humor at the door, or they could count on sharp words from her.

Such words were never needed when a child lay on the table.

She looked across at the two detectives. Barry Frost, as usual, had a sickly pallor to his face, and he stood slightly back from the table, as though poised to make an escape. Today, it was not foul smells that would make this postmortem difficult; it was the age of the victim. Rizzoli stood beside him, her expression resolute, her petite frame almost lost in a surgical gown that was several sizes too large. She stood right up against the table, a position that announced: I'm ready. I can deal with anything. The same attitude Maura had seen among women surgical residents. Men might call them bitches, but she recognized them for what they were: embattled women who'd worked so hard to prove themselves in a man's profession that they actually take on a masculine swagger. Rizzoli had the swagger down pat, but her face did not quite match the fearless posture. It was white and tense, the skin beneath her eyes smudged with fatigue.

Yoshima had angled the light onto the bundle, and stood waiting by the instrument tray.

The blanket was soaked, and icy pond water trickled off as she gently peeled it away, revealing another layer of wrapping. The tiny foot that she'd seen earlier now lay exposed, poking out from beneath wet linen. Clinging to the infant's form like a shroud was a white pillowcase, closed with safety pins. Flecks of pink adhered to the fabric.

Maura reached for the tweezers, picked off the bits of pink, and dropped them onto a small tray.

'What is that stuff?' asked Frost.

'It looks like confetti,' said Rizzoli.

Maura slipped the tweezers deep into a wet fold and came up with a twig. 'It's not confetti,' she said. 'These are dried flowers.'

The significance of this finding brought another silence to the room. A symbol of love, she thought. Of mourning. She remembered how moved she had been, years ago, when she'd learned that Neanderthals buried their dead with flowers. It was evidence of their grief, and therefore, their humanity. This child, she thought, was mourned. Wrapped in linen, sprinkled with dried flower petals, and swaddled in a wool blanket. Not a disposal, but a burial. A farewell.

She focused on the foot, poking out doll-like from its shroud. The skin of the sole was wrinkled from immersion in fresh water, but there was no obvious decomposition, no marbling of veins. The pond had been near freezing temperatures, and the body could have remained in a state of near-preservation for weeks. Time of death, she thought, would be difficult, if not impossible, to determine.

She set aside the tweezers and removed the four

safety pins closing the bottom of the pillowcase. They made soft musical ticks as she dropped them onto a tray. Lifting the fabric, she gently peeled it upwards, and both legs appeared, knees bent, thighs apart like a small frog.

The size was consistent with a full-term fetus.

She exposed the genitals, and then a swollen length of umbilical cord, tied off with red satin ribbon. She suddenly remembered the nuns sitting at the dining table, their gnarled hands reaching for dried flowers and ribbons to make into sachets. A sachet-baby, she thought. Sprinkled with flowers and tied with ribbon.

'It's a boy,' Rizzoli said, and her voice suddenly cracked.

Maura looked up and saw that Rizzoli had paled even more, that she was now leaning against the table, as though to steady herself.

'Do you need to step out?'

Rizzoli swallowed. 'It's just . . .'

'What?'

'Nothing. I'm fine.'

'These are hard to take, I know. Kids are always hard. If you want to sit down—'

'I told you, I'm fine.'

The worst was yet to come.

Maura eased the pillowcase up over the chest, gently extending first one arm and then the other so they would not be snagged by the wet fabric. The hands were perfectly formed, tiny fingers designed to reach for a mother's face, to grasp a mother's lock of hair. Next to the face, it is the

187

hands that are most recognizably human, and it was almost painful to look at them.

Maura reached inside the pillowcase to support the back of the head as she pulled off the last of the fabric.

Instantly, she knew something was wrong.

Her hand was cradling a skull that did not feel normal, did not feel human. She paused, her throat suddenly dry. With a sense of dread, she peeled off the fabric, and the infant's head emerged.

Rizzoli gasped and jerked away from the table.

'Jesus,' said Frost. 'What the hell happened to it?'

Too stunned to speak, Maura could only gaze down in horror at the skull, gaping open, the brain exposed. At the face, folded in like a squashed rubber mask.

A metal tray suddenly toppled and crashed.

Maura looked up just in time to see Jane Rizzoli, her face drained white, slowly crumple to the floor.

Ten

'I don't want to go to the ER.'

Maura wiped away the last of the blood and frowned at the inch-long laceration on Rizzoli's forehead. 'I'm not a plastic surgeon. I can stitch this up, but I can't guarantee there won't be a scar.'

'Just do it, okay? I don't want to sit for hours in some hospital waiting room. They'd probably just sic a medical student on me, anyway.'

Maura wiped the skin with Betadine, then reached for a vial of Xylocaine and a syringe. 'I'm going to numb your skin first. It'll sting a little bit, but after that, you shouldn't feel a thing.'

Rizzoli lay perfectly still on the couch, her eyes focused on the ceiling. Though she didn't flinch as the needle pierced her skin, she closed her hand into a fist and kept it tightly balled as the local anesthetic was injected. Not a word of complaint, not a whimper escaped her lips. Already she'd been humiliated by the fall in the lab. Humiliated even further when she'd been too dizzy to walk, and Frost had carried her like a bride into Maura's office. Now she lay with her jaw squared, grimly determined not to show any weakness.

As Maura pierced the edges of the laceration with the curved suture needle, Rizzoli asked, in a perfectly calm voice: 'Are you going to tell me what happened to that baby?'

'Nothing happened to it.'

'It's not exactly normal. Jesus, it's missing half its head.'

'It was born that way,' Maura said, snipping off suture and tying a knot. Sewing skin was like stitching a living fabric, and she was simply a tailor, bringing the edges together, knotting the thread. 'The baby is anencephalic.'

'What does that mean?'

'Its brain never developed.'

'There's more wrong with it than just a missing brain. It looked like the whole top of his head was chopped off.' Rizzoli swallowed. 'And the face . . .'

'It's all part of the same birth defect. The brain develops from a sheath of cells called the neural tube. If the top of the tube fails to close the way it's supposed to, the baby will be born missing a major part of the brain, the skull, even the scalp. That's what *anencephalic* means. Without a head.'

'You ever seen one like that before?'

'Only in a medical museum. But it's not that rare. It happens in about one in a thousand births.'

'Why?'

'No one knows.'

'Then it could – it could happen to any baby?'

'That's right.' Maura tied off the last stitch and snipped the excess suture. 'This child was born gravely malformed. If it wasn't already dead at birth, then it almost certainly died soon after.'

'So Camille didn't drown it.'

'I'll check the kidneys for diatoms. That would tell us if the child died by drowning. But I don't think this is a case of infanticide. I think the baby died a natural death.'

'Thank God,' Rizzoli said softly. 'If that thing had lived . . .'

'It wouldn't have.' Maura finished taping a bandage to the wound and stripped off her gloves. 'All done, Detective. The stitches need to come out in five days. You can drop by here and I'll snip them for you. But I still think you need to see a doctor.'

'You *are* a doctor.'

'I work on dead people. Remember?'

'You just sewed me up fine.'

'I'm not talking about putting in a few stitches. I'm concerned about what else is going on.'

'What do you mean?'

Maura leaned forward, her gaze tight on Rizzoli's. 'You fainted, remember?'

'I didn't eat lunch. And that thing – the baby – it shocked me.'

'It shocked us all. But you're the one who keeled over.'

'I've just never seen anything like it.'

'Jane, you've seen all sorts of terrible things in

191

that autopsy room. We've seen them together, smelled them together. You've always had a strong stomach. The boy cops, I have to keep an eye on them, because they'll drop like rocks. But you've always managed to hang in there. Until now.'

'Maybe I'm not as tough as you thought.'

'No, I think there's something wrong. Isn't there?'

'Like what?'

'You got light-headed a few days ago.'

Rizzoli shrugged. 'I've gotta start eating breakfast.'

'Why haven't you? Is it nausea? And I've noticed you're in the bathroom practically every ten minutes. You went in there twice, just while I was setting up the lab.'

'What the hell is this, anyway? An interrogation?'

'You need to see a doctor. You need a complete physical and a blood count to rule out anemia, at the very least.'

'I just need to get some fresh air.' Rizzoli sat up, then quickly dropped her head in her hands. 'God, this is some friggin' headache.'

'You whacked your head pretty hard on the floor.'

'It's been whacked before.'

'But I'm more concerned about why you fainted. Why you've been so tired.'

Rizzoli lifted her head and looked at her. In that instant, Maura had her answer. She had already suspected it, and now she saw it confirmed in the other woman's eyes.

'My life is *so* fucked up,' Rizzoli whispered.

The tears startled Maura. She had never seen Rizzoli cry, had thought this woman was too strong, too stubborn, to ever break down, yet tears were now trickling down her cheeks, and Maura was so taken aback she could only watch in silence.

The knock on the door startled them both.

Frost stuck his head into the office. 'How're we doing in here . . .' His voice trailed off when he saw his partner's damp face. 'Hey. Hey, are you okay?'

Rizzoli gave an angry swipe at her tears. 'I'm fine.'

'What's going on?'

'I said I'm *fine!*'

'Detective Frost,' said Maura, 'We need time alone. Could you give us some privacy, please?'

Frost flushed. 'Sorry,' he murmured, and withdrew, softly closing the door.

'I shouldn't have yelled at him,' said Rizzoli. 'But sometimes, he's so goddamn dense.'

'He's just concerned about you.'

'Yeah, I know. I know. At least he's one of the good guys.' Her voice broke. Fighting not to cry, she balled her hands into fists, but the tears came anyway, and then the sobs. Choked, embarrassed sobs that she could not hold back. It disturbed Maura to witness the disintegration of a woman whose strength had always impressed her. If Jane Rizzoli could fall apart, then anyone could.

Rizzoli suddenly slapped her fists on her knees

and took a few deep breaths. When at last she raised her head, the tears were still there, but pride had set her face in a rigid mask.

'It's the goddamn hormones. They're screwing around with my head.'

'How long have you known?'

'I don't know. A while, I guess. I finally did a home pregnancy test this morning. But I've sort of known for weeks. I could feel the difference. And I didn't get my period.'

'How late are you?'

Rizzoli shrugged. 'At least a month.'

Maura leaned back in her chair. Now that Rizzoli had her emotions under control, Maura could retreat into her role of clinician. The cool-headed doctor, ready with practical advice. 'You have plenty of time to decide.'

Rizzoli gave a snort and wiped her hand across her face. 'There's nothing to decide.'

'What are you going to do?'

'I can't have it. You know I can't.'

'Why not?'

Rizzoli gave her a look reserved for imbeciles. 'What would I do with a baby?'

'What everyone else does.'

'Can you see me being a mother?' Rizzoli laughed. 'I'd be lousy at it. The kid wouldn't survive a month in my care.'

'Children are amazingly resilient.'

'Yeah, well, I'm no good with them.'

'You were very good with that little girl Noni.'

'Right.'

194

'You were, Jane. And she responded to you. She ignored me, and she shrinks from her own mother. But you two were like instant pals.'

'It doesn't mean I'm the mommy type. Babies freak me out. I don't know what to do with 'em, except to hand 'em over to someone else, quick.' She released a sharp breath, as though that was that. Issue settled. 'I can't do it. I just can't.' She rose from the chair and crossed to the door.

'Have you told Agent Dean?'

Rizzoli halted, her hand on the knob.

'Jane?'

'No, I haven't told him.'

'Why not?'

'It's kind of hard to have a conversation when we hardly see each other.'

'Washington's not the other end of the earth. It's even in the same time zone. You could try picking up the phone. He'd want to know.'

'Maybe he doesn't. Maybe it's just one of those complications he'd rather not hear about.'

Maura sighed. 'Okay, I admit it, I don't know him very well. But in the short time we all worked together, he struck me as someone who takes his responsibilities seriously.'

'Responsibilities?' Rizzoli finally turned and looked at her. 'Oh, right. That's what I am. That's what this baby is. And he's just enough of a Boy Scout to do his *duty*.'

'I didn't mean it that way.'

'But you're absolutely right. Gabriel *would* do his duty. Well, to hell with that. I don't want to be some man's problem, some man's responsibility. Besides, it's not his decision. It's mine. I'm the one who'd have to raise it.'

'You haven't even given him a chance.'

'A chance to what? Get down on his knee and propose to me?' Rizzoli laughed.

'Why is that so far-fetched? I've seen you two together. I've seen how he looks at you. There's more going on than just a one-night stand.'

'Yeah. It was a two-week stand.'

'That's all it was to you?'

'What else could we manage? He's in Washington and I'm here.' She shook her head in amazement. 'Jesus, I can't believe I got caught. This is only supposed to happen to dumb chicks.' She stopped. Laughed. 'Right. So what does that make me?'

'Definitely not dumb.'

'Unlucky. And too goddamn fertile.'

'When was the last time you spoke to him?'

'Last week. He called me.'

'You didn't think to tell him then?'

'I wasn't sure then.'

'But you are now.'

'And I'm still not going to tell him. I have to choose what's right for me, not for anyone else.'

'What are you afraid he'll say?'

'That he'll talk me into screwing up my life. That he'll tell me to keep it.'

'Is that really what you're afraid of? Or are you more afraid that he won't want it? That he'll reject you before you get the chance to reject him?'

Rizzoli looked at Maura. 'You know what, Doc?'

'What?'

'Sometimes, you don't know what the hell you're talking about.'

And sometimes, thought Maura as she watched Rizzoli walk out of the office, I hit the bull's-eye.

Rizzoli and Frost sat in the car, the heater blowing cold air, snowflakes fluttering onto the windshield. The gray skies matched her mood. She sat shivering in the claustrophobic gloom of the car, and every snowflake that fell on the window was another opaque chip cutting off her view. Closing her in, burying her.

Frost said, 'You feeling better?'

'Got a headache. That's all.'

'You sure you don't want me to drive you to the ER?'

'I just need to pick up some Tylenol.'

'Yeah. Okay.' He put the car into gear, then changed his mind and shifted back into park. He looked at her. 'Rizzoli?'

'What?'

'You ever want to talk about anything – anything at all, I don't mind listening.'

She didn't respond, just turned her gaze to the windshield. To the snowflakes forming a white filigree on the glass.

'We've been together what, two years now? Seems to me, you don't tell me a lot about what's going on in your life,' he said. 'I think I probably talk your ear off about me and Alice. Every fight we have, you hear about it, whether you want to or not. You never tell me to shut up, so I figure you don't mind. But you know, I just realized something. You do a lot of listening, but you hardly ever talk about yourself.'

'There's nothing much to say.'

He thought this over for a moment. Then he said, sounding almost embarrassed: 'I've never seen you cry before.'

She shrugged. 'Okay. Now you have.'

'Look, we haven't always gotten along great—'

'You don't think so?'

Frost flushed, as he always did when caught in an awkward moment. The guy had a face like a stoplight, turning red at the first hint of embarrassment. 'What I mean is, we're not, like, *buddies*.'

'What, you want to be buddies now?'

'I wouldn't mind.'

'Okay, we're buddies,' she said brusquely. 'Come on, let's get going.'

'Rizzoli?'

'What?'

'I'm here, okay? That's all I want you to know.'

She blinked, and turned to her side window, so he wouldn't see the effect his words had on her. For the second time in an hour, she felt tears coming. Goddamn hormones. She didn't know why Frost's words should make her cry. Maybe it was just the fact he was showing such kindness to her. In truth, he had always been kind to her, but she was exquisitely sensitive to it now, and a small part of her wished that Frost was as thick as a plank and unaware of her turmoil. His words made her feel vulnerable and exposed, and that was not the way she wanted to be regarded. It was not the way you earned a partner's respect.

She took a breath and lifted her jaw. The moment had passed, and the tears were gone. She could look at him and manage a semblance of her old attitude.

'Look, I need that Tylenol,' she said. 'We gonna sit here all day?'

He nodded and put the car into gear. The windshield wipers whisked snow off the glass, opening up a view of sky and white streets. All through a blistering summer, she'd been looking forward to winter, to the purity of snow. Now, staring at this bleak cityscape, she thought she would never again curse the heat of August.

On a busy Friday night, you couldn't swing a cat in the bar at J. P. Doyle's without hitting a cop. Located just down the street from Boston PD's Jamaica Plain substation, and only ten minutes from police headquarters at Schroeder Plaza, Doyle's was where off-duty cops usually gathered for beer and conversation. So when Rizzoli walked into Doyle's that evening for dinner, she fully expected to see a crowd of familiar faces. What she didn't expect to see was Vince Korsak sitting at the bar, sipping an ale. Korsak was a retired detective from the Newton PD, and Doyle's was out of his usual territory.

He spotted her as she came in the door and gave her a wave. 'Hey, Rizzoli! Long time, no see.' He pointed to the bandage on her forehead. 'What happened to you?'

'Aw, nothing. Had a little slip in the morgue and needed a few stitches. So what're you doing in the neighborhood?'

'I'm moving in here.'

'What?'

'Just signed a lease on an apartment down the street.'

'What about your house in Newton?'

'Long story. Look, you want some dinner? I'll tell you all about it.' He grabbed his ale. 'Let's get a booth in the other room. These asshole smokers are polluting my lungs.'

'Never bothered you before.'

'Yeah, well, that's when I used to *be* one of those assholes.'

Nothing like a coronary to turn a chain-smoker into a health freak, thought Rizzoli as she followed in the wake left by Korsak's substantial frame. Although he'd lost weight since his heart attack, he was still heavy enough to double for a linebacker, which was what he reminded her of as he bulldozed through the Friday evening crowd.

They stepped through a doorway into the non-smoking section, where the air was marginally clearer. He chose a booth beneath the Irish flag. On the wall were framed and yellowed clippings from the *Boston Globe*, articles about mayors

200

long gone, politicians long dead. The Kennedys and Tip O'Neill and other fine sons of Eire, many of whom had served with Boston's finest.

Korsak slid onto the wooden bench, squeezing his generous girth behind the table. Heavy as he was, he still looked thinner than he'd been back in August, when they had worked a multiple homicide investigation together. She could not look at him now without remembering their summer together. The buzzing of flies among the trees, the horrors that the woods had yielded up, lying among the leaves. She still had flashbacks to that month when two killers had joined to enact their terrible fantasies on wealthy couples. Korsak was one of the few people who knew the impact that the case had had on her. Together, they had fought monsters and survived, and they had a bond between them, forged in the crisis of an investigation.

Yet there was so much about Korsak that repelled her.

She watched him take a gulp of ale, and flick his tongue over the mustache of foam. Once again she was struck by his simian appearance. The heavy eyebrows, the thick nose, the bristly black hair covering his arms. And the way he walked, with thick arms swinging, shoulders rolled forward, the way an ape walks. She knew his marriage was troubled, and that, since his retirement, he had far too much time on his hands. Looking at him now, she felt a twinge of guilt, because he had left several messages on her phone, suggesting they meet for dinner, but she'd been too busy to return his calls.

A waitress came by, recognized Rizzoli, and said, 'You want your usual Sam Adams, Detective?'

Rizzoli looked at Korsak's glass of beer. He had spilled it on his shirt, leaving a trail of wet spots.

'Uh, no,' she said. 'Just a Coke.'

'You ready to order?'

Rizzoli opened the menu. She had no stomach for beer tonight, but she was starved. 'I'll have a chef's salad with extra Thousand Island dressing. Fish and chips. And a side of onion rings. Can you bring it all at the same time? Oh, and could you bring some extra butter with the dinner rolls?'

Korsak laughed. 'Don't hold back, Rizzoli.'

'I'm hungry.'

'You know what that fried stuff does to your arteries?'

'Okay, then. You don't get any of my onion rings.'

The waitress looked at Korsak. 'What about you, sir?'

'Broiled salmon, hold the butter. And a salad with vinaigrette dressing.'

As the waitress walked away, Rizzoli gave Korsak an incredulous look. 'Since when did you start eating broiled fish?' she asked.

'Since the big guy upstairs whacked me over the head with that warning.'

'Are you really eating that way? This isn't something just for show?'

'Lost ten pounds already. And that's even off cigarettes, so you know it's, like, *real* weight off. Not just water weight.' He leaned back, looking just a little too satisfied with himself. 'I'm even using the treadmill now.'

'You're kidding.'

'Joined a health club. Doing cardio workouts. You know, check the pulse, keep tabs on the ticker. I feel ten years younger.'

You look ten years younger was what he was probably fishing for her to say, but she didn't say it, because it would not have been true.

'Ten pounds. Good for you,' she said.

'Just gotta stick with it.'

'So what're you doing, drinking beer?'

'Alcohol's okay, haven't you heard? Latest word in the *New England Journal of Medicine*. Glass of red wine's good for the ticker.' He nodded at the Coke that the waitress set in front of Rizzoli. 'What's with that? You always used to order Adams Ale.'

She shrugged. 'Not tonight.'

'Feeling okay?'

No, I'm not. I'm knocked up and I can't even drink a beer without wanting to puke. 'I've been busy,' was all she said.

'Yeah, I hear. What's with the nuns?'

'We don't know yet.'

'I heard one of the nuns was a mommy.'

'Where did you hear that?'

'You know. Around.'

'What else did you hear?'

'That you dragged a baby out of a pond.'

It was inevitable that the news would get out. Cops talked to each other. They talked to their wives. She thought of all the searchers standing around the pond, the morgue attendants, the crime scene technicians. A few loose lips and pretty soon, even a retired cop out in Newton knows the details. She dreaded what the morning papers would bring. Murder was fascinating enough to the public; now there was forbidden sex, a potent additive that would keep this case front and center.

The waitress set down their food. Rizzoli's order took up most of the table, the dishes spread out like a family feast. Attacking her food, she bit into a french fry so hot it burned her mouth, and had to gulp her Coke to cool things down.

Korsak, for all his self-righteous comments about fried foods, was staring wistfully at her onion rings. Then he looked down at his broiled fish, sighed, and picked up his fork.

'You want some of these rings?' she asked.

'No, I'm fine. I tell you, I'm turning my life around. That coronary might be the best thing ever happened to me.'

'You serious?'

'Yeah. I'm losing weight. Kicked the cigarettes. Hey, I think I even got some hair growing back.' He dipped his head to show her his bald spot.

If any hair was growing back, she thought, it was in his head, not on it.

'Yeah, I'm making a lot of changes,' he said.

He fell silent and concentrated on his salmon, but did not seem to enjoy it. She almost shoved her plate of onion rings toward him out of pity.

But when he raised his head again, he looked at her, not at her food. 'I've got things changing at home too.'

Something about the way he said it made her uneasy. The way he looked at her, as though about to bare his soul. She dreaded hearing the messy details, but she could see how much he needed to talk.

'What's happening at home?' she asked. Already guessing what was about to come.

'Diane and me – you know what's been going on. You've seen her.'

She had first met Diane at the hospital, when Korsak was recuperating from his heart attack. At their first encounter, she had noticed Diane's slurred speech and glassy eyes. The woman was a walking medicine cabinet, high on Valium, codeine – whatever she could beg off her doctors. It had been a problem for years, Korsak told her, yet he had stood by his wife because that's what husbands were supposed to do.

'How is Diane these days?' she asked.

'The same. Still stoned out of her head.'

'You said things were changing.'

'They are. I've left her.'

She knew he was waiting for her reaction. She stared back, not sure whether to be happy or distressed for him. Not sure which he wanted to see from her.

'Jesus, Korsak,' she finally said. 'Are you sure about this?'

'Never been more sure of anything in my whole frigging life. I'm moving out next week. Found myself a bachelor pad, here in Jamaica Plain. Gonna set it up just the way I want it. You know, widescreen TV, big fucking speakers that'll blow out your eardrums.'

He's fifty-four, he's had a heart attack, and he's going off the deep end, she thought. Acting like a teenager who can't wait to move into his first apartment.

'She won't even notice I'm gone. Long as I keep paying her pharmacy bills, she'll be happy. Man, I don't know why it took me so long to do this. Wasted half my life, but I tell you, that's it. From now on, I make every minute count.'

'What about your daughter? What does she say?'

He snorted. 'Like she gives a shit? All she ever does is ask for money. *Daddy, I need a new car. Daddy, I wanna go to Cancun.* You think I ever been to Cancun?'

She sat back, staring at him over her cooling onion rings. 'Do you know what you're doing?'

'Yeah. I'm taking control of my life.' He paused. Said, with a note of resentment, 'I thought you'd be happy for me.'

'I am. I guess.'

'So what's with the look?'

'What look?'

'Like I've sprouted wings.'

206

'I've just got to get used to the new Korsak. It's like I don't know you anymore.'

'Is that a bad thing?'

'No. At least you're not blowing smoke in my face anymore.'

They both laughed at that. The new Korsak, unlike the old, wouldn't stink up her car with his cigarettes.

He stabbed a lettuce leaf and ate silently, frowning, as though it took all his concentration just to chew. Or to build up to what came next.

'So how's it going between you and Dean? Still seeing each other?'

His question, asked so casually, caught her off guard. It was the last subject she wanted to discuss, the last thing she expected him to ask about. He'd made no secret of the fact he disliked Gabriel Dean. She had disliked him too, when Dean had first walked into their investigation back in August, flashed his FBI badge, and proceeded to take control.

A few weeks later, everything had changed between her and Dean.

She looked down at her half-eaten meal, her appetite suddenly gone. She could feel Korsak watching her. The longer she waited, the less believable her answer would be.

'Things are okay,' she said. 'You want another beer? I could use a refill on my Coke.'

'He come up to see you lately?'

'Where's that waitress?'

'What's it been? Few weeks? A month?'

'I don't know . . .' She waved to the waitress, who didn't see her signal and instead headed back to the kitchen.

'What, you haven't been keeping track?'

'I've got other things going on, you know,' she snapped. It was her tone of voice that gave it away. Korsak sat back, looking at her with a cop's eye. An eye that saw too much.

He said, 'Good-looking guy like him, probably thinks he's a hot ticket with all the ladies.'

'What's that supposed to mean?'

'I'm not as stupid as I look. I can see something's wrong. I can hear it in your voice. And that bothers me, 'cause you deserve better. A lot better.'

'I really don't want to talk about this.'

'I never trusted him. I told you that, way back in August. Seems to me, you didn't trust him back then, either.'

Again, she waved at the waitress. Again, she was ignored.

'Something sneaky about those fibbie guys. Every single one I ever met. Real smooth, but they're never straight with you. They play head games. Think they're better than cops. All that federal bigshot crap.'

'Gabriel's not like that.'

'No?'

'He's not.'

'You're only saying that 'cause you got the hots for him.'

'Why are we having this conversation?'

'Because I'm worried about you. It's like you're

falling over a cliff, and you won't even reach out for help. I don't think you got anyone to talk to about this.'

'I'm talking to you.'

'Yeah, but you're not *telling* me anything.'

'What do you want me to say?'

'He hasn't been up here to see you lately. Has he?'

She didn't answer, didn't even look at him. She focused instead on the mural painted on the wall behind him. 'We've both been busy.'

Korsak sighed and shook his head, a gesture of pity.

'It's not like I'm in love or anything.' Mustering her pride, she finally met his gaze. 'You think I'm gonna fall apart just because some guy dumps me?'

'Well, I don't know.'

She laughed, but it sounded forced, even to her ears. 'It's only sex, Korsak. You have a fling, and you move on. Guys do it all the time.'

'You telling me you're no different from a guy?'

'Don't go pulling that double standard bullshit on me.'

'No, come on. You mean there's no broken heart? He walks away, and you're fine with it?'

She fixed him with a hard stare. 'I'll be fine.'

'Well, that's good. Because he's not worth it, Rizzoli. He's not worth one minute of grief. And I'm gonna tell him that, next time I see him.'

'Why are you doing this?'

'Doing what?'

'Interfering. Bullying. I don't need this. I've got enough problems.'

'I know that.'

'And all you're doing is making things worse.'

He stared at her for a moment. Then he looked down. 'I'm sorry,' he said quietly. 'But you know, I'm only trying to be your friend.'

Of all the things he might have said, nothing could have affected her more. She found herself blinking away tears as she stared at the bald spot on his bowed head. There were times when he repelled her, times when he infuriated her.

And then there were times when she'd catch a startling glimpse of the man inside, a decent man with a generous heart, and she'd feel ashamed of her impatience with him.

They were silent as they pulled on their coats and walked out of Doyle's, emerging from the cloud of cigarette smoke into a night that sparkled with fresh snow. Up the street, a cruiser pulled out of the Jamaica Plain station, its blue lights veiled by a beaded curtain of falling flakes. They watched the cruiser swoop away down the street, and Rizzoli wondered what crisis awaited it. Somewhere there was always a crisis. Couples screaming, wrangling. Lost children. Stunned drivers huddled beside their smashed cars. So many different lives intersecting in a myriad of ways. Most people were wrapped up in their own little corners of the universe. A cop sees it all.

'So what're you doing for Christmas?' he said.

'Going to my parents' house. My brother Frankie's in town for the holidays.'

'That's the one who's a Marine, right?'

'Yeah. Whenever he shows up, the whole family's supposed to get down on our knees and worship him.'

'Ouch. Little sibling rivalry there?'

'Naw, I lost that contest a long time ago. Frankie's king of the hill. So what're you doing for Christmas?'

He shrugged. 'I don't know.'

There was an unmistakable plea for an invitation in that answer. Save me from a lonely Christmas. Save me from my own screwed-up life. But she couldn't save him. She couldn't even save herself.

'I got a few plans,' he quickly added, too proud to let the silence stretch on. 'Maybe head down to Florida and see my sister.'

'That sounds good.' She sighed, her breath a cloud of steam. 'Well, I gotta go home and get some sleep.'

'You want to get together again sometime, you got my cell phone number, right?'

'Yeah, I've got it. Have a great Christmas.' She walked to her car.

'Uh, Rizzoli?'

'Yeah?'

'I know you still got a thing for Dean. I'm sorry I said those things about him. I just think you could do better.'

She laughed. 'Like there's a line of guys waiting outside my door.'

'Well,' he said, staring up the street. Suddenly avoiding her gaze. 'There is one guy.'

She went very still, thinking: Please don't do this to me. Please don't make me hurt you.

Before she could respond, he abruptly turned to his car. He gave her a careless wave as he circled to his door and ducked inside. She stared as he drove away, his tires trailing a glittering cloud of snow.

Eleven

It was after seven that evening when Maura finally arrived home. As she turned into her driveway, she could see lights blazing in her house. Not the paltry glow of a few bulbs switched on by automatic timers, but the cheery incandescence of many lamps burning, of someone waiting for her. And through the living room curtains, she could make out a pyramid of multicolored lights.

A Christmas tree.

That was the last thing she had expected to see, and she paused in the driveway, staring at the twinkling colors, remembering the Christmases when she had put up the tree for Victor, when she had lifted delicate globes from their packing nests and hung them on branches that perfumed her fingers with the tart scent of pine. She remembered Christmases before that, when she was a child, and her father would lift her on his shoulders, so she could place the silver star on top of the tree. Not once had her parents skipped that happy tradition, yet how quickly she had let it slip from

213

her own life. It was too messy, too much work. The hauling in of the tree, the hauling out, and then it was just another dried brown discard waiting on the curb for trash pickup. She had let the troublesome aspects deter her. She had forgotten about the joy.

She stepped from the cold garage into the house, and was greeted by the scent of roasting chicken and garlic and rosemary. How good it felt to be greeted by the smells of supper, to have someone waiting for her. She heard the TV on in the living room, and she followed the sound, pulling off her coat as she headed down the hallway.

Victor was sitting cross-legged on the floor next to the tree, trying to untangle a clump of tinsel. He saw her and gave a resigned laugh.

'I'm no better at this than when we were married.'

'I didn't expect all this,' she said, looking up at the lights.

'Well, I thought, here it is, December eighteenth, and you don't even have a tree yet.'

'I haven't had time to put one up.'

'There's always time for Christmas, Maura.'

'This is quite a change. You used to be the one who was always too busy for the holidays.'

He looked up at her from the tangle of silver. 'And you're always going to hold that against me, aren't you?'

She fell silent, regretting her last comment. It was not a good way to start the evening, by bringing up old resentments. She turned to hang her coat in the closet. With her back to him, she called out: 'Can I get you a drink?'

'Whatever you're having.'

'Even if it's a girly drink?'

'Have I ever been sexist about my cocktails?'

She laughed and went into the kitchen. From the refrigerator she took out limes and cranberry juice. She measured Triple Sec and Absolut Citron into the cocktail shaker. Standing at the sink, she rattled together ice and liquor, feeling the metal container turn frosty. Shake, shake, shake, like the sound of dice in a cup. Everything's a gamble, love most of all. The last time I gambled I lost, she thought. And this time, what am I gambling for? A chance to make things right between us? Or another chance to have my heart broken?

She poured the icy liquid into two martini glasses and was carrying them out when she noticed the trash can was filled with a jumble of restaurant takeout containers. She had to smile. So Victor had not magically transformed into a chef after all. Their dinner tonight was courtesy of the New Market Deli.

When she walked into the living room, she found Victor had given up on tinsel-hanging and was packing away the empty ornament boxes.

'You went to a lot of trouble,' she said, as she set the martini glasses down on the coffee table. 'Bulbs and lights and everything.'

'I couldn't find any Christmas stuff in your garage.'

'I left it all in San Francisco.'

'You never bought your own?'

'I haven't put up any trees.'

'It's been three years, Maura.'

She sat down on the couch and calmly took a sip of her drink. 'And when was the last time *you* took out that box of bulbs?'

He said nothing, but focused instead on stacking the empty boxes. When he finally answered, he did not look at her. 'I haven't felt much like celebrating, either.'

The TV was still on, the sound now muted, but distracting images flashed on the screen. Victor reached for the remote and pressed OFF. Then he sat on the couch, a comfortable distance away, not touching her, yet close enough to leave open all possibilities.

He looked at the martini glass she'd brought him. 'It's pink,' he said, with a note of surprise.

'A Cosmopolitan. I warned you it was a girly drink.'

He took a sip. 'Tastes like the girls are having all the fun.'

They sat quietly for a moment, sipping their drinks, the Christmas lights twinkling on and off. A homey and comfortable scene, but Maura was feeling anything but relaxed. She didn't know what to expect of this evening, and didn't know what he expected either. Everything about him was disconcertingly familiar. His scent, the way his hair caught the lamplight. And the little details, which she always found endearing because they reflected his lack of pretension: the well-worn shirt, the faded jeans. The same old Timex that he'd been wearing ever since she'd met him. I can't walk into a third world country and say I'm here to help you when there's a Rolex on my wrist, he'd said. Victor as Man of La Mancha, tilting at the windmill of poverty. She may have grown weary of that fight long ago, but he was still in the thick of it.

And for that, she couldn't help but admire him.

He put down the martini glass. 'I saw more about the nuns today. On the news.'

'What are they saying?'

'The police were dragging a pond behind the convent. What's that all about?'

She leaned back, the alcohol starting to melt the tension from her shoulders. 'They found a baby in the pond.'

'The nun's?'

'We're waiting for the DNA to confirm it.'

'But you have no doubt it's her baby?'

'It has to be. Or this case gets unbelievably complicated.'

'So you'll be able to identify the father. If you have DNA.'

'We need a name, first. And even if we do establish paternity, there's always the question of whether the sex was consensual, or whether it was rape. How do you prove it, one way or another, without Camille's testimony?'

'Still, it sounds like a possible motive for murder.'

'Absolutely.' She drained the last of her drink and set down the glass. It had been a mistake to drink before dinner. The alcohol and lack of sleep were conspiring to fog her thinking. She rubbed her temples, trying to force her brain to stay sharp.

'I should feed you, Maura. You look like you've had a hard day.'

She forced a laugh. 'You know that movie, where the little boy says, "I see dead people"?'

'*The Sixth Sense*.'

'Well, I see them all the time, and I'm getting tired of it. That's what's ruined my mood. Here it is, almost Christmas, and I didn't even think about putting up a tree, because I'm still seeing the autopsy lab in my head. I'm still smelling it on my hands. I come home on a day like this, after two postmortems, and I can't think about cooking dinner. I can't even look at a piece of meat without thinking of muscle fibers. All I can deal with is a cocktail. And then I pour the drink and smell the alcohol, and suddenly there I am, back in the lab. Alcohol, formalin, they both have that same sharp smell.'

'I've never heard you talk this way about your work.'

'I've never felt so overwhelmed by it.'

'Doesn't sound like the invincible Dr. Isles.'

'You know I'm not.'

'You're pretty good at playing the part. Smart and bulletproof. Do you realize how much you intimidated your students at U.C.? They were all afraid of you.'

She shook her head and laughed. 'Queen of the Dead.'

'What?'

'That's what the cops here call me. Not to my face. But I've heard it through the grapevine.'

'I kind of like that. Queen of the Dead.'

'Well, I hate it.' She closed her eyes and leaned back against the cushions. 'It makes me sound like a vampire. Like something grotesque.'

She didn't hear him rise from the couch and move behind her. So she was startled when she suddenly felt his hands on her shoulders. She went still, every nerve ending alive and exquisitely sensitive to his touch.

'Relax,' he murmured, his fingers kneading her muscles. 'That's one thing you never learned to do.'

'Don't, Victor.'

'You never drop your guard. You never want anyone to see you as less than perfect.'

His fingers were sinking deeply into her shoulders and neck. Probing, invading. She responded by tensing even more, her muscles snapping taut in defense.

'No wonder you're tired,' he said. 'Your shields are always up. You can't just sit back and enjoy it when someone touches you.'

'*Don't.*' She pulled away and rose to her feet. Turning to face him, she could still feel her skin tingling from his touch. 'What's going on here, Victor?'

'I was trying to help you relax.'

'I'm relaxed enough, thank you.'

'You're wound up so tight your muscles feel like they're ready to snap.'

'Well, what do you expect? I don't know what you're doing here. I don't know what you want.'

'How about just to be friends again?

'Can we be?'

'Why not?'

Even as she met his gaze, she could feel herself reddening. 'Because there's too much history between us. Too much . . .' *Attraction* was what she thought, but she cut off the word. She said, instead: 'I'm not sure men and women can be just friends, anyway.'

'That's a sad thing to believe.'

'It's realistic. I work with men every day. I know they're intimidated, and I want them to be. I want them to see me as an authority figure. A brain and a white coat. Because once they start thinking of me as a woman, sex always gets in the picture.'

He snorted. 'And that would contaminate everything.'

'Yes, it would.'

'It doesn't matter what kind of authority you wave over their heads. Men will look at you, and every one of them will see an attractive woman. Unless you put a bag over your head, that's how it is. Sex is always in the room. You can't lock it out.'

'That's why we can't be just friends.' She picked up the empty glasses and walked back to the kitchen.

He didn't follow her.

She stood by the sink, staring down at the glasses, the taste of lime and vodka still tart in her mouth, his scent still a fresh memory. Yes, sex was in the room all right, performing its mischief, dangling images that she tried to shut out, but couldn't. She thought about the night they had come home late from the movies, and had started pulling off each other's clothes the instant they'd stepped into the house. How they had made frantic, almost brutal love right there on the hardwood floor, his thrusts driving so deep she'd felt taken, like a whore. And had enjoyed it.

She grasped the sink and heard her own breathing deepen, felt her body making its own decision, rebelling against whatever logic had kept her celibate all these months.

Sex is always in the room.

The front door thudded shut.

She turned, startled. Hurried into the living room to see only the twinkling tree, but no Victor. Glancing out the window, she saw him climb into his car, and heard the roar of the engine starting.

She dashed out the front door, her shoes sliding on the icy walkway as she hurried toward his car.

'Victor!'

The engine suddenly shut off, and the headlights went dark. He stepped out and looked at her, his head only a shadowy silhouette above the car roof. The wind blew, and she blinked against stinging needles of snow.

'Why are you leaving?' she asked.

'Go inside, Maura. It's freezing.'

'But why are you leaving?'

Even through the shadows, she saw the frosty cloud of his breath, exhaled in frustration. 'It's clear you don't want me here.'

'Come back. I do want you to stay.' She walked around the car and stood facing him. The wind pierced her thin blouse.

'We'd just tear into each other again. The way we always do.' He started to climb back into the car.

She reached for his jacket and tugged him toward her. In that instant, as he turned to look at her, she knew what would come next. Reckless or not, at that moment, she wanted it to happen.

He didn't have to pull her into his arms. She was already there, burrowing into his warmth, her mouth seeking his. Familiar tastes, familiar smells. Their bodies fitting together, as they always had. She was shaking now, both from cold and excitement. He folded his arms around her, and his body shielded her from the wind as they kissed their way back to the front door. They brought a dusting of snow into the house, bits of glitter that slid to the floor as he shrugged off his jacket.

They never made it to the bedroom.

Right there, in the entryway, she fumbled at the buttons of his shirt, tugging it free from his trousers. The skin beneath felt searing to her cold-numbed fingers. She peeled away the fabric, craving his warmth, desperate to feel it against her own skin. By the time they made it into the living room, her own blouse was unbuttoned, her slacks unzipped. She welcomed him back into her body. Into her life.

The lights of the tree twinkled like multicolored stars as she lay on the floor beneath him. She closed her eyes, yet even then, she still could see those lights winking above her in a firmament of colors. Their bodies rocked together in a knowing dance, without clumsiness, without the un-certainty of first-time lovers. She knew his touch, his moves, and when pleasure overtook her and she cried out, she felt no embarrassment. Three years of separation were swept away in this one act, and after it was done, and they lay together among the tangle of discarded clothes, his embrace felt as familiar as a well-worn blanket.

When she opened her eyes again, she found Victor gazing down at her.

'You're the best thing I've ever unwrapped under a Christmas tree,' he said.

She stared up at a glittering strand of tinsel hanging from a branch above. 'That's how I feel,' she murmured. 'Unwrapped. Exposed.'

'You make it sound like it's not a good thing.'

'It depends on what happens next.'

'What does happen next?'

She sighed. 'I don't know.'

'What do you want to happen?'

'I don't want to be hurt again.'

'You're afraid that's what I'll do.'

She looked at him. 'It's what you did before.'

'We hurt each other, Maura. In a lot of different

ways. People who love each other always do, without meaning to.'

'You had the affair. What did I do?'

'This doesn't get us anywhere.'

'I want to know,' she said. 'How did I hurt you?'

He rolled away to lie beside her, not touching her, his gaze focused somewhere on the ceiling. 'Do you remember the day I had to leave for Abidjan?'

'I remember,' she said. Still tasting the bitterness.

'I admit, it was a terrible time to leave you, but I had to go. I was the only one who could handle the negotiations. I had to be there.'

'The day after my dad's funeral?' She looked at him. 'I *needed* you. I needed you home with me.'

'One Earth needed me too. We could have lost that whole container of medical supplies. It couldn't wait.'

'Well, I accepted it, didn't I?'

'That's exactly the word. *Accepted* it. But I knew you were pissed off.'

'Because it kept happening. Anniversaries, funerals – nothing kept you at home. I always came in second.'

'And that's what it came down to, didn't it? I had to choose between you and One Earth. I didn't want to choose. I didn't think I should have to. Not with so much at stake.'

'You can't save the world all by yourself.'

'I can do a hell of a lot of good. You used to believe that, too.'

'But everyone burns out eventually. You spend years obsessing about people dying in other countries. And then one day you wake up, and you just want to focus on your own life for a change. On having your own children. But you never had time for *that*, either.' She took a deep breath and felt tears catch in her throat, thinking of the babies she'd wanted but would probably never have. Thinking, too, of Jane Rizzoli, whose pregnancy brought Maura's own childlessness into painful focus. 'I was tired of being married to a saint. I wanted a husband.'

A moment passed, the Christmas lights above her blurring into smears of color.

He reached for her hand. 'I guess I'm the one who failed,' he said.

She swallowed, and the colors sharpened once again to lights twinkling on a wire. 'We both did.'

He did not release her hand, but held it firmly in his, as though afraid that if he let go, there would be no second chance at contact.

'We can talk all we want,' she said, 'but I don't see that anything's changed between us.'

'We know what went wrong.'

'It doesn't mean we can make it different this time.'

He said quietly, 'We don't have to do anything, Maura. We can just be together. Isn't that enough for the moment?'

Just be together. It sounded simple. Lying beside

him, with only their hands touching, she thought: Yes, I can do this. I can be detached enough to sleep with you and not let you hurt me. Sex without love – men enjoyed it without a second thought. Why couldn't she?

And maybe this time, a cruel little voice whispered, *he'll be the one who gets his heart broken.*

Twelve

The drive to Hyannisport should have taken them only two hours, south on Route 3, and then along Route 6 into Cape Cod, but Rizzoli needed two restroom breaks along the way, so they didn't reach the Sagamore Bridge until three in the afternoon. Once across that bridge, they were suddenly in the land of seaside vacations, the road leading through a series of small towns, like a necklace of pretty beads strung along the Cape. Rizzoli's previous trips to Hyannisport had always been during the summertime, when the roads were clogged with cars, and lines of people in T-shirts and shorts snaked out of ice cream shops. She had never been here on a cold winter's day like this one, when half the restaurants were shuttered, and only a few brave souls were out on the sidewalks, coats buttoned up against the wind.

Frost turned onto Ocean Street and murmured in wonder: 'Man. Will you look at the size of these homes.'

'Wanna move in?' said Rizzoli.

'Maybe when I earn my first ten million.'

'Tell Alice she'd better get cracking on that first million, 'cause you sure aren't gonna make it on your salary.'

Their written directions took them past a pair of granite pillars, and down a broad driveway to a handsome house near the water's edge. Rizzoli stepped out of the car and paused, shivering in the wind, to admire the salt-silvered shingles, the three turrets facing the sea.

'Can you believe she left all this to become a nun?' she said.

'When God calls you, I guess you gotta go.'

She shook her head. 'Me? I would've let him keep ringing.'

They walked up the porch steps and Frost pressed the doorbell.

It was answered by a small dark-haired woman who opened the door just a crack to look at them.

'We're from Boston PD,' said Rizzoli. 'We called earlier. Here to see Mrs. Maginnes.'

The woman nodded and stepped aside to let them in. 'She's in the Sea Room. Let me show you the way.'

They walked across polished teak floors, past walls hung with paintings of ships and stormy seas. Rizzoli imagined young Camille growing up in this house, running across this gleaming floor. Or did she run? Was she allowed only to walk, quietly and sedately, as she wandered among the antiques?

The woman led them into a vast room where

floor-to-ceiling windows faced the sea. The view of gray, windswept water was so dramatic that it instantly captured Rizzoli's gaze and she did not, at first, focus on anything else. But even as she stared at the water, she was aware of the sour odor that hung in the room. The smell of urine.

She turned to look at the source of that smell: a man lying in a hospital bed near the windows, as though displayed like a piece of living art. Seated in a chair beside him was an auburn-haired woman, who now rose to greet her visitors. Rizzoli saw nothing of Camille in this woman's face. Camille's beauty had been delicate, almost ethereal. This woman was all gloss and polish, her hair cut in a perfect helmet, her eyebrows plucked into arching gull's wings.

'I'm Lauren Maginnes, Camille's stepmother,' the woman said, and reached out to shake Frost's hand. Some women ignore their own sex and focus only on the men in the room, and she was one of them, turning her full attention to Barry Frost.

Rizzoli said, 'Hi, I spoke to you on the phone. I'm Detective Rizzoli. And this is Detective Frost. We're both very sorry about your loss.'

Only then did Lauren finally deign to focus on Rizzoli. 'Thank you' was all she said. She glanced at the dark-haired woman who'd shown them in. 'Maria, could you tell the boys to come down and join us? The police are here.' She turned back to her guests and gestured toward a couch. 'Please sit down.'

Rizzoli found herself seated closest to the hospital bed. She looked at the man's hand, contracted into a claw, and his face, one side drooping into an immobile puddle, and she remembered the last months of her own grandfather's life. How he had lain in his nursing-home bed, his eyes fully aware and angry, imprisoned in a body that would no longer obey his commands. She saw such awareness in this man's eyes. He was staring straight at her, at this visitor he did not know, and she saw despair and humiliation in that gaze. The helplessness of a man whose dignity has been stolen. He could not be much older than fifty, yet already his body had betrayed him. A line of drool glistened on his chin and dribbled onto the pillow. On a nearby table were all the paraphernalia needed to keep him comfortable: cans of Ensure. Rubber gloves and Handi Wipes. A box of adult diapers. Your whole life reduced to a tabletop's worth of hygiene products.

'Our evening shift nurse is running a little late, so I hope you don't mind sitting here while I keep an eye on Randall,' said Lauren. 'We moved him into this room because he's always loved the sea. Now he can look at it all the time.' She reached for a tissue and gently dabbed the drool from his mouth. 'There. There, now.' She turned and looked at the two detectives. 'You see why I didn't want to drive all the way up to Boston. I don't like to leave him for too long with the nurses. He gets agitated. He can't talk, but I know he misses me when I'm gone.'

Lauren sat back down in the armchair and focused on Frost. 'Have you made any progress with the investigation?'

Once again, it was Rizzoli who responded, determined to hold this woman's attention, and irritated that it kept slipping away from her.

'We're following some new leads,' she said.

'But you didn't drive all the way to Hyannis just to tell me that.'

'No. We came to talk about some issues we felt more comfortable handling in person.'

'And you wanted to look us over, I imagine.'

'We wanted a sense of Camille's background. Her family.'

'Well, here we are.' Lauren waved her arm. 'This is the house she grew up in. It's hard to imagine, isn't it? Why she'd leave this for a convent. Randall gave her everything any girl could ask for. A brand-new BMW for her birthday. Her own pony. A closet full of dresses that she hardly ever wore. Instead, she chose to wear black for the rest of her life. She chose . . .' Lauren shook her head. 'We still don't get it.'

'You were both unhappy about her decision?'

'Oh, I could live with it. After all, it was her life. But Randall never accepted it. He kept hoping she'd change her mind. That she'd get tired of whatever it is nuns do all day, and she'd finally come home.' She looked at her husband, lying mute in the bed. 'I think that's why he had his stroke. She was his only child, and he couldn't believe she left him.'

'What about Camille's birth mother, Mrs. Maginnes? You told me on the phone that she was dead.'

'Camille was only eight years old when it happened.'

'When what happened?'

'Well, they called it an accidental overdose, but are any of those really accidents? Randall had already been widowed several years when I met him. I guess you could call us a reconstituted family. I have two sons from my first marriage, and Randall had Camille.'

'How long have you and Randall been married?'

'Almost seven years now.' She looked at her husband. Added, with a note of resignation, 'For better or for worse.'

'Were you and your stepdaughter close? Did she share much with you?'

'Camille?' Lauren shook her head. 'I have to be perfectly honest. We never really bonded, if that's what you're asking. She was already thirteen when I met Randall, and you know what kids are like at that age. They want nothing to do with adults. It's not that she treated me like her evil stepmother or anything. We just didn't, well, *connect*, I guess. I made the effort, I really did, but she was always so . . .' Lauren suddenly stopped, as though afraid she'd say something she shouldn't.

'What's the word you're looking for, Mrs. Maginnes?'

Lauren thought about it. 'Strange,' she said

finally. 'Camille was strange.' She looked at her husband, who was staring at her, and quickly said, 'I'm sorry, Randall. I know it's awful for me to say that, but these are policemen. They want to hear the truth.'

'What do you mean by strange?' asked Frost.

'You know how, when you walk into a party, you sometimes spot someone who's standing all alone?' said Lauren. 'Someone who won't look you in the eye? She was always off by herself in a corner, or hiding out in her room. It never occurred to us what she was doing up there. Praying! Down on her knees and praying. Reading those books she got from one of the Catholic girls at school. We're not even Catholic, we're Presbyterians. But there she was, locked in her room. Whipping herself with a belt, can you believe it? To make herself pure. Where do they get such ideas?'

Outside, the wind sprayed sea salt on the windows. Randall Maginnes gave a soft moan. Rizzoli noticed that he was looking straight at her. She gazed back at him, wondering how much of this conversation he understood. Full comprehension would be the greater curse, she thought. To know everything that was going on around you. To know your daughter, your only natural child, is dead. To know your wife feels burdened by your care. To know that the terrible odor you're forced to inhale is your own.

She heard footsteps and turned to see two young men walk into the room. Clearly they were

233

Lauren's sons, with the same reddish-brown hair, the same handsome features stamped on their faces. Though both were dressed casually in jeans and crew-neck sweaters, they managed, like their mother, to project stylish confidence. Thoroughbreds, thought Rizzoli.

She reached out to shake their hands. Did it firmly, establishing her authority. 'I'm Detective Rizzoli,' she said.

'My sons, Blake and Justin,' said Lauren. 'They're home from college for the holidays.'

My sons, she had said. Not our sons. In this family, reconstitution had not completely blended the lines of love. Even after seven years of marriage, her sons were still hers, and Randall's daughter was his.

'These are our two budding lawyers in the family,' said Lauren. 'With all the arguments they have around the dinner table, they've had plenty of practice for the courtroom.'

'Discussions, Mom,' said Blake. 'We call them discussions.'

'Sometimes I can't tell the difference.'

The boys sat down with the easy grace of athletes, and looked at Rizzoli, as though expecting the entertainment to begin.

'In college, huh?' she said. 'Where do you boys go?'

'I'm at Amherst,' said Blake. 'And Justin's at Bowdoin.'

Both within easy driving distance to Boston.

'And you want to be lawyers? Both of you?'

'I've already got my application in to law schools,' said Blake.

'I'm thinking of entertainment law. Maybe work out in California. I'm getting a minor in film studies, so I think I'm laying a pretty good foundation for it.'

'Yeah, and he wants to hang out with cute actresses, too,' said Justin. For that comment, he got a playful jab in the ribs. 'Well, he does!'

Rizzoli wondered about two brothers who could exchange such lighthearted banter while their stepsister lay, so recently deceased, in the morgue.

She asked, 'When did you two last see your sister?'

Blake and Justin looked at each other. Said, almost in unison, 'Grandma's funeral.'

'That was in March?' She looked at Lauren. 'When Camille came home for a visit?'

Lauren nodded. 'We had to petition the church to let her come home for the services. It's like asking for a prisoner's parole. I couldn't believe it when they didn't let her come home again in April, after Randall had his stroke. Her own father! And she just accepted their decision. Just did what they told her to do. You have to wonder what goes on inside those convents, that they're so afraid to let them out. What sorts of abuse they're hiding. But that's probably why she liked being there.'

'Why would you think that?'

'Because it's what she craved. Punishment. Pain.'

'Camille?'

'I told you, Detective, she was strange. When she was sixteen, she took off her shoes and went walking barefoot. In January. It was ten degrees outside! The maid found her standing in the snow. Of course, all our neighbors soon heard about it as well. We had to take her to the hospital for frostbite. She told the doctor she did it because the saints had suffered, and she wanted to feel pain, too. She thought it would bring her closer to God.' Lauren shook her head. 'What can you do with a girl like that?'

Love her, thought Rizzoli. Try to understand her.

'I wanted her to see a psychiatrist, but Randall wouldn't hear of it. He never, ever admitted that his own daughter was . . .' Lauren paused.

'Just say it, Mom,' said Blake. 'She was crazy. That's what we all thought.'

Camille's father made a soft moan.

Lauren rose to wipe another thread of drool from his mouth. 'Where is that nurse, anyway? She was supposed to be here at three.'

'When Camille came home in March, how long did she stay?' asked Frost.

Lauren looked at him, distracted. 'About a week. She could have stayed longer, but she chose to go back to the convent early.'

'Why?'

'I guess she didn't like being around all these people. We had a lot of my relatives up from Newport for the funeral.'

236

'You did tell us she was reclusive.'

'That's an understatement.'

Rizzoli asked, 'Did she have many friends, Mrs. Maginnes?'

'If she did, she never brought any of them home to meet us.'

'How about at school?' Rizzoli looked at the two boys, who glanced at each other.

Justin said, with unnecessary callousness, 'Only the wallflower crowd.'

'I meant boyfriends.'

Lauren gave a startled laugh. 'Boyfriends? When all she dreamed about was becoming the bride of Christ?'

'She was an attractive young woman,' said Rizzoli. 'Maybe you didn't see it, but I'm sure there were boys who noticed it. Boys who were interested in her.' She looked at Lauren's sons.

'No one wanted to go out with her,' said Justin. 'They'd get laughed at.'

'And when she came home, in March? Did she spend time with any friends? Did any men seem particularly interested in her?'

'Why do you keep asking about boyfriends?' said Lauren.

Rizzoli could think of no way to avoid revealing the truth. 'I'm sorry to have to tell you this. But shortly before Camille was murdered, she bore a child. A baby who died at birth.' She looked at the brothers.

They stared back at her with equally stunned expressions.

For a moment, the only sound in the room was the wind whipping off the sea, rattling the windows.

Lauren said, 'Haven't you been reading the news? All those terrible things the priests have been doing? She's been in a convent for the last two years! She's been under *their* supervision, *their* authority. You should talk to *them*.'

'We've already questioned the one priest who had access to the convent. He willingly gave us his DNA. Those tests are pending.'

'So you don't even know yet if he's the father. Why bother us with these questions?'

'The baby would have been conceived sometime in March, Mrs. Maginnes. The month she came home for that funeral.'

'And you think that it happened *here*?'

'You had a house full of guests.'

'What are you asking me to do? Call up every man who happened to visit here that week? "Oh by the way, did you sleep with my stepdaughter?"'

'We have the infant's DNA. With your help, we might be able to identify the father.'

Lauren shot to her feet. 'I'd like you to leave now.'

'Your stepdaughter's dead. Don't you want us to find her killer?'

'You're looking in the wrong place.' She walked to the doorway and called out: 'Maria! Can you show these policemen out?'

'DNA would give us the answer, Mrs. Maginnes. With just a few swabs, we could put all suspicions to rest.'

Lauren turned and faced her. 'Then start with the priests. And leave my family alone.'

Rizzoli slid into the car and pulled the door shut. As Frost warmed the engine, she gazed at the house, and remembered how impressed she'd been when she'd caught her first glimpse of it.

Before she had met the people inside.

'Now I know why Camille left home,' she said. 'Imagine growing up in that house. With those brothers. With that stepmother.'

'They seemed a lot more upset about our questions than about the girl's death.'

As they drove through the granite pillars, Rizzoli took one last backward look at the house. Imagined a young girl, gliding like a wraith among those vast rooms. A girl derided by her step-brothers, ignored by her stepmother. A girl whose hopes and dreams are ridiculed by those who are supposed to love her. Every day in that house would bring another punishing blow to your soul, more painful than the sting of frostbite as you walk barefoot in the snow. You want to be closer to God, to know the unconditional warmth of His love. For that they laugh at you, or pity you, or tell you that you're a candidate for the psychiatrist's couch.

No wonder the walls of the convent had seemed so welcoming.

Rizzoli sighed and turned to look at the road that stretched ahead. 'Let's go home,' she said.

* * *

'This diagnosis has me stumped,' said Maura.

She laid out a series of digital photographs on the conference room table. Her four colleagues did not so much as flinch at the images, for they had all seen far worse sights in the autopsy lab than these views of rat-bitten skin and angry nodules. They seemed far more focused on the box of fresh blueberry muffins that Louise had brought in that morning for case conference, an offering that the doctors were happily devouring, even as they stared at stomach-turning photos. Those who work with the dead learn to keep the sights and smells of their jobs from ruining their appetites, and among the pathologists now seated at the table was one known to be particularly fond of seared foie gras, a pleasure undimmed by the fact he dissected human livers by day. Judging by his ample belly, nothing ruined Dr. Abe Bristol's appetite, and he happily munched on his third muffin as Maura set down the last of the images.

'This is your Jane Doe?' asked Dr. Costas.

Maura nodded. 'Female, approximate age thirty to forty-five, with a gunshot wound to the chest. She was found about thirty-six hours after death inside an abandoned building. There was postmortem excision of the face, as well as amputations of the hands and the feet.'

'Whoa. There's a sick boy for you.'

'It's these skin lesions that stump me,' she said, gesturing to the array of photos. 'The rodents did some damage, but there's enough intact skin left to see the gross appearance of these underlying lesions.'

240

Dr. Costas picked up one of the photos. 'I'm no expert,' he said solemnly, 'but I'd call this a classic case of red bumps.'

Everyone laughed. Physicians flummoxed by skin lesions often resorted to simply describing the skin's appearance, without knowing its cause. Red bumps could be caused by anything from a viral infection to autoimmune disease, and few skin lesions are unique enough to point to an immediate diagnosis.

Dr. Bristol stopped chewing his muffin long enough to point to one of the photos and say, 'You've got some ulcerations here.'

'Yes, some of the nodules have shallow ulcerations with crust formation. And a few have the silvery scales you'd see in psoriasis.'

'Bacterial cultures?'

'Nothing unusual is growing out. Just *Staph. epidermidis.*'

Staph epi was a common skin bacterium, and Bristol merely shrugged. 'Contaminant.'

'What about the skin biopsies?' asked Costas.

'I looked at the slides yesterday,' said Maura. 'There are acute inflammatory changes. Edema, infiltration by granulocytes. Some deep micro-abscesses. There are also inflammatory changes in the blood vessels as well.'

'And you have no bacteria growing?'

'Both the Gram stain and Fite Faraco stains are negative for bacteria. These are sterile abscesses.'

'You already know the cause of death, right?' said Bristol, his dark beard catching the crumbs of

241

his muffin. 'Does it really matter what these nodules are?'

'I hate to think I'm missing something obvious here. We have no identification on this victim. We don't know anything about her, except for the cause of death and the fact she was covered with these lesions.'

'Well, what's *your* diagnosis?'

Maura looked down at the ugly swellings, like a mountain range of carbuncles across the victim's skin. 'Erythema nodosum,' she said.

'Cause?'

She shrugged. 'Idiopathic.' Meaning, quite simply, cause unknown.

Costas laughed. 'There's a wastebasket diagnosis for you.'

'I don't know what else to call it.'

'Neither do we,' said Bristol. 'Erythema nodosum works for me.'

Back at her desk, Maura reviewed the typed autopsy report for Rat Lady, which she had dictated earlier, and felt dissatisfied as she signed it. She knew the victim's approximate time of death, and the cause of death. She knew the woman was most likely poor, and that she had surely suffered from the humiliation of her appearance.

She looked down at the box of biopsy slides, labeled with the name Jane Doe and the case number. She pulled out one of the slides and slid it under the microscope lens. Swirls of pink and purple came into focus through the eyepiece. It was a hematoxylin and eosin stain of the skin. She saw the dark stipples of acute inflammatory cells, saw the fibrous circle of a blood vessel infiltrated by white cells, signs that the body was fighting back, sending its soldiers of immune cells into battle against . . . what?

Where was the enemy?

She sat back in her chair, thinking of what she'd seen on autopsy. A woman with no hands or face, mutilated by a killer who harvested identities as well as lives.

But why the feet? Why did he take the feet?

This is a killer who seems to operate with cool logic, she thought, not twisted perversions. He shoots to kill, using an efficiently lethal bullet. He strips the victim but does not sexually abuse her. He amputates the hands and feet and peels off the face. Then he leaves the corpse in a place where its skin will soon be gnawed away by scavengers.

It kept coming back to the feet. The removal of the feet was not logical.

She retrieved Rat Lady's X-ray envelope and slid the ankle films onto the light box. Once again, the abrupt demarcation of severed flesh shocked her, but she saw nothing new here, no clues that would explain the killer's motive for the amputation.

She took the films down, replaced them with the skull films, frontal and lateral views. She stood gazing at the bones of Rat Lady's face, and tried to envision what that face might have looked like. No older than forty-five, she thought, yet already you have lost your upper teeth. Already, you have the jaw of an elderly woman, the bones of your face rotting from within, your nose sinking into a widening crater. And scattered across your torso and limbs are ugly nodules. Just a glance in the mirror would be painful. And then to step outside, into the eyes of the public . . .

She stared at the bones, glowing on the light box. And she thought: I know why the killer took the feet.

It was only two days before Christmas, and when Maura walked onto the Harvard campus, she found it almost deserted, the Yard a broad expanse of white, scarcely marred by footprints. She tramped along the walkway, carrying her briefcase and a large envelope of X-rays, and could smell, in the air, the metallic tang of a coming snowfall. A few dead leaves clung, shivering, to bare trees. Some would view this scene as a holiday postcard with a *Season's Greeting* caption, but she saw only the monotonous grays of winter, a season she was already weary of.

By the time she reached Harvard's Peabody Museum of Archaeology, cold water had seeped into her socks and the hems of her pant legs were soaked. She stomped off the snow and walked into a building that smelled of history. Wooden steps creaked as she went down the stairwell to the basement.

The first thing she noticed, as she stepped inside the dim office of Dr. Julie Cawley, were the human skulls – at least a dozen of them, lining the shelves.

A lone window, set high in the wall, was half covered by snow, and the light that managed to seep through shone down directly on Dr. Cawley's head. She was a handsome woman, with upswept gray hair that looked pewter in the wintry light.

They shook hands, an oddly masculine greeting between two women.

'Thank you for seeing me,' said Maura.

'I'm rather looking forward to what you have to show me.' Dr. Cawley turned on a lamp. In its yellowish glow, the room suddenly seemed warmer. Cosier. 'I like to work in the dark,' she said, indicating the glow of the laptop on her desk. 'It keeps me focused. But is hard on these middle-aged eyes.'

Maura opened her briefcase and removed a folder of digital prints. 'These are the photos I took of the deceased. I'm afraid they're not very pleasant to look at.'

Dr. Cawley opened the folder and paused, staring at the photo of Rat Lady's mutilated face. 'It's been a while since I've attended an autopsy. I certainly never enjoyed it.' She sat down behind the desk and took a deep breath. 'Bones seem so much cleaner. Somehow less personal. It's the sight of flesh that turns the stomach.'

'I also brought her X-rays, if you'd rather look at those first.'

'No, I do need to look at these. I need to see the skin.' Slowly she flipped to the next photo. Stopped and stared in horror. 'Dear God,' she murmured. 'What happened to the hands?'

'They were removed.'

Cawley shot her a bewildered look. 'By whom?'

'The killer, we assume. Both hands were amputated. So were parts of the feet.'

'The face, the hands, the feet – those are the first things I'd look at to make this diagnosis.'

'Which could be the reason why he removed them. But there are other photos in there that might help you. The skin lesions.'

Cawley turned to the next set of images. 'Yes,' she murmured, as she slowly flipped through them. 'This certainly could be . . .'

Maura's gaze lifted to the row of skulls on the shelf, and she wondered how Cawley could work in this office, with all those empty eye sockets staring down at her. She thought of her own office, with its potted plants and floral paintings – nothing on the walls to remind her of death.

But Cawley had chosen to surround herself with the evidence of her own mortality. A professor of medical history, she was a physician as well as an historian, a woman who could read a lifetime's worth of miseries etched in the bones of the dead. She could look at the skulls on her shelf and see, in each, a personal history of pain. An old fracture or an impacted wisdom tooth or a jawbone infiltrated by tumor. Long after the flesh melts away, the bones still tell their stories. And judging by the many photos of Dr. Cawley taken at archaeological dig sites around the world, she had been mining these stories for decades.

Cawley looked up from a photo of one of the

skin lesions. 'Some of these do bear a resemblance to psoriasis. I can see why it was one of the diagnoses you considered. These could also be leukemic infiltrates. But we're talking about a great masquerader. It can look like many different things. I assume you did skin biopsies?'

'Yes, including stains for acid-fast bacilli.'

'And?'

'I saw none.'

Cawley shrugged. 'She may have received treatment. In which case there'd be no bacilli still present on biopsy.'

'That's why I came to you. Without active disease, without bacilli to identify, I'm at a loss as to how to make this diagnosis.'

'Let me see the X-rays.'

Maura handed her the large envelope of films. Dr. Cawley carried them to a viewing box mounted on her wall. In that office cluttered with artifacts from the past – skulls and old books and several decades' worth of photos – the light box stood out as a starkly modern feature. Cawley rifled through the X-rays and finally slid one under the mounting clips.

It was a skull film, viewed face-on. Beneath the mutilated soft tissues, the bony structures of the face remained intact, glowing like a death's head against the black background. Cawley studied the film for a moment, then pulled it down and slid on a lateral view, taken of the skull's profile.

'Ah. Here we go,' she murmured.

'What?'

'See here? Where the anterior nasal spine should be?' Cawley traced her finger down what should have been the slope of the nose. 'There's been advanced bone atrophy. In fact, there's almost complete obliteration of the nasal spine.' She crossed to the shelf of skulls and took one down. 'Here, let me show you an example. This particular skull was exhumed from a medieval grave site in Denmark. It was buried in a desolate spot, far outside the church-yard. You see here, where inflammatory changes have destroyed so much bony tissue that there's just a gaping hole where the nose would be. If we were to boil off the soft tissues from your victim there—' She pointed to the X-ray '—her skull would look very much like this one.'

'It's not postmortem damage? Could the nasal spine have been cracked off when the face was excised?'

'It wouldn't account for the severity of changes I see on that X-ray. And there's more.' Dr. Cawley set down the skull and pointed to the film. 'You've got atrophy and recession of the maxillary bone. It's so severe that the front upper teeth have been undermined and have fallen out.'

'I'd assumed it was due to poor dental care.'

'That may have contributed. But this is some-thing else. This is far more than just advanced gum disease.' She looked at Maura. 'Did you do the other X-ray projections I suggested?'

'They're in the envelope. We did a reverse Waters shot as well as a peri-apical series to highlight the maxillary landmarks.'

Cawley reached inside and pulled out more X-rays. She clipped up a peri-apical film, showing the floor of the nasal cavity. For a moment she said nothing, her gaze transfixed by the white glow of bone.

'I haven't seen a case like this in years,' she murmured in wonder.

'Then the X-rays are diagnostic?'

Dr. Cawley seemed to shake herself from her trance. She turned and picked up the skull from her desk. 'Here,' she said, turning the skull upside down to show the bony roof of the hard palate. 'Do you see how there's been pitting and atrophy of the alveolar process of the maxilla? Inflammation has eaten away this bone. The gums have receded so badly that the front teeth fell out. But the atrophy didn't stop there. Inflammation continued to chew away at the bone, destroying not just the palate, but also the turbinate bones inside the nose. The face was literally eaten away, from the inside, until the hard palate perforated and collapsed.'

'And how disfigured would this woman have been?'

Cawley turned and looked at the X-ray of Rat Lady. 'If this were medieval times, she would have been an object of horror.'

'Then this is enough for you to make a diagnosis?'

Dr. Cawley nodded. 'This woman almost certainly had Hansen's disease.'

Thirteen

The name sounded innocuous enough to those who did not recognize its meaning. But the disease had another name as well, a name that rang with ancient echoes of horror: leprosy. It conjured up medieval images of robed untouchables hiding their faces, of the shunned and pitiful, begging for alms. Of leper's bells, tinkling to warn the unwary that a monster approaches.

Such monsters were merely the victims of a microscopic invader: *Mycobacterium leprae*, a slow-growing bacillus that disfigures as it multiplies, rippling the skin with ugly nodules. It destroys nerves to the hands and feet so that the victim no longer senses pain, no longer flinches from injury, leaving his limbs vulnerable to burns and trauma and infection. With the passage of years, the mutilation continues. The nodules thicken, the bridge of the nose collapses. The fingers and toes, repeatedly injured, begin to melt away. And when the sufferer finally dies, he is not buried in the churchyard, but is banished far beyond its walls.

Even in death, the leper was shunned.

'To see a patient in such an advanced stage is almost unheard of in the U.S.,' said Dr. Cawley. 'Modern medical care would arrest the disease long before it caused this much disfigurement. Three-drug therapy can cure even the worst cases of lepromatous leprosy.'

'I'm assuming this woman *has* been treated,' said Maura. 'Since I saw no active bacilli in her skin biopsies.'

'Yes, but treatment obviously came late for her. Look at these deformities. The loss of teeth and the collapse of facial bones. She was infected for quite some time – probably decades – before she received any care.'

'Even the poorest patient in this country would have found treatment.'

'You'd certainly hope so. Because Hansen's disease is a public health issue.'

'Then the chances are this woman was an immigrant.'

Cawley nodded. 'You can still find it among some rural populations around the world. The majority of cases worldwide are in only five countries.'

'Which ones?'

'Brazil and Bangladesh. Indonesia and Myanmar. And, of course, India.'

Dr. Cawley returned the skull to the shelf, then gathered up the photos on her desk and shuffled them together. But Maura was scarcely aware of the other woman's movements. She stared at the X-ray of Rat Lady, and thought of another victim, another death scene. Of spilled blood, in the shadow of a crucifix.

India, she thought. Sister Ursula worked in India.

Graystones Abbey seemed colder and more desolate than ever when Maura stepped through the gate that afternoon. Ancient Sister Isabel led the way across the courtyard, her L. L. Bean snow boots peeking out incongruously from beneath the hem of her black habit. When winter turns brutal, even nuns rely on the comfort of Gore-Tex.

Sister Isabel directed Maura into the Abbess's empty office, then she vanished down the dark hallway, the clomp-clomp of her boots trailing a fading echo.

Maura touched the cast-iron radiator beside her; it was cold. She did not take off her coat.

So much time passed that she began to wonder if she had been forgotten, if the antique Sister Isabel had simply shuffled on down the hall, her memory of Maura's arrival fading with each step. Listening to the creaks of the building, to the gusts rattling the window, Maura imagined spending a lifetime under this roof. The years of silence and prayer, the unchanging rituals. There would be comfort in it, she thought. The ease of knowing, at each dawn, how the day will go. No surprises, no turmoil. You rise from bed and reach for the same clothing, kneel for the same prayers, walk the same dim corridors to breakfast. Outside the walls, women's hems might rise and fall, cars might take on new shapes and colors, and a changing galaxy of movie stars would appear and then vanish from the silver screen. But within the walls, the rituals continue unchanging, even as your body grows infirm, your hands unsteady, the world more silent as your hearing fades.

Solace, thought Maura. Contentment. Yes, these were reasons to withdraw from the world, reasons she understood.

She did not hear Mary Clement's approach, and she was startled to notice the Abbess was standing in the doorway, watching her.

'Reverend Mother.'

'I understand you have more questions?'

'About Sister Ursula.'

Mary Clement glided into the room and settled in behind her desk. On this bitterly cold day, even she was not immune to winter's chill; beneath her veil, she wore a gray wool sweater embroidered with white cats. She folded her hands on the desk and fixed Maura with a hard look. Not the friendly face that had greeted her on that first morning.

'You've done all you can to disrupt our lives. To destroy the memory of Sister Camille. And now you want to repeat the process with Sister Ursula?'

'She would want us to find her attacker.'

'And what terrible secrets do you imagine she has? Which sins are you now fishing for, Dr. Isles?'

'Not sins, necessarily.'

253

'Just a few days ago, you were focused only on Camille.'

'And that may have distracted us from probing more deeply into Sister Ursula's life.'

'You'll find no scandals there.'

'I'm not looking for scandals. I'm looking for the attacker's motive.'

'To kill a sixty-eight-year-old nun?' Mary Clement shook her head. 'There's no rational motive that I could imagine.'

'You told us that Sister Ursula served a mission abroad. In India.'

The abrupt change in subject seemed to startle Mary Clement. She rocked back in her chair. 'Why is that relevant?'

'Tell me more. About her time in India.'

'I'm not sure what you want to know, exactly.'

'She was trained as a nurse?'

'Yes. She worked in a small village outside the city of Hyderabad. She was there for about five years.'

'And she returned to Graystones a year ago?'

'In January.'

'Did she talk much, about her work there?'

'No.'

'She served five years there, and she never spoke of her experiences?'

'We value silence here. Not idle chatter.'

'I'd hardly consider it idle chatter to talk about her mission abroad.'

'Have you ever lived abroad, Dr. Isles? I don't mean in a nice tourist hotel, where maids change

254

the sheets every day. I'm talking about villages where sewage runs in the street, and children are dying of cholera. Her experience there wasn't a particularly pleasant topic to talk about.'

'You told us there'd been violence in India. That the village where she worked was attacked.'

The Abbess's gaze dropped to her hands, the skin chapped and red, folded on the desk.

'Reverend Mother?' said Maura.

'I don't know the whole story. She never spoke of it to me. What little I do know, I heard from Father Doolin.'

'Who is that?'

'He serves in the archdiocese in Hyderabad. He called from India, right after it happened, to tell me that Sister Ursula was returning to Graystones. That she wished to rejoin cloistered life. We welcomed her back, of course. This is her home. Naturally, this was where she came to find solace, after . . .'

'After what, Reverend Mother?'

'The massacre. In Bara village.'

The window suddenly rattled, buffeted by a gust. Beyond the glass, the day was leached of all color. A gray wall, topped by gray sky.

'That was where she worked?' asked Maura.

Mary Clement nodded. 'A village so poor it had no telephones, no electricity. Nearly a hundred people lived there, but few outsiders dared to visit. That was the life our sister chose, to serve the most wretched people on earth.'

Maura thought of Rat Lady's autopsy. Of her

skull, deformed by disease. She said, softly: 'It was a lepers' village.'

Mary Clement nodded. 'In India, they're considered the most unclean of all. Despised and feared. Cast out by their families. They live in special villages, where they can retreat from society, where they don't have to hide their faces. Where others are as deformed as they are.' She looked at Maura. 'Even that didn't protect them from attack. Bara village no longer exists.'

'You said there was a massacre.'

'That's what Father Doolin called it. Mass slaughter.'

'By whom?'

'The police never identified the attackers. It could have been a caste massacre. Or it could have been Hindu fundamentalists, angry about a Catholic nun living in their midst. Or they could have been Tamils, or any one of half a dozen separatist factions at war there. They killed everyone, Dr. Isles. Women, children. Two of the nurses in the clinic.'

'But Ursula survived.'

'Because she wasn't in Bara that night. She'd left the day before to fetch medical supplies from Hyderabad. When she returned the next morning, she found the village in ashes. Workers from the nearby factory were already there, searching for survivors, but they found none. Even the animals – the chickens, the goats – were slaughtered, and the corpses burned. Sister Ursula collapsed when she saw the bodies, and a doctor from the factory had to keep her in his clinic until Father Doolin arrived. She was the only one from Bara who survived, Dr. Isles. She was the lucky one.'

The lucky one, thought Maura. Spared from slaughter, only to come home to Graystones Abbey and find that Death had not forgotten her. That even here, she could not escape his hand.

Mary Clement's gaze met Maura's. 'You'll find nothing shameful in her past. Only a lifetime of service in God's name. Leave our sister's memory alone, Dr. Isles. Leave her at peace.'

Maura and Rizzoli stood on the sidewalk outside what had once been Mama Cortina's restaurant, and the wind sliced like an icy blade through their coats. It was the first time Maura had viewed this scene in daylight, and she saw a street of abandoned buildings, and windows that stared down like empty eye sockets.

'Nice neighborhood you've brought me to,' said Rizzoli. She looked up at the faded sign for Mama Cortina's. 'Your Jane Doe was found in there?'

'In the men's bathroom. She'd been dead about thirty-six hours when I examined her.'

'And you've got no leads on her ID?'

Maura shook her head. 'Considering her advanced stage of Hansen's disease, there's a good chance she was a recent immigrant. Possibly undocumented.'

Rizzoli hugged her coat tighter. '*Ben-Hur*,' she murmured. 'That's what it makes me think of. The Valley of the Lepers.'

'*Ben-Hur* was just a movie.'

'But the disease is real. What it does to your face, your hands.'

'It can be highly mutilating. That's what terrified the ancients. Why just the sight of a leper could send people screaming in horror.'

'Jesus. To think we have it right here in Boston.' Rizzoli shuddered. 'It's freezing. Let's get inside.'

They stepped into the alley, their shoes crunching along the icy trough that had formed from the footsteps of so many law enforcement officers. Here they might be protected from the wind, but the well of gloom between the buildings felt somehow colder, the air ominously still. Police tape lay across the threshold of the restaurant's alley doorway.

Maura took out the key and inserted it in the padlock, but it would not pop open. She crouched down, jiggling the key in the frozen lock.

'Why do their fingers fall off?' asked Rizzoli.

'What?'

'When you catch leprosy. Why do you lose your fingers? Does it attack the skin, like flesh-eating bacteria?'

'No, it does its damage in a different way. The leprosy bacillus attacks the peripheral nerves, so your fingers and toes go numb. You can't feel any pain. Pain is our warning system, part of our defense mechanism against injury. Without it, you could accidentally stick your fingers in boiling hot water, and not sense that your skin's being burned. Or you don't feel that blister building on your

258

foot. You can injure yourself again and again, leading to secondary infections. Gangrene.' Maura paused, frustrated by the stubborn lock.

'Here. Let me try.'

Maura stepped aside and gratefully slipped her gloved hands in her pockets while Rizzoli jiggled the key.

'In poorer countries,' said Maura, 'it's the rats that do the actual damage to hands and feet.'

Rizzoli looked up with a frown. 'Rats?'

'In the night, while you're sleeping. They crawl onto your bed and gnaw on fingers and toes.'

'You're serious?'

'And you don't feel a thing, because leprosy has made your skin numb. When you wake up the next morning, you discover the tips of your fingers are gone. That all you've got left are bloody stumps.'

Rizzoli stared at her, then gave the key a sharp twist.

The padlock popped open. The door swung ajar, to reveal shades of gray blending into blackness.

'Welcome to Mama Cortina's,' said Maura.

Rizzoli paused on the threshold, her Maglite beam cutting across the room. 'Something's moving inside,' she murmured.

'Rats.'

'Let's not talk any more about rats.'

Maura switched on her own flashlight and followed Rizzoli into a darkness that smelled of rancid grease.

'He brought her through here, into the dining room,' said Maura, her flashlight playing across the floor. 'They found some drag marks through the dust, probably left by the heels of her shoes. He must have grasped her under the arms and hauled her backwards.'

'You'd think he wouldn't even want to touch her.'

'I would assume he was wearing gloves, because he left no fingerprints.'

'Still, he was rubbing up against her clothes. Exposing himself to infection.'

'You're thinking of it the way the ancients did. As though one touch from a leper will turn you into a monster. It's not as transmissible as you think.'

'But you *can* catch it. You *can* get infected.'

'Yes.'

'And the next thing you know, your nose and fingers are falling off.'

'It's treatable. There are antibiotics.'

'I don't care if it's treatable,' said Rizzoli, now moving slowly across the kitchen. 'This is leprosy we're talking about. Something straight out of the Bible.'

They pushed through the swinging door, into the dining room. Rizzoli's Maglite swept a circle, and stacked chairs gleamed at the periphery. Though they couldn't see the infestation, they could hear the faint rustling. The darkness was alive.

'Which way?' said Rizzoli. Her voice now a

murmur, as though they had entered hostile territory.

'Keep going. There's a hallway to the right, at that end of the room.'

Their lights played across the floor. The last traces of the drag marks had been obliterated by the passage of all the law enforcement personnel who had since tramped through. On the night Maura had come to this death scene, she had been flanked by Detectives Crowe and Sleeper, had known that an army of CSTs were already poised to move in with their scopes and cameras and finger-print powders. That night, she had not been afraid.

Now she found herself breathing hard. Found herself staying close behind Rizzoli, acutely conscious of the fact that she had no one to watch her own back. She felt her neck hairs rise, her attention focused with exquisite sensitivity on any sounds, any hint of movement behind her.

Rizzoli halted, flashlight veering to the right. 'This is the hallway?'

'The bathroom's at that end.'

Rizzoli moved forward, light bouncing from one wall to the other. At the last doorway she paused, as though already knowing that what came next would be disturbing. She cast her light into the room and stood staring at smears of blood on the tile floor. Her light briefly slid across the walls, past the bathroom stall and porcelain urinals and rust-stained sinks. Then it returned, as though pulled by magnetic force, to the floor where the corpse had lain.

A place of death has a power all its own. Long after the body is removed and the blood scrubbed away, such a place still retains the memory of what has happened there. It holds echoes of screams, the lingering scent of fear. And like a black hole, it sucks into its vortex the rapt attention of the living, who cannot turn away, cannot resist a glimpse into hell.

Rizzoli crouched down to look at the blood-smeared tiles.

'It was a clean shot, into her heart,' said Maura, squatting down beside her. 'Pericardial tamponade, leading to rapid cardiac arrest. That's why there's so little blood on the floor. She had no heartbeat, no circulation. When he performed the amputations, he was cutting into a corpse.'

They fell silent, their gazes on the brown stains. Here in this bathroom, there were no windows. A light shining in this room wouldn't be visible from the street. Whoever wielded the knife could take his time, lingering undisturbed over the object of his butchery. There were no screams to muffle, no threat of discovery. He could cut at his leisure, through skin and joint, harvesting his prizes in flesh.

And when he was done, he left the body in this place where vermin reigned, where rats and roaches would feast, obliterating whatever flesh remained.

Maura rose to her feet, breathing hard. Though the building was frigid, her hands were sweating inside her gloves, and she felt her heart pounding.

'Can we go now?' she said.

'Wait. Let me look around some more.'

'There's nothing more to see here.'

'We just got here, Doc.'

Maura glanced toward the dark hallway and shivered. She felt an odd shift in the air, a chill breath that raised the hairs on her neck. The door, she thought suddenly. We left the door to the alley unlocked.

Rizzoli was still crouched over the bloodstains, her Maglite slowly skimming the floor, her attention focused only on the blood. She's not rattled, thought Maura. Why should I be? Calm down, calm down.

She edged toward the doorway. Wielded her light like a saber, slashing it swiftly into the dark hallway.

Saw nothing.

The hairs on the back of her neck were standing straight up.

'Rizzoli,' she whispered. 'Can we get out of here now?'

Only then did Rizzoli hear the tension in Maura's voice. She asked, just as quietly: 'What is it?'

'I want to leave.'

'Why?'

Maura stared into the dark hallway. 'Something doesn't feel right.'

'Did you hear anything?'

'Let's just get out of here, okay?'

Rizzoli rose to her feet. Said, softly: 'Okay.' She

stepped past Maura into the hallway. Paused, as though sniffing the air for any hint of a threat. Fearless Rizzoli, always in the lead, thought Maura, as she followed the detective back up the hallway and through the dining room. They stepped into the kitchen, flashlights beaming. Perfect targets, she realized. And here we come, creaking across the floor, our beams like two bull's-eyes.

Maura felt a whoosh of cold air and stared at the silhouette of a man, standing in the open doorway. She froze, a stunned observer, as voices suddenly exploded in the shadows.

Rizzoli, already in a combat crouch, screamed: 'Freeze!'

'Drop your weapon!'

'I said *freeze*, asshole!' Rizzoli commanded.

'Boston PD! I'm Boston PD!'

'Who the hell . . .'

Rizzoli's flashlight suddenly lit on the intruder's face. He raised his arm against the glare, his eyes narrowed. There was a long silence.

Rizzoli gave a snort of disgust. 'Oh shit.'

'Yeah, nice to see you, too,' said Detective Crowe. 'I guess this must be where all the action is.'

'I could've blown off your fucking head,' said Rizzoli. 'You should have warned us you were coming in . . .' Her voice trailed off. She went very still as another silhouette appeared. A tall man moved with catlike grace past Crowe, and into the circle of Rizzoli's flashlight beam. The light

264

suddenly wavered, her hand shaking too much to hold it steady.

'Hello, Jane,' said Gabriel Dean.

The darkness only seemed to magnify the long silence.

When Rizzoli finally managed to respond, her tone was strangely flat. Businesslike.

'I didn't know you were in town.'

'I just flew in this morning.'

She reholstered her weapon. Drew herself up straight. 'What are you doing here?'

'The same thing you are. Detective Crowe is walking me through the scene.'

'The FBI's coming in on this? Why?'

Dean glanced around their shadowy surroundings. 'We should talk about this somewhere else. Somewhere warm, at least. I'd like to hear how your case intersects with this one, Jane.'

'If we talk, the info has to go both ways,' said Rizzoli.

'Of course.'

'All cards on the table.'

Dean nodded. 'You'll know everything that I know.'

'Look,' said Crowe, 'Let me finish walking Agent Dean through here. We'll meet you back at the conference room. At least we'll have enough light to see each other. And we won't be standing around, freezing our asses off.'

Rizzoli nodded. 'The conference room, two o'clock. We'll see you there.'

Fourteen

Rizzoli fumbled for her car keys and dropped them in the snow. Cursed as she squatted down to retrieve them.

'Are you okay?' asked Maura.

'He took me by surprise. I wasn't expecting . . .' She stood up and huffed out a cloud of steam. 'Jesus, what is he doing here? What the *hell* is he doing here?'

'His job, I imagine.'

'I'm not ready for this. I'm not ready to work with him again.'

'You may not have a choice.'

'I know. And that's what pisses me off, that I don't have a choice.' Rizzoli unlocked her car and they both slid inside, onto icy seats.

'Are you going to tell him?' asked Maura.

Grimly Rizzoli started the engine. 'No.'

'He'd want to know.'

'I'm not sure he would. I'm not sure any man would.'

'So you're just writing off the happy ending?

Not even giving it a chance?'

Rizzoli sighed. 'Maybe, if we were different people, there would be a chance.'

'The affair didn't happen to other people. It happened to you two.'

'Right. What a surprise, huh?'

'Why?'

For a moment Rizzoli was silent, her gaze fixed on the road ahead. 'You know what my two brothers used to call me when we were growing up?' she said softly. 'The frog. They said no prince would ever want to kiss a frog. Much less marry me.'

'Brothers can be cruel.'

'But sometimes they just tell you the brutal truth.'

'When Agent Dean looks at you, I don't think he sees a frog.'

Rizzoli shrugged. 'Who knows what he sees?'

'An intelligent woman?'

'Yeah, that's really sexy.'

'To some men, it is.'

'Or so they claim. But you know what? I have a hard time believing it. Given the choice, men always go for the tits and ass.'

Rizzoli focused with angry intensity on the road as they drove down streets where dirty snow crusted sidewalks and the windows of parked cars were frosted white.

'He saw *something* in you, Jane. Enough to want you.'

'It was the case we were working. The excitement

of the hunt. It makes you feel alive, you know? When you start to close in, the adrenaline gets pumping and everything looks different, feels different. You're working with someone around the clock, working so close to him that you know his scent. You know how he drinks his coffee and how he ties his tie. Then the case turns hairy, you get angry together and scared together. And pretty soon it starts to feel like love. But it isn't. It's just two people, working in a situation so intense that they can't tell the difference between lust and the thrill of the chase. That's what I think happened. We met over a few dead bodies. And after a while, even I started to look good to him.'

'Is that all he was to you? Someone who started to look good?'

'Well, shit. He *does* look good.'

'Because if you don't love him – if you don't even care about him – then seeing him now shouldn't be all that painful. Should it?'

'I don't know!' was Rizzoli's exasperated response. 'I don't know what I feel about him!'

'Does it depend on whether he loves you?'

'I'm sure not going to ask him.'

'It's one way to get a straight answer.'

'How does that old saying go? *If you don't want to hear the answer, then you shouldn't ask the question*?'

'You never know. The answer might surprise you.'

At Schroeder Plaza, they stopped in the cafeteria to pick up coffee and carried their cups upstairs, to the conference room. While waiting for Crowe and Dean to arrive, Maura watched Rizzoli rustle through papers and search through files as though they held some secret she was desperate to uncover. At two fifteen, they finally heard the faint chime of the elevator bell, and then Crowe's laughter in the hall. Rizzoli's spine went rigid. As the men's voices drew nearer, her gaze remained fixed on the papers. When Dean appeared in the doorway, she did not immediately look up, as though refusing to acknowledge his power over her.

Maura had first met Special Agent Gabriel Dean in late August, when he had joined the homicide team investigating the slayings of wealthy couples in the Boston area. A man of imposing stature and quiet intelligence, he had quickly come to dominate that team, and his conflict with Rizzoli, the lead investigating officer, was almost guaranteed from the start. Maura had been the first to watch that conflict transform into attraction. She had noticed the first sparks of their affair, had seen their gazes meet over the bodies of victims. She had taken note of Rizzoli's blushes, her uncertainty. The first stages of love were always fraught with confusion.

As were the last stages of love.

Dean came into the room, and his gaze immediately fixed on Rizzoli. He was dressed in a suit and tie, his crisp appearance a contrast to Rizzoli's wrinkled blouse and unruly hair. When at last she looked up at him, it was almost with an air of defiance. *So here I am. Take it or leave it.*

Crowe swaggered to the head of the table. 'Okay, the gang's all here. It's time for show and tell.' He looked at Rizzoli.

'Let's hear from the FBI first,' she said.

Dean opened the briefcase he'd carried into the room. He took out a folder and slid it across the table to Rizzoli.

'That photograph was taken ten days ago, in Providence, Rhode Island,' he said

Rizzoli opened the folder. Maura, sitting beside her, had a full view of the photograph. It was a death scene photo, taken of a man curled into a fetal position inside the trunk of a car. Blood was splattered across the fawn-colored carpet. The face of the victim was surprisingly intact, the eyes open, the dependent skin suffused purple from lividity.

'The victim's name was Howard Redfield, age fifty-one, a divorced white male from Cincinnati,' said Dean. 'The cause of death was a single gunshot wound, fired through the left temporal bone. In addition, he had multiple fractures of both kneecaps, administered with a blunt weapon, possibly a hammer. There were also severe burns to both hands, which were bound with duct tape behind his back.'

'He was tortured,' said Rizzoli.

'Yes. At great length.'

Rizzoli swayed back in her chair, her face pale. Maura was the only person in the room who knew the reason for that pallor, and she watched her with concern. She saw the desperate battle play out on her face, saw her struggle against nausea.

'He was found dead in the trunk of his own car,' Dean continued. 'The car was parked about two blocks from the bus station in Providence. That's only about an hour, hour-and-a-half drive from here.'

'But a different jurisdiction,' said Crowe.

Dean nodded. 'That's why this death didn't come to your attention. The killer could very well have driven that car down to Providence with the victim in his trunk, left it there, and caught a bus back to Boston.'

'*Back* to Boston? Why do you think this is where he started from?' asked Maura.

'It's just a guess. We don't know where the killing actually took place. We can't even be sure of Mr. Redfield's movements over the last few weeks. His home is in Cincinnati, but he turns up dead in New England. He left no credit card trail, no record of where he's been staying. We do know he withdrew a large amount of cash from his account a month ago. And then he left home.'

'Sounds like someone who's on the run and doesn't want to be traced,' said Maura. 'Or someone who's scared.'

Dean looked at the photo. 'Obviously, he was right to be.'

'Tell us more about this victim,' said Rizzoli. She was back in control now, and able to gaze, without flinching, at the photo.

'Mr. Redfield was formerly a senior VP of

271

Octagon Chemicals, in charge of their overseas operations,' said Dean. 'Two months ago, he resigned from the company, ostensibly for personal reasons.'

'Octagon?' said Maura. 'They've been in the news. Aren't they currently under investigation by the Securities and Exchange Commission?'

Dean nodded. 'The SEC enforcement division has filed a civil action against Octagon, alleging multiple violations involving billions of dollars in illegal transactions.'

'Billions?' said Rizzoli. 'Wow.'

'Octagon is a huge multinational, with annual sales of twenty billion dollars. We're talking about a very big fish.'

Rizzoli looked at the death scene photo. 'And this victim was swimming in that pond. He'd know the inside scoop. You think he was a problem for Octagon?'

'Three weeks ago,' said Dean, 'Mr. Redfield made an appointment to speak with officials from the Justice Department.'

'Yep,' said Crowe with a laugh. 'He was definitely a problem for them.'

'He asked that Justice officials meet him here, in Boston.'

'Why not Washington?' asked Rizzoli.

'He told them there were other parties who wished to make statements. That it had to be done here. What we don't know is why he contacted the Justice Department, rather than go directly to the SEC, since we assume it had to do with the Octagon investigation.'

'But you don't know that for certain?'

'No. Because he never kept the appointment. By then, he was dead.'

Crowe said, 'Hey, if it looks like a paid hit and it smells like a paid hit . . .'

'What does any of this have to do with Rat Lady?' asked Rizzoli.

'I'm just getting to that,' said Dean. He looked at Maura. 'You performed the autopsy. What was her cause of death?'

'A gunshot wound to the chest,' said Maura. 'Bullet fragments penetrated her heart, and there was massive bleeding into the pericardial sac, preventing the heart from pumping. It's called pericardial tamponade.'

'And what type of bullet was used?'

Maura remembered the X-ray of Rat Lady's chest. The spray of shell fragments, like a galaxy of stars scattered through both lungs. 'It was a Glaser blue-tip,' she said. 'A copper jacket containing metal pellets. It's designed to fragment inside the body, with little chance of through and through penetration.' She paused, and added: 'It's a devastating projectile.'

Dean nodded at the photo of Howard Redfield, lying curled and bloody in the trunk of his car. 'Mr. Redfield was killed with a Glaser blue-tip. A bullet fired from the same gun that killed your Jane Doe.'

For a moment, no one spoke.

Then Rizzoli said, in disbelief, 'But you just laid

the case for a contract killing. Octagon's way of dealing with a whistle-blower. This other victim, Rat Lady—'

'Detective Rizzoli's right,' said Maura. 'Rat Lady is the most unlikely target of a corporate hit that I could imagine.'

'Nevertheless,' said Dean, 'The bullet that killed her was fired by the same weapon that killed Howard Redfield.'

Crowe said, 'That's how Agent Dean came into the picture. I requested a DRUGFIRE search on that blue-tip copper jacket you took out of her chest.'

Similar to the FBI's national AFIS database for fingerprints, DRUGFIRE was a centralized data-base for firearm-related evidence. Marks and striations found on bullets from crime scenes were stored as digitized data, which could then be searched for matches, linking all crimes committed by the same firearm.

'DRUGFIRE came up with the match,' said Dean.

Rizzoli shook her head in bewilderment. 'Why these two victims? I don't see the connection.'

'That's what makes Jane Doe's death so interesting,' said Dean.

Maura did not like his use of the word *interesting*. It implied that some deaths were not interesting, not worthy of special attention. Those victims would certainly not agree.

She focused on the photo, an ugly splash of gore lying on the conference table. 'Our Jane Doe doesn't belong in this picture,' she said.

'Dr. Isles?'

'There's a logical reason why Howard Redfield was killed. He may be a whistle-blower in an SEC investigation. The evidence of torture tells us his death wasn't just a case of robbery gone wrong. The killer wanted something from him. Retribution, maybe. Or information. But how does our Jane Doe – most likely an illegal immigrant – fit in? Why would anyone want her dead?'

'That's the question, isn't it?' Dean looked at Rizzoli. 'I understand you have a case which may tie into this as well.'

His gaze seemed to rattle her. She gave a nervous shake of the head. 'It's another one that seems completely unrelated.'

'Detective Crowe told me that two nuns were attacked in their convent,' said Dean. 'In Jamaica Plain.'

'But that perp didn't use a firearm. The nuns were bludgeoned, we think with a hammer. It looked like a rage attack. Some wacko who hates women.'

'Maybe that's what he wanted you to think. To hide any connection to these other homicides.'

'Yeah, well, it worked. Until Dr. Isles came up with Jane Doe's diagnosis of leprosy. It turns out one of the nuns who was attacked, Sister Ursula, used to work in a leper village, in India.'

'A village that no longer exists,' Maura said.

Dean looked at her. 'What?'

'It may have been a religious massacre. Nearly a hundred people were slaughtered, and the village

275

was burned to the ground.' She paused. 'Sister Ursula is the only one from that village who survived.'

She had never seen Gabriel Dean look so taken aback. Usually, Dean was the one who held the secrets and doled out the revelations. This new information temporarily stunned him into silence.

She hit him with another one. 'I believe our Jane Doe may have been from that same village in India.'

'You told me earlier you thought she was Hispanic,' said Crowe.

'It was only a guess, based on her skin pigmentation.'

'So are you changing the guess to make it fit the circumstances?'

'No, I'm changing it because of what we found at autopsy. Remember that strand of yellow thread adhering to her wrist?'

'Yeah. Hair and Fiber said it was cotton. Probably just a piece of string.'

'Wearing a loop of string around your wrist is supposed to ward off the evil eye. It's a Hindu custom.'

'India again,' said Dean.

Maura nodded. 'It does keep going back to India.'

'A nun and an illegal immigrant with leprosy?' said Crowe. 'How do we link them to a corporate hit?' He shook his head. 'Professionals don't get hired unless someone has a lot to gain.'

'Or a lot to lose,' said Maura.

'If these are all contract killings,' said Dean, 'you can be sure of one thing. That the progress of your investigations will be tracked very carefully. You need to control any and all information about these cases. Because someone's watching everything Boston PD is doing.'

Watching me too, thought Maura, chilled at the thought. And she was so visible. At crime scenes, on the TV news. Walking to her car. She was accustomed to being in the eye of the media, but now she considered the other eyes that might be watching her. Tracking her. And she remembered what she had felt in the darkness at Mama Cortina's: the prey's cold sense of dread when it suddenly realizes it is being stalked.

Dean said, 'I need to see that other death scene. The convent, where the nuns were attacked.' He looked at Rizzoli. 'Could you take me through it?'

For a moment, Rizzoli did not respond. She sat unmoving, her gaze fixed on the death photo of Howard Redfield, curled in the trunk of his car.

'Jane?'

She took a breath and sat up straight, as though she'd suddenly found some new well of courage. Of fortitude.

'Let's go,' she said, and rose to her feet. She looked at Dean. 'I guess we're a team again.'

Fifteen

I can deal with this. I can deal with him.

Rizzoli drove to Jamaica Plain with her eyes on the road, but her mind on Gabriel Dean. Without warning, he had stepped back into her life, and she was still too stunned to make sense of what she was now feeling. Her stomach was knotted, her hands numb. Only a day ago, she had thought that she was over the worst of missing him, that with a little time and a lot of distraction she could put their affair behind her. Out of sight, out of mind.

Now he was back in her sight, and very much on her mind.

She was first to arrive at Graystones Abbey. She sat in her parked car and waited for him, every nerve humming, her anxiety turning to nausea.

Pull it together, goddamn it. Focus on the job.

She saw his rental car park behind her.

At once she stepped out and welcomed the punishing wind on her face. The more brutal the cold, the better, to slap some sense into her. She watched him emerge from his car and greeted him with the crisp nod of a fellow cop.

Then she turned and rang the gate bell. No pause for conversation, no fumbling for words. She went straight to business, because it was the only way she knew how to cope with this reunion. She was relieved when a nun soon emerged from the building and began shuffling through the snow, toward the gate.

'It's Sister Isabel,' said Rizzoli. 'Believe it or not, she's one of the younger ones.'

Isabel squinted at them through the bars, her gaze on Rizzoli's companion.

'This is Agent Gabriel Dean from the FBI,' said Rizzoli. 'I'm just going to show him the chapel. We won't disturb you.'

Isabel opened the gate to let them in. It gave an unforgiving clang as it swung shut behind them. The cold sound of finality. Of imprisonment. Sister Isabel immediately returned to the building, leaving the two visitors standing in the courtyard. Alone with each other.

At once Rizzoli took control of the silence and launched into a case review. 'We still can't be sure of the point of entry,' she said. 'Snowfall covered up any footprints, and we didn't find any broken ivy to indicate he climbed the wall. That front gate's kept locked at all times, so if the perp came that way, someone inside the abbey had to let him in. That's a violation of convent rules. It would have to be done at night, when no one would see it.'

279

'You have no witnesses?'

'None. We thought, at first, that it was the younger nun, Camille, who might have opened the gate.'

'Why Camille?'

'Because of what we found on autopsy.' Rizzoli turned her gaze to the wall, avoiding his eyes, as she said: 'She'd recently been pregnant. We found the dead infant in a pond behind the abbey.'

'And the father?'

'Obviously a prime suspect, whoever he is. We haven't identified him yet. DNA tests are still pending. But now, after what you've just told us, it seems we may have been barking up the wrong tree entirely.'

She stared at the walls that encircled them, at the gate that barred the world from entry, and an alternate sequence of events suddenly began to play out before her eyes, a sequence far different from the one she had imagined when she first set foot on this crime scene.

If it wasn't Camille who opened the gate . . .

'So who let the killer into the abbey?' said Dean, eerily reading her thoughts.

She frowned at the gate, thinking of snow blowing across the cobblestones. She said, 'Ursula was wearing a coat and boots . . .'

She turned and looked at the building. Pictured it in those black hours before dawn, the windows dark, the nuns asleep in their chambers. The courtyard silent, except for the wind.

'It was already snowing when she came outside,'

she said. 'She was dressed for the weather. She walked across this courtyard, to the gate, where someone was waiting for her.'

'Someone she must have known would be out here,' said Dean. 'Someone she must have expected.'

Rizzoli nodded. Now she turned toward the chapel and began to walk, her boots punching holes in the snow. Dean was right behind her, but she was no longer focused on him; she was walking in the footsteps of a doomed woman.

A night swirling with the season's first snow. The stones are slippery beneath your boots. You move in silence because you don't want the other sisters to know you are meeting someone. Someone for whom you are willing to break the rules.

But it's dark, and there are no lamps to light the gate. So you can't see his face. You can't be sure this is the visitor you're expecting tonight . . .

At the fountain, she abruptly halted and looked up at the row of windows over the courtyard.

'What is it?' said Dean.

'Camille's room,' she said, pointing. 'It's right up there.'

He gazed up at the room. The stinging wind had made his face ruddy, and ruffled his hair. It was a mistake to stare at him, because she suddenly felt such hunger for his touch, she had to turn away, had to press her fist against her abdomen, to counter the emptiness she felt there.

'She might have seen something, from that room,' said Dean.

'The light in the chapel. It was on when the bodies were found.' Rizzoli looked up at Camille's window, and remembered the bloodstained sheet.

She awakens with her sanitary pad soaked. She climbs from bed, to use the bathroom and change her pad. And when she comes back to her room, she notices the light, glowing through the stained-glass windows. A light that should not be on.

Rizzoli turned toward the chapel, drawn by the ghostly image she now saw, of young Camille, stepping out of the main building. Shivering as she moved beneath the covered walkway, perhaps regretting that she had not pulled on a coat for this short walk between buildings.

Rizzoli followed that ghost, into the chapel.

There she stood in the gloom. The lights were off, and the pews were nothing more than horizontal slats of shadow. Dean was silent beside her, like a ghost himself, as she watched the final scene play out.

Camille, stepping through the door, just a slip of a girl, her face pale as milk.

She looks down in horror. Sister Ursula lies at her feet, and the stones are splattered with blood.

Perhaps Camille did not immediately under-stand what had happened, and thought at first glance that Ursula had merely slipped and hit her head. Or perhaps she already knew, from that first glimpse of blood, that evil had breached their walls. That it now stood behind her, near the door. Watching her.

That it was moving toward her.

282

The first blow sends her staggering. Stunned as she is, she still struggles to escape. Moves in the only direction open to her: Up the aisle. Toward the altar, where she stumbles. Where she drops to her knees, awaiting the final blow.

And when it's done, and young Camille lies dead, the killer turns back, toward the first victim. Toward Ursula.

But he doesn't finish the job. He leaves her alive. Why?

She looked down at the stones, where Ursula had fallen. She imagined the attacker, reaching down to confirm the kill.

She went very still, suddenly remembering what Dr. Isles had told her.

'The killer didn't feel a pulse,' she said.

'What?'

'Sister Ursula is missing a carotid pulse on the right side of her neck.' She looked at Dean. 'He thought she was dead.'

They walked up the aisle, past rows of pews, following in Camille's last footsteps. They came to the spot near the altar where she had fallen. They stood in silence, their gazes on the floor. Though they could not see it in the gloom, traces of blood surely lingered in the cracks between stones.

Shivering, Rizzoli looked up and saw that Dean was watching her.

'That's all there is to see here,' she said. 'Unless you want to talk to the sisters.'

283

'I want to talk to you.'

'I'm right here.'

'No, you're not. Detective Rizzoli is here. I want to talk to Jane.'

She laughed. A blasphemous sound in that chapel. 'You make it sound like I'm a split personality or something.'

'That's not too far from the truth. You work so hard at playing the cop, you bury the woman. It's the woman I came to see.'

'You waited long enough.'

'Why are you angry at me?'

'I'm not.'

'You have a strange way of welcoming me to Boston.'

'Maybe because you didn't bother to tell me you were coming.'

He sighed, huffing out a ghost. 'Can we just sit together for a moment and talk?'

She went to the front pew and sank onto the wooden bench. As he sat down beside her, she gazed straight ahead, afraid to look at him. Afraid of the emotions he stirred in her. Just inhaling his scent was painful, because of the longing it reawakened. This was the man who had shared her bed, whose touch and taste and laugh still haunted her dreams. The result of their union was growing even now, inside her, and she pressed her hand to her belly to quell the secret ache she suddenly felt there.

'How have you been, Jane?'

'I've been good. Busy.'

284

'And the bandage on your head? What happened?'

'Oh, this.' She touched her forehead and shrugged. 'Little accident in the morgue. I slipped and fell.'

'You look tired.'

'You don't bother much with compliments, do you?'

'It's just an observation.'

'Yeah, well, I'm tired. Of course I am. It's been one of those weeks. And Christmas is coming up and I haven't even bought my family any gifts yet.'

He regarded her for a moment, and she looked away, not wanting to meet his eyes.

'You're not happy to be working with me again, are you?'

She said nothing. Didn't deny it.

'Why don't you just tell me what the hell is wrong?' he finally snapped.

The anger in his voice took her aback. Dean was not a man who often revealed his emotions. Once that had infuriated her, because it always made her feel as if *she* was the one out of control, the one always threatening to boil over. Their affair had started because she had made the first move, not him. She had taken all the risks and put her pride on the line, and where did it get her? In love with a man who was still a cipher to her. A man whose only display of emotion was the anger she now heard in his voice.

It made her angry, as well.

'There's no point rehashing this,' she said. 'We

have to work together. We have no choice. But everything else – I just can't deal with that now.'

'What can't you deal with? The fact we slept together?'

'Yes.'

'You didn't seem to mind it at the time.'

'It happened, that's all. I'm sure it meant about as much to you as it did to me.'

He paused. Stung? She wondered. Hurt? She didn't think it was possible to hurt a man who had no emotions.

She was startled when he suddenly laughed.

'You are so full of shit, Jane,' he said.

She turned and looked at him – really *looked* at him – and was struck breathless by all the same things that had attracted her to him before. The strong jaw, the slate-gray eyes. The air of command. She could insult him all she wanted to, yet she'd always feel he was the one in control.

'What are you afraid of?' he said.

'I don't know what you're talking about.'

'That I'll hurt you? That I'll walk away first?'

'You were never there to begin with.'

'Okay, that's true. I couldn't be. Not with the jobs we have.'

'And it all comes down to that, doesn't it?' She rose from the bench and stamped the blood back into her numb feet. 'You're in Washington, I'm here. You have your job, which you won't give up. I have mine. No compromise.'

'You make it sound like a declaration of war.'

'No, just logic. I'm trying to be practical.' She

turned and started back toward the chapel door.

'And trying to protect yourself.'

'Shouldn't I?' she said, looking back at him.

'The whole world isn't out to hurt you, Jane.'

'Because I don't let it.'

They left the chapel. Walked back across the courtyard and stepped through the gate, which gave a resounding clang as it shut.

'Well, I don't see the point of trying to chip away at that armor,' he said. 'I'll go a long way to meet you. But you have to come halfway. You have to give, too.' He turned and started toward his car.

'Gabriel?' she said.

He stopped and looked back at her.

'What did you think would happen between us this time?'

'I don't know. That you'd be glad to see me, at least.'

'What else?'

'That we'd screw like bunnies again.'

At that, she gave a laugh and shook her head. *Don't tempt me. Don't remind me of what I've been missing.*

He looked at her over the roof of his car. 'I'd settle for the first, Jane,' he said. Then he slid inside and shut the door.

She watched him drive away, and thought: *Screwing like bunnies is how I got into this mess.*

Shivering, she looked at the sky. Only four o'clock, and already, the night seemed to be closing in, stealing the last gray light of day. She did not have her gloves, and the wind was so bitter, it stung her fingers as she took out her keys and opened the car door. Sliding into her car, she fumbled to insert the key in the ignition, but her hands were clumsy, and she could barely feel her fingers.

She paused, key in the ignition.

Suddenly thought about lepers' hands, the fingers worn down to stumps.

And she remembered, vaguely, a question about a woman's hands. Something mentioned in passing, that she had ignored at the time.

She said I was rude because I asked why that lady didn't have any fingers.

She got out of her car and went back to the gate. Rang the bell again and again.

At last Sister Isabel appeared. The ancient face that gazed through the iron bars did not look pleased to see her.

'I need to speak to the girl,' Rizzoli said. 'Mrs. Otis's daughter.'

She found Noni sitting all alone in an old classroom at the end of the hall, her sturdy legs swinging from the chair, a rainbow of crayons splayed out on the battered teacher's desk in front of her. It was warmer in the abbey kitchen, where Mrs. Otis was now preparing dinner for the sisters, and the aroma of fresh-baked chocolate chip cookies wafted even to this gloomy end of the wing, yet Noni had chosen to hole up in this cold room, away from her mother's sharp tongue and disapproving looks. The girl did not even seem to notice the chill. She was clutching a lime-green crayon in a childish grip, her tongue sticking out in fierce concentration as she drew sparks shooting from a man's head.

'It's about to explode,' said Noni. 'The death rays are cooking his brain. That makes him blow up. Like when you cook things in the microwave, and they blow up, just like that.'

'The death rays are green?' asked Rizzoli.

Noni looked up. 'Are they supposed to be a different color?'

'I don't know. I always thought death rays would be, oh, silver.'

'I don't have any silver. Conrad took mine at school and he never gave it back.'

'I guess green death rays will work, too.'

Reassured, Noni went back to her drawing. She picked up a blue crayon and added spikes to the rays, so they looked like arrows raining down on the unfortunate victim. There were many unfortunate victims on the desk. The array of drawings showed spaceships shooting fire and blue aliens chopping off heads. These were not friendly E.T.s. The girl who sat drawing them struck Rizzoli as an alien creature herself, a little gremlin with gypsy brown eyes, hiding in a room where no one would disturb her.

She had chosen a depressing retreat. The classroom looked long unused, its stark walls marred by the scars of countless thumb-tacks and yellowed Scotch tape. Ancient student desks were stacked up in a far corner, leaving bare the scuffed wood floor. The only light came from the windows, and it cast everything in wintry shades of gray.

Noni had begun the next drawing in her series of alien atrocities. The victim of the lime-green death rays now had a gaping hole in his head, and purplish blobs were shooting out. A cartoon bubble appeared above him with his dying exclamation.

AHHHHHH!

'Noni, do you remember the night we talked to you?'

The brown curls bobbed up and down in a nod.

'You haven't come back to see me.'

'Yeah, well, I've been running around quite a bit.'

'You should stop running around. You should learn to sit down and relax.'

There were echoes of an adult voice in that statement. *Stop running around, Noni!*

'And you shouldn't be so sad,' Noni added picking up a new crayon.

Rizzoli watched in silence as the girl drew gouts of bright red shooting from the exploding head. Jesus, she thought. This girl sees it. This fearless little gremlin sees more than anyone else does.

'You have very sharp eyes,' said Rizzoli. 'You see a lot of things, huh?'

'I saw a potato blow up once. In the microwave.'

'You told us some things last time, about Sister Ursula. You said she scolded you.'

'She did.'

'She said you were rude, because you asked about a woman's hands. Remember?'

Noni looked up, one dark eye peeking out from beneath the tumble of curls. 'I thought you only want to know about Sister Camille.'

'I want to know about Ursula, too. And about the woman who had something wrong with her hands. What did you mean by that?'

'She didn't have any fingers.' Noni picked up a black crayon and drew a bird above the exploding man. A bird of prey, with huge black wings. 'Vultures,' she said. 'They eat you when you're dead.'

Here I am, thought Rizzoli, relying on the word of a girl who draws space aliens and death rays.

She leaned forward. Asked, quietly: 'Where did you see this woman, Noni?'

Noni put down her crayon and gave a weary sigh. 'Okay. Since you *have* to know.' She jumped off the chair.

'Where are you going?'

'To show you. Where the lady was.'

Noni's jacket was so big on her, she looked like a little Michelin man, tramping out into the snow. Rizzoli followed in the footprints made by Noni's rubber boots, feeling like a lowly private marching behind a determined general. Noni led her across the abbey courtyard, past the fountain where snow had piled like layers on a wedding cake. At the front gate, she stopped, and pointed.

'She was out there.'

'Outside the gate?'

'Uh-huh. She had a big scarf around her face. Like she was a bank robber.'

'So you didn't see her face?'

The girl shook her head, brown curls tossing.

'Did this lady talk to you?'

'No, the man did.'

Rizzoli stared at her. 'There was a man with her?'

'He asked me to let them in, because they needed to speak to Sister Ursula. But it's against the rules, and I told him so. If a sister breaks the rules, she gets kicked out. My mommy says the sisters don't have anywhere else to go, so they *never* break the rules, because they're afraid to go outside.' Noni paused. Looked up and said with a note of pride: 'But I go outside all the time.'

That's because you're not afraid of anything, thought Rizzoli. *You're fearless.*

Noni began to tramp a line in the snow, her little pink boots marching with a soldier's precision. She cut one trough, then did an about-face and marched back, stamping out a parallel line. *She thinks she's invincible,* thought Rizzoli. *But she's so small and vulnerable. Just a speck of a girl in a puffed-up jacket.*

'What happened then, Noni?'

The girl came clomp-clomping back through the snow and came to an abrupt halt, her gaze focused on her snow-crusted boots. 'The lady pushed a letter through the gate.' Noni leaned forward and

292

whispered: 'And I saw she didn't have any fingers.'

'Did you give Sister Ursula that letter?'

The girl gave a nod that made her curls bounce like a head full of Slinkies. 'And she came out. *Right* out.'

'Did she talk to these people?'

A shake of the head.

'Why not?'

'Because when she came out, they were already gone.'

Rizzoli turned and stared at the sidewalk where the two visitors had stood, imploring a recalcitrant child to let them in the gate.

The hairs on the back of her neck suddenly bristled.

Rat Lady. She was here.

Sixteen

Rizzoli stepped off the hospital elevator, strode past the sign announcing ALL VISITORS MUST CHECK IN, and barrelled straight through the double doors into the intensive care unit. It was one A.M., and the unit lights were dimmed to allow the patients to sleep. Coming straight from the bright hallway, she confronted a room where nurses were faceless silhouettes. Only one patient cubicle was brightly lit, and like a beacon, it drew her toward it.

The black woman cop standing outside the cubicle greeted Rizzoli. 'Hey, Detective. You got here fast.'

'She said anything yet?'

'She can't. She's still got that breathing tube in her throat. But she's definitely awake. Her eyes are open, and I heard the nurse say she's following commands. Everyone seems really surprised that she woke up at all.'

The squeal of the ventilator alarm made Rizzoli glance through the cubicle doorway at the knot of medical personnel huddled around the bed. She

294

recognized the neurosurgeon, Dr. Yuen, and the internist, Dr. Sutcliffe, his blond ponytail an oddly disconcerting detail in that gathering of grim professionals. 'What's going on in there?'

'I don't know. Something about the blood pressure. Dr. Sutcliffe got here just as things started to go haywire. Then Dr. Yuen showed up, and they've been fussing with her ever since.' The cop shook her head. 'I don't think it's going well. Those machines've been beeping like crazy.'

'Jesus, don't tell me we're gonna lose her just as she wakes up.'

Rizzoli squeezed into the cubicle, where lights shone down with a brilliance that was painful to her tired eyes. She could not see Sister Ursula, who was hidden within the tight circle of personnel, but she could see the monitors above the bed, the heart rhythm skittering like a stone across water.

'She's trying to pull out the ET tube!' a nurse said.

'Get that hand tied down tighter!'

'. . . Ursula, relax. Try to relax.'

'Systolic's down to eighty—'

'Why is she so flushed?' said Yuen. 'Look at her face.' He glanced sideways as the ventilator squealed.

'Too much airway resistance,' a nurse said. 'She's fighting the ventilator.'

'Her pressure's dropping, Dr. Yuen. It's eighty systolic.'

'Let's get a dopamine drip going. Now.'

A nurse suddenly noticed Rizzoli standing in the

doorway. 'Ma'am, you're going to have to step out.'

'Is she conscious?' asked Rizzoli.

'Step *out* of the cubicle.'

'I'll handle this,' said Sutcliffe.

He took Rizzoli by the arm, and his grasp was not gentle as he led her out of the cubicle. He slid the curtain shut, cutting off all view of the patient. Standing in the gloom, she could feel the eyes of other nurses, watching her from their different stations in the ICU.

'Detective Rizzoli,' said Sutcliffe, 'you need to let us do our jobs.'

'I'm trying to do mine as well. She's our only witness.'

'And she's in critical condition. We need to get her through this crisis before anyone talks to her.'

'She is conscious, though?'

'Yes.'

'She understands what's going on?'

He paused. In the low light of the ICU, she could not read his expression. All she could see was the silhouette of his broad shoulders and the reflection of his eyes, glinting green from the nearby monitor banks. 'I'm not sure. Frankly, I never expected her to regain consciousness at all.'

'Why is her blood pressure falling? Is this something new?'

'A little while ago, she started to panic, probably because of the endotracheal tube. It's a frightening sensation, to feel a tube in your throat, but it has to stay in to help her breathe. We gave her some Valium when her pressure shot up. Then it suddenly started to crash.'

A nurse pulled back the cubicle curtain and called through the doorway: 'Dr. Sutcliffe?'

'Yes?'

'Her pressure's not responding, even on dopamine.'

Sutcliffe stepped back into the cubicle.

Through the open doorway, Rizzoli watched the drama playing out only a few feet away. The nun's hands were balled up in fists, the tendons of her arms standing out in taut cords as she fought the restraints that bound her wrists to the bed rails. The crown of her head was encased in bandages, and her mouth was obscured by the protruding endotracheal tube, but her face was clearly visible. It looked swollen, the cheeks suffused a bright red. Trapped in that mummifying mass of gauze and tubes, Ursula had the eyes of a hunted animal, the pupils dilated with fear, her gaze frantically darting left, then right, as though in search of escape. The bed rails rattled like the bars of a cage as she yanked against the restraints. Her whole torso lifted off the bed, and the cardiac alarm suddenly squealed.

Rizzoli's gaze shot to the monitor, where the line had gone flat.

'It's okay, it's okay!' Sutcliffe said. 'She just disconnected one of her leads.' He snapped the wire back in place, and the rhythm reappeared onscreen. A rapid blip-blip-blip.

'Increase the dopamine drip,' said Yuen. 'Let's push fluids.'

Rizzoli watched as the nurse opened the IV full bore, unleashing a flood of saline into Ursula's vein. The nun's gaze met Rizzoli's in a final moment of awareness. Just before her eyes started to glaze over, before the last spark of consciousness flickered out, what Rizzoli saw, in that gaze, was mortal fear.

'Pressure's still not coming up! It's down to sixty—'

The muscles of Ursula's face slackened, and the hands fell still. Beneath drooping lids, the eyes were now unfocused. Unseeing.

'PVCs,' the nurse said. 'I'm seeing PVCs!'

Gazes shot straight to the cardiac monitor. The heart tracing, which had been ticking rapidly but evenly across the screen, was now distorted by dagger thrusts.

'V tach!' said Yuen.

'I can't get any pressure! She's not perfusing.'

'Get that bed rail down. Come on, come on, let's start compressions.'

Rizzoli was shoved backwards, out of the doorway, as one of the nurses pushed toward the doorway and called out: 'We've got a Code Blue!'

Through the cubicle window, Rizzoli watched as the storm swirled around Ursula. She saw Yuen's head bobbing up and down as he performed CPR. Watched as drug after drug was injected into IV ports, and sterile wrappings fluttered to the floor.

Rizzoli stared at the monitor. The tracing was now a line of jagged teeth cutting across the screen.

'Charged to two hundred!'

In the cubicle, everyone stepped back as a nurse leaned forward with the defibrillator paddles. Rizzoli had a clear view of Ursula's bared breasts, the skin blotchy and red. It struck her as somehow startling, that a nun would have such generous breasts.

The paddles discharged.

Ursula's torso jerked, as though tugged by strings.

The woman cop standing beside Rizzoli said softly: 'I got a bad feeling. She's not gonna make it.'

Sutcliffe glanced up, once again, at the monitor. Then his gaze met Rizzoli's through the window. And he shook his head.

An hour later, Maura arrived at the hospital. After Rizzoli's phone call, she had rolled straight out of bed, leaving Victor asleep on the pillow beside her, and had dressed without showering. Riding the elevator up to the ICU, she could smell his scent on her skin, and she ached from the rawness of the night's lovemaking. She had come straight to the hospital while reeking gloriously of sex, her mind still focused on warm bodies, not cold. On the living, not the dead. Leaning back against the elevator wall, she closed her eyes and allowed herself to savor the memories for just a while longer. One more moment of remembered pleasure.

The opening of the door startled her. She jerked straight, blinking at the two nurses who stood waiting to step in, and she quickly exited, her cheeks flushing. *Do they notice it?* she thought as she walked down the hall. *Surely anyone can see, in my face, the guilty glow of sex.*

Rizzoli was in the ICU waiting room, slouched on the sofa and sipping from a Styrofoam cup of coffee. As Maura walked in, Rizzoli gave her a long look, as though she too detected something different about Maura. An unseemly flush to her face, on this night when tragedy had called them together.

'They're saying she had a heart attack,' said Rizzoli. 'It doesn't look good. She's on life support.'

'What time did she code?'

'Around one. They worked on her for almost an hour, and managed to get a heart rhythm back. But she's comatose now. No spontaneous breathing. Unreactive pupils.' She shook her head. 'I don't think there's anyone home anymore.'

'What do the doctors say?'

'Well, that's the controversy. Dr. Yuen isn't ready to pull the plug yet. But hippie boy thinks she's brain dead.'

'You mean Dr. Sutcliffe?'

'Yeah. The hunk with the ponytail. He's ordered an EEG in the morning, to check for brain activity.'

'If there's none, it'll be hard to justify maintaining life support.'

Rizzoli nodded. 'I thought you'd say that.'

'Was the cardiac arrest witnessed?'

'What?'

'Were medical personnel present when her heart stopped?'

Rizzoli looked irritated now, put off by Maura's matter-of-fact questions. She set down the cup, sloshing coffee onto the table. 'A whole crowd of 'em, in fact. I was there, too.'

'What led up to the code?'

'They said her blood pressure shot up first and her pulse went crazy. By the time I got here, her pressure was already falling. And then her heart stopped. So yeah, the whole event was witnessed.'

A moment passed. The TV was turned on, but the volume was muted. Rizzoli's gaze drifted to the CNN news banner scrolling across the bottom of the screen. *Disgruntled employee shoots four in North Carolina auto plant . . . Toxic chemical spill in Colorado train derailment . . .* A running tally of disasters across the county, and here we are, two tired women, struggling just to make it through this night.

Maura sat down on the couch beside Rizzoli. 'How're you doing, Jane? You look wiped out.'

'I feel like hell. Like it's sucking up every ounce of my energy. And there's nothing left for me.' She drained her coffee in one last gulp and threw the empty cup at the trash can. It missed. She simply stared at it, too tired to get up and retrieve it from the floor.

'The girl ID'd him,' said Rizzoli.

'What?'

'Noni.' She paused. 'Gabriel was so good with

301

her. It kind of surprised me. Somehow, I didn't expect that he'd be good with kids. You know how he is, so hard to read. So uptight. But he sat right down with her and had her eating out of his hand . . .' She looked off wistfully, then gave herself a shake. 'She recognized Howard Redfield's photo.'

'He was the man who came to Graystones? The one with Jane Doe?'

Rizzoli nodded. 'They were both there together. Trying to get in, to see her.'

Maura shook her head. 'I don't get it. What on earth did these three people have to do with each other?'

'That's a question only Urusla could have answered.' Rizzoli rose and pulled on her coat. She turned toward the door, then stopped. Looked back at Maura. 'She was awake, you know.'

'Sister Ursula?'

'Just before she coded, she opened her eyes.'

'Do you think she was actually conscious? Aware of what was going on?'

'She squeezed the nurse's hand. She was following commands. But I never got the chance to talk to her. I was standing right there, and she *looked* at me, just before . . .' Rizzoli paused, as though shaken by that thought. 'I'm the last person she saw.'

Maura walked into the ICU, past monitors pulsing with green heart tracings, past nurses who stood whispering outside curtained patient cubicles. As an intern on critical care rotation, her late-night visits to Intensive Care had always been occasions for anxiety – a patient in extremis, a crisis that required her swift decision. Even all these years later, walking at this hour into an ICU made her pulse quicken. But no medical crisis awaited her tonight; she was here to view the aftermath.

She found Dr. Sutcliffe standing beside Ursula's bed, writing in the chart. His pen slowly came to a stop, the tip pressed against the page, as though he was having trouble forming the next sentence.

'Dr. Sutcliffe?' she said.

He looked at her, his tanned face creased with new lines of fatigue.

'Detective Rizzoli asked me to come in. She said you were planning to withdraw life support.'

'You're a little premature, once again,' he said. 'Dr. Yuen's decided to hold off for a day or two. He wants to see an EEG first.' He looked down, once again, at his notes. 'It's ironic, isn't it? How there are pages and pages devoted to her last few days on earth. But her entire life takes up only one short paragraph. There's something wrong about that. Something obscene.'

'At least you get to know your patients while they're still breathing. I don't even have that privilege.'

'I don't think I'd like your job, Dr. Isles.'

'There are days I don't care for it, either.'

'Then why do you choose it? Why the dead over the living?'

'They deserve attention. They'd want us to know why they died.'

He looked at Ursula. 'If you're wondering what went wrong here, I can tell you the answer. We didn't move fast enough. We stood around watching her panic, and we should have sedated her. If we had just calmed her down sooner . . .'

'Are you saying she coded from panic?'

'That's how it started. First a spike in blood pressure and pulse. Then her pressure dropped just like that, and the arrhythmias started. It took us twenty minutes to get her rhythm back.'

'What does her EKG show?'

'An acute myocardial infarction. She's now deeply comatose. No pupillary reactions. No response to deep pain. She's almost certainly suffered irreversible brain damage.'

'It's a little early to say that, isn't it?'

'I'm a realist. Dr. Yuen's hoping to pull her through, but then, he's a surgeon. He wants his rosy statistics. As long as his patient survives the operation, he can chalk it up as one of his successes. Even if she ends up as a vegetable.'

She moved to the bedside and frowned at the patient. 'Why is she so edematous?'

'We poured fluids into her during the code, to try and bring up her pressure. That's why her face looks swollen.'

Maura looked down at the arms and saw raised and reddish wheals. 'This looks like some fading urticaria here. Which drugs did she get?'

'The usual cocktail we give during codes. Antiarrhythmics. Dopamine.'

'I think you need to order a drug and toxicology screen.'

'Excuse me?'

'This was an unexplained cardiac arrest. And this urticaria looks like a drug reaction.'

'We don't usually order tox screens just because a patient codes.'

'In this case, you should order one.'

'Why? Do you think we made a mistake? Gave her something we shouldn't have?' He sounded defensive now, his fatigue turning to anger.

'She's a witness to a crime,' Maura pointed out. 'The only witness.'

'We just spent the last hour trying to save her life. And now you're implying you don't trust us.'

'Look, I'm only trying to be thorough.'

'Okay.' He snapped the chart shut. 'I'll see the tox screen gets done, just for you,' he said, and walked out.

She remained in the cubicle, gazing down at Ursula, who lay bathed in the soft, sepulchral glow of the bedside lamp. Maura saw none of the usual litter that followed CPR. The used syringes and drug vials and sterile wrappings that always resulted from resuscitation efforts had been swept away. The patient's chest rose and fell only because of the air forced into her lungs with each whoosh of the ventilator bellows.

Maura took out a penlight and shone it into Ursula's eyes.

Neither pupil responded to the light.

Straightening, she suddenly sensed someone

watching her. She turned and was startled to see Father Brophy standing in the doorway.

'The nurses called me,' he said. 'They thought it might be time.'

He had dark circles under his eyes, and beard stubble darkened his jaw. As usual, he wore his clerical garb, but at that early hour, his shirt was wrinkled. She imagined him, newly roused from sleep, rolling out of his bed and stumbling into his clothes. Reaching automatically for that shirt as he left the warmth of his bedroom.

'Would you like me to leave?' he asked. 'I can come back later.'

'No, please come in, Father. I was just going to review the record.'

He nodded and stepped into the cubicle. The space suddenly felt too small, too intimate.

She reached for the chart, which Sutcliffe had left behind. As she settled onto a stool near the bed, she was suddenly aware, once again, of her own scent, and she wondered if Brophy could smell it too. The scent of Victor. Of sex. As Brophy began to murmur a prayer, she forced herself to focus on the nurses' notes.

00:15: Vitals: BP up to 130/90, Pulse 80. Eyes open. Making purposeful movements. Squeezes right hand on command. Drs. Yuen and Sutcliffe called about change in mental status.

00:43: BP up to 180/100, Pulse 120. Dr. Sutcliffe here. Patient agitated and trying to pull out ET tube.

00:50: Systolic BP down to 110. Flushed and very agitated. Dr. Yuen here.

00:55: Systolic 85, Pulse 180. IV rate to wide open . . .

As the blood pressure plummeted, the notes grew terser, the handwriting more hurried, until it deteriorated to a barely legible scrawl. She could picture the events as they unfolded in this cubicle. The scramble to find IV bags and syringes. The nurse, scurrying back and forth to the medication room for drugs. Sterile wrappings torn open, vials emptied, correct dosages frantically calculated. All this while the patient thrashes, her blood pressure crashing.

01:00: Code Blue called.

Different handwriting, now. Another nurse, stepping in to record events. The new entries were neat and methodical, the work of a nurse whose duty during the code was only to observe and document.

Ventricular fibrillation. DC cardioversion at 300 joules. IV Lidocaine drip increased to four mg/min.

Cardioversion repeated, 400 joules. Still in V. Fib.

Pupils dilated, but still reactive to light . . .

Not giving up yet, thought Maura. Not while the pupils react. Not while there's still a chance.

She remembered the first Code Blue that she had directed as an intern, and how reluctant she had been to concede defeat, even when it was clear that the patient could not be saved. But the man's family had stood waiting right outside the room – his wife and two teenage sons – and it was the

307

boys' faces that Maura kept thinking of as she'd slapped on the defibrillator paddles, again and again. Both boys were tall enough to be men, with enormous feet and spotty faces, but they were crying children's tears, and she had continued resuscitation efforts long beyond the stage of futility, thinking: give him one more shock. Just one more.

She realized that Father Brophy had fallen silent. Looking up, she found him watching her, his gaze so focused that she felt personally invaded.

And, at the same time, strangely aroused.

She closed the chart, a crisply businesslike gesture to disguise her confusion. She had just come from Victor's bed, yet here she was, drawn to this man, of all people. She knew that cats in heat could attract males with their scent. Was that the signal she gave off, the scent of a receptive female? A woman who has gone so long without sex that she cannot get enough of it?

She rose and reached for her coat.

He stepped toward her to help her put it on. Stood close behind her, holding it open as she slid her arms into the sleeves. She felt his hand brush against her hair. It was an accidental touch, nothing more, but it set off an alarming shiver. She stepped away, quickly buttoning up.

'Before you leave,' he said, 'I want to show you something. Will you come with me?'

'Where?'

'Down to the fourth floor.'

Puzzled, she followed him to the elevator. They stepped in and, once again, they were sharing an enclosed space that seemed far too close. She stood with both hands thrust in her coat pockets and stoically watched the floor numbers change, wondering: Is it a sin to find a priest attractive?

If not sin, then certainly folly.

The elevator door at last opened, and she followed him down the hallway, through a set of double doors, into the coronary care unit. Like the Surgical ICU, this unit had its lights dimmed for the night, and he led her through the gloom toward the EKG monitor station.

The heavyset nurse sitting in front of the monitors glanced up from the multiple cardiac tracings and her teeth shone in a smiling arc.

'Father Brophy. Making night rounds?'

He touched the nurse's shoulder, an easy, familiar gesture that spoke of a comfortable friendship. Maura was reminded of the first time she had glimpsed Brophy, crossing the snowy courtyard below Camille's bedroom. How he had laid a comforting hand on the shoulder of the elderly nun who had greeted him. This was a man who was not afraid to offer the warmth of his touch.

'Evening, Kathleen,' he said, and the soft lilt of Boston Irish suddenly slipped into his voice. 'Have you had a quiet night, then?'

'So far, knock on wood. Did the nurses call you in to see someone?'

'Not for one of your patients. We were upstairs,

in SICU. I wanted to bring Dr. Isles down here for a visit.'

'At two A.M.?' Kathleen laughed and looked at Maura. 'He'll run you ragged. This man doesn't rest.'

'Rest?' said Brophy. 'What's that?'

'It's that thing we lesser mortals do.'

Brophy looked at the monitor. 'And how is our Mr. DeMarco doing?'

'Oh, your special patient. He's being transferred to an unmonitored bed tomorrow. So I'd say he's doing great.'

Brophy pointed to bed number six's EKG line, blipping serenely across the screen. 'There,' he said, touching Maura's arm, and his breath whispered against her hair. 'That's what I wanted to show you.'

'Why?' asked Maura.

'Mr. DeMarco is the man we saved, on the sidewalk.' He looked at her. 'The man you predicted wouldn't live. That's our miracle. Yours and mine.'

'Not necessarily a miracle. I've been known to be wrong.'

'You're not in the least bit surprised that this man is going to walk out of the hospital?'

She looked at him in the quiet intimacy of darkness. 'There's not a lot that surprises me anymore, I'm sorry to say.' She didn't mean to sound cynical, but that's how it came out, and she wondered if he was disappointed in her. It seemed important to him, for some reason, that she express some sense of

310

wonderment, and all she had given him was the verbal equivalent of a shrug.

In the elevator down to the lobby, she said, 'I'd like to believe in miracles, Father. I really would. But I'm afraid you can't change the opinion of an old skeptic.'

He responded with a smile. 'You were given a brilliant mind, and of course you were meant to use it. To ask your own questions and find your own answers.'

'I'm sure you ask the same questions I do.'

'Every day.'

'Yet you accept the concept of the divine. Isn't your faith ever shaken?'

A pause. 'Not my faith, no. That, I can count on.'

She heard a faint note of uncertainty in his voice and she looked at him. 'Then what do you question?'

He met her gaze, a look that seemed to peer straight into her mind, to read the very thoughts she did not want him to see. 'My strength,' he said quietly. 'Sometimes I question my own strength.'

Outside, standing alone in the hospital parking lot, she took in punishing breaths of cold air. The sky was clear, the stars a hard glitter. She climbed into her car and sat for a moment as the engine warmed, trying to understand what had just happened between her and Father Brophy. Nothing at all, really, but she was feeling as guilty as though something *had* happened. Both guilty and exhilarated.

She drove home on streets polished with an icy

311

sheen, thinking about Father Brophy and Victor. She had been tired when she'd left the house; now she was alert and edgy, nerves humming, feeling more alive than she'd felt in months.

She pulled into the garage, and was already tugging off her coat as she walked into her house. Already unbuttoning her blouse as she moved toward the bedroom. Victor slept soundly, unaware that she was standing right beside him, shedding her clothes. In the last few days, he'd been spending more time in her house than in his hotel room, and now he seemed to belong in her bed. In her life. Shivering, she slid under sheets that were deliciously warm, and the coolness of her skin against his made him stir.

A few strokes, a few kisses, and he was fully awake, fully aroused.

She welcomed him into her, urging him on, and though she lay beneath him, it was not in submission. She took her own pleasure, just as he took his, claiming her due with a soft cry of victory. But as she closed her eyes and felt him climax inside her, it was not just Victor's face that came to mind, but also Father Brophy's. A shifting image that would not hold steady, but flickered back and forth, until she did not know whose face it was.

Both. And neither.

Seventeen

In winter, it's the clear days that are the coldest. Maura awakened to sunshine glaring on white snow, and although she was glad to see blue sky for a change, the wind was brutal, and the rhododendron outside her house huddled like an old man, its leaves drooped and folded against the cold.

She sipped coffee as she drove to work, blinking against the sunlight, longing to turn around and go home. To climb back into bed with Victor, and spend the whole day with him there, warming each other beneath the comforter. Last night, they had sung Christmas carols – he in his rich baritone, she trying to harmonize in her badly off-key alto. They'd sounded awful together, and had ended up laughing more than singing.

And here she was singing again this morning, her voice as off-key as ever, as she drove past streetlights hung with wreaths, past department store windows where holiday dresses glittered on mannequins. Suddenly, the reminders of

Christmas seemed to be everywhere. The wreaths and garlands had been hanging for weeks, of course, but she hadn't really taken notice of them. When had the city ever looked so festive? When had the sun ever glittered so brightly on snow?

God rest ye merry gentlemen, let nothing you dismay.

She walked into the Medical Examiner's building on Albany Street, where PEACE ON EARTH was displayed in huge foil letters in the hallway.

Louise looked up at her and smiled. 'You're looking happy today.'

'I'm just so glad to see sunshine again.'

'Enjoy it while it lasts. I hear we're getting more snow tomorrow night.'

'Snow on Chirstmas Eve is fine with me.' She scooped up some chocolate kisses from the candy bowl on Louise's desk. 'How's the schedule look today?'

'Nothing came in last night. I guess no one wants to die just before Christmas. Dr. Bristol has to be in court at ten, and he may go straight home after that, if you can cover his calls.'

'If it stays quiet, I think I'll leave early myself.'

Louise's eyebrow lifted in surprise. 'For something fun, I hope.'

'You bet,' Maura said with a laugh. 'I'm going shopping.'

She walked into her office, where even the tall stack of lab reports and dictations waiting to be reviewed could not dampen her mood. Sitting at her desk, she happily snacked on chocolate as she worked through the lunch hour and into the afternoon, hoping to slip out by three and head straight to Saks Fifth Avenue.

She did not count on a visit from Gabriel Dean. When he walked into her office at two thirty that afternoon, she had no inkling of how completely his visit would change her day. As always, she found him difficult to read, and once again, she was struck by the improbability of any affair between the temperamental Rizzoli and this coolly enigmatic man.

'I'm heading back to Washington this afternoon,' he said, setting down his briefcase. 'I wanted your opinion on something before I left.'

'Of course.'

'First, may I view Jane Doe's remains?'

'It's all in my autopsy report.'

'Nevertheless, I think I should see her myself.'

Maura rose from her chair. 'I have to warn you,' she said, 'this will be a difficult viewing.'

Refrigeration can only slow, not halt, the process of decomposition. As Maura unzipped the white body pouch, she had to steel herself against the odors. She had already warned Dean about the corpse's appearance, and he did not flinch when the plastic parted, revealing raw tissue where the face should have been.

'It was completely stripped off,' said Maura. 'The skin sliced along the hairline, at the crown, and then peeled downward. Freed with another incision below the chin. Like ripping off a mask.'

'And he took the skin with him?'

'It's not the only thing he took.' Maura unzipped the rest of the pouch, releasing a stench so powerful that she wished she had put on a mask and shield. But Dean had requested only a superficial viewing, not a full examination, and they had donned only gloves.

'The hands,' he said.

'They were both removed, as were parts of the feet. At first, we thought we were dealing with a collector. Body parts as trophies. The other possibility was that he was trying to obscure her identity. No fingerprints, no face. That would have been a practical reason for removal.'

'Except for the feet.'

'And that's what didn't make sense. That's when I realized there might be another reason for the amputations. It wasn't to hide her identity, but her diagnosis of leprosy.'

'And these lesions all over her skin? That's from the Hansen's disease as well?'

'This skin eruption is called erythema nodosum leprosum. It's a reaction to medical treatment. She's obviously been receiving antibiotics for the Hansen's disease. That's why we didn't see any active bacteria on skin biopsy.'

'So it's not the disease itself that's causing these lesions?'

'No. It's a side effect of recent antibiotic therapy. Based on her X-rays, she'd had Hansen's for some time, probably years, before she started receiving therapy.' She looked up at Dean. 'Have you seen enough?'

He nodded. 'Now I want to show you something.'

Back upstairs in her office, he opened his brief-case and took out a file. 'Yesterday, after our meeting, I called Interpol and requested inform-ation on the Bara massacre. That's what the Special Crimes Division of India's Central Bureau of Investigation faxed back to me. They also e-mailed some digital images that I want you to look at.'

She opened the folder and saw the top sheet. 'It's a police file.'

'From the Indian state of Andhra Pradesh, where the village of Bara was located.'

'What's the status of their investigation?'

'It remains ongoing. The case is a year old, and they haven't made much progress. I doubt this one is ever going to be solved. I'm not even sure it's high on their priority list.'

'Nearly a hundred people were slaughtered, Agent Dean.'

'Yes, but you have to take this event in context.'

'An earthquake is an event. A hurricane is an event. An entire village of people being massacred isn't an event. It's a crime against humanity.'

'Look at what else is happening in South Asia. In Kashmir, mass slaughters by both Hindus and Muslims. In India, the murders of Tamils and Sikhs. Then there are all the caste killings. Bombings by Maoist-Leninist guerillas—'

'Mother Mary Clement believes it was a religious massacre. An attack against Christians.'

'Such attacks do occur there. But the clinic where Sister Ursula worked was funded by a secular charity. The other two nurses – the ones who died in the massacre – weren't affiliated with any church. That's why the police in Andhra Pradesh are doubtful this was a religious attack. A political attack, perhaps. Or a hate crime, because the victims were lepers. This was a village of the despised.' He pointed to the file she was holding. 'There are autopsy reports I wanted you to see, as well as crime scene photos.'

She turned the page and stared at a photograph. Stunned by the image, she could not speak. She could not turn her eyes from the horror.

It was a vision of Armageddon.

Piled atop mounds of smoking wood and ash were seared corpses. The fire's heat had contracted flexor muscles, and the bodies were frozen in pugilistic attitudes. Mingled among the human remains were dead goats, their fur singed black.

'They killed everything,' said Dean. 'People. Animals. Even the chickens were slaughtered and burned.'

She forced herself to turn to the next photo.

She saw other corpses, more thoroughly consumed by the flames, reduced to piles of charred bones.

'The attack happened sometime during the night,' said Dean. 'It wasn't until the next morning that the bodies were discovered. Day shift workers at a nearby factory noticed heavy smoke rising from the valley below. When they arrived to investigate, that's what they found. Ninety-seven people dead, many of them women and children, as well as two nurses from the clinic – both of them Americans.'

'The same clinic where Ursula worked.'

Dean nodded. 'Now here's the really interesting detail,' he said.

She looked up, her attention suddenly sharpened by the change in his voice. 'Yes?'

'That factory, near the village.'

'What about it?'

'It was owned by Octagon Chemicals.'

She stared at him. 'Octagon? That's the company Howard Redfield worked for?'

He nodded. 'The one under SEC investigation. There are so many lines connecting these three victims, it's starting to look like a giant spiderweb. We know Howard Redfield was a VP of foreign operations for Octagon, which owned the factory near Bara village. We know Sister Ursula worked in Bara village. We know that Jane Doe suffered from Hansen's disease, so she may have lived in Bara village as well.'

'It all goes back to that village,' she said.

'To that massacre.'

Her gaze dropped to the photographs. 'What are you hoping I'll find in these autopsy reports?'

'Tell me if there's something the Indian pathologists missed. Something that might shed light on that attack.'

She looked at the burned corpses and shook her head. 'It's going to be difficult. Incineration destroys too much. Whenever fire's involved, the cause of death may be impossible to determine, unless there's other evidence. Bullets, for instance, or fractures.'

'A number of the skulls were crushed, according to those postmortem reports. They concluded the victims were most likely bludgeoned while asleep. The bodies were then dragged from the huts to form several different piles, for incineration.'

She turned to another photo. Another view of hell. 'All these victims,' she murmured. 'And no one was able to escape?'

'It must have happened very quickly. Many of the victims were probably crippled by disease and unable to run. It was, after all, a sanctuary for the sick. The village was cut off from society, isolated in a valley at the dead end of a road. A large group of attackers could swoop in and easily slaughter a hundred people. And no one would hear the screams.'

Maura turned to the last photograph in the folder. It showed a small whitewashed building with a tin roof, the walls scorched by fire. Lying just outside the doorway was another jumble of corpses, limbs intertwined, features burned beyond recognition.

'That clinic was the only building still standing, because it was built of cinder blocks,' said Dean. 'The remains of the two American nurses were found in that pile there. A forensic anthropologist had to identify them. He said the burning was so complete, he believed the attackers must have used an accelerant. Would you agree with that, Dr. Isles?'

Maura didn't answer. She was no longer focused on the bodies. She stared, instead, at something she found far more disturbing. Something that made her forget, for a few seconds, to breathe.

Over the clinic doorway hung a sign with a distinctive insignia: a dove in flight, its wings spread in loving protection over a blue globe. An insignia she recognized at once.

It was a One Earth clinic.

'Dr. Isles?' said Dean.

She looked up, startled. Realized that he was still waiting for her response. 'Bodies . . . aren't all that easy to incinerate,' she said. 'There's too high a water content.'

'These bodies were charred down to bone.'

'Yes. That's true. So an accelerant – you're right, an accelerant was probably used.'

'Gasoline?'

'Gasoline would work. And it's the most readily available.' Her gaze dropped back to the photos of the scorched clinic. 'Also, you can clearly see the remains of a pyre, which later collapsed. These charred branches . . .'

'Does that make a difference? Using a pyre?' he asked.

She cleared her throat. 'Raising the bodies off the ground allows melting fat to drip into the flames. It . . . keeps the fire hot.' Abruptly she swept up the photos and slid them back into the folder. Sat with her hands clasped atop the manila

321

file, its surface smooth beneath her skin, its contents gnawing a hole in her heart. 'If you don't mind, Agent Dean, I'd like some time to review these autopsy reports. I'll get back to you. May I keep the entire file?'

'Of course.' Dean rose from his chair. 'You can reach me in Washington.'

She was still staring down at the folder, and did not see him head for the door. Nor did she realize that he had turned back, and was looking at her.

'Dr. Isles?'

She glanced up. 'Yes?'

'I have another concern. Not about the case, but something personal. I'm not sure you're the one I should ask about this.'

'What is it, Agent Dean?'

'Do you talk much with Jane?'

'Naturally. In the course of this investigation—'

'Not about work. About what's been troubling her.'

She hesitated. I could tell him, she thought. Someone should tell him.

'She's always been strung pretty tightly,' he said. 'But there's something else going on. I can see she's under a lot of pressure.'

'The abbey attack has been a difficult case for her.'

'It's not the investigation. There's something else bothering her. Something she won't talk about.'

'I'm not the one you should be asking. You need to speak to Jane.'

'I've tried.'

'And?'

'She's all business. You know how she can be, a goddamn robo-cop.' He sighed. Said, quietly: 'I think I've lost her.'

'Tell me something, Agent Dean.'

'Yes?'

'Do you care about her?'

He met her gaze without flinching. 'I wouldn't be asking you this question if I didn't.'

'Then you have to trust me on this. You haven't lost her. If she seems distant, it's only because she's afraid.'

'Jane?' He shook his head and laughed. 'She's not afraid of anything. Least of all me.'

She watched him walk out of her office, and she thought: You're wrong. We're all afraid of the people who can hurt us.

As a child, Rizzoli had loved winter. She would look forward all summer long to the first flutters of snow, to the morning when she'd open her bedroom curtains and see the ground covered in white, the purity still unmarred by footprints. She'd laugh as she ran from the house, to dive into the snowdrifts.

Now, fighting heavy noontime traffic, along with all the other holiday shoppers, she wondered who had stolen the magic.

The prospect of spending Christmas Eve with her family tomorrow night did nothing to cheer her. She knew how the evening would go: everyone stuffing themselves with turkey, their mouths too full to talk. Her brother Frankie, loud and obnoxious from too much rum-spiked eggnog. Her father, TV remote in hand, turning up ESPN to drown out all meaningful conversation. And her mother, Angela, exhausted from a full day's cooking, nodding off in the easy chair. Every year, they repeated the same old rituals, but that's what made a family, she thought. We do the same things in the same way, whether or not they make us happy.

Though she had no desire to go shopping, she could put off the ordeal no longer; you simply did not show up at the Rizzolis' on Christmas Eve without the requisite armful of gifts. It didn't matter how inappropriate the gifts might be, as long as they were prettily wrapped, and everyone got one. Last year her brother Frankie, the asshole, gave her a dried toad from Mexico, its skin fashioned into a coin purse. It was a cruel reminder of the nickname he used to hurl at her. A frog for the frog.

This year, Frankie was toast.

She pushed her shopping cart through the crowds at the Target store, in search of a dried-toad equivalent. Christmas carols played over the store speakers and mechanical Santas greeted her with ho-ho-ho's as she moved with grim determination up aisles festooned with tinsel garlands. For her dad, she bought fleece-lined moccasins. For her mom, a teapot from Ireland, decorated with tiny pink rosebuds. For her younger brother Michael, a plaid bathrobe, and for his new girlfriend Irene, dangly earrings of blood-red Austrian crystal. She even bought gifts for Irene's little boys, matching snowsuits with racing stripes.

But for Frankie, the jerk, she was coming up empty-handed.

She cruised down the aisle for men's underwear. Here there were possibilities. Frankie the macho Marine in pink thong underwear? No, too disgusting; even she would never stoop that low. She kept moving, past the jockey briefs, and slowed as she reached the boxer shorts, suddenly thinking not of Frankie, but of Gabriel, in his gray suits and boring ties. A man of quiet and conservative tastes, right down to his underwear. A man who could drive a woman crazy, because she'd never know where she stood with him; she'd never know if a real heart was beating under that gray suit.

Abruptly she left the aisle and kept moving. Focus, damn it. Something for Frankie. A book? She could think of a few appropriate titles. *The Miss Manners Guide to Not Being An Asshole*. Too bad Miss Manners never wrote that one; there'd be a market for it. She cruised up the aisle, down the next, searching, searching.

And then she came to a halt, her throat aching, her fingers numb as she clutched the cart handle.

She was staring at an aisle of baby supplies. She saw little flannel sleepers embroidered with ducks. Doll-size mittens and booties and fuzzy caps topped with yarn balls. Stacks of pink and blue receiving blankets in which to swaddle newborns. It was the blankets she focused on, remembering the way Camille had swaddled her own dead infant in powder-blue wool, wrapping it with a mother's love, a mother's grief.

It took several rings before the sound of her cell phone cut through her trance. She pulled it from her purse and answered with a dazed: 'Rizzoli.'

'Hey, Detective. It's Walt DeGroot here.'

DeGroot worked in the DNA section of the crime lab. Usually Rizzoli was the one who called him, trying to goad him into a quicker turnaround on test results. Today she responded to his call with dulled interest.

'So what have you got for me?' she asked, her gaze moving back to the baby blankets.

'We ran that maternal DNA against the infant you found in the pond.'

'Yeah?'

'The victim, Camille Maginnes, is definitely the mother of that child.'

Rizzoli gave a tired sigh. 'Thanks, Walt,' she murmured. 'It's what we expected.'

'Wait. There's more.'

'More?'

'This, I don't think you expected. It's about the baby's father.'

All at once she was focused completely on Walt's voice. On what he was about to tell her.

'What about the father?' she asked.

'I know who he is.'

Eighteen

Rizzoli drove through the afternoon and into the gray of dusk, seeing the road ahead through a fog of rage. The gifts she'd just purchased were still piled on her backseat, along with rolls of wrapping paper and foil ribbon, but her mind was no longer on Christmas. It was on a young girl, walking barefoot through the snow. A girl who sought the pain of frostbite, if only to mask her deeper agony. But nothing could match the girl's secret torment, no amount of prayer or self-flagellation could silence her private shrieks of pain.

When at last she drove past the granite pillars, and into the driveway of Camille's parents, it was nearly five P.M., and her shoulders were stiff from the tension of that long drive. She stepped out of the car and inhaled a stinging lungful of salt air. She walked up the steps and rang the bell.

The dark-haired housekeeper Maria answered the door. 'I'm sorry, Detective, but Mrs. Maginnes isn't here. Was she expecting you?'

'No. When will she be home?'

'She and the boys went out shopping. She should be back for dinner. Another hour, I think.'

'Then I'll wait for her.'

'I'm not sure—'

'I'll just keep Mr. Maginnes company. If that's all right.'

Reluctantly, Maria admitted her into the house. A woman accustomed to deferring to others was not about to bar the door against law enforcement.

Rizzoli did not need Maria to show her the way; she walked across the same polished floors, past the same marine paintings, and stepped into the Sea Room. The view across Nantucket Sound was ominous, the wind-roiled water flecked by whitecaps. Randall Maginnes lay on his right side in the hospital bed, his face turned to the windows so he could see the gathering storm. A front-row seat to nature's turbulence.

The private-duty nurse sitting beside him noticed the visitor, and rose from her chair. 'Hello?'

'I'm Detective Rizzoli, Boston P.D. I'm just waiting for Mrs. Maginnes to get home. Thought I'd look in on Mr. Maginnes. See how he's doing.'

'He's about the same.'

'How's his progress since the stroke?'

'We've been doing physical therapy for months now. But the deficits are pretty severe.'

'Are they permanent?'

The nurse glanced at her patient, then made a

gesture for Rizzoli to follow her out of the room.

In the hallway, the nurse said: 'I don't like to talk about him where he can hear us. I know he understands.'

'How can you tell?'

'It's the way he looks at me. The way he reacts to things. Even though he can't talk, he does have a functioning mind. I played a CD of his favorite opera this afternoon – *La Boheme*. And I saw tears in his eyes.'

'It may not be the music. It may be just frustration.'

'He certainly has a right to feel frustrated. After eight months, he's had almost no recovery. That's a very grim prognosis. He'll almost certainly never walk again. He'll always be paralyzed on one side. And as for speech, well—' She gave a sad shake of the head. 'It was a massive stroke.'

Rizzoli turned to the Sea Room. 'If you'd like to take a coffee break or something, I'll be happy to sit with him for a while.'

'You don't mind?'

'Unless he needs some kind of special care.'

'No, you don't need to do a thing. Just talk to him. He'll appreciate that.'

'Yeah. I will.'

Rizzoli walked back into the Sea Room and pulled a chair close to the bedside. She sat down where she could see Randall Maginnes's eyes. Where he could not avoid seeing hers.

'Hi, Randall,' she said. 'Remember me? Detective Rizzoli. I'm the cop investigating your daughter's murder. You do know Camille is dead, don't you?'

She saw a flicker of sadness in his gray eyes. An acknowledgment that he understood. That he mourned.

'She was beautiful, your girl Camille. But you know that, don't you? How could you not? Every day in this house, you were watching her. You saw her grow up and change into a young woman.' She paused. 'And you saw her fall apart.'

The eyes were still staring at her, still taking in every word she said.

'So when did you start fucking her, Randall?'

Outside the window, gusts whipped across Nantucket Sound. Even in the fading daylight, the whitecaps glowed, bright pinpoints of turbulence in the dark sea.

Randall Maginnes was no longer looking at her. His gaze had shifted and he was staring downward, desperately avoiding her eyes.

'She's only eight years old when her mother kills herself. And suddenly, Camille doesn't have anyone but her daddy. She needs you. She trusts you. And what did you do?' Rizzoli shook her head in disgust. 'You knew how fragile she was. You knew why she went walking barefoot in the snow. Why she locked herself in her room. Why she ran off to the convent. She was running away from *you*.'

Rizzoli leaned closer. Close enough to catch a whiff of the urine soaking his adult diaper.

'The one time she came home for a visit, she probably thought you wouldn't touch her. That

330

for once, you'd leave her alone. You had a house full of relatives here for the funeral. But that didn't stop you. Did it?'

The eyes were still avoiding hers, still staring downward. She crouched beside the bed. Moved so close to him that no matter which way he looked, she was right there, in his face.

'It was your baby, Randall,' she said. 'We didn't even need a sample of your DNA to prove it. The baby's too close a match to its mother. It's written there, in the baby's DNA. A child of incest. Did you know you made her pregnant? Did you know you destroyed your own daughter?'

She just sat in the chair for a moment, gazing at him. In the silence, she could hear his breathing quicken, the noisy gasps of a man who is desperate to flee, but cannot.

'You know, Randall, I'm not a big believer in God. But you make me think that maybe I've been wrong about that. Because look what happened to *you*. In March, you fuck your daughter. In April, you get a stroke. You won't ever move again. Or talk again. You're just a brain in a dead body, Randall. If that's not divine justice, I don't know what is.'

He was whimpering now, struggling to make his useless limbs move.

She leaned forward and whispered in his ear. 'Can you smell yourself rotting? While you lie here, peeing in your diaper, what do you suppose your wife Lauren's up to? Probably having a very good time. Probably finding someone else to keep her company. Think about that. You don't have to die to go to hell.'

With a sigh of satisfaction, she rose to her feet. 'Have a nice life, Randall,' she said, and walked out of the room.

As she headed for the front door, she heard Maria call to her: 'Are you leaving already, Detective?'

'Yeah. I've decided not to wait for Mrs. Maginnes.'

'What shall I tell her?'

'Just that I dropped by.' Rizzoli glanced back, toward the Sea Room. 'Oh, and tell her this.'

'Yes?'

'I think Randall misses Camille. Why don't you put her photo where he can see it, all the time.' She smiled as she opened the front door to leave. 'He'll appreciate that.'

Christmas lights were twinkling in her living room.

The garage door cranked open, and Maura saw that Victor's rental car was parked inside, taking up the right side of the garage, as though it belonged there. As though this was now his house, as well. She pulled in beside it and turned off the engine with an angry twist of the key. Waited for a moment as the door closed again, trying to calm herself for what came next.

She grabbed her briefcase and stepped out of the car.

In the house, she took her time hanging up her

332

coat, setting down her purse. Still carrying the briefcase, she walked into the kitchen.

Victor smiled at her as he dropped ice into a cocktail shaker. 'Hey. I'm just mixing your favorite drink for you. Dinner's already in the oven. I'm trying to prove to you that a man really can be useful around the house.'

She watched as he rattled ice in the shaker and poured the liquid into a martini glass. He handed her the drink.

'For the hardworking lady of the house,' he said, and pressed a kiss to her lips.

She stood perfectly still.

Slowly he pulled away, his gaze searching her face. 'What's the matter?'

She set down the glass. 'It's time for you to be honest with me.'

'Do you think I haven't been?'

'I don't know.'

'If we're talking about what went wrong three years ago – the mistakes I made—'

'This isn't about what happened then. This is about now. Whether you're being honest with me now.'

He gave a bewildered laugh. 'What did I do wrong this time? What am I supposed to apologize for? Because I'll be happy to do it, if that's what you want. Hell, I'll even apologize for things I *haven't* done.'

'I'm not asking for an apology, Victor.' She reached into her briefcase for the file that Gabriel Dean had lent her, and held it out to him. 'I just want you to tell me about this.'

'What is this?'

'It's a police file, transmitted from Interpol. Concerning a mass slaughter last year, in India. In a small village, outside Hyderabad.'

He opened the folder to the first photograph, and winced at the image. Without a word, he turned to the next one, and the next.

'Victor?'

He closed the file and looked at her. 'What am I supposed to say about this?'

'You knew about this massacre, didn't you?'

'Of course I knew. That was a One Earth clinic they attacked. We lost two volunteers there. Two nurses. It's my job to know about it.'

'You didn't tell me.'

'It happened a year ago. Why should I?'

'Because it's relevant to our investigation. One of the nuns attacked at Graystones Abbey worked in that same One Earth clinic. You knew that, didn't you?'

'How many volunteers do you think work for One Earth? We have thousands of medical personnel, in over eighty countries.'

'Just tell me, Victor. Did you know Sister Ursula worked for One Earth?'

He turned and paced over to the sink. There he stood staring out the window, although there was nothing to see, only darkness beyond.

'It's interesting,' she said. 'After the divorce, I never heard from you. Not one word.'

'Do I need to point out that you never bothered to contact me, either?'

'Not a letter, not a phone call. If I wanted the latest news about you, I had to read it in *People* magazine. Victor Banks, the saint of humanitarian causes.'

'I didn't anoint myself, Maura. You can't hold that against me.'

'And then suddenly, out of the blue, you show up here in Boston, anxious to see me. Just as I start work on this homicide case.'

He turned to look at her. 'You don't think I wanted to see you?'

'You waited three years.'

'Yes. Three years too long.'

'Why now?'

He searched her face, as though hoping to see some trace of understanding. 'I've missed you, Maura. I really have.'

'But that's not the original reason you came to see me. Is it?'

A long pause. 'No. It wasn't.'

Suddenly exhausted, she sank into a chair at the kitchen table and gazed down at the folder containing the damning photograph.

'Then why did you?'

'I was in my hotel room, getting dressed, and the TV was on. I heard the news about the attack on the convent. I saw you there, on camera. At the crime scene.'

'That was the day you left the first message with my secretary. That same afternoon.'

He nodded. 'God, you were stunning on TV. All wrapped up in that black coat. I'd forgotten how beautiful you are.'

'But that's not why you called me, is it? It was the murder you were interested in. You called because I'm the ME on that case.'

He didn't answer.

'You knew one of the victims used to work for One Earth. You wanted to find out what the police knew. What I knew.'

Still there was no answer.

'Why didn't you just ask me about it? What are you trying to hide?'

He straightened, his gaze suddenly challenging hers. 'Do you have any idea how many lives we save every year?'

'You're not answering my question.'

'How many children we immunize? How many pregnant women get their only prenatal care from our clinics? They depend on us, because they have no alternatives. And One Earth survives only because of the goodwill of its benefactors. Our reputation has to be spotless. One whisper of bad press, and our grant money dries up like *that*.' He snapped his fingers.

'What does that have to do with this investigation?'

'I've spent the last twenty years building One Earth from nothing, but it's never been about me. It's always been about *them* – the people no one else cares about. They're the ones who matter. That's why I can't let anything endanger our funding.'

Money, she thought. It's all about money.

She stared at him. 'Your corporate donor.'

'What?'

'You told me about it. That you got a huge grant last year, from a corporate donor.'

'We get grants from a lot of sources—'

'Was it Octagon Chemicals?'

The look of shock on his face answered her question. She heard his sudden intake of breath, as though he was preparing to deny it, but then he exhaled without saying a word, the futility of argument leaving him silent.

'It's not hard to confirm,' said Maura. 'Why don't you just tell me the truth?'

He looked down. Gave a tired nod. 'Octagon is one of our major donors.'

'And what do they expect from you? What does One Earth have to do in return for that money?'

'Why do you think we have to do anything? Our work speaks for itself. Why do you think we're welcomed in so many countries? Because people trust us. We don't proselytize, and we don't muck around in local politics. We're just there to help them. That's all that matters in the end, isn't it? Saving lives?'

'And Sister Ursula's life? Does that matter to you?'

'Of course it does!'

'She's now on full life support. One more EEG, and they'll probably pull the plug. Who wants her dead, Victor?'

'How should I know?'

'You seem to know a lot that you never bothered to tell me. You knew one of the victims worked for you.'

'I didn't think that was relevant.'

'You should have let me decide that.'

'You said you were focusing on the other nun. The young one. *She* was the only victim you talked about. I assumed the attack had nothing to do with Ursula.'

'You concealed information.'

'Now you're talking like a goddamn cop. Are you going to whip out the badge and handcuffs next?'

'I'm trying *not* to get the police involved. I'm trying to give you a chance to explain.'

'Why bother? You've already passed judgment.'

'And you're already acting guilty.'

He stood very still, his gaze averted, one hand clutching the granite countertop. The seconds ticked by in silence. And she suddenly focused on the wooden block of knives resting just within his reach. Eight Wusthof chef's knives, which she always kept well honed and ready for use. Never before had she felt afraid of Victor. But the man standing so close to those knives was someone she did not know, did not even recognize.

She said, quietly, 'I think you should leave.'

He turned to face her. 'What are you going to do?'

'Just leave, Victor.'

For a moment he didn't move. She stared at him, her heart hammering, every muscle tensed. Watching his hands, waiting for his next move, the whole time thinking: *No, he wouldn't hurt me. I don't believe he'd ever hurt me.*

And, at the same time, frighteningly aware of the strength of his hands. She wondered if those same hands would ever reach for a hammer and crush a woman's skull.

'I love you, Maura,' he said. 'But there are some things more important than either one of us. Before you do anything, think about what you might be destroying. How many people – innocent people – you might be hurting.'

She flinched as he moved toward her. But he didn't stop; he walked right past her. She heard his footsteps move down the hallway, and then the front door slammed shut.

At once she rose and went into the living room. Through the window, she watched his car back out of the driveway. She went to the front door and turned the deadbolt. Then she bolted the door leading to the garage. Locking Victor out.

She returned to the kitchen to lock the back door as well, her hand shaking as she slid the chain in place. She turned and gazed at a room that now seemed foreign to her, the air still reverberating with the echoes of threat. The cocktail that Victor had poured for her was sitting on the countertop. She picked up the drink, which was no longer chilled, and poured it down the sink, as though it was contaminated.

She felt contaminated now, by his touch. By his lovemaking.

She went straight to the bathroom, peeled off her

clothes, and stepped into the shower. There she stood under the stream of hot water, trying to wash away all traces of him from her skin, but she could not purge the memories. She closed her eyes and it was still his face she saw, his touch she remembered.

In the bedroom, she stripped the sheets, and his scent wafted up from the linen. Yet another painful reminder. She made the bed with fresh sheets that did not smell of their lovemaking. Replaced the towels in the bathroom, towels he had used. Went back to the kitchen and discarded the takeout food he had left warming in the oven – a casserole of eggplant parmesan.

She ate no dinner that night; instead she poured a glass of zinfandel and carried it into the living room. She lit the gas fireplace and sat staring at the Christmas tree.

Happy holidays, she thought. I can crack open a chest and bare the contents of a torso. I can slice off slivers of lung, and through the microscope, diagnose cancer or tuberculosis or emphysema. But the secret of what lies inside a human heart is beyond the reach of my scalpel.

The wine was an anesthetic, deadening her pain. She finished the glass and went to bed.

In the night, she awakened with a start, and heard the house creaking in the wind. She was breathing hard, her heart racing, as the last shreds of a nightmare tore away. Burned bodies, stacked like black twigs on a pyre. Flames, casting their glow on a circle of standing figures. And she, trying to stay in the shadows, trying to hide from the firelight. Even in my dreams, she thought, I can't get away from those images. I live with my own private Dante's inferno in my head.

She reached out to feel cool sheets beside her, where Victor had once slept. And she missed him then, his absence suddenly so painful to her that she crossed her arms over her stomach, to quell the emptiness there.

What if she was wrong? What if he was telling her the truth?

At dawn, she finally climbed out of bed, feeling drugged and unrested. She went to the kitchen to make coffee, and sat down at the table, sipping from her mug in the gloomy light of morning. Her gaze fell to the folder of photographs, still lying on the table.

She opened it, and saw the inspiration for last night's nightmares. The burned bodies, the charred remains of huts. So many dead, she thought, killed in one night's paroxysm of violence. What terrible rage must have driven the attackers to slaughter even the animals? She gazed at dead goats and humans, mingled in a common tangle of corpses.

The goats. Why the goats?

She mulled this over, trying to understand what could motivate such senseless destruction.

Dead animals.

She turned to the next photo. It showed the One Earth clinic, its cinder block walls scorched by fire, the pile of burned bodies lying in front of the doorway. But it was not the bodies she focused on;

341

it was the clinic roof, made of corrugated tin, still intact. She had not really looked at the roof before. Now she studied what appeared to be fallen leaves. Dark blots were scattered atop the ridged metal. They were too small for her to make out any detail.

She carried the photo into her office and switched on the lights. Hunting in her desk, she found a magnifying glass. Under the bright desk lamp, she studied the image, focusing on the tin roof, her lens bringing out every detail of the fallen leaves. The dark blots suddenly took on a terrible new shape. A chill whispered up her spine. She dropped the magnifying glass and sat stunned.

Birds. They were dead birds.

She went into the kitchen, picked up the phone, and paged Rizzoli. When her phone rang a few minutes later, she jumped at the sound.

'There's something I need to tell you,' said Maura.

'At six-thirty?'

'I should have told Agent Dean yesterday, before he left town. But I didn't want to say anything. Not until I could talk to Victor.'

'Victor? That's your ex-husband?'

'Yes.'

'What does he have to do with anything?'

'I think he knows what happened in India. In that village.'

'He told you that?'

'Not yet. That's why you have to bring him in for questioning.'

Nineteen

They sat in Barry Frost's car, parked just outside the Colonnade Hotel. Frost and Rizzoli were in the front seat, Maura in the back.

'Let me talk to him first,' said Maura.

'It'd be better if you stayed right here, Doc,' said Frost. 'We don't know how he'll react.'

'He'll be less likely to resist if I speak to him.'

'But if he's armed—'

'He won't hurt me,' said Maura. 'And I don't want you to hurt him, is that clear? You aren't arresting him.'

'What if he decides he doesn't want to come?'

'He'll come.' She pushed open the car door. 'Just let me handle it.'

They took the elevator to the fourth floor, sharing the ride with a young couple who probably wondered about the grim trio standing beside them. Flanked by Rizzoli and Frost, Maura knocked on the door to room 426.

A moment passed.

She was about to knock again when the door

finally swung open and Victor stood looking at her. His eyes were tired, his expression infinitely sad.

'I wondered what you'd decide,' he said. 'I was starting to hope that . . .' He shook his head.

'Victor—'

'But then, I suppose I shouldn't be surprised.' He looked at Rizzoli and Frost, standing in the hallway. Gave a bitter laugh. 'Did you bring handcuffs?'

'There's no need for handcuffs,' said Maura. 'They only want to talk to you.'

'Yes, of course. Just talk. Should I call a lawyer?'

'It's up to you.'

'No, you tell *me*. Am I going to need a lawyer?'

'You're the only one who knows that, Victor.'

'That's the test, isn't it? Only the guilty insist on a lawyer.'

'A lawyer is never a bad idea.'

'Then just to prove something to you, I'm not going to call one.' He looked at the two detectives. 'I need to put on my shoes. If you have no objections.' He turned and walked toward the closet.

Maura said to Rizzoli, 'Could you wait out here?' She followed Victor into the room, letting the door swing shut behind her for one last moment of privacy. He was sitting in a chair, lacing up his boots. She noticed his suitcase was lying on the bed.

'You're packing,' she said.

'I'm booked on a flight home at four. But I guess those plans are about to change, aren't they?'

'I had to tell them. I'm sorry.'

'I'm sure you are.'

'I didn't have a choice.'

He stood. 'You had a choice, and you made it. I guess that says it all.' He crossed the room and opened the door. 'I'm ready,' he announced. He handed Rizzoli a key ring. 'I assume you'll want to search my rental car. It's the blue Toyota, parked in the garage, third floor. Don't say I didn't cooperate.'

It was Frost who walked Victor down the hall. Rizzoli tugged on Maura's sleeve, holding her back as the two men continued toward the elevators.

'Here's where you have to back off,' Rizzoli said.

'I'm the one who gave him to you.'

'That's why you can't be part of this.'

'He was my husband.'

'Exactly. You have to step away and let us handle this. You know that.'

Of course she did.

She followed them downstairs anyway. Climbed into her own car and tailed them to Schroeder Plaza. She could see Victor in the back seat. Only once, as they waited at a stoplight, did he turn and look at her. Their gazes met, just for an instant, through the window. Then he turned away and did not look at her again.

By the time she found a parking spot and

walked into Boston PD headquarters, they had already brought Victor upstairs. She took the elevator to the second floor and headed straight for the Homicide Unit.

Barry Frost intercepted her. 'You can't go back there, Doc.'

'He's already being questioned?'

'Rizzoli and Crowe are handling it.'

'I *gave* him to you, goddamn it. At least let me hear what he has to say. I could watch from the next room.'

'You have to wait here.' He added, gently, 'Please, Dr. Isles.'

She met his sympathetic gaze. Of all the detectives in the unit, he was the only one who, with just a kind look, could silence her protest.

'Why don't you sit over there, at my desk?' he said. 'I'll bring you a cup of coffee.'

She sank into a chair and stared at the photo on Frost's desk – his wife, she assumed. A pretty blonde with aristocratic cheekbones. A moment later, he brought her the coffee and set it in front of her.

She didn't touch it. She just kept gazing at the photo of Frost's wife, and thought of other marriages. Of happy endings.

Rizzoli did not like Victor Banks.

He sat at the table in the interrogation room, calmly sipping from a cup of water, his shoulders relaxed, his posture almost casual. A good-looking man, and he knew it. *Too* good-looking.

346

She eyed the worn leather jacket, the khaki trousers, and was reminded of an upscale Indiana Jones, without the bullwhip. He had a medical degree to boot, with solid-gold humanitarian credentials. Oh yeah, the girls would go for this one. Even Dr. Isles, always so cool and levelheaded in the autopsy lab, had lost her heart to this man.

And you betrayed her, you son of a bitch.

Darren Crowe sat to her right. By earlier agreement, she would do most of the talking. So far, Victor had been chilly but cooperative, answering her introductory questions with the curt responses of a man who wished to make quick work of this. A man who had no particular respect for the police.

By the time she was finished with him, he'd respect her, all right.

'So you've been in Boston for how long, Mr. Banks?' she asked.

'It's Dr. Banks. And I told you, I've been here about nine days. I flew in last Sunday night.'

'You said you came to Boston for a meeting?'

'With the dean of the Harvard School of Public Health.'

'The reason for that meeting?'

'My organization has work-study arrangements with a number of universities.'

'Your organization being One Earth?'

'Yes. We're an international medical charity. We operate clinics around the world. Of course we welcome any medical and nursing students who want to volunteer at our clinics. The students get

347

some real-life experience in the field. We, in return, benefit from their skills.'

'And who set up this meeting at Harvard?'

He shrugged. 'It was just a routine visit.'

'Who actually made the call?'

A silence. *Gotcha.*

'You did, didn't you?' she said. 'You called Harvard two weeks ago. Told the Dean you'd be coming to Boston anyway, and could you drop by his office.'

'I need to keep my contacts fresh.'

'Why did you really come to Boston, Dr. Banks? Wasn't there another reason?'

A pause. 'Yes.'

'And that was?'

'My ex-wife lives here. I wanted to see her.'

'But you haven't spoken to her in – what? Nearly three years.'

'Obviously she's already told you everything. Why do you need to talk to me?'

'And suddenly you want to see her so desperately that you fly across the country, without even knowing if she'll see you?'

'Love sometimes demands we take risks. It's a matter of faith. Believing in something you can't see or touch. We just have to take the leap.' He looked her in the eye. 'Don't we, Detective?'

Rizzoli felt herself flush, and for a moment could not think of anything to say. Victor had just reversed the question, twisting it so that she suddenly felt the conversation was about her. *Love demands risks.*

Crowe broke the silence. 'Hey, nice-looking lady, your ex-wife,' he said. Not hostile, but in the casual tone of one guy to another, the two of them now ignoring Rizzoli. 'I can see why you'd fly all this way to try and patch things up. So did you manage to?'

'Things were working out between us.'

'Yeah, I hear you've been staying at her house for the last few days. Sounds like progress to me.'

'Why don't we just get down to the truth,' Rizzoli cut in.

'The truth?' asked Victor.

'The real reason you came to Boston.'

'Why don't *you* tell me which answer you're fishing for, and I'll just give it to you? It'll save us both time.'

Rizzoli dropped a folder on the table. 'Take a look at those.'

He opened it and saw it was the set of photographs from the devastated village. 'I've already seen these,' he said, and closed the folder again. 'Maura showed them to me.'

'You don't seem very interested.'

'It's not exactly pleasant viewing.'

'It's not meant to be. Take another look.' She opened the folder, fished out one of the photos, and slapped it on top. 'This one in particular.'

Victor looked at Crowe, as though seeking an ally against this unpleasant woman, but Crowe simply gave him a what-can-you-do? shrug.

'The photo, Dr. Banks,' said Rizzoli.

'Exactly what am I supposed to say about it?'

'That was a One Earth clinic in that village.'

'Is that so surprising? We go where people need us. Which means we're sometimes in uncomfortable or even dangerous situations.' He was still not looking at the photo, still avoiding the grotesque image. 'It's the price we pay as humanitarian workers. We take on the same risks our patients do.'

'What happened in that village?'

'I think it's pretty obvious.'

'Look at the picture.'

'It's all in the police report, I'm sure.'

'*Look* at the goddamn picture! Tell me what you see.'

At last his gaze fell on the photograph. After a moment, he said: 'Burned bodies. Lying in front of our clinic.'

'And how did they die?'

'I'm told it was a massacre.'

'Do you know that for a fact?'

His gaze snapped up to hers. 'I wasn't there, Detective. I was at home in San Francisco when I got the phone call from India. So you can hardly expect me to provide the details.'

'How do you know it was a massacre?'

'That was the report we got from the police in Andhra Pradesh. That it was either a political or religious attack, and there were no witnesses, since the village was relatively isolated. People tend to avoid having much contact with lepers.'

'Yet they burned the bodies. Don't you find that odd?'

'Why is it odd?'

'The bodies were dragged into large piles before they were set on fire. You'd think that no one would want to touch a leper. So why stack the bodies together?'

'It would be more efficient, I suppose. To burn them in groups.'

'Efficient?'

'I'm trying to come at this logically.'

'And what's the logical reason for burning them at all?'

'Rage? Vandalism? I don't know.'

'All that work, moving the dead bodies. Hauling in the cans of gasoline. Building wooden pyres. And the whole time, the threat of discovery was hanging over them.'

'What are you getting at?'

'I'm saying the bodies *had* to be burned. To destroy the evidence.'

'Evidence of what? It's clearly a massacre. No fire's going to hide that.'

'But a fire would hide the fact it's not a massacre.'

She was not surprised when his gaze dropped away, his eyes suddenly reluctant to meet hers.

'I don't know why you're asking me these questions,' he said. 'Why don't you believe the police report?'

'Because either they got it wrong, or they were bribed.'

'You know this, do you?'

She tapped the photo. 'Look again, Dr. Banks.'

'I'd rather not.'

'These aren't just human corpses burned here. The goats were slaughtered and burned as well. So were the chickens. What a waste – all that nutritious meat. Why kill goats and chickens, and then burn them?'

Victor gave a sarcastic laugh. 'Because they might have had leprosy too? I don't know!'

'That doesn't explain what happened to the birds.'

Victor shook his head. 'What?'

Rizzoli pointed to the clinic's corrugated tin roof. 'I bet you didn't even notice this. But Dr. Isles did. These dark blots on top of the roof here. At first glance, they just look like fallen leaves. But isn't it strange, that there are leaves here, when there don't seem to be any trees nearby?'

He said nothing. He was sitting very still, his head bowed so that she could not read his face. His body language alone told her he was bracing for the inevitable.

'They're not leaves, Dr. Banks. They're dead birds. Some kind of crows, I believe. Three of them are lying there at the edge of the photo. How do you explain that?'

He gave a careless shrug. 'They could have been shot, I suppose.'

'The police didn't mention any evidence of gunfire. There were no bullet holes in the building, no recovered cartridge cases. No bullet fragments found in any of the victims. They did report that several of the corpses had fractured skulls, so they

352

assumed the victims were all clubbed to death while they slept.'

'That's what I would assume, too.'

'So how do we explain the birds? Surely those crows didn't just sit on that roof, waiting for someone to climb up there and whack them over the head with a stick.'

'I don't know what you're getting at. What do dead birds have to do with this?'

'They have everything to do with it. They weren't clubbed, and they weren't shot.'

Victor gave a snort. 'Smoke inhalation?'

'By the time that village was torched, the birds were already dead. Everything was dead. Birds. Livestock. People. Nothing moving, nothing breathing. It was a sterilized zone. All life was wiped out.'

He had no response.

Rizzoli leaned forward, getting right into his face. 'How much did Octagon Chemicals donate to your organization this year, Dr. Banks?'

Victor lifted the cup of water to his lips and took his time sipping it.

'How much?'

'It was in the . . . tens of millions.' He looked at Crowe. 'I could use a refill of water, if you don't mind.'

'Tens of millions?' said Rizzoli. 'Why don't you try eighty-five million dollars?'

'That could be right.'

'And the year before that, they gave you nothing. So what changed? Did Octagon

353

suddenly develop a humanitarian conscience?'

'You should ask them.'

'I'm asking you.'

'I really would like some more water.'

Crowe sighed, picked up the empty cup, and walked out. Only Rizzoli and Victor were left in the room now.

She leaned even closer, a frontal assault on his comfort zone. 'It's all about that money, isn't it?' she said. 'Eighty-five million dollars is one hell of a big payoff. Octagon must have had a lot to lose. And you obviously have a lot to gain, by co-operating with them.'

'Cooperating in what?'

'Silence. Keeping their secret.'

She reached for another file folder and tossed it on the table in front of him.

'That was a pesticide factory they were operating. Just a mile and a half away from Bara village, Octagon were storing thousands of pounds of methyl isocyanate in their plant. They closed down that plant last year, did you know that? Right after the village of Bara was attacked, Octagon abandoned that factory. Just packed up all their personnel and bulldozed the plant. Fear of terrorist attack was their official explanation. But you don't really believe that, do you?'

'I have nothing more to say.'

'It wasn't a massacre that destroyed the village. It wasn't a terrorist attack.' She paused. Said, quietly: 'It was an industrial catastrophe.'

Twenty

Victor sat unmoving. Not looking at Rizzoli.

'Does the name "Bhopal" mean anything to you?' she asked.

It was a moment before he responded. 'Of course it does,' he said softly.

'Tell me what you know about it.'

'Bhopal, India. The Union Carbide accident in nineteen-eighty-four.'

'Do you know how many people died in that event?'

'It was . . . in the thousands, I believe.'

'Six thousand people,' she said. 'The Union Carbide pesticide plant accidentally released a toxic cloud that rolled over the sleeping town of Bhopal. By the next morning, six thousand were dead. Hundreds of thousands were injured. With so many survivors, so many witnesses, the truth couldn't be hidden. It couldn't be suppressed.' She looked down at the photo. 'The way it was in Bara.'

'I can only repeat myself. I wasn't there. I didn't see it.'

'But I'm sure you can guess what happened. We're just waiting for Octagon to release a list of their employees at that plant. One of them is eventually going to talk. One of them is going to confirm it. It's the night shift, and some overworked employee gets careless. Or he falls asleep at the switch, and poof! Up goes a cloud of poisonous gas, to be carried off by the wind.' She paused. 'Do you know what acute exposure to methyl isocyanate does to the human body, Dr. Banks?'

Of course he knew. He had to know. But he didn't answer her.

'It's corrosive, and just touching it can burn your skin. So imagine what it does to the lining of your airways, your lungs, when you breathe it in. You begin to cough, and your throat hurts. You feel dizzy. And then you can't catch your breath, because the gas is literally eating away your mucous membranes. Fluid leaks through, flooding into your lungs. It's called pulmonary edema. You drown, Dr. Banks, in your own secretions. But I'm sure you know that, since you're a doctor.'

His head dipped in a defeated nod.

'That Octagon factory knew it too. It wouldn't take long for them to realize they've made a terrible mistake. They know that methyl isocyanate is denser than air. That it will collect in low areas. So they hurry out to check the leper village in the valley, just downwind of them. The village of Bara. And what they find is a dead zone. People, animals – nothing left alive. They're staring at the corpses of almost a hundred people, and they know they're responsible for those deaths. They know they're in trouble. There'll certainly be criminal charges, and possibly arrests. So what do you think they did next, Dr. Banks?'

'I don't know.'

'They panicked, of course. Wouldn't you? They wanted the problem to go away. They wanted it to vanish. But what to do with all that evidence? You can't hide a hundred bodies. You can't make a village disappear. Plus, there were two Americans among the dead – two nurses. Their deaths weren't going to be ignored.'

She spread the photos across the table, so all were visible at once. Three views, three separate piles of corpses.

'They burned them,' she said. 'They got to work covering up their mistakes. Maybe they even cracked a few skulls, to confuse the investigators. What happened in Bara didn't start off as a crime, Dr. Banks. But that night, it turned into one.'

Victor pushed back his chair. 'Am I under arrest, Detective? Because I'd like to leave now. I have a plane to catch.'

'You've known about this for a year, haven't you? But you've kept quiet, because Octagon paid you off. A disaster like this would have cost them hundreds of millions of dollars in fines. Add in law-suits and stock losses, not to mention criminal charges. Buying you off was the far cheaper option.'

'You're talking to the wrong person. I keep telling you, I wasn't there.'

'But you knew about it.'

'I'm not the only one.'

'Who told you, Dr. Banks? How did you find out?' She leaned closer, gazing across the table at him. 'Why don't you just tell us the truth, and maybe you'll still have time to catch that plane to San Francisco.'

He was silent for a moment, his gaze on the photos spread out before him. 'She called me,' he finally said. 'From Hyderabad.'

'Sister Ursula?'

He nodded. 'It was two days after the . . . event. By then, I'd already gotten word from Indian authorities that there'd been a massacre in the village. That two of our nurses had been killed in what they believed was a terrorist attack.'

'Did Sister Ursula tell you otherwise?'

'Yes, but I didn't know what to make of her call. She sounded scared and agitated. The factory doctor had given her some tranquilizers, and I think the pills were adding to her confusion.'

'What did she say to you, exactly?'

'That something was all wrong with the investigation. That people weren't telling the truth. She'd spotted some empty gasoline containers in one of the Octagon trucks.'

'Did she tell the police?'

'You have to understand the situation she was in. When she got to Bara that morning, there were burned bodies everywhere – the bodies of people she knew. She was the only survivor, and she was surrounded by factory employees. Then the police arrived, and she took one of them aside and pointed out the gasoline cans. She assumed it would be investigated.'

'But nothing happened.'

He nodded. 'That's when she got frightened. That's when she wondered if the police could be trusted. It wasn't until Father Doolin drove her all the way to Hyderabad that she felt safe enough to call me.'

'And what did you do about it? After that call?'

'What could I do? I was half a world away.'

'Come on, Dr. Banks. I can't believe you just sat there, in your office in San Francisco, and let it drop. You're not the kind of man who'd hear a bombshell like that, and not do anything about it.'

'What was I supposed to do?'

'What you ended up doing.'

'What would that be?'

'All I have to do is check your phone records. It should be there, somewhere. The call you made to Cincinnati. To Octagon corporate headquarters.'

'Naturally I called them! I'd just been told their employees burned down a village, with two of my volunteers.'

'Who did you speak to at Octagon?'

'A man. Some senior vice president.'

'Do you remember this man's name?'

'No.'

'It wasn't Howard Redfield, was it?'

'I don't remember.'

'What did you tell him?'

Victor glanced at the door. 'What's taking that water so long?'

'What did you tell him, Dr. Banks?'

Victor sighed. 'I told him there were rumors about the Bara massacre. That employees from their factory may have been involved. He said he didn't know anything about it, and promised to check into it.'

'What happened then?'

'About an hour later, I got a call back from Octagon's CEO, wanting to know where I'd heard that rumor.'

'Is that when he offered your charity a multi-million dollar bribe?'

'It wasn't put that way!'

'I can't blame you for cutting the deal with Octagon, Dr. Banks,' said Rizzoli. 'After all, the damage was already done. There's no bringing back the dead, so you might as well use a tragedy for the greater good.' Her voice dropped, and turned almost intimate. 'Is that how you saw it? Rather than hundreds of millions of dollars going into the pockets of lawyers, why not put the money directly to good use? It only makes sense.'

'You said it, Detective. I didn't.'

'And how did they buy Sister Ursula's silence?'

'You'd have to ask the Boston archdiocese that question. I'm sure a deal was made with them, as well.'

Rizzoli paused, suddenly thinking of Graystones Abbey. The new roof, the renovations. How could an impoverished sisterhood of nuns hold onto, and restore, such a valuable piece of real estate? She remembered what Mary Clement had said:

that a generous donor had come to the rescue.

The door opened, and Crowe walked in with a fresh cup of water, which he placed on the table. Victor quickly took a nervous gulp. The man who had started off so calm, even insolent, now looked wrung out, his confidence destroyed.

Now was the time to squeeze out the last drops of truth.

Rizzoli leaned closer as she launched her final assault. 'Why did you really come to Boston, Dr. Banks?'

'I told you. I wanted to see Maura—'

'Octagon asked you to come. Didn't they?'

He took another sip of water.

'*Didn't* they?'

'They were concerned.'

'About what?'

'They're the target of an SEC investigation. It has nothing to do with what happened in India. But because of the size of the grant One Earth received, Octagon was concerned it might come to the attention of the SEC. That questions might be raised. They wanted to make sure that we were all reading from the same script, in case we were questioned.'

'They were asking you to lie for them?'

'No. Just to stay silent. That's all. Just not to . . . bring up India.'

'And if you were asked to testify? If you were asked directly about it? Would you have told the truth, Dr. Banks? That you took money to help cover up a crime?'

'We're not talking about a crime. We're talking about an industrial accident.'

'Is that why you came to Boston? To convince Ursula to stay silent as well? To maintain a united front of lies.'

'Not lies. Silence. There's a difference.'

'Then somehow, it all gets complicated. An Octagon senior vice president named Howard Redfield decides to turn whistle-blower, and talk to the Justice Department. Not only that, he produces a witness from India. A woman he's brought back from India to testify.'

Victor's head came up and he stared at her with genuine bewilderment. 'What witness?'

'She was there, at Bara. One of the lepers who survived. Does that surprise you?'

'I don't know about any witness.'

'She saw what happened in her village. She saw those men from the factory drag bodies into piles and light the fires. She saw them smash the skulls of her friends and family. What she saw, what she knew, could bring Octagon to its knees.'

'I don't know anything about this. No one told me there was a survivor.'

'It was all about to come out. The accident, the cover-up. The payoffs. You might be willing to lie about it, but what about Sister Ursula? How do you induce a nun to lie under oath? That's the trick, isn't it? One honest nun could bring it all crashing down. She opens her mouth, and there goes eighty-five million dollars, right out of your hands. And the whole world sees Saint Victor fall off his pedestal.'

362

'I think I'm finished here.' He rose to his feet. 'I have a plane to catch.'

'You had the opportunity. You had the motive.'

'Motive?' He gave a disbelieving laugh. 'For murdering a *nun*? You might as well accuse the archdiocese, since I'm sure they got paid off quite nicely.'

'What did Octagon promise you? Even more money if you came to Boston and took care of the problem for them?'

'First you accuse me of murder. Now you're saying that Octagon hired me? Can you see any executive personally risking a murder charge, just to cover up an industrial accident?' Victor shook his head. 'No American went to jail for Bhopal. And no American will go to jail for Bara, either. Now, am I free to leave or not?'

Rizzoli shot a questioning glance at Crowe. He responded with a dispirited nod, an answer that told her he had already heard back from the Crime Scene Unit. While she was questioning Victor, CSU had been searching the rental car. Obviously they had turned up nothing.

They did not have enough to hold him.

She said, 'For now, you're free to go, Dr. Banks. But we need to know exactly where you are.'

'I'm flying straight home to San Francisco. You have my address.' Victor reached for the door. Stopped, and turned back to face her. 'Before I leave,' he said, 'I want you to know one thing about me.'

'What's that, Dr. Banks?'

'I'm a physician. Remember that, Detective. I save lives. I don't take them.'

Maura saw him as he left the interrogation room. He walked with his gaze straight ahead, not even glancing her way as he drew near the desk where she was sitting.

She rose from the chair. 'Victor?'

He stopped, but didn't turn toward her; it was as though he could not stand to look at her.

'What happened?' she said.

'What do you think happened? I told them what I know. I told them the truth.'

'That's all I was asking from you. That's all I've ever asked.'

'Now I've got a plane to catch.'

Her cell phone rang. She looked down at it, wanting to fling it away.

'Better answer that,' he said, an angry bite to his voice. 'Some corpse might need you.'

'The dead deserve our attention.'

'You know, that's the difference between you and me, Maura. You care about the dead. I care about the living.'

She watched him walk away. Not once did he look back.

Her phone had stopped ringing.

She flipped it open and saw that the call had come from St. Francis Hospital. She'd been waiting to hear the results of Ursula's second EEG, but she could not deal with that right now; she was still absorbing the impact of Victor's last words.

Rizzoli emerged from the interrogation room and came toward her, an apologetic look on her face. 'I'm sorry we couldn't let you listen in,' Rizzoli said. 'You understand why, right?'

'No, I don't understand.' Maura dropped the phone into her purse and met Rizzoli's gaze. 'I gave him to you. I handed you the answer.'

'And he confirmed it all. The Bhopal scenario. You were right about the dead birds.'

'Yet you shut me out of the room. As if you didn't trust me.'

'I was trying to protect you.'

'From what, the truth? That he used me?' Maura gave a bitter laugh and turned to leave. 'That, I already knew.'

Maura drove to St. Francis Hospital through a gathering flurry of snow, her hands calm and steady on the wheel. The Queen of the Dead, on her way to claim another subject. By the time she pulled into the parking garage, she was ready to play the part she'd always played so well, ready to don the only mask she allowed the public to see.

She stepped out of the Lexus, black coat sweeping behind her, boots clipping across the pavement as she walked through the parking garage, toward the elevator. Sodium lights cast the cars in an eerie glow, and she felt as if she was moving through an orange mist. That if she just rubbed her eyes, the mist would clear. She saw no one else in the garage, and heard only her own footsteps, echoing off concrete.

In the hospital lobby, she walked past the

Christmas tree, sparkling with multicolored lights, past the volunteers' desk, where an elderly woman sat with a red Santa's elf cap jauntily perched on her gray hair. 'Joy to the World' was playing over the sound system.

Even in the ICU, the holiday spirit twinkled in ironic good cheer. The nurses' station was draped with fake pine garlands, and the ward clerk had tiny gold Christmas bulbs dangling from her ears.

'I'm Dr. Isles, from the Medical Examiner's office,' she said. 'Is Dr. Yuen here?'

'He just got called into emergency surgery. He asked Dr. Sutcliffe to come in and turn off the ventilator.'

'Has the chart been photocopied for me?'

'It's all ready for you.' The ward clerk pointed to a thick envelope on the counter, with 'Save for Medical Examiner' scrawled across it.

'Thank you.'

Maura opened the envelope and took out the photocopied chart. She read through the sad accumulation of evidence that Sister Ursula was beyond saving: two separate EEGs had shown no brain activity, and a handwritten note by the neurosurgeon Dr. Yuen admitted defeat:

Patient remains unresponsive to deep pain, with no spontaneous respirations. Pupils remain mid-position and fixed. Repeat EEG shows no brain activity. Cardiac enzymes confirm myocardial infarction. Dr. Sutcliffe to inform family of status.

Assessment: Irreversible coma secondary to prolonged cerebral anoxia after recent cardiac arrest.

She turned, at last, to the pages of lab results. She saw neatly printed columns of cell counts and blood and urine chemistries. How ironic, she thought as she closed the chart, to die with most of your blood tests perfectly normal.

Maura crossed to Cubicle #10, where the patient was getting her final sponge bath. Standing at the foot of the bed, Maura watched the nurse peel back the sheets and remove Ursula's gown, revealing not the body of an ascetic, but of a woman who had heartily indulged in meals, generous breasts spilling sideways, pale thighs heavy and dimpled. In life, she would have appeared formidable, her stout figure made even more imposing by her voluminous nun's robes. Now, stripped of those robes, she was like any other patient. Death does not discriminate; whether saints or sinners, in the end, all are equal.

The nurse wrung out the washcloth and wiped down the torso, leaving the skin slick and shiny. Then she began to sponge the legs, bending the knees to clean beneath the calves. Old scars pocked the shins, the ugly aftermath of infected insect bites. Souvenirs of a life lived abroad. Finished with her task, the nurse picked up the washbasin and walked out of the cubicle, leaving Maura alone with the patient.

What was it you knew, Ursula? What could you have told us?

'Dr. Isles?'

She turned to see Dr. Sutcliffe standing behind her. His gaze was far more wary than the first time they'd met. No longer the friendly hippie doctor with the ponytail.

'I didn't know you'd be coming in,' he said.

'Dr. Yuen called me. Our office will assume custody of the body.'

'Why? The cause of death is pretty obvious. You only have to look at her cardiogram.'

'It's just protocol. We routinely take custody whenever there's a criminal assault involved.'

'Well, I think it's a waste of taxpayer money, in this case.'

She ignored his comment and looked at Ursula. 'I take it you've spoken to the family about withdrawing life support?'

'The nephew agreed to it. We're just waiting for the priest to get here. The sisters at the convent asked that Father Brophy be present.'

She watched Ursula's chest rise and fall with the cycling of the ventilator. The heart continued to beat, the organs to function. Draw a tube of blood from Ursula's vein, send it down to the laboratory, and none of their tests, none of their sophisticated machines, would reveal that this woman's soul had already fled her body.

She said, 'I'd appreciate it if you could forward the final death summaries to my office.'

'Dr. Yuen will be dictating it. I'll let him know.'

'And any last lab reports that come in as well.'

'They should all be in the chart by now.'

'There was no tox screen report. The test was done, wasn't it?'

'It should have been. I'll check with the lab and call you with the results.'

'The lab needs to send the report directly to me. If it wasn't done, we'll do it at the morgue.'

'You do tox screens on everyone?' He shook his head. 'Sounds like another waste of taxpayer money.'

'We only do them when indicated. I'm thinking about the urticaria I saw, the night she coded. I'll ask Dr. Bristol to draw the tox screen when he does the autopsy.'

'I assumed you'd be doing it.'

'No. I'm going to hand this case over to one of my colleagues. If you have any questions after the holidays, you should speak to Dr. Abe Bristol.'

She was relieved when he didn't ask her why she was not doing the autopsy. And what would she have said? *My ex-husband is now a suspect in this death. I cannot let there be even a whisper of a question that I've been less than thorough. Less than complete.*

'The priest is here,' said Sutcliffe. 'I guess it's time.'

She turned and felt her cheeks flush when she saw Father Brophy standing in the doorway. Their eyes locked in instant familiarity, the gaze of two people who, at that somber moment, have suddenly recognized the sparks between them. She dropped her gaze as he stepped into the cubicle. She and Sutcliffe withdrew to allow the priest to administer last rites.

Through the cubicle window, she watched as Father Brophy stood over Ursula's bed, his lips

369

moving in prayer, absolving the nun of her sins. And what of my sins, Father? she wondered, as she gazed at his striking profile. Would you be shocked to learn what I am thinking and feeling about you? Would you absolve me, and forgive me for my weaknesses?

He anointed Ursula's forehead, traced the sign of the cross with his hand. Then he looked up.

It was time to let Ursula die.

Father Brophy emerged, to stand beside Maura outside the window. Sutcliffe and a nurse now entered.

What happened next was disturbingly matter-of-fact. The flip of a few switches, and that was all. The ventilator went silent, the bellows wheezing to a stop. The nurse turned her gaze to the heart monitor as the blips began to slow.

Maura felt Father Brophy move close beside her, as though to reassure her that he was there, should she need comfort. It was not comfort he inspired, but confusion. Attraction. She kept her gaze focused on the drama playing out beyond the window, thinking: Always the wrong men. Why am I drawn to the men I cannot, or should not, have?

On the monitor, the first stumbled heartbeat appeared, then another. Starved of oxygen, the heart struggled on, even as its cells were dying. A stuttering of beats now, deteriorating to the last twitches of ventricular fibrillation. Maura had to suppress the instinct to respond, ingrained by so many years of medical training. This arrhythmia

370

would not be treated; this heart would not be rescued.

The line, at last, went flat.

Maura lingered by the cubicle, watching the aftermath of Ursula's passing. They wasted no time on mourning or reflection. Dr. Sutcliffe pressed a stethoscope to Ursula's chest, shook his head, and walked out of the cubicle. The nurse turned off the monitor and disconnected the cardiac leads and IVs, in preparation for the transfer. Already, the morgue retrieval team was on its way.

Maura's task here was done.

She left Father Brophy standing by the cubicle, and returned to the nursing station.

'There's one more thing I forgot to mention,' she said to the ward clerk.

'Yes?'

'For our records, we'll need contact information for the next of kin. The only number I saw in the chart was the convent's. I understand she has a nephew. Do you have his phone number?'

'Dr. Isles?'

She turned and saw Father Brophy standing behind her, buttoning up his coat. He gave an apologetic smile.

'I'm sorry, I didn't mean to listen in, but I can help you with that. We keep all the family contact information for the sisters in our parish office. I'll look up the number for you, and call you about it later.'

'I'd appreciate that. Thank you.' She picked up the photocopied chart and turned to leave.

371

'Oh, and Dr. Isles?'

She glanced back. 'Yes?'

'I know this may not be the most appropriate moment to say it, but I wanted to, anyway.' He smiled. 'Have a merry Christmas.'

'And a merry Christmas to you too, Father.'

'You'll come by for a visit someday? Just to say hello?'

'I'll certainly try,' she replied. Knowing, even as she said it, that it was a courteous lie. That to walk away from this man and never look back was the most sensible move she could make.

And that's what she did.

Stepping out of the hospital, the blast of cold air shocked her. She hugged the chart close to her and headed into the wind's icy teeth. On this holy night, she walked alone, her only companion the bundle of papers she now carried. Crossing through the garage, she saw no one else, and heard only her own footsteps, echoing off concrete.

She quickened her pace. Paused twice to glance back and confirm she was not being followed. By the time she reached her car, she was breathing hard. I've seen too much death, she thought. Now I feel it everywhere.

She climbed into her car and locked the doors.

Merry Christmas, Dr. Isles. You reap what you sow, and tonight, you've reaped loneliness.

Pulling out of the hospital parking lot, she had to squint against a pair of headlights shining in her rearview mirror. Another car was leaving right behind hers. Father Brophy? she wondered. And where would he go on this Christmas Eve, home to his parish residence? Or would he linger in his church tonight, to minister to all the lonely members of his flock who might wander in?

Her cell phone rang.

She dug it out of her purse and flipped it open. 'Dr. Isles.'

'Hey, Maura,' said her colleague, Abe Bristol. 'What's with the surprise I hear you're sending me from St. Francis Hospital?'

'I can't do the autopsy on this one, Abe.'

'So you hand it over to me on Christmas Eve? Nice.'

'I'm sorry about this. You know I don't usually pass the buck.'

'This is the nun I've been hearing about?'

'Yes. There's no urgency. The postmortem can wait till after the holiday. She's been hospitalized since the assault, and they discontinued life support just a little while ago. There's been extensive neurosurgery.'

'So the intracranial exam won't be very helpful.'

'No, there'll be post-op changes.'

'Cause of death?'

'She coded early yesterday morning, from a myocardial infarction. Since I'm familiar with the case, I've already taken care of the preliminaries for you. I've got a copy of the chart, and I'll bring it in day after tomorrow.'

'May I ask why you're not handling this one?'

'I don't think my name should be on the report.'

'Why not?'

She was silent.

'Maura, why are you taking yourself off this case?'

'Personal reasons.'

'Did you know this patient?'

'No.'

'Then what is it?'

'I know one of the suspects,' she said. 'I was married to him.'

She hung up, tossed the cell phone on the seat, and turned her attention to getting home. To retreating to safety.

Snowflakes were falling, as fat as cotton balls, by the time she turned into her own street. It was a magical sight, that thick curtain of snow, the silvery drifts blanketing front lawns. The stillness of a sacred night.

She lit a fire in her hearth and cooked a simple meal of tomato soup and melted cheese on toast. Poured a glass of zinfandel and brought it all into the living room, where the Christmas tree lights twinkled. But she could not finish even that small supper. She pushed aside the tray, and sipped the last of her wine as she gazed at the fireplace. She fought the urge to pick up the phone and try to reach Victor. Had he caught that plane to San Francisco? She didn't even know where he was tonight, or what she would say to him. We've betrayed each other, she thought; no love can survive that.

She rose, turned off the lights, and went to bed.

Twenty-one

A pot of veal sauce had been simmering for nearly two hours on the stove, and the fragrance of plum tomatoes and garlic and fork-tender stew meat overwhelmed the blander aroma of the eighteen-pound turkey now sitting, browned and glistening, in its roasting pan on the countertop. Rizzoli sat at her mother's kitchen table, beating eggs and melted butter into a warm bowl of potatoes that she had just boiled and mashed. In her own apartment, she seldom took the time to cook, and her meals were thrown together from whatever she managed to excavate from her cupboard or freezer. But here, in her mother's kitchen, cooking was never a hurried affair. It was an act of reverence, in honor of the food itself, no matter how humble the ingredients. Each step, from chopping to stirring to basting, was part of a solemn ritual, up to the climactic parade of dishes being carried out to the table, there to be greeted with properly appreciative sighs. In Angela's kitchen, there were no shortcuts.

And so Rizzoli took her time adding flour to the bowl of mashed potatoes and beaten eggs, mixing it with her hands. She found comfort in the rhythmic kneading of the warm dough, in the quiet acceptance that this process could not be rushed. She was not accepting of many things in her life. She expended too much energy trying to be faster, better, more efficient. It felt good, for once, to surrender to the unyielding demands of making gnocchi.

She sprinkled in more flour and kneaded the dough, focusing on its silky texture as it slid between her fingers. In the next room, where the men were gathered, the TV was tuned to ESPN with the volume at full blast. But in here, buffered by the closed kitchen door from the roar of stadium crowds and the chatter of the sportscaster, she worked in serenity, her hands working the now-elastic dough. The only break in her concentration came when one of Irene's twin sons toddled through the swinging door into the kitchen, banged his head on the table, and started screaming.

Irene ran in and scooped him up. 'Angela, are you *sure* I can't help you two with the cooking?' Irene asked, sounding a little desperate to escape the noisy living room.

Angela, who was deep-frying cannoli shells, said: 'Don't you even think about it! You just go take care of your boys.'

'Michael can keep an eye on them. He's not doing anything else in there but watching TV.'

'No, you go sit down in the living room and take it easy. Janie and I have everything under control.'

'If you're really sure . . .'

'I'm sure, I'm sure.'

Irene gave a sigh and walked out, the toddler squirming in her arms.

Rizzoli began to roll out the gnocchi dough. 'You know, Mom, she really does want to help us out in here.'

Angela scooped crisp and golden cannoli shells from the oil and set them on paper towels to drain. 'It's better if she watches her kids. I've got a system going. She wouldn't know what to do in this kitchen.'

'Yeah. Like I do?'

Angela turned and looked at her, her slotted spoon dripping oil. 'Of course you know.'

'Only what you taught me.'

'And that's not enough? I should've done a better job?'

'You know that's not how I meant it.'

Angela watched with a critical eye as her daughter cut the dough into one-inch pieces. 'You think Irene's mother taught her how to make gnocchi like that?'

'I doubt it, Mom. Since she's Irish.'

Angela snorted. 'There's another reason not to let her in the kitchen.'

'Hey, Ma!' said Frankie, banging through the door. 'You got any more nibbles or anything?'

Rizzoli looked up to see her older brother

swagger in. He looked every bit the Marine he was, his over-pumped shoulders as wide as the refrigerator he was now peering into. 'You can't have finished that whole tray already.'

'Naw, those little brats got their grubby hands all over the food. I ain't eating it now.'

'There's more cheese and salami on the bottom shelf,' said Angela. 'And some nice roast peppers, in that bowl over on the counter. Make up a new tray, why don't you?'

Frankie grabbed a beer from the refrigerator and popped the top. 'Can't you do it, Ma? I don't wanna miss the last quarter.'

'Janie, you fix them up a tray, okay?'

'Why me? It's not like he's doing anything useful,' Rizzoli pointed out.

But Frankie had already left the kitchen and was probably back in front of the TV, chugging his beer.

She went to the sink to rinse the flour from her hands, the serenity she'd felt only moments earlier now gone, replaced with a familiar sense of irritation. She cut cubes of creamy fresh mozzarella and paper-thin slices of salami and arranged them on a platter. Added a mound of roast peppers and a scoop of olives. Any more than that, and the men would ruin their appetites.

God, I'm thinking like mom now. Why the hell should I care if they ruin their appetites?

She carried the platter into the living room, where her dad and her two brothers sat like slack-jawed lunks on the couch, glassy eyes staring at

378

the TV. Irene was kneeling on the floor by the Christmas tree, picking up cracker crumbs.

'I'm so sorry,' Irene said. 'Dougie dropped it on the carpet before I could catch it—'

'Hey, Janie,' Frankie said. 'Can you move outta the way? I can't see the game.'

She set the platter of antipasti on the coffee table and picked up the tray which was now contaminated with toddler germs. 'You know,' she said, 'Someone *could* help Irene watch those boys.'

Michael finally looked up, eyes glazed over. 'Huh? Oh, yeah . . .'

'Janie, *move*,' said Frankie.

'Not till you say thank you.'

'For what?'

She snatched up the plate of snacks, which she'd just set down. 'Since you didn't even notice . . .'

'Okay, okay. Goddamn it. *Thank* you.'

'You're *welcome*.' She set the plate down again, hard, and headed back to the kitchen. In the door-way she paused and looked back at the scene in the living room. The Christmas tree, twinkling with lights, had a mountain of gifts piled up beneath it, like offerings to the great god of excess. The three men planted in front of the TV were stuffing their mouths with salami. The twins were spinning around the room like two tops. And poor Irene painstakingly searched for every stray cracker crumb as strands of her beautiful red hair came loose from her ponytail.

Not for me, thought Rizzoli. I'd rather die than let myself be trapped in this nightmare.

She fled into the kitchen and set down the tray. She stood there for a moment, taking deep breaths, shaking off a terrible sense of claustrophobia. Aware, at the same time, of the fullness pressing down on her bladder. I can't let it happen to me, she thought. I can't turn into Irene, worn out and dragged down by grubby little hands.

'What's the matter?' said Angela.

'Nothing, Mom.'

'What? I can tell something's wrong.'

She sighed. 'Frankie really pisses me off, you know that?'

'You can't think of a nicer word?'

'No, that's exactly the word for what he does to me. Don't you ever see it, what a jerk he is?'

Angela silently scooped out the last of the cannoli shells and set them aside to drain.

'Did you know he used to chase me and Mikey around the house with the vacuum cleaner? Loved scaring the shit outta Mike, telling him he was gonna suck him into the hose. Mike used to scream his head off. But you never heard it, because Frankie always did it when you were out of the house. You never knew how nasty he was to us.'

Angela sat down at the kitchen table and gazed at the little nuggets of gnocchi dough that her daughter had cut. 'I knew,' she said.

'What?'

'I knew he could have been nicer to you. He could have been a better brother.'

'And you let him get away with everything. That's what bothered us, Mom. It still bothers Mike, that Frankie was always your favorite.'

'You don't understand about Frankie.'

Rizzoli laughed. 'I understand him just fine.'

'Sit down, Janie. Come on. Let's do the gnocchi together. It goes faster that way.'

Rizzoli gave a sigh and sank into the chair across from Angela. Silently, resentfully, she began dusting the gnocchi with flour, squeezing each piece to make an indentation with her finger. What more personal mark can a chef leave but her own angry fingerprint, pressed into each morsel?

'You have to make allowances for Frankie,' said Angela.

'Why? He doesn't make any for me.'

'You don't know what he's been through.'

'I've heard more than I ever want to hear about the Marines.'

'No, I'm talking about when he was a baby. What happened when he was a baby.'

'Something happened?'

'It still gives me the chills, how his head hit the floor.'

'What, did he fall out of the crib?' She laughed. 'It might explain his I.Q.'

'No, it's not funny. It was serious – very serious. Your dad was out of town, and I had to rush Frankie to the emergency room. They did X-rays, and he had a crack, right there.' Angela touched the side of her head, leaving a smear of flour in her dark hair. 'In his skull.'

'I always said he had a hole in his head.'

'I'm telling you, it's not funny, Jane. He almost died.'

'He's too mean to die.'

Angela stared down at the bowl of flour. 'He was only four months old,' she said.

Rizzoli paused, her finger pressing into soft dough. She could not imagine Frankie as an infant. She could not imagine him helpless or vulnerable.

'The doctors had to drain some blood from his brain. They said there was a chance . . .' Angela stopped.

'What?'

'That he might not grow up normal.'

A sarcastic remark automatically popped into Rizzoli's head, but she held it back. This, she understood, was not an occasion for sarcasm.

Angela was not looking at her, but was now staring down at her own hand, clutching a lump of dough. Avoiding her daughter's gaze.

Four months old, Rizzoli thought. There's something wrong here. If he was only four months old, he couldn't crawl yet. He couldn't climb out of his crib, or squirm out of his high chair. The only way for an infant that young to fall is to be dropped.

She looked at her mother with new comprehension. She wondered how many nights Angela had awakened in horror, remembering the instant when she'd lost her grip, and her baby had slid from her arms. Golden boy Frankie, almost killed by his careless mother.

She reached out and touched her mother's arm. 'Hey. He turned out okay, didn't he?'

Angela took a breath. She began dusting and pinching more gnocchis, suddenly working at record speed.

'Mom, of all of us, Frankie's the toughest one in the bunch.'

'No, he isn't.' Angela set a gnocchi on the tray and looked up at her daughter. 'You are.'

'Yeah, right.'

'You are, Jane. When you were born, I took one look at you, and I thought: This one I never have to worry about. This one's gonna fight back, no matter what. Mikey, I know I probably should have protected better. He's not so good at defending himself.'

'Mike grew up a victim. He's always gonna act like one.'

'But not you.' A faint smile tugged at Angela's lips as she gazed at her daughter. 'When you were three, I saw you fall and hit your face on the coffee table. You cut yourself right there, under the chin.'

'Yeah, I still got the scar.'

'The cut was so bad you had to get stitches. You were bleeding all over the carpet. And you know what you did? Guess what you did.'

'I screamed a lot, I imagine.'

'No. You started hitting the coffee table. Punching it, like that!' Angela whacked the table with her fist, sending up a puff of flour. 'Like you were furious at it. You didn't come running to

383

me. You didn't cry about all the blood. You were too busy fighting back at the thing that hurt you.' Angela laughed and wiped her hand across her eyes, leaving a streak of white on her cheek. 'You were the strangest little girl. Of all my kids, you made me the proudest.'

Rizzoli stared at her mother. 'I never knew that. I had no idea.'

'Ha! Kids! You have no idea what you put your parents through, either. Wait till you have your own, you'll see. That's when you'll know what it really feels like.'

'What what feels like?'

'Love,' said Angela.

Rizzoli looked down at her mother's worn hands, and suddenly her eyes burned and her throat ached. She rose and went to the sink. Filled a pot of water in which to cook the gnocchi. She waited for the water to heat, thinking: Maybe I don't really know what love feels like. Because I've been too busy fighting it. Just as I fight everything else that might hurt me.

She left the pot on the stove, and walked out of the kitchen.

Upstairs, in her parents' bedroom, she picked up the telephone. Sat on the bed for a moment, holding the receiver, trying to gather up enough nerve to make the call.

Do it. You have to do it.

She began to dial.

The phone rang four times, and then she heard the recording, brief and matter-of-fact: 'This is

Gabriel. I'm not home right now. Please leave a message.'

She waited for the beep and took a deep breath.

'This is Jane,' she said. 'I have something to tell you, and I guess it's better this way, over the phone. It's better than talking to you in person, because I don't think I really want to see your reaction. So anyway, here goes. I . . . screwed up.' She suddenly laughed. 'Jesus, I feel really stupid, making the world's oldest mistake. I'll never joke about dumb bimbos again. What happened is, well . . . I'm pregnant. About eight weeks, I think. Which, in case you're wondering, means it's definitely yours. I'm not asking you for anything. I don't want you to feel obligated to do whatever it is men are supposed to do. You don't even have to return this call. But I did think you had a right to know, because . . .' She paused, her voice suddenly thick with tears. She cleared her throat. 'Because I've decided to keep the baby.'

She hung up.

For a long time she didn't move, but just stared down at her hands as she rode a twister of emotions. Relief. Fear. Anticipation. But not ambivalence – this was a choice she felt absolutely right about.

She rose, feeling suddenly weightless, released from the burden of uncertainty. There was so much to worry about, so many changes to prepare for, yet she felt a new lightness in her step as she walked down the stairs and went back into the kitchen.

The water on the stove was now boiling. The rising steam warmed her face, like a mother's caress.

She added two teaspoons of olive oil, then slid the gnocchi into the pot. Three other pots already were simmering on the stove, each releasing its own fragrance. The bouquet of her mother's kitchen. She inhaled the smells, aching with new appreciation for this sacred place, where food was love.

She scooped up the potato dumplings as they floated to the surface, set them on a platter, and ladled on veal sauce. She opened the oven and pulled out the casserole dishes that had been left warming inside: Roast potatoes. Green beans. Meatballs. Manicotti. A parade of plenty, which she and her mother carried out in triumph to the dining room. And last, of course, the turkey, which sat in royal isolation at the center of the table, surrounded by its Italian cousins. It was more than their family could ever eat, but that was the point; an abundance of both food and love.

She sat at the table, across from Irene, and watched the twins being fed. Only an hour ago, when she had looked at Irene in the living room, she had seen a tired young woman whose life was already over, whose skirt sagged from the constant tugging of small hands. Now she looked at that same woman, and she saw a different Irene, one who laughed as she spooned cranberry sauce into little mouths, whose expression turned tender and unfocused as she pressed her lips to a head of curly hair.

I see a different woman because I'm the one who's changed, she thought. Not Irene.

After dinner, as she helped Angela brew coffee and pipe sweet whipped cream into the cannoli shells, she found herself looking with fresh eyes at her mother as well. She saw new streaks of silver in her hair, and a face starting to sag at the jowls. Do you ever regret having us, Mom? she wondered. Do you ever stop and think that you've made a mistake? Or were you as sure as I am now, about this baby?

'Hey, Janie!' yelled Frankie from the living room. 'Your cell phone's ringing in your purse.'

'Can you get it?' she yelled back.

'We're watching the game!'

'I've got whipped cream all over my hands! Will you just answer it?'

He stalked into the kitchen and practically thrust the phone at her. 'It's some guy.'

'Frost?'

'Naw. I don't know who it is.'

Gabriel was her first thought. *He's heard my message.*

She crossed to the sink and took her time rinsing off her hands. When at last she picked up the phone, she was able to answer with a calm, 'Hello?'

'Detective Rizzoli? It's Father Brophy.'

All the tension suddenly whooshed out of her. She sank into a chair. She could feel her mother watching her, and she tried to keep the disappointment from her voice.

'Yes, Father?'

'I'm sorry to call you on Christmas Eve, but I can't seem to get through to Dr. Isles's phone, and – well, something has come up that I thought you should know about.'

'What is it?'

'Dr. Isles wanted contact information for Sister Ursula's next of kin, so I offered to look it up for her. But it turns out our parish records are a little out of date. We have an old phone number for a brother in Denver, but that phone's been disconnected.'

'Mother Mary Clement told me the brother died.'

'Did she tell you that Sister Ursula also has a nephew living out of state?'

'The Abbess didn't mention him.'

'It seems he's been in touch with the doctors. That's what the nurses told me.'

She looked at the platter of filled cannoli, now getting soggy with their filling of sweet cream. 'Where are you going with this, Father?'

'I know this seems like a minor detail, tracking down some nephew who hasn't seen his aunt in years. And I know how hard it is, to locate someone who's out of state, if you don't even know their first name. But the church has resources even the police don't have. A good priest knows his flock, Detective. He knows their families and the names of their children. So I called the priest in the Denver parish where Sister Ursula's brother lived. He remembers the brother quite well. He performed his funeral Mass.'

'Did you ask him about her relatives? About this nephew?'

'Yes, I did.'

'And?'

'There is no nephew, Detective. He doesn't exist.'

Twenty-two

Maura dreamed of funeral pyres.

She was crouched in shadow, watching orange flames lick at bodies stacked like cordwood, watching flesh consumed in the heat of the fire. The silhouettes of men surrounded the burning corpses, a circle of silent watchers whose faces she could not see. Nor could they see her, for she was hidden in darkness, cowering from their sight.

Sparks flew up from the pyre, fed by its human fuel, and spiralled into the black sky. The sparks lit the night, illuminating an even more terrible sight: The corpses were still moving. Blackened limbs thrashed in the torment of fire.

One among that circle of men slowly turned and stared at Maura. It was a face she recognized, a face whose eyes were empty of any soul.

Victor.

She came awake in an instant, her heart ramming against her chest, her nightshirt soaked with sweat. A gust buffeted the house, and she could hear the skeletal clatter of shaking windows, the groan of the walls. Still wrapped in the panic of the nightmare, she lay perfectly still, the sweat beginning to chill on her skin. Was it only the wind that had awakened her? She listened, and every creak of the house sounded like a footstep. An intruder, moving closer.

Suddenly she tensed, alerted to a different sound. A scratching against the house, like the claws of an animal trying to get in.

She looked at the glowing face of her clock; it was eleven forty-five.

She rolled out of bed, and the room felt frigid. She groped in the darkness for a robe, but did not turn on the lights, to preserve her night vision. She went to her bedroom window and saw that it had stopped snowing. The ground glowed white under moonlight.

There it was again – the sound of something rubbing against the wall. She pressed as close to the glass as she could, and spied a flicker of shadow, moving near the front corner of the house. An animal?

She left the bedroom, and in her bare feet, she felt her way down the hallway, moving toward the living room. Edging around the Christmas tree, she peered out the window.

Her heart nearly stopped.

A man was climbing the steps to her front porch.

She could not see his face, for it was hidden in shadow. As though he sensed her watching him, he turned toward the window where she stood, and she saw his silhouette. The broad shoulders, the ponytail.

She pulled away from the window and stood wedged against the prickly branches of the Christmas tree, trying to understand why Matthew Sutcliffe was here, at her door. Why would he come at this hour without calling first? She still hadn't shaken off the last strands of fear from her nightmare, and this late night visit made her uneasy. It made her think twice about opening her door to anyone – even a man whose name and face she knew.

The doorbell rang.

She flinched, and a glass bulb fell from the tree and shattered on the wood floor.

Outside, the shadow moved toward the window.

She didn't move, still debating what to do. I just won't turn on the light, she thought. He'll give up and leave me alone.

The doorbell rang again.

Go away, she thought. Go away and call me back in the morning.

She released a sigh of relief when she heard his footsteps descending the porch steps. She inched toward the window and looked out, but could not see him. Nor could she see any car parked in front of the house. Where had he gone?

Now she heard footsteps, the crunch of boots in snow, moving around toward the side of the house. What the hell was he doing, circling her property?

He's trying to find a way into the house.

She scrambled out from behind the tree and bit back a cry of pain as she stepped on the broken bulb, and a shard of glass pierced her bare foot.

His silhouette suddenly loomed in a side window. He was staring in, trying to see into the dark living room.

She retreated into the hall, wincing with every step, the sole of her foot now damp with blood.

It's time to call the police. Call nine-one-one.

She turned and hobbled into the kitchen, hands brushing across the wall, searching for the phone. In her haste, she knocked the receiver off its cradle. She snatched it up and pressed it to her ear.

There was no dial tone.

The bedroom phone, she thought – was it off the hook?

She hung up the kitchen phone and limped back into the hallway, the shard of glass stabbing even deeper into her sole, retracing a floor now wet with her blood. Back into the bedroom, her eyes straining to see in the darkness, her feet now moving across carpet until her shin bumped up against the bed. She felt her way up the mattress to the headboard. To the phone on the nightstand.

No dial tone.

Terror blasted through her like an icy wind. *He's cut the phone line.*

She dropped the receiver and stood listening, desperate to hear what he would do next. The house creaked in the wind, obscuring all sounds except the drum of her own heartbeat.

Where is he? Where is he?

Then she thought: my cell phone.

She scurried over to her dresser, where she'd left her purse. Dug into it, pawing through its contents, searching for the phone. She pulled out her wallet and keys, pens and a hairbrush. Phone, where's the fucking phone?

In the car. I left it on the front seat of the car.

Her head snapped up at the sound of breaking glass.

Had it come from the front of the house, or the rear? Which way was he coming in?

She scrambled out of the bedroom and into the hall, no longer registering the pain as the shard of glass drove deeper into her foot. The door to the garage was right off the hallway. She yanked the door open and slipped through, just as she heard more glass breaking and scattering across the floor.

She pulled the door shut. Backed away toward her car, her breaths coming in quick gasps, her heart galloping. *Quiet. Quiet.* Slowly she lifted the car door handle and cringed when she heard the *clunk* as the latch released. She swung open the door and slid in behind the wheel. Gave a strangled groan of frustration when she remembered the car keys were still in her bedroom. She couldn't just start the engine and drive away. She glanced at the passenger seat, and by the glow of the dome light, she spotted her cell phone, wedged in the crack.

She flipped it open and saw the glow of the full battery signal.

Thank you, God, she thought, and dialed 911.

'Emergency Operator.'

'This is twenty-one thirty Buckminster Road,' she whispered. 'Someone's breaking into my house!'

'Can you repeat the address? I can't hear you.'

'Twenty-one thirty Buckminster Road! An intruder – ' She went dead silent, her gaze fixed on the door leading into the house. A sliver of light now glowed beneath it.

He's inside. He's searching the house.

She scrambled out of the car and softly pushed the door shut, extinguishing the dome light. Once again, she was in darkness. The house's fuse box was only a few feet away, on the garage wall, and she considered flipping all the circuit breakers and cutting off power to the lights. It would give her the cover of darkness. But he would surely guess where she was, and would immediately head into the garage.

Just stay quiet, she thought. Maybe he'll think I'm not at home. Maybe he'll think the house is empty.

Then she remembered the blood. She had left a trail of blood.

She could hear his footsteps. Shoes moving across the wood floor, following her bloody footprints out of the kitchen. A confusing smear of them, up and down the hallway.

Eventually, he would follow them into the garage.

She thought of how Rat Lady had died,

remembered the bright spray of pellets scattered throughout her chest. She thought of the path of devastation that a copper-jacketed Glaser bullet cuts through the human body. The explosion of lead shot tearing through internal organs. The rupture of vessels, the massive hemorrhage of blood into the chest cavity.

Run. Get out of the house.

And then what? Scream for the neighbors? Pound on doors? She didn't even know which of her neighbors was home tonight.

The footsteps were moving closer.

Now or never.

She ran toward the side door and cold air blasted in as she pulled it open. She bolted out into the yard. Her bare feet sank calf-deep into snow, which cascaded in, blocking the jamb, so she could not close the door behind her.

She left it ajar, waded to the gate, and yanked up the coldstiffened latch. The cell phone tumbled from her grasp as she strained on the gate, trying to pull it open against the barrier of deep snow. At last she swung it just far enough so that she could squeeze through, and she stumbled into the front yard.

All the houses on her street were dark.

She ran, bare feet churning through snow. Had just reached the sidewalk when she heard her pursuer also wrenching on the gate, straining to open it wider.

The sidewalk was mercilessly exposed; she veered between hedges, into Mr. Telushkin's front yard. But here the drifts were even deeper, almost to her knees, and she had to struggle just to move forward. Her feet were numb, her legs clumsy from the cold. Against the bright reflection of moonlight on snow, she was an easy target, a stark black figure against a sea of pitiless white. Even as she stumbled forward, her legs mired, she wondered if he was, at that moment, taking aim.

She sank into a thigh-deep drift and fell, tasting snow. Rose to her knees and began to crawl, refusing to surrender. To accept death. On senseless legs she tunneled forward, hearing footsteps crunch toward her. He was moving in for the kill.

Light suddenly cut through the darkness.

She looked up and saw the glitter of approaching headlights. A car.

My only chance.

With a sob, she sprang to her feet and began to run toward the street. Waving her arms, screaming.

The car skidded to a stop just in front of her. The driver stepped out, a tall and imposing silhouette, moving toward her across the spectral whiteness.

She stared. Slowly began to back away.

It was Father Brophy.

'It's all right,' he murmured. 'Everything's all right.'

She turned and looked toward her house, but saw no one. *Where is he? Where did he go?*

Now more lights were approaching. Two more cars pulled to a stop. She saw the pulsing blue of a police cruiser, and raised her hand against the glare of headlights, trying to make out the silhouettes walking toward her.

She heard Rizzoli call out: 'Doc? Are you okay?'

'I'll take care of her,' said Father Brophy.

'Where's Sutcliffe?'

'I didn't see him.'

'The house,' said Maura. 'He was in my house.'

'Get her in your car, Father,' said Rizzoli. 'Just stay with her.'

Maura still hadn't moved. She stood frozen in place as Father Brophy stepped toward her. He pulled off his coat and draped it over her shoulders. Wrapped his arm around her and helped her toward the passenger seat of his car.

'I don't understand,' she whispered. 'Why are you here?'

'Shhh. Let's just get you out of this wind.'

He slid in beside her. As the heater blasted at her knees, her face, she hugged his coat tighter, trying to get warm, her teeth chattering so hard she could not talk.

Through the windshield, she saw dark figures moving on the street. She recognized Barry Frost's silhouette as he approached her front door. Saw Rizzoli and a patrolman edging toward the side gate, their weapons drawn.

She turned to look at Father Brophy. Though she could not read his expression, she felt the intensity of his gaze, as surely as she felt the warmth of his coat. 'How did you know?' she whispered.

'When I couldn't get through, on your phone, I called Detective Rizzoli.' He took her hand. Held it in both of his, a touch that brought tears to her eyes. Suddenly she couldn't look at him; she stared straight ahead, at the street, and saw it through a blur of colors as he pressed her hand to his lips in a warm and lingering kiss.

She blinked away tears, and the street came into focus. What she saw alarmed her. Running figures. Rizzoli, silhouetted by flashing blue lights as she darted across the road. Frost, weapon drawn, dropping to a crouch behind the cruiser.

Why are they all moving toward us? What do they know that we don't?

'Lock the doors,' she said.

Brophy looked at her, bewildered. 'What?'

'Lock the doors!'

Rizzoli was yelling at them from the street, shouts of warning.

He's here. He's crouched behind our car!

Maura twisted sideways, hand scrabbling across the door in search of the button, frantic because she could not find it in the darkness.

Matthew Sutcliffe's shadow reared outside her window. She flinched as the door swung open and cold air rushed in.

'Get out of the car, Father,' said Sutcliffe.

The priest went very still. He said quietly, calmly: 'The keys are in the ignition. Take the car, Dr. Sutcliffe. Maura and I are both getting out.'

'No, just you.'

'I won't step out unless she does, too.'

399

'*Get the fuck out, Father!*'

Her hair was wrenched sideways, and the gun bit into her temple. 'Please,' she whispered to Brophy. 'Just do it. Do it now.'

'Okay!' Brophy said in panic. 'I'm doing it! I'm getting out . . .' He pushed open his door and stepped outside.

Sutcliffe said to Maura, 'Get behind the wheel.'

Shaking, clumsy, Maura climbed over the gear shift, into the driver's seat. She glanced sideways, out the window, and saw Brophy still standing beside the car, staring at her helplessly. Rizzoli was shouting at him to move away, but he seemed paralyzed.

'Drive,' said Sutcliffe.

Maura put the car in gear and let out the brake. She pressed her bare foot to the gas pedal, then lifted it again.

'You can't kill me,' she said. The logical Dr. Isles was back in control. 'We're surrounded by the police. You need me as a hostage. You need me to drive this car.'

A few seconds passed. An eternity.

She sucked in a gasp as he lowered the gun from her head and pressed the barrel, hard, against her thigh.

'And you don't need your left leg to drive. So do you want to keep your knee?'

She swallowed. 'Yes.'

'Then let's go.'

She pressed the accelerator.

Slowly the car began to roll forward, past the

parked cruiser where Frost was crouched. The dark street stretched ahead of them, unobstructed. The car kept moving.

Suddenly she saw Father Brophy in her rearview mirror, running after them, lit by the strobelike flashes of the cruiser's blue lights. He grabbed Sutcliffe's door and yanked it open. Reaching in, Brophy clawed at Sutcliffe's sleeve, trying to drag him out.

The blast of the gun sent the priest flying backwards.

Maura shoved open her own door and threw herself out of the rolling car.

She landed on icy pavement, and saw bright flashes as her head slammed against the ground.

For a moment she could not move. She lay in blackness, trapped in a cold and numbing place, feeling no pain, no fear. Aware only of the wind, blowing feathery snow across her face. She heard a voice calling to her from across a great distance.

Louder, now. Closer.

'Doc? *Doc?*'

Maura opened her eyes and winced against the glare of Rizzoli's flashlight. She turned her head away from the light and saw the car a dozen yards away, its front bumper rammed against a tree. Sutcliffe was lying face-down on the street, struggling to get up, his hands cuffed behind him.

'Father Brophy,' she murmured. 'Where is Father Brophy?'

'We've already called the ambulance.'

Slowly Maura sat up and looked down the

401

street, where Frost was crouched over the priest's body. No, she thought. No.

'Don't get up yet,' said Rizzoli, trying to hold her still.

But Maura pushed her away and rose, her legs unsteady, her heart in her throat. She scarcely felt the icy road beneath her bare feet as she stumbled toward Brophy.

Frost looked up as she approached. 'It's a chest wound,' he said softly.

Dropping to her knees beside him, she tore open the priest's shirt and saw where the bullet had penetrated. She heard the ominous sound of air being sucked into the chest. She pressed her hand to the wound, and felt warm blood and clammy flesh. He was shaking from the cold. Wind swept down the street, its bite as sharp as fangs. And I am wearing your coat, she thought. The coat you gave me to keep me warm.

Through the howl of the wind, she heard the wail of the approaching ambulance.

His gaze was unfocused, consciousness fading.

'Stay with me Daniel,' she said. 'Do you hear me?' Her voice broke. 'You're going to live.' She leaned forward, tears sliding onto his face as she pleaded into his ear.

'Please. Do it for me, Daniel. You have to live. You have to live . . .'

Twenty-three

The TV in the hospital waiting room was tuned, as always, to CNN.

Maura sat with her bandaged foot propped up on a chair, her gaze fixed on the news banner crawling across the bottom of the screen, but she did not register a single word. Though she was now dressed in a wool sweater and corduroy slacks, she still felt cold, and did not think she would ever feel warm again. Four hours, she thought. He has been on the operating table for four hours. She looked at her hand and could still see Daniel Brophy's blood under her fingernails, could still feel his heart throb like a struggling bird against her palm. She did not need to see an X-ray to know what damage the bullet had done; she'd seen the lethal track that a Glaser blue-tip had torn in Rat Lady's chest, and knew what the surgeons now faced. A lung sliced by exploding shrapnel. Blood pouring from a dozen different vessels. The panic that grips the staff in the O.R. when they see life hemorrhaging out, and the surgeons cannot snap on clamps fast enough.

She looked up as Rizzoli came into the room, carrying a cup of coffee and a cell phone. 'We found your phone by the side gate,' she said, handing it to Maura. 'And the coffee's for you. Drink it.'

Maura took a sip. It was too sweet, but tonight she welcomed the sugar. Welcomed any source of energy into her tired and bruised body.

'Is there anything else I can get you?' asked Rizzoli. 'Anything else you need?'

'Yes.' Maura looked up from her coffee. 'I want you to tell me the truth.'

'I always tell the truth, Doc. You know that.'

'Then tell me that Victor had nothing to do with this.'

'He didn't.'

'You're absolutely certain?'

'As sure as I can be. Your ex may be a major-league prick. He may have lied to you. But I'm pretty sure he didn't kill anyone.'

Maura sank back against the couch and sighed. Staring down at the steaming cup, she asked: 'And Matthew Sutcliffe? Is he really a doctor?'

'Yes, as a matter of fact. M.D. from the University of Vermont. Did his internal medicine residency in Boston. It's interesting, Doc. If you've got that M.D. behind your name, you're golden. You can walk into a hospital, tell the staff that your patient's just been admitted, and no one questions you. Not when the patient's relative calls and backs up your story.'

'A physician who works as a paid killer?'

'We don't know that Octagon paid him. In fact, I don't think the company had anything to do with these murders. Sutcliffe may have done it for his own reasons.'

'What reasons?'

'To protect himself. To bury the truth about what happened in India.' Seeing Maura's bewildered look, Rizzoli said, 'Octagon finally released that list of personnel working at their plant in India. There was a factory doctor.'

'He was the one?'

Rizzoli nodded. 'Matthew Sutcliffe, M.D.'

Maura stared at the TV, but her mind was not on the images playing across the screen. She thought of funeral pyres, of skulls savagely fractured. And she remembered her nightmare of fire consuming human flesh. Of bodies, still moving, still writhing in the flames.

She said, 'In Bhopal, six thousand people died.'

Rizzoli nodded.

'But the next morning, there were hundreds of thousands who were still alive.' Maura looked at Rizzoli. 'Where were the survivors at Bara? Rat Lady couldn't have been the only one.'

'And if she wasn't, what happened to the others?'

They stared at each other, both of them now understanding what Sutcliffe had been desperate to conceal. Not the accident itself, but the aftermath. And his role in it. She thought of the horror that must have greeted him that night, after the

405

poisonous cloud had swept across the village. Entire families, lying dead in their beds. Bodies sprawled outside, frozen in their final agonies. The factory doctor would have been the first sent out to assess the damage.

Perhaps he did not realize that some of the victims were still alive until after the decision was made to burn the corpses. Perhaps it was a groan that alerted him, or the twitching of a limb, as they dragged bodies to the flaming pyre.

With the smell of death and seared flesh rising in the air, he must have regarded the living with panic. But by then they could not turn back; they had already gone too far.

This is what you didn't want the world to know: what you did with the living.

'Why did he attack you tonight?' asked Rizzoli.

Maura shook her head. 'I don't know.'

'You saw him at the hospital. You spoke to him. What happened there?'

Maura thought about her conversation with Sutcliffe. They had stood gazing down at Ursula, and had talked about the autopsy. About lab tests and death summaries.

And toxicology screens.

She said, 'I think we'll know the answer when we do the postmortem.'

'What do you expect to find?'

'The reason why she went into cardiac arrest. You were there that night. You told me that just before she coded, she was panicking. That she looked terrified.'

406

'Because he was there.'

Maura nodded. 'She knew what was about to happen, and she couldn't speak, not with a tube in her throat. I've seen too many codes. I know what they're like. Everyone crowding into the room, so much confusion. Half a dozen drugs going in at once.' She paused. 'Ursula was allergic to penicillin.'

'Would it show up on the drug screen?'

'I don't know. But he'd worry about that, wouldn't he? And I was the only person insisting on the test.'

'Detective Rizzoli?'

They turned to see an OR nurse standing in the doorway.

'Dr. Demetrios wanted you to know that everything went well. They're closing him up now. The patient should be moving to the surgical ICU in about an hour.'

'Dr. Isles here has been waiting to see him.'

'It will be a while before he can have any visitors. We're keeping him intubated and under sedation. It's better if you come back later in the day. Maybe after lunchtime.'

Maura nodded and slowly rose to her feet.

So did Rizzoli. 'I'll drive you home,' she said.

It was already dawn by the time Maura walked into her house. She looked at the trail of dried blood she'd left on the floor, the evidence of her ordeal. She walked through each room, as though to reclaim it from the darkness. To reassert that this was still her home, and that fear had no place within these walls. She went into the kitchen, and found that the broken window had already been boarded up against the cold.

Jane's orders, no doubt.

Somewhere, a phone was ringing.

She picked up the receiver on the wall, but there was no dial tone. The line had not yet been repaired.

My cell phone, she thought.

She went into the living room where she'd left it. By the time she reached the phone, the ringing had stopped. She punched in her code to hear the message.

The call had been from Victor. She sank onto the couch, stunned to hear his voice.

'I know it's too soon for me to be calling you. And you're probably wondering why the hell you should listen to me, after . . . well, after everything that's happened. But now it's all out in the open. You know I have nothing to gain by this. So maybe you'll believe me when I tell you how much I miss you, Maura. I think we could make it work again. We could give it another chance. Give *me* another chance, won't you? Please.'

For a long time she sat on the couch, holding the phone in numb hands, and staring at the cold fireplace. Some flames cannot be rekindled, she thought. Some flames are better left dead.

She slipped the phone back into her purse. Rose to her feet. And went to clean the blood off her floor.

* * *

By ten A.M., the sun had finally broken through the clouds, and as she drove home, Rizzoli had to squint against the brilliance of its reflection on the newly fallen snow. The streets were quiet, the sidewalks a pristine white. On this Christmas morning, she felt renewed. Cleansed of all doubt.

She touched her abdomen and thought: I guess it's just you and me, kid.

She parked the car in front of her building and stepped out. Paused there, in the cold sunshine, to take a deep breath of crystalline air.

'Merry Christmas, Jane.'

She went very still, her heart thumping hard. Slowly she turned.

Gabriel Dean stood near the front entrance to her apartment building. She watched him walk toward her, but she could think of nothing to say to him. Once, they had been as intimate with each other as a man and a woman could be, yet here they were, as tongue-tied as strangers.

'I thought you were in Washington,' she finally said.

'I got in about an hour ago. I took the first flight out of D.C.' He paused. 'Thank you for telling me,' he said quietly.

'Yeah, well.' She shrugged. 'I wasn't sure you'd even want to know.'

'Why wouldn't I?'

'It's a complication.'

'Life is a series of complications. We have to deal with each one as it comes.'

Such a matter-of-fact response. *The man in the*

gray suit had been her initial impression of Gabriel when they'd first met, and that was how she saw him now, standing before her in his dark overcoat. So calm and detached.

'How long have you known about it?' he asked.

'I wasn't sure until a few days ago. I took one of those home pregnancy tests. But I think I've suspected it for a few weeks.'

'Why did you wait so long to tell me?'

'I wasn't going to tell you at all. Because I didn't think I was going to keep it.'

'Why not?'

She laughed. 'For one thing, I'm lousy with kids. Someone hands me a baby, I don't know what to do with it. Do you burp it or change its diaper? And how am I supposed to go to work if I've got a baby at home?'

'I didn't know cops took a vow of childlessness.'

'But it's so *hard*, you know. I look at other moms, and I don't know how they do it. I don't know if I can do it.' She huffed out a cloud of white and straightened. 'At least, I've got my family in town. I'm pretty sure my mom will be thrilled to baby-sit. And there's a daycare a few blocks from here. I'm going to check it out, see how young they'll take them.'

'So that's it, then. You've got it all planned.'

'More or less.'

'Right down to who's going to watch our baby.'

Our baby. She swallowed, thinking of the life growing inside her, a part of Gabriel himself.

410

'There are still details I need to figure out.'

He was standing perfectly straight, still playing the man in the gray suit. But when he spoke, she heard a note of anger that startled her. 'And where do I come in?' he asked. 'You've made all those plans, and you didn't mention me once. Not that I'm surprised.'

She shook her head. 'Why do you sound so upset?'

'It's the same old act, Jane. The one you can't stop playing. Rizzoli in charge of her own life. All safe in your suit of armor. Who needs a man? Hell, not *you*.'

'What am I supposed to say? Please, oh *please* save me? I can't raise this baby without a man?'

'No, you probably could do it all on your own. You'd find a way, even if it killed you.'

'So what do you want me to say?'

'You do have a choice.'

'And I've made it. I told you, I'm keeping the baby.' She started toward her front steps, wading fiercely through the snow.

He grasped her arm. 'I'm not talking about the baby. I'm talking about us.' Softly, he said: 'Choose me, Jane.'

She turned to face him. 'What does that mean?'

'It means we can do this together. It means you let me past the armor. That's the only way this can work. You let me hurt you, and I let you hurt me.'

'Great. And we both end up with scars.'

'Or we end up trusting each other.'

'We barely know each other.'

'We knew each other well enough to make a baby.'

She felt heat flood her cheeks, and suddenly she could not look at him. She stared down at the snow.

'I'm not saying we'll be able to pull it off,' he said. 'I'm not even sure how to make this work, with you here, and me in Washington.' He paused. 'And let's be honest. Sometimes, Jane, you can be a real bitch.'

She laughed. Brushed her hand across her eyes. 'I know. Jesus, I know.'

'But other times . . .' He reached out and touched her face. 'Other times . . .'

Other times, she thought, you see me for who I am.

And that scares me. No, it terrifies me.

This may be the bravest thing I will ever do.

At last she raised her head and looked at him. She took a deep breath.

And she said, 'I think I love you.'

Twenty-four

Three months later.

Maura sat in the second row of pews in St. Anthony's church, and the sound of the organ stirred memories from her childhood. She remembered Sunday Mass with her parents, and how hard and unforgiving the church benches had felt, after sitting on them for half an hour. How she had fidgeted, trying to get comfortable, and how her father had swept her up into his lap, the best perch of all, for it came with a pair of protective arms. She would look up at the stained-glass windows, at images that frightened her. Joan of Arc, tied to the stake. Jesus on the cross. Saints, bowed down before their executioners. And blood, so much blood, spilled in the name of faith.

Today, church did not seem forbidding. The organ music was joyful. Garlands of pink flowers festooned the aisles. She saw children happily bouncing on parents' knees, children untroubled by images of suffering etched into stained glass.

The organ began to play Beethoven's 'Ode to Joy.'

Down the aisle came two bridesmaids wearing light gray pantsuits. Maura recognized both of them as Boston PD cops. The pews were filled with cops today. Glancing back, she spotted Barry Frost and Detective Sleeper in the row just behind her, both of them relaxed and happy. Too often, when cops and their families gathered together in church, it was to mourn one of their own. Today, she saw smiles and bright dresses.

Now Jane appeared, on her father's arm. For once her dark hair had been tamed into a stylish knot. Her white satin pantsuit, with its oversize jacket, could not quite disguise the swelling abdomen. As she reached Maura's row of pews, their gazes briefly met, and Maura saw Jane roll her eyes with a look of *can you believe I'm doing this?* Then Jane's gaze turned toward the altar.

Toward Gabriel.

Sometimes, thought Maura, the stars line up, the gods smile, and love gets a fighting chance. Just a chance – that's all it can really hope for. No guarantees, no certainties. She watched Gabriel take Jane's hand. Then they turned and stood facing the altar. Today they were united, but surely there'd be other days when angry words would fly, or silence would freeze the household. Days when love would barely stay aloft, like a bird fluttering on one wing. Days when Jane's quick temper and Gabriel's cooler nature would send them spinning to their own corners, and they would both question the wisdom of this match.

Then there would be days like today. Perfect days.

It was late afternoon when Maura stepped out of St. Anthony's. The sun was shining, and for the first time she felt a breath of warmth in the air. The first whisper of spring. She drove with her window down, the scents of the city blowing in, heading not toward home, but toward the neighborhood of Jamaica Plain. To the church in the parish of Our Lady of Divine Light.

Stepping through the massive front door, she found it dim and silent inside, the stained-glass windows catching the day's last sunlight. She saw only two women, seated together in the front pew, their heads bent in prayer.

Maura moved quietly to the alcove. There she lit three candles for three women. One for Sister Ursula. One for Sister Camille. And one for a faceless leper whose name she would never know. She did not believe in heaven or hell; she was not even sure she believed in the eternal soul. Yet she stood in that house of worship and lit three flames and took comfort from it, because what she did believe in was the power of remembrance. Only the forgotten are truly dead.

She emerged from the alcove and saw that Father Brophy was now standing beside the two women, murmuring words of comfort. He looked up. As the last jewel tones of sunlight glowed through the windows, their gazes met. For just a moment in time, they both forgot where they were. Who they were.

She raised her hand in a farewell salute.

Then she walked out of his church, and back into her own world.

THE END